COPPER THRONE

Book Three in the Mapmaking Magicians Series

EMMA STERNER-RADLEY

SIGN UP

Thank you for purchasing Copper Throne.

I often hold sales and giveaways, to find out more about these great deals (and what I'm working on) please sign up to my mailing list by clicking the link below:

https://www.subscribepage.com/emmasternerradley

To my grandmother Ingeborg Persson, who was not only one of the kindest people to ever walk this earth, but who also found her family through adoption.

ACKNOWLEDGMENTS

Thank you to Kit Eyre and Cheri Fuller for editing and proofreading. Also, thank you to my sensitivity/continuity readers: Tom Hawkins, Miira Ikiviita, Carol Hutchinson, and Aisling Harrison Bond.

As always, thank you to my patient family. And, of course, my wife Amanda who STILL lifts me so I can reach for my dreams. (And the cookies on the top shelf.)

In memory of:
Malin Sterner
1973-2011
Who never liked fantasy books but who would've loved Eleksander.

CAST OF CHARACTERS

- Avelynne Ironhold
- Eleksander Aetholo
- Hale Hawthorn
- Sabina Rosenmarck
- Captain Octavius Naseer
- Second in Command Aurea Heraclius
- Taferia Palm, (sailor and member of the Twelve.)
- Jero, a Lakelander sailor
- King Lothiam
- Kae Tarvin The Peakdweller royal advisor (also, high-ranking member of the Twelve)
- The Northern royal advisor and Hall of Explorers official (also, high-ranking member of the Twelve)
- The Lakelands royal advisor (also, high-ranking member of the Twelve)
- The Woodlands royal advisor (also, high-ranking member of the Twelve)
- Tutor Elya Hathleen

- Tutor Ithikiel Myle
- (Former Tutor) Atha Santorine
- (Former Tutor) Royal Knight Coth Rogan
- The Baroness and Baron of the North
- The Grand Count and Grand Countess Ironhold of the Peaks
- The Duchess and Duke Phamaro of the Lakelands
- The Warden of the Woodlands
- Ekon Aetholo
- Elebna Aetholo
- Ellenaria Aetholo
- Elissee Aetholo
- Kall, a snowtiger
- Nore, an icewolf

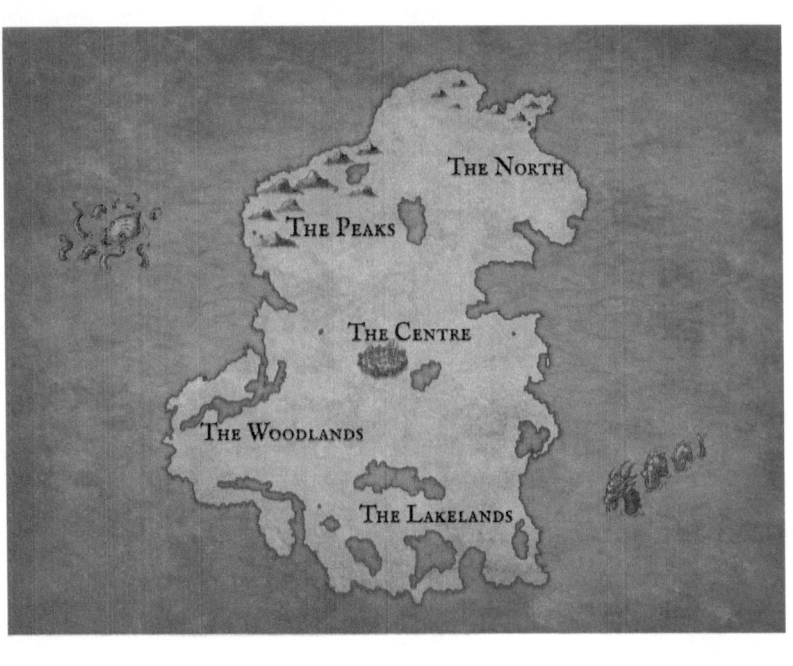

Chapter One

FOUR MORE DAYS AT SEA

Hale Hawthorn was done. Beyond done. In fact, he was beyond done times ten. He wiped his brow while mumbling, "Shitting silver beast sea," at the never-ending waves. They glinted in the scorching afternoon sun, taunting him. The crews of the Qetesh and the Parataxia were on the second day of ship repairs from the damage of the tempest. Which meant that, if Captain Naseer's estimates were right, and they weren't delayed by lack of winds, they'd be back in Cavarra—with the king, the Twelve, and their uncertain futures—in three to four days. Hale could finally plant his feet on land. His land. Not that it felt like it after all they'd learned about their kingdom's history and how they had been manipulated their entire lives. Solstice born. Whatever the shit that all meant.

His head hurt. Not just from those thoughts but from the drink. Curse that Hethklian rum. But how else was he to stop hearing the screams of drowning sailors every night? *His* drowning sailors, and he hadn't even learned all their names.

1

He tried to shake that off and picked up his hammer. There was practical work to be done. He worked alongside the Hethklish sailors, trying to learn their work songs and laughing along when they claimed he sang off-key. When they paused to have a drink and a rest, he had some water too. No rest, though. He couldn't sit still.

There was something he could do, should do. Shitty task as it was, at least it was better than sitting around brooding about their past, their uncertain future, and their wreckage of a present. He took a deep breath, rolled his shoulders, and went in search of one of the most uncomfortable conversations of his life.

Chapter Two

OAKENBERRY AND ABANDONMENT

Eleksander's whole body was getting sore. A group of Hethklish sailors and he had been stooped over the sails with needle and thread for hours. He'd been terrible at it first, never having held a sewing needle in his life. But Hale, who like all Woodlanders had sewn his own clothes, had stopped by and shown him how to do it. Sewing was soothing and Eleksander decided to do more of it when he got home. If he got home. A breeze touched his face. When they had sailed from Cavarra, spring had been just starting. Now, it must be quite warm in the Centre where the Hall of Explorers and the king's court awaited them. Back home in the Lakelands, however, it would already be as warm as summer.

The Lakelands.

He stopped sewing. How could his birthfather be the Duke of the Lakelands? What would he do when he met him? Because if he made it back to Cavarra, he surely would at some point. Since he'd already paused, he decided to take a break and walk around a little to stretch out his

3

hips and legs. A few steps away, he heard Hale's voice on the other side of some stacked up crates. Eleksander always stopped in his tracks at the sound of that voice. Deep, rough, and with that Woodlander lilting accent.

"You know how hard it is for me to talk about emotions, but I've got to do it now."

Eleksander winced. Sabina had complained of having gotten an unpleasant habit of overhearing others' conversations on this journey and said that it was the close quarters on a ship making you hear and see everything. It was true, privacy was a lost luxury. Now Eleksander was faced with her problem too, although he did have the option of walking away. Guilt grew in his belly; he shouldn't eavesdrop. However, he was worried about Hale, about his drinking and reluctance to talk about his guilt, grief, and worry. He was dying to know about Hale's emotions and to whom he would confide them in.

The voice that answered, "I know, dearest, go ahead," was Avelynne's.

Of course. Eleksander clenched his jaw. He could imagine two ways this was about to go. The bad outcome was that Hale would've decided that Avelynne—his ideal woman on paper—was a better option for him than romancing another lad. After all, Hale might be happy to experiment while out at sea, but when returning to Cavarra, would want a lass on his arm. The good outcome would be that Hale was about to have that conversation about loving someone else that he, due to some misguided sense of honour, had said he must have with Avelynne.

Eleksander closed his eyes. He should leave. He shouldn't listen.

"It won't take long," Hale said. "I just," he coughed, "wanted to say sorry."

"Oh? For what?"

"Uh. For my promises of lifelong love. I mean, um, for making you think I loved you. For making myself think I loved you. Shit, I mean, I do love you," he hastened to add, "but not..."

"Not in a romantic way?"

Hale made an unsure sound. "More like, not in the huge way I've realised I can love. Not in the way that makes you want to spend your life with someone."

"Good," Avelynne said.

Eleksander found the relief in her voice almost as wonderful as Hale's words. His own relief and joy made him want to jump up and down.

"Being the way I am, I could never love you the way you wanted anyway," Avelynne said, in that warm and caring tone of hers. "Besides, as I told you before we sailed, if I must force myself into an exclusive, romantic relationship, it will be with Sabina. I love all three of you, but she is the one I simply cannot be without."

"I know. You said that," Hale snapped. The indignation in his speech soon faded, his tone contented as he said, "I'm glad that is all out in the open."

"Me too. Now, are we going to discuss how lucky you are that our lovely Sander has fallen for you?" Avelynne said.

"I know," Hale said with an embarrassed chuckle. "He's smart, strong, talented, rich, but still so shittingly humble and kind. What's even worse, he's stunning. I never realised that men could be stunning, you know?"

Eleksander's heart soared.

Hale groaned. "But..."

"But?" Avelynne said, right as Eleksander thought it.

"I don't deserve him."

"Oh, you're not half as terrible as you think. Simply do your best to treat him right and put him first. That way, you will deserve him. Just remember that you have to tell him things, Hale."

"I'll try."

The guilt became too strong and Eleksander walked away to avoid overhearing more. Back by the sail, one of the sailors he'd been sewing with stood and said, "We're out of thread. Fancy coming with me as a human shield for when I tell Captain Naseer that we need to nick some of the Parataxia's already low thread stash?" He indicated their sister ship with his thumb.

"Sure," Eleksander said. "Although, I recommend we ask Aurea instead. I can barter some information with her."

"All right."

The sailor didn't ask what he would barter with and Eleksander wouldn't have told him anyway. Sabina, Aurea, and Avelynne clearly had some sort of complicated and possibly painful attraction triangle going on and deserved privacy to sort it out. Still, he had seen how Aurea yearned for the other two and sympathised. He could no doubt get a lot of favours if he bartered harmless information about Avelynne and Sabina to her. There were two things he wanted when he was enamoured with someone.

1. To be with them all the time.
2. To know everything about them, from what

their favourite berry was to what their biggest fear was.

Oakenberry and abandonment, he thought as he looked in Hale's direction, aware that he must be smiling like he had just struck gold.

THREE MORE DAYS AT SEA

This morning Avelynne awoke to a ruckus. She took little notice. That was life onboard a busy ship. The sailors worked in shifts and, while otherwise very lovely, were not much for being considerate, so there was no fully quiet time. In fact, she had struggled to fall asleep last night as two sailors a couple of hammocks away were bedding each other loudly and unashamedly. She, however, had been quite shamed, but only by how much hearing it aroused her and how much she wanted to climb into Sabina's hammock and try to convince her to take their lead. Avelynne had been too tired though, and not wanted Sabina's first time to be in front of an audience. She'd stuck to letting her fingers massage the need away and, after her climax, had fallen deep asleep.

Now, the noises continued, and her hammock swayed more than usual, nearly bumping into Sabina's. The Northerner lay with an arm over her eyes, mumbling in her sleep. Bleary-eyed, Avelynne watched her slumber. A knot formed in her stomach. She held so much affection for

Sabina, but it wasn't the kind that Sabina wanted. Avelynne had plenty of aunts, uncles, and family friends that were in deep and passionate love affairs even after decades together. And yet, she found no desire to have that for herself. She didn't even want the sort of impenetrable two-person bond, reaching beyond friendship or blood ties, that her otherwise emotionless parents had. She saw the Grand Count and Grand Countess Ironhold in her mind's eye. How would they react if she met them again? Would they shun her, keeping to their ban on her ever returning? Had they even grieved when they thought her dead?

The shouts on deck grew louder and stole her attention. Was that the usual orders about hauling sails or scrubbing decks? Something smashed into the ship. "No," Avelynne said under her breath. She clambered out of her hammock and approached Sabina's, clasping her shoulder and saying, "Wake up, snowdrop."

Sabina leant up on her elbows and opened her mouth to speak.

Avelynne cut her off. "I fear something collided with the ship. Come on!"

Together they hurried to the stern where sailors had gathered and were shouting to one another. As Avelynne ran, she hoped with every drop of her blood that this wouldn't be another sea monster like the one that had sunk their ship and most of their sailors with it. Or whatever had destroyed the first wave's ship and lives. When at the stern, she heard Sabina whisper, "Sea serpents."

Due to a long spell of unconsciousness after the ship-wreck, Avelynne hadn't seen these creatures as much as the others had. For some reason, she had assumed they only attacked on land. The sea serpents shooting through the water at great speed and ramming the ship proved otherwise. Luckily, they weren't large enough to cause much damage. Not yet anyway, but she counted at least a dozen of them, and they kept thumping into the Qetesh. How much could a ship handle, particularly one that was still being patch-repaired after that collision with its sister ship in the storm? She tried to think of what to do as she watched the shimmering monsters' impact. They didn't give off that strange smoke while in water, but they looked just as deadly and much more agile.

"Doldrums! They must be starved to attack a ship of our size."

The shout came from Captain Naseer, running towards the stern with a grave expression. The moment he got close enough, he flung magic at the beasts, rousing the shocked sailors as well as Avelynne and Sabina who joined him in firing volleys of magic at the attacking creatures. The sea serpents kept ramming the Qetesh, though, making the ship judder with each impact. Soon other sailors entered the fray, shooting harpoons and arrows at the slithering beasts, but that was stopped by Aurea who told them to save their ammunition and added, "Secure the water and food supplies. We cannot afford to lose a single barrel or crate overboard."

A lengthy magic barrage later, the sea serpents either lay belly up with dead eyes or slunk back down into the depths.

Octavius Naseer still appeared grim and squinted down to where the sea serpents had attacked.

A sailor next to him squawked, "Are we taking in water, Captain? Did they breach the stern?"

"I shall find out. Stay here in case the ones that fled return," Naseer said before taking off running down below deck.

Aurea grabbed a small crate and followed him, shouting for Avelynne and Sabina to come along. When down there, they could see that the timber of the hull had splintered but held. Still, water bled in through the cracks and Avelynne's heart was in her throat. Joining her in a state of utter fright were the ship's goats, who lived here in a roped off area behind where Avelynne stood. They bleated as if their last moment had come but stared at the people, not the cracks where the water was entering.

"Quickly now," Naseer said, calmy but firmly, to his second in command.

In response, Aurea opened the crate to reveal what looked like a spatula and a glass jar two-thirds full of something black. Avelynne moved closer to see but stayed out of their way. Sabina, meanwhile, had sensibly fetched two wooden buckets and put them under the biggest drips.

Aurea popped open the glass jar and stuck the spatula into it, bringing up what resembled black wax with little glistening spots–a starry night sky bottled. She applied it liberally to where the leaks were, and the water stopped coming in. Soon the starry wax became matte and evenly black.

When Aurea had repeated the procedure with all the cracks, Naseer blew out a long breath. "Phew. All right. Get the repair team down here with whatever planks we still have and some nails. Hopefully they can get this all secured before the sealing wax weakens."

Aurea nodded and headed back up with Avelynne and Sabina trailing behind her like fearful ducklings after a duck.

Avelynne had to ask, "Will that hold all the way to Cavarra?"

"With proper repairs and no further accidents, it should get us to land." Aurea's shapely brow furrowed. "It certainly won't get us back to Hethekla afterwards, though."

She called forth three sailors, the ones assumedly specialised in ship mending.

"I'm sure it'll be fine," Sabina said. "Cavarra will allow you to at least make repairs before you sail off." She sounded as unsure as Avelynne felt.

Still, if anyone was able to make it happen, it was Aurea and Sabina. More capable, brave, and ingenious people Avelynne had never met. All that and gorgeous to boot. She slapped her thigh, chiding herself for drooling over these two. Yes, she wanted them physically, but she also wanted to be their friend. It was all so wrong. She should either pick one of them and try to love her—the natural choice being Sabina— or step aside and let them fall in love and have a traditional relationship with each other.

"Little Countess," Sabina said. "Are you going to stand there watching us help the repair team or are you going to pitch in?" She smirked and poked a finger toward Avelynne's side.

Avelynne dodged the poke. "I shall if you stop hoarding all the planks."

Down below deck, it was easy to work next to these two,

despite her lingering weakness after her infirmity. They made her feel as strong, healthy, and as brave as they were. She could go on any adventure, face any threat, mend any hurt, if she was with them.

A few moments later, Captain Naseer came down and said, "Progress report?"

"All done," Aurea said, standing up and wiping her hands on her thighs. "We had enough spare planks and nails left. The repairs aren't pretty but they're solid."

"That's good news." Naseer ran a hand over his weathered face. "Let's hope it gets us to Cavarra. I'd hate for us to fail when we're so close."

Chapter Four

STILL THREE DAYS AWAY FROM CAVARRA

Sabina ducked a blow and grinned so her cheeks hurt. "Too slow, little lad."

"All part of the plan," Hale said. "I'm wearing you out. And call me 'little lad' once more and I'll make you take my deck swabbing shift."

"Ha! I'd like to see you try."

She and Hale were sparring on a quiet part of the deck, her with Grimfrost and him with a spear he had borrowed from the Hethklish. It reeked of fish from its usual use. Hale now jabbed with it and Sabina slammed the blunt end of Grimfrost at the spearhead, knocking it aside.

"I see you are making good use of our fishing tools," Naseer said good-naturedly from behind them.

"Oh hey," Sabina said. "We're making sure not to blunt it, don't worry."

She wasn't sure that was fully true and immediately brimmed with guilt.

"I would not fret too much over that," he replied with a frown. "We are not using it much for fishing lately."

Hale relaxed out of his fighting stance. "No?"

"No. I fear that's another problem we have been encountering in the last few days. The closer we get to Cavarra, the more we find the waters empty of anything worth catching. Over-fished, I assume."

As she sheathed Grimfrost, Sabina groaned. "Aye, they would be. I think I told you before, our fishermen have stuck to the coast due to the tales of what lives in the deeper waters. And with other food dwindling due to the silver beasts, many commoners live on fish and other sea life only."

"I thought it might be something of that ilk," Naseer said. "Anyway, it means we are catching scant fresh fish, which is what we mainly rely on."

Aurea and Avelynne walked over from the captain's quarters with rolled up maps under their arms.

"You have quite a lot of food stores left," Hale said to Naseer.

"Not for two crews," Aurea said. "Sorry if I'm inserting myself into a conversation uninvited again. Bad habit. But we are low on stores, especially if we have to travel back from Cavarra without re-supplying."

Sabina ground her teeth. There it was again. The shameful fact that their brute of a king and his terrible court were happy to let Cavarrians starve and suffer and would probably be even happier to see it happen to foreigners. As long as they themselves were fed, clad in golden rings, and merry, who cared about others? Or even the future for all living things?

"It's not just that the stores are at risk of running out." Captain Naseer pensively peered at the brooding, bruised clouds gathering above them. "Living off only korkorand acorns and dried meats, both stored since we were on the islands, is a sure way to get illnesses and fatigue."

Hale scratched the back of his sunburnt neck. "You don't have anything else? What about the goats?"

"We need them for the milk," Naseer said. "We will slaughter them if we must, but they are worth more to us as milk providers and, unlike us, they can live off the orris seaweed we gather each morning, so they aren't a drain on our food supplies."

Sabina considered the meals they had eaten so far. "What about that hard bread?"

"We ran out yesterday," Aurea said. "We had travelled quite a way when you met us back on that island. And while we gathered lots of korkorand acorns and hunted all the wildlife possible, with this many mouths to feed we do need fish."

Sabina bit her lip. The Hethklish hadn't mentioned that. They had just done the calculations that they had enough food if they included the daily fishing and then, without hesitation, sailed far away from safe havens to take their guests home. Feeding those extra mouths all the while. This was what Sabina wished Cavarrians were like and maybe they could be, with less selfish leaders setting the tone.

"And I assume fish contains more liquid so you would have to use less of your precious drinking water with it," Avelynne said, astute as ever.

"True." Aurea reshuffled her grip on the maps that she and Avelynne had presumably meant to discuss with

Naseer. "We must resupply our water stores soon too, though."

They stood in silence for a while.

"Chin up, everyone," Octavius Naseer said. "We do at least have good news regarding fresh water, it looks like it's going to rain. And when it comes to food, well, we'll find something to eat. In worst case, we are not far from shore and can go hungry for a few days."

He was supposing they would be allowed to restock in Cavarra, then? Or perhaps he was just pretending to. Sabina wished she had any idea what awaited them on those shores. They had been gone for much longer than expected and must, like the first wave, be assumed dead. When only the captains and two sailors returned, with a large number of foreigners who were unmistakably superior when it came equipment, resources, and inventions, how would they be welcomed? Would they be seen as heroes or villains?

Without warning, the sky erupted, proving Naseer right. Sabina knew the drill by now and wasn't surprised when everyone who wasn't busy with vital tasks stopped at the sound of the rain. Even sleeping sailors were roused with shouts to collect drinking water and to wash. First any available buckets or containers were opened to gather up the sweet water. Then, portions of soap were handed out and people began scrubbing their clothes and then taking them off—the Hethklish didn't see nakedness as necessarily something sexual or shameful—to wash their skin and hair under the downpour. As Sabina stood there, enjoying the pattering of water against her skin and listening to the rhythm of it hitting the deck, she wrung out her soapy clothes. She couldn't help but moan with pleasure at the relief of not having to wash in dehydrating, fishy saltwater. No dry itches for the next few days.

Eleksander and Jero, with the love for hygiene of the Lakelanders, used up their soap despite that it lasted for longer than the Cavarrian kind did. The Hethklish soap was superior in every way compared to their own ash and tallow mix ones, which weren't much use and usually smelled... less than exciting. The Hethklish kind softened and cleaned better as well as being scented by herbs and plants. The crew of the Parataxia and the Qetesh had brought three sorts of soap, two were scented with herbs with long Hethklish names that she couldn't pronounce, but the third one was familiar: pine. That was Aurea's favourite and was what she often smelled of. It reminded Sabina of the snow-clad forests back home in the North.

When the torrent faded into a drizzle, the sailors swept rain off the deck and hung wet clothes on ropes between the masts, and then returned to their earlier tasks.

Sabina, meanwhile, put her wet clothes back on. It was a warm day; they would dry soon enough. She re-braided her hair before crossing the deck to where Avelynne was off to the side with Captain Naseer. They were both wet but dressed and Naseer was holding a book and tapping it with his forefinger. Whatever he was saying, it was leaving Avelynne flushed and agape.

When Sabina was close enough, she heard Naseer say, "The physician who wrote this discovered it. She says that it is not an illness or flaw in any way, in fact, it's quite common. Some people simply are not designed to enjoy romantic love, while some do not like bedding others. Some like neither."

Avelynne was fidgeting with her necklace. "And that is really not a flaw or a problem?"

"Why should it be? The world has more than enough bedplay and babies that have been made during it," he said with a friendly chuckle. "You should read the book. It tells of large amounts of people like you. And, having read it, I realise that I've known many like you back home. Variation in a society is a strength, not a weakness. Someone needs to keep a level head while the rest of us lose our heads by falling in love or lust."

Avelynne laughed and there was such relief in that laugh that it lit up the whole deck. "As someone who falls in lust, I fear I lose my head often. But I take your point. From the bottom of my heart, thank you."

Sabina turned and left before they had time to spot her. She wasn't meant to hear this conversation. Most of all, she wasn't sure she wanted to hear this conversation. Her chest ached as she hurried away to busy herself with work.

Chapter Five

TWO MORE DAYS AT SEA

Avelynne, Taferia, and Jero stood by the stern, scouring the waves for any sign of something edible. The high sun seemed to pulse out its blistering light and Avelynne had to look away, instead glancing at the other two. It was chilling to think they were the only surviving sailors of the second wave's crew. Thank the skies that they were now with experienced sea-travellers who could keep people alive.

Her stomach soured at how the king had made four inexperienced nineteen-year-olds captains and then forced them to sail, lacking proper equipment and without finishing their training. Still, the deaths lay at their feet as well, even if they had been accidental. Avelynne couldn't forgive herself but was slowly realising that they had been all but set up to fail. Hale was drinking his problems away, but would no doubt soon get to his anger phase and take it out on the king. Sabina struggled much more, probably because it added to her guilt over Tutor Rete's death. Or was it that she put so much pressure on herself to get everything right? Avelynne was certain of Eleksander's reasons for struggling—his low self-esteem. He often spoke of not being strong enough to lead and not being enough. Not enough to save more sailors than he had or to avoid the dangers.

She hoped Taferia and Jero saw that their young captains had done all they could and that it wasn't only their fault. Considering Taferia was a high-ranking member of the Twelve and knew a lot about them, and about the king, she probably did. Jero, a son of Lakelander weavers who had grown up far away from the Centre and its dangers, was a different matter. He had wanted a fun adventure and so had volunteered as a sailor, only to end up on a mission where most of his compatriots drowned or were eaten. However, he seemed to still have faith in his former captains. Stars knew why.

Jero mumbled something.

"Pardon?" Avelynne said.

"S-silver beasts."

"Yes," she replied. "We'll be back home with those fiends soon, won't we? Hopefully with our new information about the deal between Lothiam and the monster in the lake, we can do something about them and—"

"No! There's a silver beast right there," he screamed, pointing to a flash of silver flying towards them.

Taferia picked up a spyglass and pointed it towards the movement. "He's right. Shitting ragworts, there's three of them!"

Three? Silver beasts rarely travelled together. Even swarming insects, like bees or wasps, lived alone when they had been transformed. Perhaps it made sense since eating habits, living arrangements, and everything else changed in the transformation. They went from a useful part of nature to unnatural monsters who seemed as miserable as their victims.

Avelynne wouldn't make the same mistake as during the sea serpent attack. This time she sounded the alarm right away and then got ready to defend the ship. She reminded herself that she could do this and squared her shoulders. She raised her hands, magic swirling around her fingers, waiting for the fiends to be within shooting distance. She thought she saw the other two do the same, but her focus was too set on the silver beasts to be certain. The fiends must've been something like dragonflies once but were now nearly unrecognisable as they had the classic silver beast traits: razor sharp teeth, metal skin and wings, massively increased size, and an eerie magic-silver glow. To her surprise, the beasts weren't coming for them. They were hunting a flock of seagulls. The birds squawked in panic as the beasts, about twice the size of the gulls, chased them and took bites off their tail feathers while still in flight.

Sailors crowded around and, from the corner of her eye, Avelynne saw Aurea jostling her way through while carrying a bow and shouting, "Someone get the captain to swing over from the Parataxia!"

When she was next to the three Cavarrians, Aurea asked in awed tones, "Are those...?"

"Silver beasts," Taferia said. "Three big flying ones, which are the most dangerous."

Hale had made his way past the sailors too, Eleksander right behind him. "No time to talk about them," Hale bellowed. "Shoot the shitting things before they finish with the gulls and come for us and our food."

He threw his magic to create a cage for encapsulating one of the beasts. He acted too soon, though. The silver beasts had swerved in their hunt and were out of reach.

Avelynne bided her time, taking the chance to explain what to do to the Hethklish. "Their skin is nigh impenetrable so shooting them with arrows or penetrating volleys of magic rarely works. The arrows bounce off and the magic volleys, well, silver beasts usually absorb that magic energy and grow stronger and bigger."

Stars only knew how the fiends would grow if they absorbed their golden magic, they couldn't risk using that. If they could even get it to work again.

"What do we do, then?" Aurea said, putting an arrow back into her quiver.

"Hard, bludgeoning impact. Kills them every time," Sabina said from somewhere in the crowd. "You either use magic to capture the beasts, so you can beat them to death with a regular weapon, or you shape the magic as a bludgeon. No matter what you use, I would aim for the head and club with all your might."

In demonstration, Sabina fired off a volley that was shaped as a dense ball at the nearest silver beast. She hit it but only with a glancing blow. She cursed as the beast shook itself off and flew towards her. Luckily, Eleksander warded it off by shooting a magic cage at it, however, the fiend dodged the cage by diving below the Qetesh's railing.

"Stay away from their wings and teeth," Eleksander said. "Both will be razor-sharp. Some of these monsters have large stingers or needle claws too. Oh, and shield your face, they go for the eyes."

Hale had managed to capture one, but it fought against the cage of silvery magic as he tried to lower it to the ship. Sabina unsheathed her war axe and got ready to club the beast with Grimfrost's blunt side once Hale got the creature onto the deck.

Meanwhile, Avelynne fired off her own cage towards a silver beast which swooped low in its chase, but the stream was intercepted by Taferia's magic, and the beast got away. Jero and Eleksander were shooting volleys at the third one, which still seemed preoccupied with the seagulls.

The Hethklish stood back. They were usually such skilled, fierce fighters but now they seemed incapacitated at the sight of this foreign enemy. A heartbeat later, Avelynne understood why. Aurea hadn't given them their orders yet. Was she waiting for Captain Naseer or simply planning their attack?

Avelynne gave her a beseeching look and that made Aurea act. She planted her feet, raised her hands, and shouted, "All hands to attention. All on my left side, fetch bludgeoning implements. All on my right side, trap the silver beasts with magic and bring them on deck. We'll show them the pain of Hethklian metal."

Her sailors roared and either began fetching hard objects or slinging magic nets and cages up at the beasts. Avelynne worried that their magic would interrupt one another's, like hers and Taferia's had, but the Hethklish were better at aiming and correlating their attacks. Their magic was stronger too, thus when they caged one of the beasts it didn't stand a chance of wiggling out. Both silver beasts were trying to eat the powerful magic, however, doubling Avelynne's panic.

"Bring them down immediately, before they absorb your magic," she called. The sailors obeyed her without consulting Aurea or the recently arrived Naseer.

The two beasts stuck in Hethklish nets of magic were lowered onto the deck. A group of sailors holding oars or rigging chains stood about, ready to strike. One of the beasts had eaten parts of its magic prison, though, and was not only free but now larger and glowing silver with swelling magic. It made that metal-pincers-clicking sound that she abhorred. Avelynne's stomach rose into her throat as she recalled the silver beast that had eaten of her grandmother's dead body, seeing the memory repeating in her mind. No. She mustn't vomit and mustn't think of that. She must act.

The beast flew towards Aurea. Avelynne gathered her magic into a hard ball about the size of her own head and launched it at the beast. It hit home. The fiend screeched and fell to the deck, laying there on its back with its skull caved in. She heard the sailors beating it anyway, just to be safe, she assumed.

Avelynne rushed to Aurea. "Are you hurt?"

"Its wing," she said, dazed. "It cut my ear."

Blood streamed from her ear and cheek. Avelynne used her tunic sleeve to mop the blood up and found a scratch from Aurea's aging scars up to one of her pointed ears. Luckily, the wound wasn't deep. Captain Naseer was there in an instant, calling for things to clean the cut with. So, Avelynne just caressed Aurea's other cheek and told her she would be taken care of, then she had to see to the silver beasts. This was a Cavarrian problem, they should be the ones to handle it. Considering all the Hethklish had done for them, it was the least they could do.

The other silver beast that the Hethklish had caught was dead. It had been clubbed to death by oars and Jero wielding a spear with a particularly heavy tip. Good. Now, where was the third? She was about to start searching but recalled that Hale and Sabina had been fighting that one. She worked her way over to them and saw that something had gone wrong. Their silver beast must've also ingested magic as it was larger now, about the size of a human two-year-old. No oar clubbing was going to do the trick here. It skittered across the deck, clicking and flapping its sharp wings despite not being airborne.

Eleksander stepped forward. "We need to all shoot magic at its head at the same time. It should be enough to—"

He didn't get any further. The silver beast had focused on him and launched itself with great speed. Right for his face. Avelynne had a heartbeat to worry about his features, not just his eyes, for a beast of this size might damage more than that, but then two things happened at once. Hale threw himself at Eleksander, knocking him out of the beast's path. And a volley of magic with such force and size that it knocked the silver beast aside struck true.

"You lot have had enough blood from us," Aurea said, staggering a little after the immense magic expulsion.

Impressed and worried as she was, Avelynne had no time to check on her. Or on poor Eleksander. She and the others turned their magic towards the remaining silver beast and did what Eleksander had suggested. The magic volleys and the clubbing with actual tools did the job; silvery ichor and pieces of iron-hard carapace splattered across the deck and hit everyone near the beast. The bits of shell struck the legs and feet of people but that was better than sliced open faces or devoured eyes.

Avelynne kicked one of the legs of the large fiend. It was dead. All three of them were. She searched the skies. Was this going to keep happening? Would they have to fight silver beasts all the way back home to Cavarra?

Hale was still slumped over Eleksander after throwing himself at him. Avelynne rushed to them, just in time to hear Hale say, "Did it get you?"

"No. Thanks to you and Aurea, it didn't." Eleksander sat up. "It was close enough that I smelled the stink of it, though."

"Shitting silver beasts!" Hale ran a hand over his lover's face. "I... thought we lost those pretty eyes of yours."

Eleksander's shy, lopsided smile came out in full force. "Pretty?"

"Don't fish for compliments, Lakelander."

"I wasn't. I merely don't believe I heard you right."

Hale glanced around at the gathered crowd, then quietly mumbled something about the most beautiful, big brown eyes he had ever seen. After that, he stood and raised his voice to say, "What do we do with the silver beast corpses? They tend to attract other beasts if left in the open air."

"Weigh them down and sink them, I suppose." Naseer handed the wound cleaning supplies to the quartermaster, but was smiling at Aurea as he added, "Make sure my brawler of a second in command here gets her wounds cleaned."

Naseer went to check on the rest of the crew, starting with those who had taken bits of carapace to the ankles or had been grazed by passing silver beast wings.

Aurea stood still so the quartermaster could clean her still bleeding cut but said, "So, those were silver beasts?"

"Some of their kind, yes," Eleksander said. "They have evolved from all types of insects and so come in all insect shapes. The flying ones are most common in the Peaks, but all breeds plague Cavarra from shore to shore. Well, no, except for the Centre. King Lothiam has actually bothered spending the coin on exterminating them from there."

Aurea winced and Avelynne wasn't sure if it was from the wound cleaning or the conversation. "Are some of them evolved from the insects with many legs? You know, like spiders or wood lice?"

"Of course," Hale said, using a cloth to wipe ichor off his boots. Had he kicked one of them? "The first silver beast I ever killed was a millipede. It was the size of my shitting arm, and its countless legs were like arrows."

Aurea shivered visibly. "I can handle pretty much anything, but things with more legs than four? Ugh. They make my skin crawl."

"Let's hope we don't come across any of them," Avelynne said, spinning the silver quill of her necklace around in her fingers. "I was surprised that we met sea serpents so close to Cavarra. But now..." She considered the silver beast corpse. "I'm starting to feel right at home as we come across more familiar monsters."

Naseer came back. "Well, there is some good news," he

said. "The silver beasts drove the seagulls towards us, making them fly close to my sailors, and arrows don't bounce off them." He indicated a heap of dead birds being piled up by the sailors. "I think stray magic attacks killed some of them too. Anyway, seagulls may not be tasty or have much meat on them, but I think we have enough for some seagull soup tonight."

"The hungry eat what comes their way," Aurea said in the tones of someone quoting an old saying.

Avelynne couldn't help but look at her. That was some extraordinary magic throwing she had done. It made Avelynne tingle in ways she shouldn't.

Sabina sheathed Grimfrost and strode over to Aurea. "Are you all right?"

"I'm fine." Aurea put a hand on Sabina's arm. "Thank you for asking."

"That was an incredible magic attack," Sabina said, flushing a tad.

No one else could surely tell, but Avelynne knew Sabina well enough to think she had experienced that awestruck, aroused tingle too.

Aurea shrugged. "We have stronger magic. And I was furious."

"Still," Sabina said, "the power combined with the aim? It was really quite something."

Avelynne clasped a hand to her chest. Because the look that Aurea and Sabina shared right now... that was quite something too.

Chapter Six

WOODSFOLK

Hale was on the port side of the Qetesh, leaning over the railing and sipping from a half-empty bottle of rum. The sails above hung useless and doleful. There wasn't even the tiniest gust of wind and hadn't been one since yesterday when the silver beasts had attacked. Becalmed. That was apparently the word for when the sky and sea was this shittingly still. He blinked up at the scorching sun and mumbled curse words at it before taking a gulp of rum. First sea serpents, then silver beasts, and now the shit-stinking combination of running out of food and a delay in reaching land. It was like nature didn't want them to go home.

"That is a frown to rival all other frowns."

He turned, finding that the speaker was Taferia. His fellow Woodlander wasn't frowning but wore her unusual smile. It was... Oh, the others would know the word. It was like there was so much darkness that she'd decided she couldn't rail against or cry at it all, and so might as well smile at it.

"Most of us frown a lot these days," Hale said.

"Sabina certainly does," she said. "That lass will grow old before her time. Avelynne and Eleksander worry, as always. You, however, you are meant to be the carefree one."

Taferia had aged in the last months too. The faint wrinkles at the side of her eyes had deepened and had there always been grey streaks in her hair? She wasn't even that old, right? Early thirties? He could never tell ages.

He stuck to replying, "Shitting silver beasts, I wasn't aware I had a role."

"We all have roles in our groups, especially us Woodsfolk with our tightknit communities."

He had to smile at that. Only Woodlanders used the term Woodsfolk, and hearing it made him homesick. "I know my role here on the Qetesh, at least," he replied. "Something between honoured guest and lowly deck swabber, which suits me fine."

That was here. What about on Cavarra? If they made it home, what awaited him there? Time in the dungeon for failing to occupy new land and for getting their crew killed? Or a hero's welcome for finding the islands and the Hethklish? He assumed the first option. Their shit-heap of a king didn't want trade partners, especially not superior ones. If they weren't imprisoned, would they be sent right back out by King Lothiam to find more land? Maybe Taferia would know.

"We're so close now," he said. "If the wind picks up, which Naseer seems to think it will, we should be back home in a day or two at the most."

"Yes." Taferia leaned against the railing, squinting out at sea and towards Cavarra. "You know, last night I dreamt we were blown off course and ended up at Hethekla instead. I woke up happy."

"What? You don't want to go home?"

"I do. Most of my adult life I have fought for Cavarra to be a fairer nation, doing it from the shadows and being constantly afraid of getting caught. Ever since my brother's death," her voice wavered and Hale remembered what the king and his dungeon did to Taferia's brother, "ever since his death, I have tried to wrestle Cavarra into something like a safe, fair home. But shitting silver beasts, Hale, I am so tired of how that fight gets me nowhere."

Hale wasn't sure what to say and so stayed quiet.

"I've spent our journey with the Hethklish learning about Hethekla," she said with a faraway expression. "It is a society built on peace, trade, and progress – be that in exploring the world or in advances of science. They have a more equal society, where the rich *must* help the poor. Hethekla and its politics clearly have their faults, but even with that, they have achieved things that I have long dreamed of for Cavarra."

"Mm. Cavarra does need changing. Maybe we can be part of that." He decided to bring it back to what he had been wondering. "All depending on what *his highness the royal ragwort* orders us to do next. Do you think we'll be welcomed back to Cavarra? Or tossed into a labour camp?"

Taferia's body grew rigid. "I doubt he will imprison you. However, he did expect you to come back with the first wave safe and sound, and that you would somehow have

managed to colonise new land during the rescue mission."
She tsked. "He's a spoiled child with no awareness of what
is plausible."

Hale didn't ask what that made the Twelve, considering
they wanted something similar, except they expected a
rebel base on *uninhabited* land.

"Yes, he is. Our homecoming will be shittingly different.
We couldn't even save the first wave or our own sailors."
Hale took a deep gulp of the rum.

Taferia tapped a fingertip against the bottle. "Don't you
think you're having a little too much of that stuff?"

"Oh, I have a big old shit-heap of it," he said, taking
another sip.

"I'm glad you're aware. Have you considered stopping?"

"I will when the nightmares stop."

"I see," she said, her tone neutral. "Does the booze help
with that?"

"I'm less aware of things and I don't dream as much."

"But when you do?"

"Same nightmares."

She clicked her tongue. "Three things, then. Firstly, the
drink isn't doing what you want it to, so you need something else to get through this. Secondly, your nightmares
are about the guilt over our lost crew, right?"

"Most of them, yes."

There was no need to tell her of the ones about their
future, about what the king hid in that lake, or Hale's
worries about what other Woodlanders would say when
they knew he shagged a lad.

"Well, I was there, Hale. Both when that sea monster

attacked and when we went over the waterfall. There was no way for you, or anyone, else to avoid it. They were calamities of the sea, no more stoppable than a wave."

"Do you think I don't know that? I'm shittingly aware! But I could've reacted better when they happened."

She didn't acknowledge his shouting but said, "The only thing that might have helped was if we had some sort of safety equipment. Which, of course, King Lothiam decided we didn't need." He saw her expression tighten but she kept talking. "Or if you had more experience of the sea and more nautical training – which Lothiam decided there was no time for you, or the first wave, to have."

She had a point, Lothiam was at the heart of all of this. Shit. Hale was going to peel the skin off that maggot of a king with a dull knife when he next saw him.

Taferia clicked her fingers to get his attention back. "But even if you had had all of that, you still cannot do anything against natural disasters. Those sailors signed up knowing they might die. I know because I was one of them. It's not your fault. And finally," she slapped his upper arm, "stop being a selfish shit, the Hethklish are running out of rum."

He regarded the bottle, then slowly handed it over to her. "I was tired of the mussy head and hangovers anyway."

Not to mention that he was struggling to keep up the work on his muscles.

"Makes sense. We'll all be glad you're not so moody anymore, too." She held up the bottle. "Where's the cork?"

"Kall ate it."

"Why would a snowtiger eat a bottle top?"

He shrugged. "Variety?"

She raised her eyebrows but said nothing. She probably assumed the drunken failure before her had dropped it somewhere.

"The booze did help me cope with that, though." He glared at the waves below. "I hate the sea. All it does is kill things and... lay there. Bare. Uncontrollable. Dull."

"Everyone would no doubt agree with uncontrollable, but I doubt the sea life would agree with it being bare." She took a sip of the rum. "And Sabina and Avelynne were just last night talking about how exciting they found the sea, so they would disagree with 'dull,' I wager."

"Sab and Ave have strange tastes. Neither of them fancy me."

That made her laugh. "For what it's worth, boyo, neither do I. You're about ten years too young, not to mention too much like myself." She spun to look behind her. "Ah, here comes someone who might fancy you, though."

Hale followed her gaze and saw someone he knew *did* fancy him. And, shitting silver beasts, the feeling was mutual. If someone had told him he'd feel like this about another lad before he came to the Hall of Explorers, he wouldn't have believed them. Now everything had changed, and it was dizzying.

Eleksander approached, carrying a full barrel of fresh water. Those swimmers' muscles of his were growing even further with all the sailor's work. If he wasn't careful, Eleksander would start to rival his own muscle mass. Shit. He couldn't put up with that.

Putting the barrel down, Eleksander panted, "Hey you

two. We're moving all the water here so we can keep a closer eye on what we have and how much we're using."

"I see why they put you on that job," Taferia said. "Trees above, lad, if it wasn't for the nigh identical eyes and nose, I'd never think the small and fine-boned Queen Lea was the author of such a well-built piece of work."

"Have a care," Hale said to her, something niggling in his belly. "He's just as ten years too young as I am. Besides, you're betrothed, aren't you?"

Taferia's good humour fell away. "Yes. I am. I just don't know if the man I'm to wed is still alive."

Hale bit the inside of his cheek. Why did he have to open his hopeless mouth?

Eleksander wiped his brow and softly asked, "He's part of the Twelve, right? Working undercover?"

"He's the king's envoy to the Peaks. Most of his time is taken up by Twelve work, though, trying but failing to rally people against the king," she said, a deep line between those black eyebrows. "He lacks patience and so is not as careful as he should be. Before we sailed, he sent me a letter saying that some Peakdwellers had reacted badly to his talk about thwarting Lothiam and might report him."

Hale sucked in air through his teeth. Even questioning Lothiam's decisions could get you thrown in a dungeon or a labour camp. Or killed in an "accident."

"King Lothiam is a monster," Eleksander said, nostrils flaring.

"He is," Taferia said. "And what we have found out explains how he manages to be one and yet people do not notice or care. But how do we make people believe us? I need to discuss it with the rest of the Twelve."

"I keep thinking about the old idea that Cavarra, the actual land and not the population, chose Lothiam's blood-line," Eleksander said, leaning against the railing too. "That the reason the Centre has more surviving crops and cattle is because the land chose him and his forbearers. Not the obvious fact that he spent much of his tithes having the silver beasts driven out of the Centre."

Hale clenched his fists. He'd forgotten that old-fashioned idea, since no one under the age of forty ever mentioned it. Still, it was in the back of their minds, he supposed. *The soil chooses its crownbearer.* What absolute oxen-shit.

Taferia sighed. "He, and his ancestors before him, have spun many lies. That creature in the lake and the murder of the queen being only two laying on top of the heap. I cannot wait to inform the rest of the Twelve about that."

"How are we going to get to talk to them? In private, I mean," Eleksander said. "And what is our next step? How do we reveal the king's lies? Does the Twelve still need another base to plan the overthrowing? Are we going to go with Aurea's idea of printing pamphlets and spreading them?" His voice was getting agitated. "Does the Twelve have a plan? They, *you*, never tell us anything."

"Secrecy is the backbone of what we do. It's how we've stayed alive," Taferia said. "I'm sorry this has meant you've been kept in the dark."

Hale huffed. They all knew that the main reason they had been kept out of the loop was their age. He was done with that. No matter what happened when, or should he say *if*, they returned to Cavarra, he'd no longer be used as a helpless tool just because of his age. His time of wallowing and self-loathing was over. He was going to make changes in how Cavarra was run. And he was going to make that worm-eating villain of a king pay.

Chapter Seven

BACK ON COURSE

Avelynne sat on the middeck next to Eleksander, both leaning against stacks of crates as they drew maps of the islands they had been marooned on. There was no ship work to be done in this lull so they may as well see to their mapmaking. Their other project, kept secret because they didn't know how Hale and Sabina would respond, was finished. Right in time too, as they were approaching Cavarra.

"My hand is cramping. I'm going to go talk to Captain Naseer," Eleksander said and stood, wiping down his behind and legs. "I keep wondering why he's so sure that there is more wind coming."

After having spoken to sailors, Avelynne thought it had to do with the patterns of the weather in this general area during this time of year but didn't want to sound like a know-it-all. Seafaring was a fascinating craft and she had much to learn.

"Sure. Ask him and tell me what he said, please."

"Will do," he said, heading for where Naseer stood.

Avelynne made a mental note to ask to borrow the book that Naseer had showed her, the one about people like her. For now, she should focus on her map. She took Eleksander's ink pot since hers was nigh empty. Another thing they were running out of.

A moment later, Aurea approached, carrying a bucket. "Sabina and I have just fed the goats. Can you believe that Kall actually ate some of the orris seaweed? Sabina is still down there mopping up snowtiger vomit."

Avelynne put her quill down and closed the ink pot. "Poor little kitten. Kall has a strong stomach but not quite as ironclad as goats' ones."

"True. So, you have goats on Cavarra too?"

"Yes," she said, stretching out her ink-stained fingers and her wrist. "Although they aren't that beautiful mossy green like yours but just grey, white, black, or brown. The ones still alive that is, the silver beasts often rend and debilitate them to steal the goats' food."

A warm gust, a zephyr as Aurea had once called such winds, caught some of Aurea's short hair and tousled it adorably. It took Avelynne a moment to understand why Aurea was so thrilled about that.

"There we go," Aurea trilled, smoothing her hair with triumph. "No more lull for us."

Above them, the sails shuddered into life with the increasing winds and slowly filled to the shapes of pregnant stomachs. The sailors on deck cheered, shouting "tails" and "tailwinds" in the usual Hethklish exultation, and got to work with the rigging and many other things Avelynne still didn't quite grasp.

Avelynne, aided by Aurea's outstretched hand, stood up

and squinted in the direction where Cavarra lay. "How long do you think it will be until we reach land?"

"We were about a day away when we were becalmed."

Stars and peaks above. Only a day. She could imagine the dockworkers and fishermen's shocked expressions when two so advanced and foreign ships came towards them. Then what? Should she and the other Cavarrians onboard try to set the Hethklish up with somewhere to repair and restock and then get carriages back to the Hall of Explorers? Doing anything so ordinary felt odd and, quite frankly, dull. It wouldn't all be ordinary, though. Her pulse picked up as she thought of what the Hall of Explorers' officials and the king may say about their failure and all the poor dead souls they had lost.

She firmed the grip on Aurea's hand, which she for some reason hadn't let go of since the ever-chivalrous Hethklishwoman had helped her up. "What can I do? Please put me to work."

Aurea squeezed her hand, her eyes full of understanding. "Of course."

Chapter Eight

THE LAST EVENING AT SEA

The stars above Sabina resembled small, sharp, shards of glass as they glinted in the light of the ship's nearest lantern. She growled at them and got back to work. She was on the Qetesh's starboard side, sanding down a railing that had been damaged in the collision and forgotten in the repairs. The ship was quiet, only a few sailors on duty. She wished they would sing or chat, it was too quiet for someone desperately trying not to think. Or to look in Cavarra's direction, despite that she wasn't even sure where that was in this darkness. Not that she'd ever admit that to anyone. She should know, though. Maybe... west? Oh, never mind. She had a task to complete.

"There you are," Avelynne said, startling her. "I awoke and wasn't able to find you."

"Sorry." She didn't stop sanding. "Couldn't sleep so I came here to see to some minor repairs."

Avelynne seemed to search her face. "What's wrong?"

"Nothing."

"Something is obviously awry. Can you tell me about it? Or should I leave and mind my own matters?"

"Aye. Or no. Or, um, I don't know."

"Would you like to try telling me? I'm worried about you."

"Fine." Sabina stopped sanding and faced her. "I overheard you talking to Naseer about how you can't love."

Avelynne looked like she'd gut-punched her. "Snowdrop, I can. I love you."

"Yes. Of course. I'm sorry. You do love me. But merely as a friend."

"Deeper than friendship. I... simply cannot love you the way I see couples loving each other."

"How's that?"

Avelynne was gesturing as if searching for words. "Being clingy or jealous or wanting to be just the two of you forever? That feels foreign and uncomfortable to me. I'm happy when I have people around that I really care for, that I can be physically intimate with, and spend time with *when it feels right*. But that is as close as I get to a traditional relationship." She grabbed a fistful of her sleep-tousled hair, looking perplexed and lost. "I cannot make myself want to be part of a 'couple.' I've struggled with this since I came to the Hall of Explorers. Before then I thought I hated relationships because of my parents trying to marry me off or putting pressure on me regarding who I spent time with. Or because I simply hadn't met the right person." She took Sabina's free hand. "But at the Hall of Explorers, I met the right person. You. And I've tried to make our relationship work, but I'm not made that way."

Sabina wasn't sure if the weight on her chest was from

heartbreak or guilt for making Avelynne go against her nature. "And now Naseer has told you that this is a common thing on Hethekla?"

She nodded enthusiastically with her sleepy eyes opened wide, that in combination with her ruffled hair and half-dressed state made her look so young. "In fact, at the start of the conversation he was saying that he suspects it's common everywhere. But many societies are so focused on people becoming a couple and having children that people force themselves into that. Whether they want to or not."

"I'm glad you have found," Sabina weighed her words, "that the way you are isn't a problem and that you're not alone."

It was true. Conversely, it was also true that she was terrified for what this meant for *her*, selfish as that was. She took her hand back and fixedly checked the sanded railing as she said, "So, I suppose I should release you from your promise to try to have some sort of exclusive relationship with me?"

"No, snowdrop," Avelynne said. "When I spoke of wanting people around that I care for, can be physically intimate with, and spend time with when it feels right – I meant you. Granted, I would like to be free to be with others too, but the most of my time and the most of the bedplay, I want with you. Just not all of it. Or within the confines of a romantic relationship."

Sabina drew herself up. "All right. I'll take what I can get. I just don't want to lose you."

"I know you don't. And you never will. However," she slumped against the railing, "you also deserve a committed, romantic relationship, which for you will not be a confinement but a fulfilment."

"That's impossible now. Don't be sad about that, though. I'm lucky to get to love you and wouldn't change that."

Avelynne seemed about to say something else but refrained.

Someone else did instead. "Excuse me, lovely ladies. One of my sailors told me that two Cavarrians were sanding my ship unbidden. May I ask why you're doing that at midnight? Alone? In sleepwear?"

Aurea stood behind them and, with clear amusement, pointed from the tools that Sabina had used, up to their borrowed sleeping tunics. She herself was fully dressed and wide awake. She must be on the night shift. Had she swung in from the Parataxia or had she just been out of sight this whole time? Sabina wished she would have known Aurea was up. She would have asked her to tell more tales of Hethekla and what ship chores needed doing. Anything to keep busy, anything to not be alone.

"Well, someone had to do it." Sabina patted the railing. "No matter the time nor their outfit."

"Really? That jaggedness had to be sanded down right now?"

Sabina scratched the back of her head. "Sure. You know, splinters. Dangerous."

"Mm-hm. Perhaps leave that for another time? We should get some rest. Tomorrow, we will reach Cavarra. Unless my calculations are all wrong."

"They're not," Avelynne said. "You are excellent at that

sort of thing. Furthermore, Naseer doublechecked them, did he not?"

"He did," Aurea admitted. "I was just covering myself in case we're both wrong as donkeys in jam."

Sabina's tired brain tried to unravel that one. "Donkeys in... Ah, you can explain what that means tomorrow. You're right, let's put these tools away and then go get some sleep."

Or try at least. Sabina suspected she wouldn't get more than brief fits of unconsciousness. If that. To her left, she was sure she could feel Cavarra looming in the distance.

Chapter Nine

ARRIVING AT CAVARRA

How could they be almost home? It seemed impossible to Sabina. She stood at the stern, the warming sun high in the sky and her belly full after a midday meal of seagull in korkorand sauce. How the Hethklish could make that taste good she had no idea, although she suspected it was due to the spices they'd picked up from all the countries they'd visited. Now here she stood, unease in her stomach despite its pleasant fullness. She squinted towards the shore of Cavarra, taking it in for the first time in what felt like a lifetime.

The other five Cavarrians joined her in looking to the horizon.

"Home," Sabina whispered.

Jero hummed in agreement. "Are you gladdened to see it, Captain Rosenmarck?"

"Aye. In some ways. In others, no. Our first trip has been so short and such a disaster."

Avelynne sought her gaze. "And you do know that was not your fault, don't you snowdrop?"

Not wanting to reply, Sabina said, "It's odd to be going home when there is so much more to explore and to learn out here."

"All in good time," Eleksander said, putting an arm around her shoulders.

"Aye," she said, resting against his broad chest.

Avelynne had picked up a spyglass, but after aiming it at the shore, lowered it quickly with a strangled cry. Her face was bloodless. "Taferia, I think King Lothiam might have intercepted your messenger raven."

Sabina snatched the spyglass and saw that beyond the pebbled shoreline stood line after line of the king's army.

As Avelynne told the others what she had seen and the spyglass was passed round to horrified gasps, Sabina considered that Avelynne was right. The king had been warned that they and two Hethklish ships would return at some point today. Was he planning to kill them all? Or was he merely capturing them? If they convinced him they had followed his orders, would he let them live?

Hethklish sailors stopped their work and gathered around to see what had upset the Cavarrians.

Sabina stared desperately through the spyglass to get a better view. There were too few soldiers for it to be the full army, but it was a battalion with more soldiers than they had crew on these ships. Foremost was a row of soldiers crouching with polearms. Behind them were soldiers on horseback, most with swords and lances. Around a dozen of them, though, had bows and what were clearly burning arrows. Farther behind on a hill were two flagbearers on massive Woodlander horses and—raised up enough that she could see the sunlight glint off his golden crown with all its massive jewels—was King Lothiam. He was here? He was famed for cowering at home when there was danger about. Had he come to ensure they had no time to speak to the waiting army?

She wasn't sure if it was her imagination, but she could swear she heard the king's banners flapping in the wind and the neighing of horses and quiet speech from their riders.

"A few nights ago, I had a nightmare about the king meeting us with an army," Avelynne said, quietly and shakily. "In the dream, it was a cold early morning with salt-stained fog and the smell of blood in the air. Not this beautiful, cheerful afternoon. Also, it seemed like a scenario dredged out of my most anxious depths. Not... a reality."

Sabina took Avelynne's hand and found it shaking as much as her own. Was it possible to ask the Hethklish to turn the ship around and go back to their quiet little island? Or all the way to Hethekla? The cowardly thoughts passed. Cavarra was her home. The Rosenmarck family had been the warrior protectors of their small Northern town since time began. The North supplied wood, salt, and manpower for King Lothiam, meaning her people had bled and sweated into Cavarra's soil, which was more than their useless crownbearer ever had done. He could not scare her away from it. Not even with an army. Or a sword to her throat.

"What do we do?" Avelynne whispered.

"I don't know what the Hethklish will do," Hale said. "Maybe they'll drop us in boats here and sail off. Or surrender. But..." he drew himself up, his features firm, "all my life, I've been building my stamina, my muscles, and my skills for the fight to end all fights. And here it is. So, I'll fight and either win, die, or be captured. I think you'll do the same?"

"I will fight to win or to die," Taferia said. "The Twelve are trained to commit suicide rather than be captured. Our secrets cannot reach the king."

The idea of Taferia's death was unbearable. Sabina's muscles flexed without her meaning for them to, as about nineteen years of warrior training kicked in. She would protect what was left of her crew. "Aye, I'll fight," she said.

Eleksander and Avelynne agreed to fight too, with fear in their voices but resolute body language.

Even Kall at her feet pinned his ears back and growled with the loudness only a snowtiger could achieve. Although that was probably just because he picked up on her rage.

Aurea approached them with her mouth slightly ajar. "Your king comes to meet you and you assume he's here to kill you?"

"The arse-maggot brought a good portion of his army," Hale said. "And they're set up in fighting stance with spears pointed and bows nocked. He's not here to offer us a welcome home feast."

"He probably doesn't know it's you. He saw a foreign ship and assumed it was a threat," Aurea suggested.

"I can see his face," Avelynne said as she watched through the spyglass. "And considering his own spyglass, I know he can see mine and what is left of my Hall of Explorers uniform. He's looking right at us. He knows we're on this ship."

"Maybe he worries about us foreigners and that we may

have abducted you? Perhaps he will attack us and welcome you home with open arms?"

Sabina didn't know how to tell her but was spared by Taferia doing it. "If he knows to be here now and has had the two to three days needed to gather part of his army, he has intercepted my message and decoded it." Taferia paused, no doubt wondering if the code had been broken by breaking a member of the Twelve. "Additionally, it was sent to another member of the Twelve. Not to the king's court, which it would have been if the second wave was still loyal to him." She rubbed her furrowed brow. "I can only hope against the odds that the message reached the Twelve too. Maybe they can at least come up with a way to save you five," she nodded to the second wave and Jero.

Sabina saw no self-pity on her face, just resoluteness. Death would probably be better than what the king would do if he caught a member of the Twelve.

Aurea scowled. "Bloody doldrums."

Captain Naseer had arrived at her side with much the same expression. "What sort of leader sends four youths out to do his most difficult work and then has soldiers waiting to kill them when they come home?"

"We did inform you of what he is like," Avelynne said with a wince. "To be honest, I am surprised he has not had his archers loosen burning arrows onto the ship. Or tried to break the hull with magic volleys."

Sabina was about to suggest what they should do but then thought better of it. She was meant to be letting go of her addiction to being responsible and, besides, she wasn't even sure what was best. Instead, she regarded the others. Hale's teeth were bared, the veins on his muscled neck protruded, and his black eyes stared unblinking, making him resemble an iceboar raring to draw blood. Avelynne, well, she was still shaking. Eleksander, though, squinted at the shore with a calculating look. She asked, "What should we do, Sander?"

He was so focused that he didn't seem to remember to be diffident. "I suggest that when we disembark, we're ready to be attacked but that we do not attack," he tapped his fingers against the railing, the sound like miniature war drums. "There is a small chance Lothiam only means to frighten us back into loyalty. Thus, we wait to do anything until we see what he does. If there is going to be blood spilled today, it will be on *his* hands."

Hale grunted. "Oh, the bag of shit will attack all right. We'll have to fight." He grunted again. "If only we could put up more of an effort! We're tired, underfed, and outnumbered. I count well over a hundred soldiers."

"Well," Naseer said, "tallying up the crew of both ships, we are currently eighty-one Hethklish and you six Cavarrians. I have fought with worse odds."

"You will fight with us?" Eleksander asked.

"Did you expect anything else?" Aurea said, her tone injured.

Sabina released her held breath.

"We are here and so will be pulled into this one way or another," Octavius Naseer said. "And I believe in doing the right thing and fighting for underdogs, particularly a group of underdogs I have come to respect and care for during our journey," he said with a sad smile.

"True, you are in this fight either way," Taferia said. "Besides, considering you Hethklish are better magic wielders and less prone to the exhaustion after magic use, you should be able to go through this without many losses. Certainly not as many as the king's forces will suffer, that's for sure."

Eleksander, ever worried about injustice, turned to the sailors crowding around them. "This is not your war. Your captain has graciously offered to fight with us. Nevertheless, I must ask, do *you* wish to?"

Not only did they receive nods and verbal agreements but there were also several excited whoops and even some shouts of "tails" or "tailwinds" with fists pumping the air.

Aurea clapped the nearest sailor on the shoulder. "We've had quite a slow year, haven't we, rascals? Hethekla doesn't have war anymore, but we were all made to train for it. Now would be a good time to put that training to proper use." She raised her fist. "Who's ready to fight something other than overgrown barnacles and stinking sea serpents?"

The sailors hollered and bellowed even louder. Sabina's chest filled with affection for this foreign people but also with cautious smidgeons of hope. Could they walk away from this, alive and free?

"Get below deck and bring up the weaponry," Naseer said. "Arm yourselves to the teeth. Aurea, write down a quick explanation then magic that missive over to the Parataxia."

He seemed less excited than the others. Sabina would wager he had more experience with battles and its costs than his crew did.

As the Hethklian sailors went below deck to fetch weapons, Sabina let Jero and Taferia go with them but stopped her fellow mapmakers. Before she spoke, she noted that they were all glancing towards the shore. Those soldiers were here for them. Not the Hethklish. Not Jero. And only partly for Taferia. The king had come for them. For the secret power he, thanks to the intercepted missive, now knew they held. He didn't know details about the golden magic, but he surely wouldn't stop until he did.

"Be prepared, they will target us four," she said, drawing Grimfrost. The sign of a proper Northern weapon, the snowflake carved into the white-grey steel, caught the sunlight. "We need to take the brunt of this battle and, so, need to be extra prepared and armed."

Aurea was the last of the Hethklish to leave and she must've overheard because she called back, "We have extra weaponry if you require some? No doubt they will be inferior to your weapons, though. As I say, we have little practise in warcraft and tend to rely on our magic."

"We will take whatever you have," Avelynne said.

"We have bows for hunting. The rest is large knives and axes that we use for cutting and chopping. Oh, also there's spears and harpoons for fishing and for sea serpent attacks."

Hale started patting his torso and hip. "If the Hethklian weapons are not enough, I still have three knives strapped to my body. I can give away two of those to anyone in need."

Avelynne and Eleksander shared a look that Sabina couldn't read.

Dipping her head solemnly, Avelynne said, "You should fetch it, Sander. Do you need help carrying?"

"No. It will be fine." He left, only to return with an armful of fabric and metal. "These are the pieces of our Hall of Explorers uniforms that survived our ordeals.

Avelynne and I have been mending and cleaning them best we could. We worried that we might need them one day."

Hale scowled at the uniforms and Sabina felt her own face contort. She grasped why Avelynne and Eleksander hadn't told them about mending the garb. Those uniforms had meant so much and had been such a source of pride, especially to her and Hale. Now they were nought but bad memories and symbols of the lies they had been fed by the Hall of Explorers, by their king, by their whole society. Sabina recalled how the mail vest and the heavy leathers had dragged her and Avelynne down when she had tried to get them back up to the surface after the fall. Her lungs now ached with the phantom pains of drowning.

They pulled the outfits on unenthusiastically. The warm day certainly didn't make them any more comfortable. Eleksander and Avelynne accepted bows and arrows from the Hethklish with weary, polite smiles. Sabina noted that Hale's mail vest had indeed been mended, but poorly. Torn mail. Cracked leather. Worn hunting bows. Small daggers or far too long sailor's spears. Blunt axes. What was all that going to do against trained, rested soldiers in full armour and a plethora of honed weapons? No, they wouldn't be able to rely on weapons, they would have to use their magic. Perchance even their golden magic. If that would work on land.

Sabina crossed her arms over her chest and stared right at their crownbearer on that ostentatious horse. "You know, I keep remembering when Lothiam came to watch us fight."

Eleksander gave a hollow chuckle. "Mm. Taunting us

and telling us that we should be ready to kill or be killed for him."

"Exactly," Sabina said. "Now here he is, the foul potato-head just sitting there on his shiny horse. Waiting to take our lives or our freedom because we know too much and we're inconvenient. Or mayhap because he wants to use our new skill. So, what are *we* going to do?"

"I suggest we show him that skill. Show him what this mission taught us and just who he's dealing with," Hale said. He sprung to the railings and streamed a line of silvery magic in the water ahead of them.

Sabina understood what he meant. Was it a good idea, though? They'd show their cards. But then, she was so tired of sneaking and being afraid. It would do her good to be the one with power for once.

Eleksander lifted his large hands, silver playing at his fingertips, but hesitated. "I suppose we could do this? As long as we don't use too much magic and wear ourselves out."

"We shan't," Sabina said. "We'll just do enough to show him that we are not the controllable young killing machines that he thought. That we will not be used or lied to anymore." She joined her magic to Hale's.

Eleksander followed suit. His face showed cold determination as he stared right at the man who, Sabina now remembered, had killed his birthmother.

"Should we not think this through?" Avelynne said. "Perchance save this secret weapon for a more opportune moment?"

"He might shoot those shitty fire arrows at us and kill us any moment. We can't wait," Hale said. "Besides, it might not work without saltwater, remember? As soon as we're on land, we could have lost our chance to stab fear into his feeble bones."

"I suppose you are right," Avelynne said, fretting with her necklace. "This would send a message and also unnerve the soldiers before the battle."

She dropped the necklace, approached, and threw a powerful stream of magic into the mix. Gradually, the silvery streams changed to gold until the sea around the ship gleamed with it, glinting in the afternoon sun. This time the golden magic was stronger than when they fought the sea monster. It spread further around the two ships, gilding the sea as far as they could see. Too late did Sabina worry it might encapsulate the ships, as it did with the sea monster, and immobilise them. It didn't. It coated the bottom of the ships and drove them forward at greater speed.

"For the lost crews of the first wave and the second wave," Hale roared.

The other three of them repeated his words. Sabina's chest tightened at the thoughts of the dead, trying to see the faces of the sailors under her command in her mind to honour them and to grieve for them.

The Hethklish sailors surrounded them and roared with frankly uncomfortable glee and fighting frenzy. These people had forgotten what battle was: death, regret, and pain.

Sabina focused back on the dead as she blinked away tears. She wasn't tired or drained yet and so didn't pull her magic back. Neither did the others, it streamed out of them and pooled in brightest gold across the waves as if with no effort. They were near enough to the shore now that Sabina could see the horses draw back at the blinding glimmer of gold. This shone much stronger than that pathetic king's crown. The Hethklish were crowding around them now, still bellowing and whooping.

Taferia elbowed them out of the way until she was by the second wave and shouted, "No, you should have saved that and caught him unawares!"

It was too late for that, though. Lothiam would know what he was facing. Sabina was tired of obeying her elders.

Then, in a sobering jolt, Naseer shouted to his sailors to drop anchor and to prepare to disembark. The biggest fight of Sabina's life was here.

Chapter Ten

THE FIGHT COMMENCES

With a thrashing heart, Eleksander stepped off the ship. Soon, the Hethklish, the six Cavarrians, and a snowtiger had all disembarked and stood in front of the waiting army. At least the bowmen hadn't shot them as they alighted.

It was hard not to speak to those who awaited them on that shore. Eleksander knew that seeing what the king would do and *then* responding was the best plan. However, he found himself wanting to question what was happening, wanting to scream, wanting to know how he could get everyone to safety.

Their crownbearer merely glowered from behind two rows of his soldiers, who waited with professional, blank expressions. Finally, King Lothiam called to them, "Insolent, untrustworthy whelps. How dare you return to my shores without the crew I gave you but instead with a horde of armed, long-faced, foul barbarians?" He sneered at the Hethklish in front of him and then back to the second wave. "Tell me you at least found me land and resources."

"Only small islands," Avelynne said, gaze down. "However, through trade Cavarra may yet win resources. When it comes to our crew and the first wave, I fear they—"

"Silence, traitor," he interrupted. "My advisors intercepted your message. It took a lot of torture of the message's recipient to break the code, but when we did, I knew you had turned on me." He adjusted his seat on the horse to lean forward. "Tell me, do you seek the throne for yourself? Or to slay all Cavarrians with that vile golden sorcery you did out there?"

Lothiam didn't care at all what had happened to them or their crew. Eleksander wondered why he was even a tad surprised at that.

There was a loud scoff and Hale roared, "You know nothing about our magic and nothing about us. Underestimating us will be your death, old man."

"Oh, but I do know things, savage little Woodlander. After reading the message about the second wave's 'special weapon,' I had my underlings venture into the reformatories and contact someone who dares oppose me but who also knows more about you than anyone else." He held his double chin high. "Your former tutor. Atha Santorine, I believe her name is."

Eleksander heard Avelynne gasp but endeavoured to not give Lothiam the pleasure of a reaction.

"Since nearing starvation, she has been known to mumble in her sleep," Lothiam said, smugness replacing the anger in his expression. "Mainly about a special power the Hall of Explorers' second wave have. People confined in the same cell reported it to the guards in return for food and word of it reached me."

More like his advisors, who did the thinking for him.

"Everyone believed her to be gibbering," he said, waving a hand wearing so many rings that he probably couldn't even hold the crossbow strapped to his saddle. "I, however, saw that there was more. Her ramblings of a new ability that may be possible to weaponize echoed what was in the intercepted message."

"Is there a point to this?" Hale called. "Other than you trying to prove that you have at least a baby's turd of a clue what's going on here?"

The king spoke over Hale's comment, sure as ever of his right to be heard over all others. "I will learn more about this new ability of yours and how it can serve me. For now, I am preoccupied by your manner of return. The only way I can pardon you arriving with armed heathens is that you have enslaved them and bring them to me as a gift."

This dimwit actually thought they could simply colonise any people they met? Even ones that travelled on such advanced ships? The only explanation Eleksander found was that this fool believed his own propaganda about Cavarrians being a superior people.

Taferia stood behind Eleksander and whispered, "One of the advisors is a leader of the Twelve and she is still here, therefore clearly undetected, and has signalled to me."

She wasn't the only one with power. Eleksander saw several influential Lakelanders on horseback on either side of the king. They, even more than the soldiers, needed to be told the truth since they could spread it farther. But then, if Lothiam was coercing them via some sort of spell, would they even listen? And who would they listen to? Not the Hethklish. One of the six Cavarrians, then. Hale would be the one to stand up to the king without fear. Sabina would be the one to step up and lead, even though she didn't want to. Avelynne would be the one to have the measured, intelligent answers and methods. Taferia was the one with experience and knowledge. Jero was the calm, sensible one. They all had more reason to answer the king than Eleksander did.

Yet, they turned to him, and he found he had the answer ready. "We have not, nor will ever, enslave anyone. And, even if we tried, we could not do that with these people who are ten times more developed as a society than us Cavarrians."

The soldiers opposite grumbled and huffed with faces like thunder. Their discontent prickled at his skin, but Eleksander fought through it. "They are a peaceful and scientific people from a country called Hethekla."

He quickly explained the history of how the Hethklish had left Cavarra many generations ago and their two peoples' shared history. The king was about to interject but Eleksander knew what would grab his, and the other Cavarrians, attention. "And, as Avelynne tried to tell you earlier, we followed the order to find the first wave."

"Are they alive?" an archer called. "Is my little girl still alive?"

Sorrow made Eleksander so heavy he might sink into the ground. "No. We found their shipwreck. We think they sailed straight into rocky waters and were sunk. When vulnerable, they were possibly attacked by sea monsters." He cleared the shakiness out of his voice. "They were unprepared for the task. As we were. Without the Hethklish, we would all have died. As our crew did and as the whole first wave's crew did."

A man he recognised all too well, Coth Rogan, rode up to Lothiam. Their former tutor wore the garb of a royal knight, a chosen protector of the crownbearer. He whispered something to the king.

Lothiam nodded, then drew himself up and said, "It sounds like you are casting the blame for not keeping your crew alive. Can you look these fine men and women in the eye and say that it wasn't your incompetence that got their children killed?"

Rogan whispered something else and the king added, "Or were they killed by these outlanders that you claim came from our continent, a likely story by the way, and you are covering up for them? Mayhap because you are under their thrall. Or they have threatened you into telling their lies."

The soldiers around the king called their agreement with his words and Eleksander's heart sank. He noted weapons being raised on both the Cavarrian side and the Hethklian one.

A hand was suddenly on the small of his back. A strong, steady hand. Eleksander got goosebumps but also an infusion of strength at Hale's touch. He braced himself. "I'll give you the truth."

He got ready to speak fast—so that the king didn't interrupt, or the soldiers became restless—then he revealed their losses and how they had tried everything but were too ill equipped, too few, too young, too out of their depth. How they had been manipulated into their roles by puppeteering adults on both sides. Here the king began to disrupt but he quieted when Eleksander got to how they discovered their puzzling golden magic. Eleksander gave no direct details away about that, though, instead switching to talking about how none of it had to be this way. How the king could have let them finish their education, sent them with better weapons, better ships, done more recognisance, and given them better advisors. How all those sailors didn't have to die but how he would carry their deaths on his shoulders for the rest of his life.

Lothiam was about to interrupt again so Eleksander rounded up with the words, "And that is as it should be. They were under my charge. But maybe they shouldn't have been, not like that, not so soon? Either way, I am sorrier than I can ever say for the losses you have suffered, and I beg your forgiveness."

The soldiers looked less hostile now, instead appearing sombre and forlorn. But no one spoke. And no one lowered their weapons.

"You should indeed beg their forgiveness," the king said. "And mine for not doing what you were asked to do. We Cavarrians die here on these silver beast infested shores. You were meant to save the first wave and find us new land. You failed in both ways *and* brought dangerous enemies upon us. You should fall to your knees and plead for my leniency."

The king leaned forward on his horse again and gave him a long, intense look. Eleksander noticed something inside him shifting in an instant. His thoughts were stranger, colder, starker.

Shouldn't he listen to his king and kneel? Wasn't the king right? Wasn't Eleksander a sad excuse for a subject who should apologise for what he had done to his monarch and to his nation?

The mind fog cleared. Obviously he shouldn't do any of

that. He knew that was ridiculous and, yet, for a beat it had seemed like the truth.

He faced the king, fixing their gazes tight. This man would have been his stepfather if he hadn't killed his own wife. Eleksander knew little of his birthmother, but he was sure she would want him to never yield to this man, the way she was forced to. Eleksander stood unbent and stared right at the man who would happily sacrifice everyone's life if it gave him even a moment of pleasure or gain.

The king's intense gaze wavered, and he blinked those dull, bovine eyes.

"Your sorcery won't work," Hale called. "We cannot be swayed like that, shit-sack."

The king seemed flabbergasted but then sat back and sneered. "So, my... charms are lost on you. No matter. That is why I brought these fine members of my army." He indicated them with a sweeping gesture. "Is it not impressive that I brought such an appropriate number to best you but not too many as to leave my territories unprotected? Clever calculation on my part."

"Lucky guesses by your advisors, you mean," Avelynne muttered.

Eleksander glanced to the others and saw that Taferia and Jero were straightening up, they had almost kneeled. So, continuously reminding each other that the king was not what he seemed only worked so far. But the four of them, the second wave, were impervious. Was it that they were solstice born?

"Look, I do not want to slaughter you," Lothiam said with a theatrical frown. "Simply retrieve your lost loyalty, lay down your weapons and kneel. Then, tell the strangers you have met, in whatever language they speak, to do the same."

"They speak our language. Weren't you listening?" Sabina said.

The king glanced at her as if she was nothing more than a bothersome gnat. "They, and their whole people, will submit to me or die. I will, however, deal with them later. First, you four will be brought to my court for experiments. We will see what can be done with your so-called golden magic and how it can serve me. Or simply be transferred to me."

Exactly how dim-witted was this man? Or rather, how stupefied with power was he? Then, as Lothiam focused that intense gaze on the Hethklish, Eleksander wondered if he had misjudged his intelligence. If the Hethklish had been Cavarrians once, would his sorcery work on them?

Eleksander thought hard and fast. Should they pretend to obey the king? Let him capture them and take them for experiments and, while there, try to convince the Twelve to work with Aurea and spread those leaflets with the use of her printing press back on Hethekla. But if the king could control the Hethklish? All would be lost.

There was only one way out.

"I believe we must fight him," Eleksander whispered to the others. "Right now. Before he turns everyone against us."

"Yes," a voice croaked. It was Jero. He held his Hethklish spear with white knuckles and a desperate expression. "He almost took over my mind. I shan't allow him to try again." Without waiting for a plan of action, he charged the first row of soldiers, shouting, "For the crew of the Wolfsclaw!"

Being nearest him, Avelynne tried to grab on to his sleeve, but he shook her off easily. Now everything happened lightning fast and Eleksander struggled to take it all in.

The archer next to the king fired. With unbelievable luck, Jero had sidestepped a rock at that point, meaning the arrow hit him in the arm instead of square in the chest. Hale roared a battle cry and ran in with his knives held high, covering Jero. Meanwhile, Sabina shot a volley of magic at the man who had fired at Jero and that set off the battle everywhere around them. Right away, it was a cacophony of sound and movement. Blinding streams of magic and cries filled the air. It came to Eleksander like a bucket of ice water over the head – so many people would die here today. The smell of blood, sweat, and loosened bowels from the fighting and the dying infested his nostrils. Eleksander loosened arrows at everyone who attacked him or those on his side, happy that the Cavarrians wore the king's uniform so he could tell who was who. Even then, he knew that the people he was firing at—that he was hurting and killing—were his own kind. Many of them had the Lakelands flag on their uniforms. He fired his final arrow at a rider and, only when unseating her from her horse, realised that she was a friend of his father's. She had been to dinner at their house, and he vaguely recalled that she had bought him a set of marbles for one of his birthdays. Now, he might have killed her.

He had little time to dwell on it as a Northern soldier's ice wolf attacked. Eleksander fought the beast off, trying very hard to incapacitate it without killing it. He threw his now useless bow away and instead hit the wolf over the head with a small amount of magic. It struck true and the wolf lay unconscious but, thankfully, still breathing. A heartbeat later, its owner attacked. Eleksander had just enough time to draw the dagger Hale had given him.

And so it continued. There was no rest, scarce time to think, and none of the glory and feeling of purpose he had read about in the history books. In fact, nothing was like in the books. There they always had a plan of attack. Charging from different flanks, trying to take out the archers, and so on. Here, it was just a dirty and miserable dogfight. It was only the enemy you had in front of you. Only the volley of magic that came towards you and how you would fight it off. It was only surviving for as long as you could.

A Peakdweller soldier with a broadsword hissed through gritted teeth that her nephew had been on the Wolfsclaw and Eleksander went nerveless for a beat, guilt spreading through him like a numbing poison. Fortunately, Hale was there and counterattacked, using his magic to encapsulate the Peakdweller's sword and almost yanking it out of her hands. Eleksander hit her with a magic volley of his own, knocking her flat on her back.

"By the waters, I am glad to see you unharmed," Eleksander panted, grabbing Hale's arm.

"Likewise, soft-heart."

Or had he said "sweetheart"?

Either way, Eleksander wanted to kiss him. To hold him close and breathe in the calming pepper scent of him. But there was no time. Another two soldiers attacked and Eleksander had to dodge a crossbow bolt.

Hale now stayed by his side and Eleksander noted that he was limping a little. Despite that, Hale's skilled movements, so much quicker than his own, meant they could take on three or four soldier at a time and allowed Eleksander to occasionally shake out his strained hands or to blink.

The king's army was indeed well-trained, well-armed, and had the advantage of numbers. But, as he had hoped, the stronger magic of the second wave and of the Hethklish meant they were more efficient in battle and didn't tire as much as standard Cavarrians after magic use. Taferia's and Jero's magic of course had the same energy and forcefulness as their enemies, but Eleksander had lost track of where Taferia fought and had no idea where Jero had gone after his injury. They were good fighters, though, and would be protected by both his fellow mapmakers and the Hethklish. Still, he could only beg fate to have kept them alive.

Now, he used his stronger magic to shoot off two streams at once while spinning, knocking out four Woodlanders brandishing axes and swords. One of them fell with his head hitting a rock. Eleksander knew for sure he had killed that one and nearly vomited, his heart aching like it was being strangled.

After that, the crowd where he and Hale stood momentarily thinned out. Eleksander took the chance to breathe and check Hale and himself for injuries. Hale's limping turned out to be due to a, in Hale's words, "blow from a shitting flail." Luckily, the flail hadn't been the spiked kind and had only hit his thigh. Nevertheless, Eleksander worried about permanent damage.

He looked around for the others. No sight of Taferia or Jero or any of the Hethklish that he knew by name. After a while, he did spot Avelynne and Sabina, though. They were a good distance away and fighting alongside someone else, from his location he couldn't see who, but assumed it was Aurea. They stood in a small circle with their backs to each other. It seemed a good tactic. He was about to call to them to gather up. Perchance if Avelynne and Sabina were with him, they could pool their magic again and through the golden magic propel a large swathe of the soldiers away and end this. Assuming the king would stop the fighting if he lost a sizeable amount of his soldiers, of course. And if Lothiam was even here and hadn't gone back to his castle to nap and listen to his lute players. Or to gather the rest of his army.

However, before Eleksander had a chance to call Sabina's name, soldiers were upon him and Hale. Eleksander didn't even have time to duck or raise his dagger before a soldier had grabbed his tunic and pointed her long, well-honed sword at him, the tip poking at the base of his throat. What should he do? Talk to her? No, she was under Lothiam's spell. Action, then. Could he slap the sword away with his dagger? Attempt to yank it away with magic? Duck or dodge? Try to punch her? No. Any violence was out of the question. That sword was already piercing his skin and any movement could drive it in further. In fact, he was surprised she hadn't already shoved it through his neck and ended him in one gory thrust.

Hale wasn't able to help. Eleksander saw him from the corner of his eye, fully engaged in frenzied battle with two soldiers.

"Face me, traitorous scum," the soldier who was pointing a sword at him said. "How dare you sell out

Cavarra to these savage-looking outlanders? Drop your dagger."

Eleksander obeyed.

Did he imagine it or was the sword's metal cold against his skin? He was certain that the warmth of his dripping blood was real, either way. Only after he'd noticed the dribble of blood did the pain register. Despite that, the thrum of his pulse left his ears, and all was quiet for a beat. The pain and fear didn't much seem to matter anymore.

So. This was how he would die.

Dying in battle was meant to be a heroic, noble death to be written about or sung about. Eleksander didn't feel like a hero. Not brave. Not glorious. There wasn't even a whisper of his birthmother's noble blood making him take pleasure in entering the history books. He was only a nineteen-year-old merchant's son who dropped his focus to make sure his friends were all right and, because of that, was going to die.

He looked into the eyes of his killer and found them the same colour as his sister Ellenaria's. If he was to die, he would pretend they were Ellenaria's eyes and she was here with him, ready to comfort him like when they were little.

Out of nowhere, Hale rushed forward and stabbed an already blood-drenched dagger into the soldier's forearm. Screaming, the soldier dropped the sword, releasing Eleksander. Hale pushed Eleksander aside, taking his spot as the soldier started getting back up.

Eleksander had lost his balance when pushed aside and fell, landing on his back. Painfully, the air went out of his lungs, and he had a few moments where he couldn't catch his breath. As he struggled to collect himself, he saw the soldier give a bellow of rage again while picking up her sword with her good arm. She attacked just as Hale lifted his dagger—where was his other one?—to deflect the blow. Despite the size difference in their weapons, Hale managed it. And now he was in a position to attack. Eleksander watched as sword and dagger clanged against one another. Hale was dodging and swiping, dancing like a leaf in the wind despite his limp. The soldier, distracted by cuts and stabs and already looking tired, jabbed her sword again, but this time slower due to the weight of her weapon. Hale, however, seemed finally in his natural element. Eleksander was just about to fire off a volley of magic to push the soldier back when he realised that Hale didn't need him to. As always, his Woodlander enjoyed this dance of battle. He was an artist at work as he jabbed his dagger into the seam between the soldier's breastplate and shoulder armour and drove it deep into the flesh. As the screaming soldier tried to cover her wound, Hale slit her throat without hesitation. It was only when the soldier fell in a boneless heap and Hale mumbled, "May trees grow where you land," that he looked pained and as if he hated this battle as much as Eleksander did.

Hearing that phrase brought home a fact. Hale just had to kill another Woodlander. Had he known her? Had he known any of the others he had been forced to kill today? Should they have surrendered after all?

Decisions. Always these heavy, impossible decisions.

Eleksander got to his feet, glancing about him. How many of these soldiers were merely under the king's spell and how many actually believed in the justice of killing the second wave and the Hethklish? Could enough of them have been made to see reason and put their weapons down? It was all quite hypothetical as they had no time to speak to their attackers before they were fighting for their lives.

"Are you all right?" Hale said, grabbing his arm. "You look dazed. Did you hit your head when I pushed you? Sorry about that, by the way. I had to make sure you were safe."

"No need to apologise. And no, I didn't hit my head. I was just trying to find a way out of this without... You know what, never mind. We may be attacked any moment now so let me just say thank you for saving my life."

Hale adjusted his clothes and took the fighting stance again, even though the combatants around them were all busy with each other. "Don't thank me for something so obvious. The second wave protect each other. Shitting silver beasts, people on the same side in a war protect each other."

"I know. I want to convey my gratitude anyway." Eleksander examined the battlefield, checking that no one was coming at them. "Especially as we might not survive this."

"I'll always protect you. I've chosen to tie my life to yours. There's a link between our hearts now," Hale said. "That link cannot be broken, not even by death. I won't allow it."

With ease, Hale turned to throw magic at an approaching soldier, like he had said nothing out of the ordinary, like that one sentence hadn't rose-tinted Eleksander's whole world.

But this was not the time to think of that.

Eleksander picked up his dagger and headed back into the fray when Hale's calloused, strong hand pulled him back toward him. Eleksander had no time to ask why as his speech was silenced by a kiss. A panicked and sloppy kiss, but still unmistakably a very visible and *public* kiss. It was as rough as it was heartfelt, and it filled Eleksander from his toes to his braids with the will to live.

They broke apart as fast as they had come together. "Are you sure you want to be doing that here?" Eleksander panted.

"Because we should be fighting or because people can see us?" Hale asked with a wild grin.

"Both!"

"Well, there was a lull in the fighting long enough for a kiss."

With one eye on the busy combatants around them, Eleksander asked, "And the second bit?"

Hale pulled his torn mail vest into place. "Constantly being about to die puts shit into perspective. Even more so when I saw you almost slain. If anyone has a problem with me loving another lad, that's their shitting problem." He wiped the worst of the blood and gore off his dagger. "When we go back to the Woodlands or the Lakelands, we'll probably get hounded for it. Still, my gut says that it'll be worth it, and you taught me to listen to that."

The word "loving" thrummed along with the high pulse in Eleksander's ears. "I taught you to listen to your gut instinct?"

"Of course. That's why I got the tattoo."

Eleksander would've asked what he meant about the tattoo, right before he said that he loved Hale too. Except another wave of soldiers surged towards them, and the world became noise, blood, and frenzy. Thank the waters that the vile Tutor Rogan had made them go through such extensive battle training. Eleksander had hated it then but now it was keeping him alive.

Soldiers filled his vision. He was struggling to keep focused on every flank and quite a few blows from his enemies were hitting home. So far, it was all flesh wounds, bruises, and bumps but he was terrified he'd soon feel a sword or axe penetrate his leather and mail. He was even more terrified that would happen to Hale, who now fought behind him, meaning they were back-to-back. Both his and Hale's desperation grew as this new surge of soldiers didn't let up. Had there been reinforcements? He tried to think of a way to get the upper hand or at least even the odds. But, planner as he was, he found nothing. All he could do was keep slinging magic, keep parrying blows with his dagger, and beg fate for this not to be the end of them. For him to get a chance to show Hale how much he loved him and to try for a life with him.

He was exhausted, his arms heavy as stone and his legs weak and throbbing from repeatedly stepping around and dodging down. He heard his own breathing, ragged and pathetic. Then that was drowned out by an almighty noise from the west. It was loud enough to make the combat cease as all fighters turned towards the sound.

Chapter Eleven

THE SHIFT

Sabina planted her feet firmer and saw the other two do the same. She, Avelynne, and Aurea had made a circle without discussing it when the fighting began. It was as natural and easy as when the three of them spoke or worked together. And now, here they were, a united front as they fought for their lives, the truth, the future, and every other accursed thing that had fallen onto their shoulders.

Through blood, scattered sand, and sweat, enemy after enemy was defeated. Kall stayed by Sabina's feet, clawing and biting as many enemies as she subdued. Although she had to stop him from simply attacking anyone in sight since he had gone into some sort of blood-thirsty frenzy.

Aurea's lack of weapon and battle training was obvious, but her quick reflexes and incredible magic skills made up for it. As time went on, the enemies were able to get closer before being defeated though. And, yes, the injuries to their trio were adding up. When she heard Avelynne yelp in pain and Aurea pant as her energy levels dropped, Sabina's fear rose along with her stomach into her throat. She couldn't let them die. She couldn't lose this battle. This was so much bigger than them and she had already failed far too many times.

So, she swung Grimfrost harder and threw her magic more viciously, feeling her usual fits of panic at the blood on her hands. Every person she maimed or killed threatened to bring back the memory of Tutor Rete's death and the guilt that filled her nightmares.

"How much longer do we have to keep this up?" Aurea wheezed.

How much longer they'd be *able to* was a better question. Sabina had known they might die here today. Nonetheless, knowing that with your head and now understanding it with your heart were two different things.

"Just keep going," Avelynne called. "You are doing wonderfully."

Sabina had no time for replies. Her current foe, a helmeted Peakdweller of indeterminate gender, was ferocious. And Kall was busy fighting a furious icewolf in her periphery and could not help. Sabina ducked a quick blow, feeling the blade swish above her head. When she looked down, long and thick strands of white were strewn around her feet. Her enemy had cut off some of the hairs that had escaped her braid, right at her scalp.

Sparring and training had prepared her for the fighting, but not for the blinding panic, the chilling rush, the hopelessness, or the flashes of hate.

Enraged to her marrow, Sabina's level-headed warrior calculation vanished. She screamed and lunged with Grimfrost, the bloodied battle axe hacking at her foe without mercy. It helped to think of it as the axe acting. She paused only to shoot off some magic, managing to knock off the other's already damaged breastplate.

That provoked the soldier— just as enraged and as skilled as Sabina— and their sword sang against Grimfrost, over and over. No one got the upper hand. They were too well-matched.

Then the soldier, out of nowhere, kicked wide and somehow managed to knock Sabina's knee to the side. She wobbled and unwillingly gave the soldier an in. That sword came for her and in an inelegant countermove, Sabina sliced with Grimfrost at a desperate, awkward angle. It was such an unexpected blow that the Peakdweller wasn't even protecting their exposed torso. The axe's blade cut through the clothing and buried itself deep in flesh. With battle craze in her blood and a roar on her lips, Sabina pulled the axe out and blood spurted all over her.

The soldier staggered back and collapsed, half-sitting and half-slumped, and pulled the helmet off.

Sabina now guessed the broad-shouldered Peakdweller was a woman, probably only half a handful years older than herself. She fell to her knees next to her foe. She'd knocked many a soldier out today and surely maimed and slayed plenty, but she hadn't so viciously and obviously killed someone as she just had this one. Because, yes, judging by that long axe gash across her chest and how it was bleeding, this woman was dead. She simply hadn't caught up to it yet.

The Peakdweller's gaze found Sabina's. "I don't w-want to die."

For some reason, Sabina tried putting pressure on the

gushing wound. "I know. Oh, shit. None of us do. I'm sorry. You came at me... I.... had to."

The screams and clangs of weaponry were so loud, and the woman replied so faintly that Sabina only caught the word, "Fault."

Panic and self-reproach made Sabina's eyesight blur. Yes, it was her fault. She had made that same unforgivable mistake again; she had taken lives. Blood was all over her and spouting out between her fingers on the woman's chest. Did this woman have a family? Parents? A spouse? Children? Had she perchance grown up with Avelynne?

"Yes," Sabina panted, blinking away tears.

"It's n-not yours. The king? W-why did I believe..." Her lips fell open and her eyes glazed over.

For a moment, Sabina heard and saw nothing.

The spell, did its power fade at death? Something else in Sabina clicked. *Not yours.*

Kall came back to sit by her, blood all over him too. Distractedly, she checked him for wounds but found only grazes.

"Snowdrop! Are you all right?" Avelynne asked between magic volleys at a Northerner and his iceboar.

"What? Oh." She scrambled up, running a shaking, grimy hand over her face. "Um. Physically, yes."

Sabina was torn away from the conversation by a burly attacking soldier with the flag of the Peaks on his uniform. Had he seen Sabina slay his fellow Peakdweller? She picked up the bloodied Grimfrost to parry the blow, and another battle took all her focus. The two of them struck, ducked, and fought, more desperately for each strike. Kall could now help, equalising the fight despite the man's massive frame. Sabina blinked away not only sweat but blood that dripped from her forehead, hoping the blood wasn't her own.

There was a reverberating noise, and in a heartbeat, all fighting stopped.

Even the soldier in front of her lowered his quarterstaff to face the west, where the noise came from. It was the sound of countless hooves.

What Sabina saw wasn't exactly an army, it was an immense mishmash of peoples. She first spotted frenzied riders on wide, thick-furred Northern horses and some extra brave ones riding reindeer. Keeping pace with the quick riders were Northerners companions: iceboars, snow-bears, icewolves and, of course, snowtigers. She gasped with rapture at seeing such power from her home, despite that these fighters would no doubt be under the king's spell and be coming to kill everyone she cared for.

Next to the Northerners rode Woodlanders on those svelte, large horses made for the heat of jungles and deserts. They rode hard and fast but still in formation, both riders and horses looking battle-hewn, confident, and fierce. Just like Hale.

At their side but a little further back, Sabina saw elegantly straight-backed riders in immaculate livery and tabards, all in the pale Lakelander blues and bright white. Behind them, she was sure she could spot Peakdweller banners and their trademark gleaming helmets and armour on top of their equally armed horses. They weren't hurrying. Those cursed Peakdwellers and their love for dignity and deliberateness, even when people were dying.

This wasn't the royal army, which was made up of

soldiers trained at the Centre, clad in the king's gold and scarlet uniforms and armour, with only a flag to tell you what county they came from. *These* were the armies of the four individual counties, the ones that the king could call in at times of war. She understood now that it was his spell that allowed him to so often make them war with each other and give him most of the spoils.

Why had they come, though? If the king wanted reinforcements, he could simply call upon the rest of his royal soldiers and have another thousand, loyal fighters leave the Centre for the short ride over here. The counties' armies would take days to arrive.

Her heart juddered. If they had come to aid their monarch, the last of the second wave's hope was gone. And they would have doomed the Hethklish along with themselves.

Kall paced around her feet, and she distractedly placed a hand on his back. Did he pick up on her fretting? Or was the killing frenzy still in his blood?

Avelynne had been shouting over the clamour, explaining to Aurea who these people were. She now finished with, "They should be loyal to the king. Yet, I cannot see why they would be here to aid him."

"I see," Aurea croaked. She stared at the armies, holding her throat and the right side of her jawbone. There was no blood there, but some was at her lips and now dripped onto her chin. Sabina gently wiped it off, not doing much good since her hands were sodden with the stuff already. "Aurea, look at me. Did you take a blow to the head?"

"What?" Aurea noted the blood. "Oh, that's only from

where I bit my cheek after I got a jab to the jaw. I'm all right."

Sabina nodded, again preoccupied with the approaching armies and the throbbing pain and exhaustion. The dazed realisation that there was nowhere to run, no extra trick to bring out, overcame her. Not unless they could find Eleksander and Hale and get the golden magic to work, despite the lack of water. She hadn't seen her adopted brothers for a long time though. Were they even alive?

"We must get ready to fight," Avelynne said in a hollow voice.

"Aye."

With that, she, Aurea, and Avelynne returned to their fighting circle. For a moment they held each other's bloodied hands. Then they gripped their weapons and prepared themselves.

The armies of the four counties neared. When the first Woodlander entered the fray, his long, notched sword wasn't aimed at the Hethklish or at the second wave. It was brought down against one of the king's soldiers.

Sabina gaped as the armies of the counties attacked her enemies. Was this a mirage? How could these people not be fighting for the king after the enthrallment of the spell, endless propaganda, and generations of history and tradition?

She stopped thinking and allowed a glimmer of relief and hope to stream into her battered mind. Now they were not only the ones with the strongest magic and the ones fighting for their lives; they were the ones in *majority*. With fresh vigour, she threw magic at the brawny enemy she had been fighting before, knocking him far back. He didn't get up again and she didn't check on him. If guilt kept her incapacitated, she had no chance of survival. She felt the body heat of the other two women, near but far enough to give room to manoeuvre. Or perhaps she wasn't actually feeling their body heat but only conscious of their presence and, snow help her, of how much she loved them. The three of them, with the aid of Kall, worked well together and soon they were fighting soldiers as a team. Sabina swung Grimfrost and sent enemies right into Aurea's streams of magic or into the pike Avelynne had picked up from a defeated enemy. It wasn't the beloved war scythe she had lost at sea, but she seemed happy to have some sort of polearm in her hands again.

Their fighting prowess was obviously drawing attention, as the ones who attacked them now were the riders who had flanked the king. Sabina countered another blow while pondering where the king was. He'd probably retreated to a safe place and sat quaffing from a wineskin. His inner circle, however, was attacking with force and she was happy to knock them off their beautiful horses. However, they were more experienced fighters and kept bringing out additional weapons from hidden sheaths and holders on their saddles. And there were at least a dozen of the riders. There were no Hethklish around them at the moment either, not that Sabina could see through the commotion anyway. She thought about shouting for the Northern army, knowing the strength of her own people and their companions would solve their quandary. She never got that far.

Four soldiers had joined up and pooled their magic to

create a stream strong enough to knock not only Sabina, but also Aurea, Kall, and Avelynne, to the ground. Sabina landed badly. She could tell that much despite the sudden confusion and ringing in her ears. She blinked to clear her vision. She had to get up. Had to fight. There was a throbbing right where her neck met her head which wouldn't let her get control of herself, though.

Her eyesight darkened and when it came back, something silvery flashed before her. Was it another magic assault? Or a sword coming straight for her face? For a befuddled moment she even worried it was a silver beast. Then she blurrily saw Eleksander, standing over her and throwing magic at the soldier who had attacked her. He was blooded and wincing, but thankfully he was alive and fighting fit.

When the foe was vanquished, he bent towards her. Through the fading ringing in her ears, she heard him ask, "Are you all right, Sab? Can you stand?"

Sabina clambered to her feet, still blinking away confusion. Everyone was already up? Avelynne was fighting a reedy soldier and clearly winning. Aurea was leaning over with hands on her thighs as if about to vomit. Kall was biting at the jugular of one of the soldiers that had thrown the magic. The other two soldiers were somehow already defeated.

"How long was I out? Everything went black and—"

"No time, older sister," Hale grunted. "We need your help but, first, answer his question. Are you all right?"

Sabina tried to check herself. Her ears no longer rang and her eyesight was back to normal. Only the pain at the base of her skull lingered. "I'm well enough."

"Thank the shitting silver beasts," Hale said.

Eleksander brushed back Sabina's hair, which was now more out of the braid than in it, checking the back of her neck. "No open wound or blood, only a bump."

"Aye, great," Sabina dismissed. "What did you need aid with?"

"There's too many soldiers around the king," Eleksander said. "Weapons and normal magic cannot get through. Sorry to rush you after your fall, but can you join your magic to ours? We must draw the king out."

"And we better hurry," Hale said. "Before Lothiam manages to use the shitty spell to make the Hethklish and the armies of the counties turn on us."

They were trying the golden magic, then? That would certainly get the king's attention.

Sabina rubbed the painful part of her head and neck. There truly was a massive bump forming there. Marvellous. She picked up and sheathed Grimfrost, then squared her shoulders. "Aye. Let's do it."

Chapter Twelve

ATOP A BED OF GOLD

With unease biting at her, Avelynne watched Eleksander raise his hands and pitch magic down into the ground. Hale soon added his stream of magic to his lover's, while Sabina held her blood-spattered hands out and said, "Right then, let's see if this works without water."

No matter how desperate they were, and despite the urgency, Avelynne couldn't join them. "Wait. Since we are not certain how the golden magic works, ought we really do this now? What if we hurt someone? Particularly, of course, those on our side."

Hale frowned at her. "We're shooting it into the ground, Ave."

"I obviously understand that," Avelynne said, battle having worn away her usual patience. "However, when we did this the first time, it coated the sea monster until it was frozen, or maybe even strangled, then drowned it. The second time, on the way here, it propelled the ship towards our enemies."

"And?" Hale said.

"We do not know how it works, other than that it either follows our unspoken wishes or that it merely seeks to destroy and harm," she said, looking at the fighting going on around them. "If it is the first option, everything will be fine. If it is the second, the magic may come out of the ground and coat every person and kill them."

While checking that no enemies were approaching, Avelynne noted that Aurea was called away and watched her leave with worry growing in her stomach.

Eleksander paused his magic throwing in what was probably the wise decisions to conserve energy. "I don't think it's the latter. If it was, the magic would've coated and sunk the second Hethklish ship when we were coming here, not propelled it and ours to shore. While we cannot consciously control the golden magic, I think we unconsciously can."

So many times, Avelynne had thought they should practise with the golden magic, to test its limits and its methods. But she had feared it. Mentioning the golden magic to the others had proved that they were afeared too. It always made them hurry to ask her to focus on the here and now and not fret about everything else. Also, they had all been up to their ears in the new and the intimidating, and so, she hadn't pushed and neither had anyone else. Now, she wished they would have conquered that fear and experimented.

A royal soldier was about to kill a Hethklish man next to them. Hale spun to the side and stuck his dagger into the soldier's neck, then turned back to the second wave. "We have to try something. We have the advantage for now but as soon as the king starts using his spell to convince everyone, we're lost."

Sabina was rubbing the back of her head. "How about we start shooting the golden magic into the ground next to a dying soldier? There's bound to be quite a few," she said with palpable sadness. "If the magic kills the soldier, we know we can't trust or control it and we need to come up with another way to draw the king to us."

"And if it doesn't kill them, we'll know our unconscious wishes are controlling it?" Avelynne filled in, optimism seeping into her like a hot drink on a freezing day.

"Let's try it. And fast," Eleksander said with a surprising air of confidence and leadership. After a while of scouring the battlefield, he pointed to a moaning woman wearing the king's scarlet and gold who lay a small distance away from the combat. They rushed over to the soldier and found her fatally hurt but not dead.

"We need to kill her," Hale said. "She's suffering."

Avelynne swallowed hard, not believing she was about to say this. "We will end her misery, but first we must do the test."

The cruelty of battle was too much for her and the matter-of-factness in her own voice added to it. She had to keep from throwing up or crying, though, the future of Cavarra was at stake.

Sabina held out her hands. "Make haste, then."

They all followed her lead and shot streams of magic into the ground. There was a beat where nothing happened, except for precious magic energy being wasted. Then, the streams mingled and turned golden. Avelynne sighed with relief, this at least was effortless, no magic-use fatigue, no pain in the muscles from swinging a weapon. The gold spread across the ground, but it was somewhat duller and more sluggish than usual.

Out of the corner of her eye, Avelynne saw Aurea come running. She was carrying something. A Peakdweller helmet? Aurea walked near the golden magic without fear and, holding the helmet like a bowl, threw its contents at the magic. Like a bolt of lightning, the magic there brightened and spread with its normal speed.

Aurea held up the helmet. "The ocean provides. Shall I fetch more water?"

"You clever thing," Avelynne breathed, overcome with the wish to kiss her.

"Aye, please get more water," Sabina said. She sounded just as infatuated as Avelynne felt.

"All right. I'll go find something bigger to hold more of it."

She left and Eleksander said, "Thank the waters the golden magic didn't hurt her. Now, we must carry on with the test."

And so they did. The magic neared the groaning soldier and Avelynne placed all her desire to not have the magic slay the soldier to the forefront of her mind. Wait. They planned to mercy kill this woman later. What if, unconsciously, they wanted to kill the soldier to put her out of her misery? Or because this was a war and she the enemy who had been trying to kill them? She cursed herself inwardly. She mustn't lose faith. They wanted the soldier to survive the golden magic, she had to focus on that!

The gold spread to the prone woman, solidifying and covering the blood around her, just like it had spread across the sea and then coated the monster. Avelynne's breath hitched. It was happening again. That poor soldier was going to be covered and die a painful death.

No. The gold spread around her but not onto her body. Instead, it looked like the soldier was writhing as before, but now atop a bed of gold.

The combat around them had ceased. County soldiers, king's soldiers, and Hethklish had all stopped mid-fight to stare at the gold. Only the county armies hadn't seen it before and yet *everyone* reacted as if it was a new phenomenon, as frightening as it was striking. Although, Avelynne assumed it was different seeing gold spread across the waves and seeing it on your land, approaching your very feet.

Riders drew nearer, slowly and unsure by the sound of their hoofbeats. When Avelynne gazed up, she saw it was the king's advisors and his flagbearers. The king could not be far behind.

"Not only is the test done. I think we got the shit-stain's attention," Hale muttered.

He lowered his hands and the golden magic turned into merely three streams of silver, making the others stop casting magic as well.

With his gaze fixed on the soldier, Hale took out his dagger.

Avelynne grabbed his arm. "No. I am the one who made her wait. I should be the one who commits the act."

Before he had time to argue, which he would considering he wanted to protect her from everything, Avelynne took the soldier's own sword out of her limp hand. Avelynne was trembling and her stomach roiled. She noted the flag on the woman's chest and said the Woodlander words she had heard Hale mumble after every discernible death, "May trees grow where you land."

Then she brought the sword down over the woman's neck. It was the quickest death she knew she could accurately perform. When the sharp blade cut through most of the woman's throat, Avelynne heard herself keen like a wounded animal. It was one thing to slash and stab at soldiers during a battle, it was another to execute someone while composed. Still, it was the right thing to do, and she had no other choice. Lothiam had left her with no other choice.

Through tears, she looked up to the riders approaching. She had seen a few of them back at Ironhold castle when they had attended her parents' feasts or celebrations; they had always demanded supplies from the Peaks and the king's ever-growing tithes before leaving. One of them, a severe man about ten years older than her, had even been a candidate for marriage. With them was Tutor Rogan on his scarred war horse.

She had feared these people. Now, she held up the soldier's sword, trying not to look at what it was covered in, and glared at them. "Where is your puppet master hiding, huh? Does the king not want to see the golden magic that he was so eager to experiment with? That he wanted to take from us for himself?"

She felt Sabina at her side and saw the gleam of Northern steel as Grimfrost was held out. "Answer her."

One of the advisors, Avelynne's would-be suitor, sneered. "Do you truly expect us to answer to traitors?"

"Look around," Hale said from where he stood next to

the advisor's horse. "We've outnumbered you and out-magicked you. All this fighting is achieving is more death, *your* death. Now, will your useless coward king show up? Or do we have to cut our way to him?" With that, he slashed through the strap of the advisor's saddle. The haughty man fell off his horse, to the laughter of anyone on the second wave's side.

There was a different mood on the air. Not the rush and commotion of war, but the feeling of a conflict having come to a head. And everyone was watching the four of them. Avelynne found she neither minded nor shrank under their gaze.

Chapter Thirteen

THE KING

Sabina heard a voice shout, "You dare! You dare do this to me?"

The king came riding over, quivering like a leaf on his horse. She wasn't sure if he was shaking with rage, fear, or simply the shock of not everything going the way he wanted.

Hale shouted back, "Get off that Woodlander horse, which you have not earned, and fight me, shit-heap!"

Sabina stifled a smile. That horse had been a sore point with Hale since the first time they met the king. Her merriment died as the king seemed to gather himself, breathing faster and audibly through his nose. Then, he held his hands out. Everyone fell silent.

In his most booming voice, King Lothiam called, "To everyone gathered. These four young traitors have deceived and lied to you all." He pointed to a group of Hethklish near him. "Yes, even you foreign sailors. You see their strange magic? That is not natural, not the way nature intended it. Tis wrong and unwholesome. It cannot be controlled and so will kill us all."

Sabina felt something, a niggling fear. A feeling that the king was probably right. They were a threat. Their very presence meant death and destruction. Who knew what they would do next? Who they would hurt?

Oh, snow above. He was using his power and he was putting all his effort into it this time, considering how hard those words had struck her.

The others must have felt it too because Eleksander raised his hands and shouted, "Hurry!"

They joined their magic to his, even though Sabina at least had no idea what they were doing. She only knew she wanted to keep the king from talking, keep him from turning everyone against them.

The magic crept up the horse's legs but didn't linger on them, instead moving to the saddle and the man in it. As it crawled up Lothiam's body and coated it, she heard those around him gasp, murmur, or give cries of "stop" or "no." He screamed too, shouted for aid, for someone to seize these vile traitors and free him of the spell. All while swatting at the gold and even trying to slice at it with his sword. The four of them sped up the magic best they could and, finally, his mouth was covered. Soon after that, he was fully coated.

Now what?

"Get him off that horse," Hale said through tight jaws.

And yes. Why not?

Sabina focused and assumed the others did too. The magic, still covering Lothiam in gold, lifted him off the horse and slammed him down to the ground with a thud. There, it kept him immobile.

How would they keep him from talking, though? They couldn't hold him covered in golden magic forever; it would suffocate him. Sabina jolted. She could kill him, thereby ending all of this. That was what they had trained her to do. What a warrior was meant to do, right? What Lothiam would do.

She looked at her bloody hands and the unique magic they were creating.

It hit her then, clear as glass. She got to choose this time. And, of course, she wouldn't kill. She wasn't a killer, no matter how this man and his actions had made her take lives. She wasn't a monster for killing Rete or any of the others. She had killed. But only because she had no other choice. Now, she had a choice and that would show who Sabina Rosenmarck really was. Everyone from her uncle back home to Aurea had claimed that the use of self-defence hadn't made Sabina a murderer, but she hadn't believed them until now. Until she saw war where everyone killed each other, whether they wanted to or not. They killed to survive and to make sure those they protected survived.

Just like her.

It wasn't right and it was a tragedy. But it wasn't her fault.

Someone she hadn't seen for a while came up to where the gilded king lay. Captain Naseer, in all his calming glory. He was carrying saddle bags which seemed full of water. "Looks like you don't need these anymore," he said, setting them down.

Behind him came Aurea with bags of her own. She put them down next to Naseer's and, after one look to Sabina and Avelynne, said, "Perhaps you wish to stop throwing that magic and we can quickly tie up and—more importantly—*gag* this pest?"

A gag. Sabina emptied her lungs of her tense breaths. Thank the snow for the level-headed Hethklish.

"I dare not stop the golden magic," Eleksander said. "You heard him speak. What if the moment we let him go, everyone here throws themselves at us and starts to kill us for our 'unwholesome, unnatural magic?' We cannot risk it."

"Yes, you can."

Speaking as she stepped forward was the pepper and salt-haired woman that Taferia had pointed out right before the battle begun: the undercover member of the Twelve who had given Taferia their secret signal. In a clear and precise manner of speech and with an unmistakable Peakdweller accent, she said, "Stand down, mapmakers. You have done more than enough today." She smiled, showing a few beautifully shaped wrinkles. "There are a number of us here who have practised the art of reminding each other of the king's true nature, thereby counteracting his powers of persuasions. We will help you."

As she spoke, a set of people had gathered rope and were standing around the king. In silence, they pulled up their sleeves, showing the silver tattoos of the Twelve.

Sabina and the other three glanced at each other and then, on an unspoken signal, dropped their hands and let their magic fade. The Twelve members immediately bound and gagged Lothiam, with help from Naseer and Aurea.

The Twelve representative nodded to them and then threw herself up on the king's tall horse, so she could be seen by more of the onlookers. She whistled for attention. "I am Kae Tarvin. Most of you know me as a proud and prominent daughter of the Peaks and royal advisor to King Lothiam. I am something else as well. I am a member of an underground organisation."

In a much more distinct way than Sabina ever could, this royal advisor told them all about the Twelve. How it was founded and why. Sabina threw a glance to Eleksander when Kae said that the murdered queen had started their organisation. His throat bobbed as he swallowed hard. After being prodded in the ribs by Avelynne, Hale hurried to wrap an arm around Eleksander's waist.

Kae sat forward on the horse. "One of our main reasons for upholding our organization, despite the risk of death and torture, was to counteract our king's evil deeds. Yes, I said evil. We do not know how he managed to do the things he did, but we suspect dark sorcery."

Taferia stepped up to the horse. "We have found some answers to fill in the gaps during our travels. However, it is a long conversation and we have wounded and dying people on this shore. We must tend to them before more answers are given."

Kae nodded. "My co-member is right. We will inform you all of everything we know later. No longer will our nation be kept in the dark and lied to. However, now, we must see to our wounded. And all will be treated the same, as long as you accept that the king is defeated, and the battle is over?"

Sabina saw soldiers and sailors call their agreement

and sheath their weapons. Soon, people began to tend to the injured and speak in low voices. The contrast from the hubbub of battle was striking.

Her gaze went to the king, bound and rolling around on the ground while grunting and screaming into his gag. Kall went over and growled in the burly man's face. The king stopped his grousing and lay still.

Eleksander, all politeness and decorum, was formally introducing himself to Kae and the group of Twelve members that had gathered, all showing their silver tattoos. There was no reason to hide now, she supposed. He motioned to the other mapmakers, and they came over. However, before Eleksander could finish introducing them, Kae kindly said, "Yes. We know who you are, where you come from, who your families are. We even know how you did on your acceptance tests into the Hall of Explorers."

Sabina remembered with a jolt that these people had helped manoeuvre them, four solstice born students, into their positions. Both with the aim of defeating the king and to, one day, get Eleksander onto the throne, with the three of them to back his claim and aid him. Now, the Twelve were reaping the benefits of their work. The king was defeated. Although, gagging him was only the start. They still had a nation in his thrall, no one to rule, and a continent starved and plagued by silver beasts. Perhaps knocking the king off his horse was the easy part?

"Well," Eleksander said. "You won't know these two people." He indicated Captain Naseer and Aurea.

Kae bowed to them and thanked them for their help in bringing the second wave home.

"It was our pleasure," Aurea said. "We have learned a lot from your mapmakers."

"And, thanks to Captain Rosenmarck," Naseer nodded to Sabina, "we have begun talks of diplomacy and trade. Ones that I look forward to continuing when things settle down here on Cavarra."

"We would be honoured, I'm sure," a large male member of the Twelve said.

Introductions over, Naseer said, "I must go see to my wounded sailors."

Sabina regarded the battlefield, fearing there would be Hethklish worse off than simply wounded.

Eleksander clasped Naseer by his upper arm. "Thank them for their sacrifice. And thank you again for your aid."

"I will," the captain said. "Well fought, lad."

Sabina watched him go, noting he was limping and holding his shoulder. Thank the snow he survived the fight. What other adult had ever listened to them, trusted them, as he had?

Avelynne addressed Kae. "How did you know we were coming? I thought the king intercepted the raven's message? And, if I may ask, how did you get the county armies to help?"

"Let me start with answering your last question. Atha Santorine."

Sabina's head swam and, for some reason, she found herself frantically looking around for their old tutor. That night when they confronted Rete and Santorine began repeating in her mind and she tried to shut it out. She couldn't deal with her attacks of guilt and panic now, not after having made such progress today. She pulled back, let go of control, and allowed the others to speak without her while she focused on breathing calmly and reminding herself that she hadn't done anything wrong.

Chapter Fourteen

A THEORY PROVED

Hale ran his hands through his short-cropped hair. It had blood splatter on it. Everything did. He regarded his hands, red again despite that he had kept wiping them on his clothes. He could smell blood and sweat on himself, still, that was the stench of victory. His three compatriots all looked severe and sad and Hale understood why. But... they had won! He had shown himself as the skilled warrior he had always wanted to be.

It had made him tired as all shit, though, and his eyes wanted to close. He shook his head to rouse himself and realised he had missed some of the conversation.

"Tutor Santorine?" Avelynne said. "What did she have to do with this?"

The Twelve woman—what was her name again? Oh yes, *Kae*—answered, "Atha Santorine cracked how to counteract whatever magic it is the king uses. While imprisoned, she carried out experiments on her fellow prisoners."

Eleksander balked. "What?"

"Nothing invasive or immoral, of course," Kae said, getting off that handsome Woodlands horse. "She merely theorised that, if you kept repeating to each other what the king did, every day, the hearers built up some immunity to the lie that the king wants what is best for us. She took inspiration from us in the Twelve."

Ever these repetitions, they made Hale itch with impatience.

"Yes, yes," he said. "Taferia told us all of that and we found the reason why."

"Ah. You hinted to having answers before," Kae said, squinting at him. "Why don't you tell me all while the others see to the wounded."

Oh no. None of that.

"Answer our questions first," Hale said. "How did you get the armies of the counties here?"

Kae smiled at him, some sort of appreciation there, he thought. "After Atha had experimented with reminding certain prisoners of the king's deceit, she passed on her findings. In the last few weeks, we implemented the method with the leaders of the four counties. Positioning our members around them so we could remind them at least two or three times daily."

Hale crossed his arms over his chest. "How does that explain why the armies of the four counties showed up?"

Avelynne and Eleksander glared at him, but it was Sabina who he expected to tell him not to be so rude and impatient. She, however, looked lost in her own world. Instead, Aurea nudged him with her elbow.

"Maybe if we gave her a chance to keep talking, we'd find out."

Her tone was jesting and her expression kind, so he didn't feel told off. This lass, she was a good addition to their group. He just wasn't sure how she fit into the whole Sabina and Avelynne thing. If, indeed, she did. Relationships were odd and confusing as snail-shit.

One of the other Twelve members, a man with hair as blond as his beard and an icewolf said, "Three days ago, we managed to get a raven to Santorine's prison window. Her reply told us that the king had, through torture and informants, found out about her research into the second wave and your solstice magic." He glowered down at the bound king. "She also said that it was clear from his questions that Lothiam had intercepted one of our messages and she told us roughly what it must have said."

Kae nodded. "We immediately contacted our stationed members in each county and asked them to tell the leaders to gather their armies and come here to fight the king."

Eleksander was fidgeting with one of his sleeves, which was half sliced off. "And that worked?"

"Aye. Despite our doubts, the process of daily reminders must've served its function," the Northern man said. "Without the spell in action, the leaders of the counties remembered hating the king, both for the high tithes and the constant demands for supplies and soldiers."

"Not to mention his refusal to do anything about the silver beasts anywhere but here in the Centre," Kae said in a matter-of-fact voice.

Hale didn't like that detached tone. The silver beast issue wasn't the only time Lothiam put the needs of the

Centre first. Were these people aware of how little coin for aid, food, or education Lothiam had allowed into the four counties? It was hard for Hale not to think of his parents, who might've lived if there had been a physician around.

Another Twelve member—wrinkled like a raisin and with so many amazing tattoos she must've struggled to hide them—said, "I reckon the information that they had to act to protect not only Cavarra, but their children - symbolised by you four, roused them. They were all happy to quickly gather as much of the armies as possible and rush to this shore."

Avelynne gave a quiet whimper. She was staring at a corner of the battlefield. Kae followed her gaze. "Yes. In your case, you didn't merely symbolise all Peakdweller children for the leaders of the Peaks. Your parents knew they were fighting for you. In fact, they were the first to join the cause."

Hale took in the people in question. A moustachioed, tall, slim man in neat armour was nearest, sitting ramrod straight on a grey-dappled horse. Riding up next to him, similarly armoured and also on a grey-mottled horse, was a short but even thinner woman with her chin held high and the coldest facial expression Hale had ever seen. The horses were wearing far too much iron armour. Shit, that must be uncomfortable for the animals after their long ride here and all the battle. The Ironholds faced each other, speaking only a few words judging by the lip movements and then sheathing their blooded weapons at exactly the same time. So, these were the pus-filled boils that had treated their only child like filth on their fancy boots. The grand count and grand countess were looking in their direction, ignoring their wounded Peakdweller soldiers. They hadn't come to check on Avelynne either. Or even nodded or waved to her. They merely sat there like statues and watched. Hale shook his head. All those years when he had wished he still had living parents, he had dreamed of warmth and laughter. He doubted these shitty people had a drop of either in those pale, rigid, skinny bodies. Still, they had at least come to fight. Even been first to join the cause.

He was pulled out of his thoughts and into the conversation again when Kae smacked her hands together and kept them pressed before her. She wore an expression that he couldn't read. Need? Desperation?

"Now, please answer the question we of the Twelve have been dying, often literally, to know," she said. "How does the king's propaganda spell work?"

With Sabina still standing to the side and Avelynne casting shy glances over at her parents, it was up to him, Aurea, or Eleksander to reply.

"Where to begin?" Eleksander said, running a hand over his now untidy braids. "Lothiam's ancestors entered a pact with some magical, ancient creature that apparently dwells within the lake between the castle and the Hall of Explorers. In return for sacrifices of the people that anyone of Lothiam's bloodline loved, a spell would be cast over Cavarra."

Hale watched him, as mesmerised as a silver beast is by magic. Eleksander's words were pretty and fancy as ever, while his poor, gorgeous face was serious and blood-spattered. It was so hard not to reach out and wipe that blood away, stroking that bruised cheek and that determined, strong jaw. His Lakelander. His lover. His... loved one. No more holding back. Come what may, Eleksander was his person, and he would follow him into fire or flood. Gently, Hale dabbed away the blood.

"A spell? Of what sort?" Kae said with an air of impatience.

"One that ensures Cavarrians believe the lies the king tells," Eleksander replied, taking Hale's blood-wiping hand and holding it. "And that they have a deep-rooted belief that the king wants what is best for them, making them inclined to want to obey him."

"Also, somehow, the spell created the silver beasts," Hale added. "Since that's gotten worse with the years, I bet the royal maggot did something else to worsen that, though."

He gave Lothiam a kick to the chins, enjoying the curses coming from that gagged mouth.

Their group stood there, listening to Lothiam grumbling and Kall washing with that massive purplish tongue of his. Meanwhile, Hale thought hard. The easiest idea? Force the truth out of Lothiam. Except, letting the shit-stain speak was dangerous. They were better off going to the creature in the lake, since that had to be dealt with anyway. Lothiam was only a mouthpiece, it was the creature that had doomed their nation and Hale was willing to bet it would be much harder to defeat.

Kae rubbed her chin. "Anyone in Lothiam's bloodline could carry on this pact with the monster? That may explain the rumours of him feverishly trying, but failing, to father children with any female courtiers, milk maids, or harlots available."

"Why did he not take a new wife and try to officially extend his royal line?" Aurea said.

Eleksander hummed, a crease between his brows as he looked at anything but Lothiam. "If he developed any sort of affection for said wife, he would have to sacrifice her to the creature in the lake. Like he did my birthmother. Mayhap even selfish, entitled, power-mad monarchs experience guilt?"

"Or he couldn't be a decent enough human to hold up even an arranged relationship," Hale said and spat in front of Lothiam's face.

"This is no time for details," Taferia said. "We must inform the leaders of the four counties of the salient points. Before they either begin warring with each other or return home."

"True enough." Kae clicked her tongue. "We shall invite the other Twelve members residing in the Centre too. They must be told that everything has changed. We no longer need a base to stage the rebellion, nor the rest of our meticulous nine-step plan. Whether or not we're ready... the cards have been dealt and the game started."

The liberally tattooed member shuffled, in true old lady manner, towards Avelynne's parents while saying, "Soon I shall go search out the Lakelanders, *my* duke and duchess are sure to be cleaning up in the sea. First, I'll speak to the Peakdwellers, though, since they're right there."

That snapped Avelynne's full attention back. "Wait. You mention discussing it with the rest of the Twelve and with the county leaders. What about us?"

The Twelve members looked at each other. Kae was the one to finally reply. "We will reconvene with you later. You ought to get cleaned up and go somewhere safe to heal and await further orders."

Hale bristled. "Wait a shitting moment. Does that mean you'll make all the decisions and then return only to tell us what to do?"

"Like we are nought but wayward children in need of controlling?" Eleksander added.

"You are not children," the vast Twelve member said. "You are, however, young and must be fatigued after all the responsibility weighing on your shoulders. You will be needed later when we place you, young Master Aetholo, on the throne."

Bone-tired as Hale was, he wouldn't be used as a pawn and then shoved away in a drawer when decisions about his future were being made. As he had decided on the ship, they had come too far and conquered too many perils to sit quietly out of the way.

"Old people tire much faster and yet you call us too 'young and fatigued'?" Hale pulled himself up to full height. "The only people able to use golden magic, that's what we are, you arrogant ragwort. We're the people who took your shitty king out."

"Of course. Not on your own, though, dear lad," the tall and bulky man said, infuriatingly patient and with what Hale finally placed as a Woodlander accent. One that had nearly been scrubbed away. "You required us to have prepared the county leaders to withstand the spell and to bring their soldiers to overpower the king's forces. Without that, Lothiam's soldiers would have stormed you the moment your golden magic struggled its way up his horse."

Struggled? It had flowed like water!

Eleksander put a hand on the small of Hale's back. "Hale is right about who we are. I might add, however, that we're also the only people with experience of journeying away from Cavarra and to have connections with a foreign race. Except for Taferia, who, by the way, will be precisely as tired as us. If you involve her in the talks, you should allow us to at least sit in."

Without hesitation, Taferia said, "Young or not, they should be part of this. They have not only the experience and information, but good heads for calculation and planning. Besides, if we hope to have Sander as king one day, he should start on the path of governing right away."

"Taferia," Kae said. "you have doubtlessly become attached to these four during your voyage. Nevertheless, you know as well as I do that they have endured much for folk not yet turned twenty. What is more, you're aware that we of the Twelve have been working on this for longer than they have been alive."

That lecturing note? Judging by her grimace, Hale would wager Taferia hated that as much as he did.

"I'm not saying they should make the decisions instead of us or that they should make them at all. But they should *be in the room* as they are made." Taferia set her jaw. "Furthermore, I believe an emissary from Hethekla should be present for the first reform talks. Not to intervene, but to listen and to tell us their experience as a more advanced nation."

The large Woodlander, the blond Northerner with the icewolf, and the elderly, much-tattooed Lakelander all looked to Kae. There seemed, again, to be some sort of silent communication. Only now did Hale note that the youngest one of them must be more than twice his age. *Shittingly ancient.*

"I suppose for these first talks we can be a larger group," Kae said slowly. "We can handle the details in smaller clusters subsequently."

So, that meant that the more involved chats would take place without them, huh? They'd have to see about that.

"First things first," Kae said, studying the battlefield. "We should join the others in seeing to the injured and the dead. Everyone should make sure to drink some water and see to any wounds of your own before you help anyone else."

Avelynne fidgeted with her necklace and still threw glances at her parents as she said, "Someone must offer the Hethklish shelter. It would not say much for our hospitality if they had to rough it on their battered ships. Perchance they could take some of the many free bedchambers at the Hall of Explorers?"

Oh shit. He hadn't thought of where they'd all stay. After this group chat was over, would they all be expected to return home to their counties? If so, he would be parted from Eleksander! And from Sabina and Avelynne, who by the way might still be banned from the Peaks?

First to answer was the icewolf-owner, who, now that Hale looked closer, was one of the Hall of Explorers officials. "Aye, they can take the guest quarters since we now have plenty of soldiers to place there to make sure our visitors..."

Behave, Hale thought.

However, the Northerner finished with, "Are comfortable. And you of the second wave will obviously lodge there too. Hopefully we shall have enough food for everyone."

They all agreed and dispersed.

Under the heat of the sun, they cleaned up the grim mess that warring humans make.

Chapter Fifteen

AFTER THE BATTLE

After having helped some wounded, Sabina had to go sit down. She leaned against a tree and slowly sank to the ground. Despite the spring warmth, she shivered, and her head swam. Fatigue, shock, and grief, she guessed. The fighting was finally over, both the battle and the debate on whether they could be part of the debrief and future planning. Nevertheless, Sabina found it hard to believe that they were out of danger. Every movement spotted out of the corner of her eye might be a threat, an oncoming blow, a sword, a volley of magic. She took deep breaths, trying to calm her battle-heated pulse.

When calmer, she closed her eyes. Her head still hurt. So much pain. So much death. How did one move on after all of this?

She opened her eyes at the sound of footfalls. Aurea came rushing towards her. Sabina blinked repeatedly, trying to shake her headache and the idea of Aurea being far too beautiful with her short, copper hair dishevelled and eyes shining with worry.

Crouching beside her, Aurea cupped her face. "Sab, are you all right? Doldrums, that was quite the knock you took back in that battle."

It had been, hadn't it? She was lucky to be alive. Aurea's hands on her cheeks were cool and calming. Sabina tried to smile to reassure her, but it probably came out as a grimace. "Aye, I'm fine. Just a bad bump."

Aurea moved to see the back of Sabina's head. "More than just a bump. Your head is bleeding."

"I'm fine." She put her hands over Aurea's. "I promise."

"Thank the tailwinds for that," Aurea said on an exhale.

Then, with hummingbird fast movements, she leaned in and placed a kiss on Sabina's mouth. Their lips just brushed before Aurea pulled away again with a shocked expression.

"Sorry! I was so worried about you! And then I was, I don't know, so feverish and excited and terrified and all these things that the battle brought about. And, and, and I can't seem to calm down again. And so, I do things I shouldn't."

Sabina loved when the words came this fast from those pretty Hethklish lips. "It's all right."

"No. I didn't have your consent."

With emotions warring in her and her gaze searching around for Avelynne, Sabina said, "I think we've been close to kissing quite a few times. You know I wanted to."

"I thought so, yes." Aurea moved from crouching to sitting. "But, I mean, I know you and Avelynne are being exclusive."

So, they were having this conversation here and now? Sabina wasn't sure she was in good enough shape for it.

"Aye," she said. "I'm in love with Ave. However, she cannot love the way I do. I've started to come to terms with that, but it's all very confusing."

Mainly the fact that she thought she would never love anyone but her lovely countess. But Aurea, so different from Avelynne, had crept into her thoughts and her heart when she wasn't paying attention. What did that mean? Was she terrible for being attracted to two people at the same time?

"That's fine," Aurea said, drawing circles in the sand with a finger. "I have no expectations of you. I was just so attracted to you immediately. I've never felt that way before. I take a long time before I fall for someone and, when I do, I stay stuck on them for years. With you, though, I was instantly spellbound." She brushed off her sandy fingers, avoiding eye contact. "However, I don't want to disrupt anything. Whatever sort of love it is, it's clear how deep the bond between you and Avelynne is." Her expression grew awed. "I understand why, she's so intelligent, lovely, and kind. And, of course, painfully beautiful."

Sabina looked down at her bloodied hands. "Aye, Avelynne is special. There's no one like her and that is sort of mesmerising."

Aurea put a finger under her chin and lifted her face to lock their gazes. "You're special and mesmerising too. Your strength, your accountability, your loyalty, your bravery, and the way you see things. I find you just as fascinating, if not more, then Avelynne."

Sabina was stunned. The idea that someone could find plain old her more fascinating than the unique, ethereal Countess Avelynne Ironhold of the Peaks was gobsmacking. Someone other than Avelynne, of course, since she thought everyone was better than herself.

Seeming self-conscious, Aurea ran a hand through her hair, making some of it stand on end. Sabina reached out to smooth it down. "Thank you. Truly. That means so much to me. Oh, and thank you for everything you did in this battle. We would surely be dead without your aid."

"It was fine. You would do the same for me without any hesitation. Speaking of the battle though, I should return to checking on my sailors. Will you be all right here on your own?"

"No need to fret, sweetest Aurea. I shall look after her," Avelynne said.

Both Sabina and Aurea whipped their heads towards the third lass, who stood to their right with the sun backlighting her. When had she appeared? How much had she heard?

Aurea stood with an unsure smile. "Good."

Stepping nearer with a smile anything but unsure, Avelynne said, "I add my thanks to Sabina's. We are forever in your debt."

She wasn't acting jealous, but she also wasn't acting quite normal. Had she seen the kiss? If so, had she even minded?

"No need to thank me," Aurea said, gaze flitting around. "Are... you all right?"

"Cuts, bumps, and bruises. Otherwise, I am fine." Avelynne gave a little laugh. "It astounds me, actually. I was certain I would be killed in the first few blows but clearly the Hall of Explorers' training and your instruction during our sea journey has improved me."

"You give yourself too little credit," Aurea said, just as Sabina was thinking it.

Avelynne tilted her head, in her usual gesture of examination. "And you perchance give me too much. Either way, I thank you for your kindness."

Aurea nodded and went off towards where the Hethklian sailors were gathered.

Then, the two of them were alone.

Avelynne sat down next to her, with such care and grace that she might be at a tea party rather than a battlefield. She had a long, barely clotted over gash on her neck and blood on her ruined clothes, though, proving what she had actually been doing.

She also had that look in her eye.

Sabina knew it well. She'd seen it in the mirror after Tutor Rete's death. Something broke inside you the first time you had killed, even if it was self-defence or on a battlefield. Sabina wasn't sure if it ever could be fixed again. Or if it even should be.

Avelynne brushed her hair away from her face. That sleek mane had grown quite a bit these few weeks, she should have tied it up before battle. "Are you all right, snowdrop?"

"Aye, I'm fine. Didn't you... hear me tell Aurea that?"

Smiling sadly, Avelynne said, "No. I came to overhear the conversation around when you explained that I was incapable of loving you the way you love me and how that confuses you. My apologies for not alerting you both to my presence, I froze."

Sabina had known she'd be honest. It still stunned her

to hear her own words parroted back to her in those posh speech patterns of Avelynne's.

"So, then I guess you gathered that Aurea and I..." She couldn't say the words.

"Are attracted to each other? Yes. That has been apparent for weeks, though." Avelynne gazed up at the cloudless sky. "You know, I cannot help wondering if this gets easier with time. Is attraction a more solid, clear, reliable thing after the age of twenty? Or after thirty? Does it get easier to know your own heart and to control it?"

"I don't know. And it doesn't matter much. I'm in this complicated situation right now and I wish I wasn't," Sabina said, scrubbing a hand over her face. "Our world has just been turned upside down for the hundredth time this year. Or at least that's how it feels. I can't be handling all these emotions too."

Avelynne caressed her cheek. "I know, my dearest, and I am sorry for it. At the moment, we all seem to be in such a muddle."

Sabina looked over to Hale and Eleksander, who were helping wounded Hethklian sailors while sharing affectionate glances. "I don't know. Those two seem to be getting somewhere. They've had their share of confusion and heartbreak, but it seems to be settling. They just need the chance to start their relationship and figure it out as they go along. You, me, and Aurea on the other hand..."

Avelynne's lips quirked up. "Don't let Hale hear you say that. You know our dear Woodlander would say something clumsy about women being more complicated than men."

Sabina knew full well that he would blurt out something like that but with brusquer language. "True. I hope Sander is up for the job of keeping that one in check."

"He is," Avelynne said with a maternal smile towards both lads. "I think he may be the only one who can steer Hale right. And Hale knows that too and will find ways to prove his gratitude and appreciation, I'm sure." She returned her attention to Sabina. "Now, may I see that head injury of yours, snowdrop?"

"Sure."

Avelynne began gently examining the area. It hurt like frostbite, but Sabina tried to be brave and not show it.

"Hm. There's a gash, which is where the blood is coming from, and below it you have a large bump. Having recently had a head injury of my own, I must ask what Naseer asked me when I awoke. Do you have a headache?"

"I did. But it was just around the bump and it seems to be lessening."

"Are you nauseous or struggling to stay awake?"

"No."

Avelynne looked into her eyes. "Any memory loss or issues with movement, hearing, or vision?"

"Not that I've noticed."

"Good. We shall see how you get on and keep an eye on that bump." Avelynne sat down in front of Sabina. "She's utterly charming, isn't she?"

"What?"

"Aurea. That infectious joy, charisma, boundless energy, generosity, and curiosity. You feel better just being around her."

"Aye," Sabina said, unable to meet her gaze.

"I find her physically attractive too. She's got a unique

sort of appeal that transcends gender and fashion. She's so captivating that it's hard to take one's eyes off her."

"It is." Sabina pretended to be fascinated by a strip of cloth sliced half from her tunic hem.

"Maybe you ought to be with her?" Avelynne said in tones as slow as they were sad. "She eases your troubles and makes you less hard on yourself. She brings out the best in you. Furthermore, she could love you the way you want to be loved."

"You are the one I'm with."

"We've been over this, sweet snowdrop. A conventional relationship locks one into living one's life with someone and only them. It expects more than erotic friendship, it expects a connection that I cannot feel."

"Aye, I know that and my feelings *have* adjusted. I don't want to trap you in a relationship, but I do want to be with you somehow. We have been through so much together."

"Indeed," Avelynne said wistfully. "First coming to the academy and settling into that strange life. Then there was my secret."

"Then the conspiracy and the deaths."

"The confrontation with Rete and Santorine," Avelynne added. "Finding out about the Twelve and about the king."

"After that, sailing and losing our sailors and our ship, meeting a new race, finding out more truths from Taferia and the Hethklish history book," Sabina finished. Hadn't she missed a few hundred points, though?

"It has been," Avelynne moved close enough to place her forehead against Sabina's, "a lot. We understand each other like no one else can."

"You have certainly understood me for a long time.

Before you and Aurea, no one had ever understood me. Or even tried, I think." An ache was spreading through her chest, a deep, sharp one. She pressed her forehead harder against Avelynne's and wrapped her arms around her. "Whatever you can offer me, I will stay with you. Unless you tell me to go."

"I know, my sweet," Avelynne said with misery pouring off every word.

They sat like that in silence until Taferia came to ask them to help carry wounded to the makeshift physician's camps being set up. Taferia was holding hands with a handsome, pudgy man and kissing his hand between her sentences. He watched her with such ardent affection that no one could mistake that this was her betrothed. He'd survived and they had been reunited, thank the snow. That chest ache increased as Sabina watched them. This was what mutual, marital love looked like. But how it felt? That she would never know.

Chapter Sixteen

THE FIRST MEETING

Eleksander examined a multi-coloured bruise covering most of Hale's arm. It was fading as expected, considering it was five days after the battle on the beach. "If you're careful, and don't hurt yourself while sparring or training, this should be gone soon."

Hale rolled his eyes. "Careful is for old people."

"Careful is how you survive to be old people," Eleksander countered, quietly so the others in the room wouldn't be disturbed by their conversation.

Hale looked about to argue but then grudgingly nodded.

They were gathered at the Hall of Explorers, in the grand hall that had given the institution its name to be exact. It was a natural place for the meeting to discuss Cavarra's future. It had been a rough few days to get here, though. Not only because of the grieving for the dead and the healing of wounds, but because every citizen they encountered meant hard work. The people either had to be convinced of the king's wickedness, and told not to be loyal to him, or threatened by the armies of the four counties into allowing the interim leaders—the four members of the Twelve who had been royal advisors—to rule until a government could be formed. Eleksander wasn't sure why he had thought that after the king was silenced, people would stop blindly defending and adoring him. Even if the spell was to be removed fully, generations of propaganda and traditions would remain. However, the spell wasn't broken. That mysterious creature lingered deep in its lake and Lothiam's deal with it held firm. Still, one problem at a time.

Eleksander regarded the attendants.

There was the second wave, sitting close to one another, determined not be thrown out. Next to them were Captain Naseer and Aurea, who seemed unsure if they should be here. Tutor Hathleen and Tutor Myle were also present, both timid and as useless as ever. Fortunately, Tutor Rogan had been imprisoned for his complicity and unyielding support of the king. And finally, there were the four most high-ranking members of the Twelve who had also been royal advisors. They were the ones they had met after the battle. Kae was the only one who had given her name. The other three were the large man hiding his Woodlander heritage, the Northerner with the icewolf, and the overly-tattooed Lakelander.

Eleksander had asked the old lady how she had hidden her silver tattoos for those many years, and she answered, "No one looks all that closely at an unobtrusive, little grandmother. Lothiam certainly never looked at anyone but curvy, fertile maidens. Besides, my wrinkles hid some of the tattoos and my oversized royal advisor garb did the rest." She had grinned wickedly. "Never underestimate a hooded cloak, lad. They let you get away with everything."

Now, the tutors and the members of the Twelve sat speaking in sombre voices as they waited. Eleksander was doing everything he could not to think about who they were waiting for. In fact, he had tried everything to postpone this meeting, including ducking into alcoves when he heard the approach of the entourage of the duchy. However, today, he had to face his birthfather.

Eleksander sat between Sabina and Hale on the left side of the long table that divided the hall. He tried to get comfortable on the padded bench and to focus on his surroundings to distract himself. As for every meal they had ever had here, the table was set with perfectly polished pewter plates, tankards, cutlery, and candelabras with long candles. The difference was that those candles had always been scarlet, the king's shade of red, but now they were the Hall of Explorers' emerald green. Another difference was to be seen on the walls. Woven banners still hung on them, but not the main one – their former crownbearer's over-sized one. Its gilt threads and rubies had always caught the light from the candles and the hall's huge fireplace. Now, its spot gaped empty. Eleksander wondered why they hadn't replaced it. Was leaving the space blank meant to be symbolic? Or were they just waiting for the next crown-bearer's banner?

He heard Kae say, "Oh, by the way, Taferia. We have finally been given access to all of Lothiam's affairs."

Taferia snorted. "I assume that was interesting reading?"

"Interesting is one word for it. That callous, short-sighted fool not only seized more tithes than even he could squander but also made truly witless purchases and investments. Not a plan, or even a thought, in sight."

"I'm not surprised. Without the spell, someone would have replaced him on that golden throne of his long ago."

Eleksander considered how the king had sent them out unprepared and with low resources and still expected miracles. He was knocked out of his thoughts by Sabina nudging him and whispered, "Look, the baron and baroness!"

Two genderless people in furs and leather marched in without any pomp. The Northerners were broad-shouldered with short hair and pale, weather-beaten faces. In short, they were as rugged, strong, and unpretentious as Sabina. And as Ivar had been. Thinking about the old sailor and how his life had ended in the jaws of that sea monster squeezed Eleksander's heart like a vice. Was Sabina thinking about that too? If anyone would be, it was her. Just in case, Eleksander put his hand over hers on the table.

She gave him a fleeting smile and mouthed, "Are you all right?"

He mouthed back, "Yes. You?"

She nodded before her usual serious expression returned as her attention went back to the new arrivals.

When the baron and baroness were seated, their animal companions—an iceboar for him and a snowbear for her—sat on either side. The giant bear, almost too big for its spot in the room, laid its head on the baroness's shoulder. She tilted a little under the weight but bore the giant head with the dignity of someone used to it, even moving her face so her cheek rested against the bear's nose.

Eleksander leaned close to Sabina and whispered, "Why don't Northerners who have snowbears ride on them?"

"They are *companions*. Not mounts," Sabina said sharply.

"Right. Sorry."

He'd never grasp what companions were. Not pets. Not guard dogs. Not mounts. Never mind, he didn't have to understand something to respect it.

Another party entered. These people were dressed in layers of clothing with luxurious fabrics cut in strict fashions, all in muted hues of iron-grey and dark purple. They had all the pomp that the Northerners did not, with finely dressed pages escorting them in and pulling out their chairs for them before bowing and scurrying back out. Eleksander heard Avelynne gasp as a haughty woman promenaded in with her hand held up in the merest grasp of a pockmarked, moustachioed man who was very tall for a Peakdweller. The woman was an older and even thinner version of Avelynne, with the same pallid skin, calculatedly graceful movements, and sleek red-black hair, hidden partially under a charcoal hennin headdress. The couple had, like their daughter, the narrow and grey eyes of Peakdwellers. But their eyes were darker and lacked the shy kindness of Avelynne's, those eyes also never looked in the direction of their only child.

They had barely sat down when a muscled woman with light brown skin and deep scars stormed into the room with an air of someone in a hurry to get a small errand over with before continuing with more important business. She wore linen clothing with a leather harness for weapons and accessories. This had to be the Woodlander's Warden, the only leader on Cavarra who was voted for instead of being born into her position.

Eleksander let go of Sabina's hand to adjust his clothes and check his braids. They now waited for the Duke and Duchess of the Lakelands. The pair were as known for their beauty, culture, wealth, and intellectual status as the Lakelands itself. But, equally, the Lakelands' shallowness, self-interest, and drama. Naturally, they would keep everyone waiting to make a grand entrance.

Eleksander's hands shook as they pulled his tunic into place.

His father by blood. No one had talked about that in the last few days. Taferia and the others of the Twelve only went on and on about him being the late Queen Lea's son. She was the one who carried him, who birthed him, and probably gave him milk before he was handed off to the wet nurse. She had missed and loved him until her death by the king's orders. Duke Phamaro had been a boy with a crush who got a girl from another county with child and never bothered to check back with her. Or maybe he had and she didn't tell him about the baby? Eleksander knew little about Queen Lea's personality, but everyone in the Lakelands knew everything about their duke, Phamaro had made sure of that. He must have gone straight from Lea to his duchess, marrying a Lakelander girl so similar to himself that they could have been twins. Aristocratic. Beautiful. Distant. Elegant. Vain. Ambitious. *Cold*. The duke and duchess had soon begun having children and taking over the running of the duchy from Phamaro's parents. Those parents who had cleaned up his mess by trying to have an accidental baby hidden, and then to have it killed.

Eleksander wondered how many times this had happened throughout history, countless probably. He was glad he loved only men and wouldn't have to worry about babies, unless he wanted them, of course. It was odd to him, that men could create a child and then be so divorced from it in every way. One act of lovemaking and then nothing. Well, not quite nothing, Eleksander had ended up being raised in the Lakelands due to Phamaro being a Lakelander.

Some people shouldn't have children. Others absolutely should, like Ekon Aetholo who came across a petrified five-year-old and dropped everything, including one of the most important copper deals of his life, to try to find the boy's parents. Not finding any, despite many years searching, he gladly and proudly raised Eleksander as his own.

Eleksander wiped his hands, which were clammy despite the icy chills that raced through him. He had seen the duke before. It was unavoidable since the Aetholos were influential merchants and often invited to the duke's palace. However, he'd never seen Duke Phamaro and known that this was his sire.

The duke hadn't known anything about him as a baby. Had someone told him since? If so, did he, like everyone else, think that Eleksander had been drowned by that nurse?

The doors opened and nausea started deep in Eleksander's gut. As ever, there were bowls with dried rose petals and spices on the table, filling the air with warming sweet scents. Normally, Eleksander loved that but now it made him dizzy and turned his stomach. He stared at the nearest bowl. It was easier than facing the people he heard appearing. If he looked up now, *right now*, he would see his birthfather and the woman who could've been his step-mother head on. He stared at the pewter bowl, filled with blood-red flowers and browned spice leaves, and then to the empty tankards and large decanters filled with water in the middle of the long table. Anything to distract himself.

A sudden, high-pitched sound made him look up.

It was a slender silver flute, played by a young boy who led a procession of deferential servants in Lakelander blues and whites. After them came a stunning couple, as tall as the Peaks' grand count but with the healthy builds, smooth skin, and exquisitely sculpted faces of statues in brown marble. They glided in, followed by three beautiful, tall lasses, who walked with the same superiority and sophistication as their parents. One of them could only be a couple of years younger than himself while the youngest must be about four or five. Or maybe her height made her look older than she was, because she was sucking her thumb. Eleksander vaguely remembered that there had been still-born sons before this youngest daughter and one new-born who famously died by being partly eaten by a silver beast. He shivered, brought back to their purpose here. Break the king's spell, stop the silver beasts, find someone to rule Cavarra, and make it safe for all.

"Of course the Lakelanders would bring a whole theatre troupe with them," the Baron of the North said with a guffaw. "Some of us left our children in charge of our county. As it should be."

Eleksander kept his gaze locked on his sire. The duke wore delicate, flowing silks in blues and whites with silver threads in the patterns of waves. A necklace with a large teardrop-shaped sapphire rested between defined chest muscles. Phamaro had a multitude of braids, as Lakelands' fashion dictated. But his were slimmer and more elegantly made then Eleksander's own, with silver thread braided into them. On top of his head rested a slim wreath of silver swirls that matched the waves on his hose, britches, and unlaced tunic. To Eleksander, he resembled the pictures of elven kings in books. More importantly, this man looked like a more refined version of himself. The shape of the face, the braids that were the exact same shade of brownish black as his own, their skin colour only a shade lighter than their hair, and that same tall and broad build. The only question was if their wide shoulders were due to traits in their blood or a shared love of swimming?

Hale leaned in and mumbled, "Have you ever seen folk so beautiful it sort of turns ugly? They're all too shittingly perfect."

Eleksander tried not to take offence. Hale was Hale. But he did ask, "You don't think *he* looks like me?"

"Hm. I suppose," Hale said, sounding like he was only now considering it. "But you're comelier. More human, with nicer eyes. His beauty is bloodless, nothing to heat up the groin."

The youngest girl said something as they were sitting down, and the duke briefly smiled at her. Eleksander didn't spend much time looking in mirrors but even he recognised that lopsided smile.

"Shitting silver beasts, you have exactly the same—"

"Yes. Shh," Eleksander whispered, stopping the conversation to not draw attention.

No wonder the duke's parents had panicked as baby Eleksander developed more and more features like his father, wearing his blood traits like an outfit for everyone to behold. Taferia had said his eyes and nose were like his mother's? Well, the rest of him was the spitting image of this man. Yet, that was no reason for the old duke and duchess to order their grandson to be drowned, was it? Did little him have to die?

He ground his teeth at his own insecurity about the matter. Why was he able to fight against any injustice in the world but faltered when the injustice was about him? Obviously, he didn't deserve to die just because of who his biological parents were. By the waters, he had been only a handful years old! He glared at the duke. Did he know? If not, Eleksander was going to tell him.

"Hey, are you all right?" Hale whispered, placing a hand on Eleksander's thigh.

"I will be," he said through half-clenched teeth. He would explain to Hale later, this was neither the time nor the place.

Hale squeezed his thigh. "Can I, um, help in any way? Just let me know if there's anything you need me to do. Get you some water. Or brandy. Maybe punch him?"

When Eleksander didn't reply, Hale grumbled, "I'm shit at these things, but I really want to be of use to you. Please tell me what to do?"

"Stay with me, close to me. No matter what happens."

"Snowtigers couldn't drag me away," Hale said as if it was obvious.

"And... keep that hand there, please." The touch was steadying.

He put his own hand over Hale's, worried that his beloved would get embarrassed about being with a lad again and pull his hand away. Hale instead gripped the thigh tighter and sat closer, so their shoulders touched. It wasn't the kiss or arm around the shoulders Eleksander had secretly hoped for, but it helped.

From the corner of her mouth, Sabina said, "Are you all right, Sander?"

"I'll be fine, Sab. Please don't draw more attention to me."

"All right. Just say if I can help in any way."

Avelynne leaned forward to make eye contact. "Same goes for me. This is a strange day, indeed."

Eleksander gave her an acknowledging nod. It was odd that two of them had ended up having county leaders as birthparents. No. Perhaps not that odd. The Twelve's schemes and plans had been extensive. It wouldn't surprise him if they found out that the four of them had some sort of links to the counties' leading families. He was glad at least that Kae had said they should keep back the fact of him being the son of Queen Lea and Duke Phamaro for later. He didn't know her motives, maybe she was keeping information as bartering goods, but he was glad that he could decide when and how his family connections would be disclosed.

Family connections.

With sudden force, Eleksander missed his parents and sisters. Not some heroic dead queen and this extravagant fop, but his real mother, who would braid his hair and practice archery with him. And his real father who would take Eleksander with him to the merchant's guild to outsmart all the pompous trade tycoons together. By the waters, he even wanted his sisters to force him to study harder and tease him about boys. He hadn't had this need for his family even when he was drowning out at sea. Nor when he was near death during battle. Now, it was a physical ache in his chest.

He squeezed Hale's hand tighter, and the chest ache loosened a little as Hale said, "I'm right here."

On Eleksander's other side, Sabina sniffed and said, "That haughty duke isn't even returning the nods and greetings from the other leaders. It's a good thing you didn't grow up with him, you might not have been the great person you are now if you had."

"I find it hard to believe that anything could make our Eleksander anything but great," Avelynne said simply.

Eleksander relaxed a little. He had some of his family here. The found family that the Hall of Explorers and the Twelve gave him. Including, *hopefully*, a future husband.

Meanwhile, tension had filled the hall like heavy mist, mirroring the foreboding day outside. Through the hall's arrow slits he could see rain lashing down from the looming, cloud-crammed sky. It was nigh dark as night out there.

Inside everyone was finally seated, and all greetings were concluded. The leaders of the four counties were sat on the same side as the tutors, meaning the opposite side to the second wave. Eleksander avoided looking too much at the duke. He wasn't sure what he'd do if their gazes connected.

Now, someone in this room of enemies and strangers had to speak.

The first one to brave it was Kae. "Welcome everyone. It has been a tumultuous time with many questions left unanswered. I know none of us expected Lothiam to be defeated so swiftly." She glanced to the second wave. "Nor for our mapmakers to return with a foreign race and a new form of magic. Let us begin by listening to our four young mapmakers. One of you, please stand and tell your tale."

With that, she extended a hand towards the four of them. By the waters, why had no one told them they would have to give a sort of presentation? They glanced at each other, all looking equally lost as to who should speak.

After a painful amount of silence, Aurea, seated on the other side of Avelynne cleared her throat. "I have heard the whole account and know it's a long and painful one. Perhaps the four can all tell a part each? Hale, why don't you start with when your sail date was moved up because of the missing first wave?"

Eleksander sighed with relief. Aurea had chosen well; Hale was the least nervous. Partly due to his personality, partly because of his lack of respect for the gathered company—except his warden—but mainly because he was the least invested in this conversation.

Hale sat up straighter, but didn't stand, and began telling everyone about their sailing date being moved forward.

Chapter Seventeen

WHO WILL LEAD

Sabina kept swallowing air. Hale had, without any sign of unease, rattled through the start of their journey and handed over to Avelynne. Clearly nervous, but with her usual storytelling flair, Avelynne then detailed the middle. She made everyone hang on her every word when she got to the part where they beat the sea monster with their golden magic and how the magic's existence had shocked them. She finished with the plummet over the waterfall and the guIlt and grief over how many of their sailors were lost. Eleksander subsequently covered the largest part, everything from after the waterfall up to when they were attacked by the silver beasts on the way home. He was looking at her now. "Sab, do you want to take over?"

Like she had much of a choice.

She stood, feet planted wide and hands behind her back, like a true Northern warrior. "We sailed the last bit home on patch-repaired ships with the lack of both wind and food as our enemy. When we got to the shore, there was a worse enemy awaiting us, Lothiam and some of his army." Was she scowling? She tried to look neutral. "We came ashore armed, but kept our weapons sheathed in hope of peace. However, Lothiam gave us no other option than to either surrender to experiments, torture, and probable death, or to fight. You know the rest." She placed her closed fists on the table and leaned on them until she was at eye level with the county leaders. "The important thing about my part of the tale is how the Hethklish helped us home. And how they fought with us without any offer of payment or promise of being spared. They are fair, decent, generous people that we should reward and that we can trust. I truly believe that, and I think their actions show as much."

With that, Sabina sat back on the bench with a relieved thump.

Taferia applauded, the others joining in with varied enthusiasm.

Kae stood again. "Quite a story, with such heartache and bravery. Thank you for sharing it. You four have done Cavarra proud. We will help you write condolence letters to the sailors' families and will delve further into the mystery of your golden magic. Other than that, we shall not ask more of you until you are older." Kae bowed to them, then faced the others. "Now, it has been a confusing few days since Lothiam's fall. We have been left somewhat lost and drifting. Today, we start charting the course for Cavarra's future."

There was louder applause at that.

Sabina let her gaze travel the room, surveying every person and marking how they had their own agenda and ambitions, and then fastened it back on Kae. Officially, the

Twelve had no leader but it was clear for anyone with eyes that Kae Tarvin was in charge.

Kae adjusted her robe. She no longer wore the red and gold royal advisor garb but had, like the rest of her associates, borrowed emerald tutor robes. "We four Twelve members in attendance have backgrounds as advisors. First to Queen Lea and then to the king, guiding, commanding, and keeping some of Lothiam's worst atrocities from occurring. Throughout all of this, we were also leaders of the rebellion." She clasped her hands before her. "Furthermore, between the four of us, we represent all the counties. In short, whether temporarily or permanently, we are fit and willing to rule."

When she said "temporarily", she had surreptitiously glanced at Eleksander, and Sabina felt him stiffen at her side.

"Fit to rule? I disagree," the grand countess said. "We do not even know what you have been doing in the shadows. Why did it take four youths a mere moment to topple Lothiam when you have apparently been trying for decades?"

The Duchess of the Lakelands gave a regal hand gesture. "For once, the Peakdwellers speak true. We cannot trust you to rule."

Taferia Palm held out her hands. "Who will, then? Some random aristocrat that you pick after much warring? You county leaders? Whether you vote for a single leader, take turns, or try to rule together, we'll end up with ceaseless wars again."

The duke raised his sculpted eyebrows. "In no time nor realm will I sit back and be ruled by Peakdwellers. They cannot be trusted not to take all power for themselves. No offence, *dear* grand count and grand countess," he said with a nonchalant hand gesture and the sincerity of a healing salve salesman.

"Ha, you're one to speak of that," countered the Baron of the North. "You have even more ambitions for the throne than the Peakdwellers and twice as much history of deceit. None of you can be trusted."

The Warden of the Woodlands leaned her elbows on the table. "Well now, this squabbling is a fine thing. You're proving Lothiam right in that we cannot rule without him."

"Pray pardon an outsider weighing in," Aurea said, her voice shaking. "But have you considered making a council to rule, at least until you find a permanent leader?"

"What type of council, lass?" asked the wizened Twelve member.

"One with representatives from all factions present in this hall. Everyone gets a vote, and you make the decisions together?" Aurea was clearly noting the sharp scepticism on the faces around them as she swallowed visibly. "I don't wish to be repetitive here. Many of you have sought me out to ask questions about Hethklish society and I know I've pestered you about the benefits of deciding by vote. And how letting citizens vote has helped us Hethklish and you Woodlanders," she nodded to the warden, "to trust in their leaders."

Sabina stared at Aurea. She'd been talking to the Twelve and the leaders of the counties? Sabina had spent the last five days healing her broken body, grieving, and brooding about the past, the future, and her love life. Not to mention trying to catch up on sleep lost during nights brimming with nightmares and startling awake every hour. She hadn't seen Aurea much but had simply assumed she was down at the dockyard, seeing to the ship repairs.

Everyone squirmed, even the Lakelander children, who had all picked up books and embroidery earlier but now focused on what was happening in the room.

In the end, it was the giant Twelve member who patted his beer belly and said, "You have indeed spoken about voting and as I told you yesterday, Cavarra is not ready for its people to vote on matters. A council of us is another matter, I reckon."

"You don't know what Cavarra is ready for," Eleksander said so quietly that only those around him could hear.

"B-but who will be on this council? Everyone in this room?" Tutor Hathleen asked in that delicate voice of hers. Her pointy face reddened with every word. At least she dared to speak at all. Tutor Myle hadn't said more than a meek hello.

"We gathered here, of course," the Baroness of the North boomed while petting her snowbear. "Well, without our young heroes and the foreigners."

Everyone eyed the two Hethklish.

"She's right. We are out of place here," Naseer said. "We only came because Taferia asked us to sit in and advise. We shall let you have this meeting alone." He stood, bowed, and walked away with Aurea following a step behind.

Taferia stopped them at the door. "Please do not leave." She faced everyone at the table. "At sea, I saw Captain Naseer and Aurea's wisdom and experience. As we have seen from Aurea's suggestion about the council, we can use some guidance from outsiders. Too long have we tried the same methods and had the same results."

"Perchance it would be better if they sat in on one of the smaller meetings we will have after this one?" asked the Northern member of the Twelve, his tone making it clear that the word "perchance" was a mere curtesy. "Their presence, and that of the four youths, is merely symbolic today. For the more vital meetings, they need not attend. Mayhap not you either, Taferia."

Sabina balked. Hadn't they had the discussion about them being involved in future decisions and won?

"I strongly disagree," Taferia said to the blond man. "Every following meeting should have representatives of all those attending today. And we cannot dally to have these 'vital' meetings. How rarely have these people agreed to be in the same place, huh?" She indicated the four leaders with a hand. "We ought to make the big decisions while we are all here. While change still feels possible and before we have all sunk back into our old habits. The moment is now and we need everyone present."

"You are but a junior member of the Twelve, Taferia, are you certain you know what we need?" the Northerner said, one hand stroking his beard and the other on the head of his growling icewolf.

"Yes! Look at this group. In it we have all kinds, rich and poor, young and old, scholars and workers, people from all four counties, and two people from another continent. This full group should be voting, not only the older, richer, and more educated attendees."

Sabina wondered if exploring mapmakers were workers. Had she changed her societal class? That could be answered another time, what was happening here was far more urgent. And more infuriating.

"Taferia, have a care and mind your tone," Kae said. "Even without the youths and the foreigners, we still have plenty of diversity."

In a stopping gesture, Taferia held up her hands. On them, were calluses from many years of working in the dockyard. "I disagree."

So did Sabina, and surely the rest of the second wave too. What was worrying was how obvious it was that the rest of the room didn't and how Taferia had lost the respect of the elders. Those scowls deepened while the haughty sniffs grew louder.

Captain Naseer and Aurea stayed standing, clearly unsure of what to do.

The question of the Hethklish attending wasn't crucial since Naseer and Aurea surely didn't care either way. But the second wave wanted their seats at the table and now they were apparently only here as symbols and would later be excluded? Sabina wanted to scream. They had been seen as able to captain the first expedition beyond Cavarra's borders. Able to lead a crew. Able to start trade and diplomatic liaisons. Able to, in Lothiam's mind, commit genocide and colonise. Most of all, they had been seen as able to die for this nation. Was then a say in its future such an absurd request? After all, the second wave would be part of that future for longer than the others in this room. Sabina didn't want to scream after all, she wanted to remind these people of a few things. Like how the tutors had been cowed by Lothiam into training youths to be colonising fiends or how the county leaders had been enthralled by his spell and paid him the tithes that their own people needed. And, most of all, how the Twelve's rebellion had ended up as an ineffective and murderous mess despite that they weren't under the spell. Age and experience clearly wasn't everything.

"You can ignore everything else I say if you wish," Taferia said. "But heed me when I say that there are those who must be here for every meeting."

Sabina sat back, waiting to see how Taferia would champion their cause.

"The Hethklish must have at least one representative on it," Taferia said. "Someone to serve as a link between our nations and to show us new ways of governing. To help us alter every last rotten bit of Cavarra."

Angry rumblings and whispered conversation within the groups travelled around the table like rustling through leaves.

The grand count very loudly said, "If your sword is blunted and has a worn handle, you do not toss it by the wayside and purchase a new one. You have the handle mended and the blade honed. Then, you ensure you take better care of it in the future."

"She's making them all defensive, turning them against the idea of any type of reform," Eleksander whispered.

"Never mind that," Sabina hissed back. "What about the fact that she isn't mentioning us?"

He was right, though. Taferia's attitude made sense to Sabina who knew about Hethklish society and that Taferia had seen the future she wanted for Cavarra in the way Hethekla was laid out. Nevertheless, this was the wrong way to do this.

"Alter Cavarra? What are you suggesting, Taferia?" The Northern Twelve member knitted his bushy, blond brows. "Because if I didn't know you better, I'd say you wanted to let the Hethklish simply make us a part of Hethekla?"

The rain picked up. It pelted the Hall of Explorers and some droplets even came in through the arrow slits. Heavy, rain-chilled winds followed, making the flames in the hall's stone hearth dance. The two tutors scurried to cover the arrow slits and the room darkened.

Inside, the quarrel which had long hung in the air, descended fully.

The Duchess of the Lakelands asked, in a disgusted drawl, "why do we not simply hand the Hethklish the keys to the treasury and all the supplies of Cavarra while we are at it?"

The Warden of the Woodlands, not one for such sarcasm, instead roared about how they had just dethroned one leader who did not love Cavarra and now risked stepping under the yoke of another.

Avelynne's father stood iron-spike straight, his deep frown lines looking carved into stone, and with an authoritative tone said, "There can be no doubt that this is the warden's work. Tis a wicked plot to remove ruling by birthright and forcing the process of voting in leaders on to all four counties."

"Oh, stop being paranoid, you joyless gobshite," the warden called back.

"No, no, the grand count makes a fair point. This unknown newcomer," the Baroness of the North pointed to Taferia, "is by the sounds of her accent a Woodlander and she is the one who wants us to become a colony of

Hethekla. This stinks of Woodlander schemes, trying to strong-arm the rest of us."

"Ah. There it is." The Duke of the Lakelands steepled his fingers, looking calm but for the fury on his pretty features. "Peakdwellers and Northerners coming together to hand out blame. You always do come together don't you, be it in a meeting or in your beds."

The grand countess's head shot towards them. "What exactly are you implying?"

Her voice was as glacial as Avelynne's was warm and far more high-pitched, Sabina realised. The speech patterns were the same, though.

"I'm merely noting that the North and the Peaks have ever been such bosom bedfellows," the duke said with a smirk tugging at his lips.

The baroness and baron both laughed as if that was the most ludicrous thing ever, until the baroness collected herself enough to say, "Does your frustrated little mind really imagine we'd want to touch those two musty, cold eels? Our fingers would get either dust mites or frostbite."

She said something else, but it was drowned out by the grand count loudly asking the Lakelanders, "How dare you imply we bed those hairy barbarians?" On the last words, his voice rose to a shout while his moustache quivered and blue veins protruded on his forehead.

"You do not share a bed with those snow-beasts, then?" the duchess said innocently and languidly. "Shame. I was aching to ask you which one is the woman and which is the man. Or are they both the same gender? I know you Northerners and Peakdwellers enjoy that sort of thing."

"Bigoted cod," replied the baroness. "And in front of your own children too."

The Peakdwellers, however, didn't answer the Lakelanders. Instead, the grand count, with measured movements, drew his sword. The icy metal whisper of it leaving its sheath was heard even over the quibbling of the Twelve.

"And now we get to the violence," the duchess said to her husband. "Mayhap we Lakelanders *should* join with Hethekla. The rest of Cavarra is a violent and carnal bunch, so far below us. Wouldn't you say, water of my soul?"

"Indeed, my pearl," the duke said, eyeing the sword as if it was a mildewed piece of fruit brought before him. "Far below us."

The young Lakelander duchesses didn't even flinch either, so sure that they were untouchable.

The grand count raised the sword, but the grand countess stayed his arm and told him not to stoop to the Lakelander's petty level. Something which started the screaming match again. The baron even threw an empty tin tankard at the warden, who was making to leave while growling curse words.

Shouted accusations echoed in the vast hall, increasing Sabina's irritation.

The members of Twelve now stopped bickering with each other and turned to the leaders of the counties. With waggling fingers, they told them that they were like unruly children, spoiling for a fight and overreacting.

Which, in fact, was quite accurate to Sabina's mind.

Meanwhile, Tutor Myle and Tutor Hathleen were trying to stop everyone from knocking over the carved benches or throwing the bowls of spices and herbs. They failed with the bowl idea, since the warden threw one of them at the grand countess after she suggested the Woodlanders had started the last four wars out of boredom. It rained dried leaves and spices on that side of the table and Sabina saw the poor snowbear sneeze repeatedly. The iceboar, however, gobbled up the bowl's contents with glee.

The furious babble increased and, to Sabina's surprise, one of the loudest voices was Taferia. She kept insisting that the Hethklish should have a deciding vote on this new council.

The duchess, who had lost her superior drawl and was now quite shrill, screeched, "The nerve! Next you'll want those four snotty younglings on the council and a whole shipload of Hethklish to boot. I shan't allow it."

With a ferocious glower, Taferia leaned over the table to get closer to the duchess. "Who are you to allow anything? Here in the Centre, you county leaders have about as much power as I do."

That brought forth outcries and gasps across the room.

The grand countess, seeming to keep her temper fixed with nothing but her iron self-discipline, pointed to the Twelve members with such speed that strands of red-black hair fell out of her headdress. "This entire shambles is your fault. You ought to have begun reminding us about Lothiam earlier. Then we could have pooled our armies and defeated him decades ago!"

Her high, icy voice was so jarring and the replies, agreements, and disagreements, were too loud. Sabina resisted the urge to cover her ears and considered how they could end this and move on. She didn't want to have to be the one to handle this. The back of her head still throbbed, she was exhausted from sleepless nights, and she was so tired of taking responsibility.

Yet, she'd once again have to.

She sighed and went to stand up to get attention. Gentle hands landed on hers. Over the din, Eleksander said, "I'll do it this time, Sab."

He stood, clearly trembling, and used those big lungs of his to call, "Has anyone considered that the Hethklish do not have to be *on* the council?"

Everyone turned to look at him and his trembling increased. Sabina willed him on.

He blinked repeatedly. "Can, um, can they not aid the forming of the new Cavarra without being a part of the council?"

"How?" asked Taferia.

Naseer stepped over to Eleksander's side but addressed Taferia. "I could stay in Cavarra and advise only when required, that way being a connection between our countries without serving on your new council. I appreciate your faith in us Hethklish, Taferia, but tis not right for us to be deciding the fate of your nation."

Aurea grabbed his sleeve and loudly whispered, "What are you saying? You're our captain, how could you stay here?"

"Easy," he answered. "You would captain the ships back to Hethekla. When there, you would inform our government of our new discovered acquaintances and that I stayed behind as a show of good faith and diplomacy."

She gaped at him. He smiled and said, "We can discuss that more later."

Kae was eyeing Naseer. "Yes, I am more comfortable with you staying as an advisor."

"I'm sure we all are," said the baron, petting his iceboar. It seemed to calm him, and Sabina found herself stroking Kall too, getting the same result.

Taferia seemed deflated and argued no more.

"Back to us Cavarrians, then," Kae said. She turned to Tutor Myle and Hathleen. "Does the Hall of Explorers want a member of your faculty on our new council?"

Sabina rolled her eyes. *They* could be the representatives from the Hall of Explorers but not the second wave? If she, Hale, Eleksander, and Avelynne had been in charge, they would have wrapped this whole ruling council question up by now up and been on their way to the lake to speak with the creature there. Or to fight it. Whatever might be required.

Myle looked to Hathleen with panic in his watery eyes.

"Not the two of us," Elya Hathleen quickly replied. "But, um, perchance the former Tutor Santorine?"

There were once more gasps around the table.

Tutor Hathleen hurried to explain. "Her crimes must surely have been repaid by her imprisonment and torture in the king's labour camps? Besides, her research has been essential to uncovering the truth and to beating the crownbearer."

"Santorine was essential to fighting the king?" Sabina said so only the second wave could hear. "What about us?"

The leaders of the four counties all agreed, with scant enthusiasm, to include Santorine on the council.

"It is settled," Kae said. "The council will consist of the leaders of the four counties, Tutor Santorine, the members of the Twelve here in attendance, and the occasional advisory input from Captain Octavius Naseer of Hethekla."

Sabina turned to Hale. Why wasn't he screaming and shouting about their non-inclusion? Because leadership wasn't to his taste? Or due to his loathing of debates in stuffy rooms? Eleksander was equally disengaged. After his father by blood had looked right at him during his query about Naseer being on the council, Eleksander had drawn in on himself and stared into the middle distance. Avelynne was no help either. As soon as her parents—the people who had locked her up, starved her, belittled her, and then disowned her when she objected—had become angry, she had shrunk into her seat. Besides, Avelynne gave herself such little credit that she no doubt felt she shouldn't be allowed on the council.

If they wanted representation here, it was up to Sabina. And it was vital that they got it. Fear and worry ate away in her belly at the idea of trusting these people, *their respected elders*, who had not been able to solve anything on their own. More than that, who had not helped any of the mapmakers but had manipulated them or ignored them. These people, all so ready to act now, had stood by while the first wave were sent out to die and when the second wave were sent after them to the same possible fate.

Busy with these thoughts, Sabina only distantly heard the Woodlands Twelve member say, "Now that this council is formed, we must decide what to do with the former king."

"Keep him mouldering down in the dungeons," suggested the baroness. "Let us forget about the wee maggot."

The duke shook his head, making his braids dance under their circlet. "No. Lothiam must go on trial for his crimes, ensuring the people hear what he did. Otherwise, they shall never accept that he had to be overthrown."

"The king can wait," Kae said. "We cannot convince the people of what happened unless the spell is broken. Therefore, we need to confront the monster in the lake and make it undo the spell that kept the king loved and created the silver beasts."

The warden nodded. "That is our first step. The monster. After that, the feckless, former king. Wait, will we be needing the king to call forth the beast?"

"Aye, we might. We must have a care, though," said the baroness, her shoulder once more weighed down by the head of her snowbear. "If Lothiam is allowed to speak, he may enchant us all again before we have time to stop him."

Her husband put an arm around her in a gesture of agreement, nearly flicking the nose of the snowbear. "Stopping the spell is crucial. We must also ensure this creature does not interfere in Cavarra business again."

"We should drive it out," the grand countess said. "With fire and magic or with ice and iron. Whatever it fears and whatever hurts it the most. Killing it publicly would obviously be preferable."

How did so much casual cruelty fit in that threadlike body? And how in all snowstorms did she come to have such a kind-hearted daughter?

"We ought to speak to it. The creature may be useful and we should not always resort to violence first," said the duke.

He ignored it when the grand count muttered about

peace needy Lakelanders, merely placing one of his bejewelled hands on the table and saying, "We must see what it wants. Perchance it wishes to be freed from the lake?" One of his daughters sneezed and he distractedly handed an ornate handkerchief to her. "Or perhaps it will want to work with us? By the waters, we have no clue what sort of relationship the former king had with this creature. He might have been controlling it as much as it was controlling him."

"We must find out," said Kae. "I propose we arm ourselves and speak to the lake monster to uncover its motives and methods. Anyone on our new council is welcome to join this expedition, if you are willing to risk it."

Only those on the council were going to the lake? What in all the snow? Sabina started planning out her arguments for them being on the council. She mustn't forget to mention that they weren't ordinary nineteen-year-olds but ones with unique experience, education, and they were solstice born. The latter giving them untapped powers beyond anyone in the room. Would that be enough to convince everyone? She was terrible at speechmaking normally but now when panic made her grow hotter and more flustered? She must get this right, state her arguments in a logical way and avoid getting frustrated. No one listened to a young woman who was emotional. She tried to slow her breathing and clear her head.

She need not have bothered with any of this.

Avelynne stood, her slender frame first bent but then she straightened, the full poise of someone raised as the Countess Ironhold on show. The firelight threw shadows over her face, showing how gaunt she still was since her bout of unconsciousness. But also, to Sabina's eyes, how her ordeals had toughened her. There was something about the set of the mouth that looked stronger. "If you are to speak to the creature, we should be present."

"You four? As a mother, I must point out how terrible a notion that is," the duchess said, eyeing Avelynne with a scowl. "This situation calls for adults."

"Respectfully, we may not have turned twenty yet, but we are not children. Unlike anyone else on Cavarra, we have experience in fighting unidentified creatures," Avelynne said, voice as clear and strong as ice. "Furthermore, our magic defeated the king in an instant, and it can do so much more than regular silver magic. It is a weapon you will need against a threat like the lake creature and only we can wield it."

Sabina couldn't be prouder. She wanted to applaud. She also wanted to, much like the warden, throw a bowl of spices at the grand countess, who cut those stony eyes towards her daughter and subtly gestured for Avelynne to sit down. While the grand count's lips twitched under his moustache, with obvious shame and disgust.

Avelynne didn't look at her parents, though, her gaze moved over the other leaders. "With all due respect, if you trust us to make your maps, find your land, make contact with new civilisations, and fight your king, then you can trust us to be part of this."

The grand countess stopped gesturing for Avelynne to sit and the grand count's lips stilled.

"When called for, you came here to fight Lothiam and you saw what we four can do," Avelynne added, standing straight as Sabina knew she was raised to do, but speaking louder than she had surely ever been allowed. "Now a new danger awaits us. Let us face it together and you will once more see what our magic and experience can achieve."

"To be sure, we don't doubt your skill, lass," the warden said. "Nor your impressive, new magic." She smiled with open warmth. "We are keeping you out of this because we never should have let Lothiam send nineteen-year-olds out to do our dirty work. You have done enough."

Sabina doubted that was the others' reason. Certainly not the Peakdwellers, the Lakelanders, and the Twelve, who had openly made it clear they didn't trust young people. Murmuring broke out, everyone shaking their heads and now discussing if the second wave should perhaps be kept back as a last resort.

With Avelynne's bravery as tinder for her fire, Sabina made her decision. She'd never get to the point where she had perfect, logical arguments and her window was closing. She banged her fist on the table, as much to get silence as attention.

"It doesn't matter why you don't want us involved, we want to be, and we'll have to be. This power came to us, and aye, we're young and have much to learn. You still need us. Not only to fight this monster but to sit on the council. We offer a different perspective, one you need." She tapped that fist on the table, hammering her point home. "What have you got to lose, anyway? It's not like we could vote you down, we would be in minority."

"Mind the table *and* your tongue, wee lassie," the Northern Twelve member said.

She really did have to learn this arsehole's name.

"She has a right to speak," Hale roared, finally invested, even if it was just in protecting his adopted sister.

It was the Woodlands Twelve representative who answered, "Only if she respects her elders."

That was it.

"Respect my elders?" Sabina said, standing firmer. "What have my elders done for me? Instead of a childhood, my parents had me raise my siblings while also training to be a warrior. Lothiam, and through him some of you, sent me to kill and die for you." There were protests but she spoke over them. "The Twelve manipulated me into being where, and what, they wanted so I'd be able to fight their cause. You all had me travel out to sea where you did not dare go." Sabina shook her head. "My elders have done nought but use me. And the young of our nation feel as let down as I do, so I will speak for them. I'm sure there are better people for the task, but I'm here and not gagged by familial connections like some of the other second wavers. And, so," she leaned down on both of her fists now, the table's oak unyielding against her knuckles, "I refuse to not be heard. Cavarra needs a council with younger people on it, ones who have seen some of the world out there, ones with open eyes and clean hearts."

Silence filled every portion of that great hall, pressing against the walls.

"She may have a point," the warden said, rubbing her scarred chin.

"There's no 'may' about it. I do."

Low mumbling and fidgeting in seats met her words but Sabina didn't stop. Couldn't stop. Sure, she had to learn to let go of control and responsibility, but not now. These people were not to be trusted. She picked up the pace, frightened of being stopped. "We have seen and done things you haven't, gone places you couldn't. On top of having experiences that you don't, we also know this country and its people better than many of you do."

"Especially those of us who grew up among the people and not the coin-hoarding upper crust," Hale said, putting words on what Sabina hadn't thought wise to say out loud.

"Must we listen to this?" the grand count said, smoothing his moustache with those long, uncalloused fingers.

"If I may give my advice as your new advisor, these four are the future," Naseer said, sounding apologetic for getting involved. "It may be a good idea to let them be heard. Both now and on the council."

"Aye," Sabina said. "At least let Eleksander be part of the council. He is after all the heir to the throne by blood."

All the murmuring and fidgeting halted, fast as a candle blown out. Everyone stared at her.

The warden sat forward. "He's the what now, lass?"

Sabina froze. Snow below, had she said that out loud? She slumped down on the bench with a murmured, "So sorry," in Eleksander's direction.

Chapter Eighteen

BLOOD HEIR

Eleksander was face to face with an utterly crushed Sabina. Guilt poured off her.

"It's all right," he said, putting a hand on her shoulder. "It had to come out sooner or later."

She put her hand over his, her teary frown lessening somewhat.

The rain outside kept thrashing the stone walls and the hatches in front of the arrow slits. Only the rain could be heard in the tense, weighted silence of the hall.

Kae sighed. "We were going to make this information known at a time when we and young Eleksander were ready. But it seems it must be now?" She looked to him and he nodded for her to go ahead. "Some of you voiced concerns about the Twelve working in the shadows and keeping secrets. Well, we had to. Most of the four counties were under the spell's thrall."

Angry mumblings filled the hall, but no one could disagree.

"So," Kae continued, "we kept secrets. One of them was

that, before King Lothiam sacrificed Queen Lea to the lake monster, she had not only learned his family secret regarding the spell and the creature. She had also, as a lass about the age of the second wave, born a child."

Sharp inhales and the word, "What?" came from several directions.

With bloodless lips, the grand countess said, "How have we not been told of this before?"

Eleksander watched his birthfather, who was staring at Kae. Had the duke's warmly brown skin turned ashier or was that just in his imagination? It was hard to tell in a hall now lit only by the fireplace.

Kae interlaced her fingers and clasped her hands before her. "When Eleksander here took the tests to enter the Hall of Explorers, Atha Santorine recognised in his skills a solstice born and began researching his past."

Tutor Santorine. So much came back to her. Eleksander thought back to how much he had liked her when she was their tutor and how kind she had been to him, until that awful night ruined everything.

"She found out that he had been raised in the Lakelands by a high standing merchant family," Kae continued. "His arrival with them matched the timing of when the queen's son was said to have been drowned by his wet nurse in a river in the Lakelands. The wet nurse later admitted to having disobeyed the order to drown him and instead sent him off in the hopes he would survive."

"Again, we ought to have been informed of all of this," the grand countess sniped before pinching her lips together, making them even paler.

Kae ignored her. "I will be completely honest, the

Twelve were standing by to aid the queen's son in gaining entrance into the Hall of Explorers. The plan was that when he sailed to find new lands, we would tell him everything and then ask him and his cohorts to give said land to the Twelve for us to build a base on." She didn't heed the questioning outbursts in the room but once more spoke on. "On said base we would, with him as the future heir, launch a rebellion against Lothiam. Luckily, we didn't need to interfere as Eleksander was by far the best candidate from the Lakelands and was accepted on his own. All the solstice born did, since heightened skills in all fields, but especially magic, seems to be inherent to them."

She didn't mention how all their lovely plans about telling him the truth never came to fruition. Partly because of their order to sail being moved up, partly because the second wave was avoiding the Twelve, and partly because these people were so used to hiding in the shadows that they didn't dare step out of them for an instant. Not until the second wave got rid of Lothiam. They, and the squabbling county leaders, could not be left to rule alone.

"You mean to tell me that the queen's son is one of the wee bairns you have lined up next to you?" the baron asked, squinting curiously at the four mapmakers.

Taferia, who had been quiet for a long time, said, "Yes." She got up and walked over to where he sat, putting her steady hands on his shoulders. "This excellent scholar, brave explorer, born diplomat, and skilled mapmaking magician is Eleksander Aetholo. Son by birth of the late queen and, in accord with the succession laws of Cavarra that acknowledges three bloodlines, a viable heir to the throne. And, in my opinion, an excellent heir."

She let go of him and went back to her seat, leaving him alone to face the stares.

Eleksander's mouth and throat were suddenly sand-dry. He coughed to clear it, cursing the physical reaction. The last thing he wanted now was more attention. Sabina clapped him on the back to help his cough but then left her arm draped there. It, in combination with Hale's hand on his leg, would normally have been comforting, but now they might just as well not have been there. The leaders of the four counties were observing him as if he was a new type of bug they had pinned down and were about to dissect. Eleksander tried to shrink in on himself by leaning back into the sisterly arm Sabina had placed around him, but he felt too big and too obvious to hide anywhere.

The Warden of the Woodlands slapped Tutor Myle lightly on the arm. "Light some tapers, bookworm. I can't see my own hand in here."

When Tutor Myle had dutifully fetched and lit some candles, the warden said, "Huh. Are you talking about that meek boyo sitting there like a shrinking flower? You're claiming that's the bold Queen Lea's wee'un?"

Hale's grip on his leg tightened and Eleksander was sure his Woodlander was about to stand up and scream about Eleksander not being a shrinking flower. But he was, wasn't he?

"Well, there is a family resemblance," said Avelynne's mother, squinting at Eleksander. "Look at his eyes. And the shape of that nose. I dare say the rest of him looks extraordinarily like his... father, though." There was a tone of gossiping glee in the grand countess' cold voice, which grated even more on Eleksander's shocked system. With studied slowness, she moved her iron-eyed gaze to the duke.

"Aye, similar like a pair of snow cherries," said the baron with a chuckle. "Aren't you, Duke Phamaro?"

The duke grabbed onto the table so hard he made it shake. "I know not of what you speak."

Kae's expression soured. "To some extent, you must do. Many have heard the rumours that you were in a dalliance with our late queen back when she was merely Lea Tarvin, a highborn daughter of The Peaks."

Tarvin. Eleksander had never known Queen Lea's surname. She had been related to Kae? Then he was too? This was all too much to take in.

The duke's eyes had shot wide. "Gossip. You have no proof. I have no sons, only daughters."

The words hit Eleksander as if his birthfather had thrown a slab of rock at his chest. He told himself that the man was in shock. Perhaps even feeling guilty at having left Lea behind so fast, even if he didn't know she was with child. It was likely that the duke would've reacted differently to this news if there wasn't a room full of judging former enemies gawking at him.

Still. The fact that Duke Phamaro didn't look at him but kept repeating, "I have no son," hurt in a way that made Eleksander want to curl into a ball. This was what he had always expected. That his birthparents wouldn't want him, that they had left him intentionally. That they would be ashamed at the mere idea of him being their son. That he wouldn't be good enough. Those fears had faded when Taferia had told him of Queen Lea and how she had only given him up to save him from Lothiam's murderous fury and how she had missed him. How she'd wanted to keep him.

Now, he saw the rejection he had been expecting in that face so like his own on the other side of the table.

Kae scoffed. "I do have proof, Duke Phamaro. Queen Lea gave your name as the father. Furthermore, you can ask anyone close to your parents. They decided to hide the child from you and then, when their nerve failed them, to order your son's death. All to avoid Lothiam's jealousy, any scandal, and any disfavour at court."

"Just look at the lad," the warden said. "His whole face and body are proof, you gobshite."

"You cannot say that. Faces prove nothing," the duke said. He kept glancing towards his wife and his daughters. None of whom were speaking but only glaring at him.

"Oh, be quiet, you whingy water weed," the baroness muttered at the duke. "We can discuss later how you have your head so far up your arse that you're more worried about having a bastard than you are proud to have a hero for a son. We were discussing whether the young mapmakers can come along to confront the monster."

"And if we can be on the council," Sabina shot in.

"Aye, and as my young subject so determinately points out, the possibility of a seat on the council," the baroness said with clear appreciation. The Northerners did value tenacity, Eleksander distractedly remembered.

"Yes," Taferia said. "They should be involved in both. To convince you of why, I'd like to explain more about the golden magic."

Good. Taferia had finally shifted from fighting for Hethklish inclusions to *their* inclusion. Something which

Eleksander should have been doing earlier, if only he hadn't been so incapacitated by his birthfather's presence. Was it warming in here? He was sweating and his heart raced.

"About time. Tell us how it works," the warden said, eyes glinting with interest.

Taferia explained about that special solstice and about Santorine's experiments. She moved on to how the golden magic only works when all four of them intentionally mix their magic, and that it seems to grow stronger when water —possibly only saltwater—is involved. Then, on to how it is less controllable than silver magic but also less draining. She probably said many more things, since she seemed to speak forever, but Eleksander struggled to keep focused. He grew more lightheaded, more overheated. He sat there, feeling everyone's gazes still on him despite Taferia speaking of things that should interest them. Those gazes were measuring him. Occasionally, the county leaders whispered to each other about him.

His birthfather was the only one pretending that Eleksander wasn't in the room. He sat, chin now held high, staring unseeingly at Taferia. Eleksander saw his throat bob as he swallowed, over and over.

Eleksander knew that feeling at least. His mouth was even drier than before, and his tongue felt too big for his mouth. His breaths came in gulps and his rapidly beating heart was squeezed, as if there was a weight on his chest. Was he breathing too fast? How long was a breath meant to be? His eyesight narrowed. The only things tethering him to something else than the sudden feeling that he was either dying or fainting were Sabina's hand rubbing calming circles on his back and Hale's hand still gripping his leg.

"Is he all right?" he heard Avelynne whisper.

Someone replied but Eleksander couldn't make it out over the blood singing in his ears. He tried to detachedly count the pulse beats. As if they were drumbeats in a song, not his heart hammering out of his chest. It worked a little and soon he could at least hear again.

Taferia rounded up with, "Considering all this, I not only advocate for the second wave to be on the council and on the team confronting the monster, but I also propose that we waste no time in crowning Eleksander Aetholo as the new ruler of Cavarra."

There was a strangled sound, and it took time before Eleksander realised it came from his own mouth. His eyesight blurred so he was barely able to make it out when someone pushed a tankard of water in front of him.

"Drink. You'll feel better. I'm right here. Have a sip of water, love."

It was Hale's voice. So, of course, he obeyed. The water was cold and he focused on that. The difference between his overheated body and the cold water. When he was composed enough to look back up at the people in the room, he found the duke still gazing sightlessly at Taferia, who had quieted.

Everyone else continued to watch Eleksander, without any hint of discretion now. He heard the Ironholds mutter to each other about him not looking fit to be any sort of king. The Baron and Baroness of the North were smiling pityingly. The warden seemed to be measuring him still with those sage deep-set eyes of hers.

The Duchess of the Lakelands slowly stood, the only sound the rustling of her long gown. "As my husband is too thunderstruck to speak, I shall do so in his stead. I agree that we prepare this young man to take the throne."

This was it. Eleksander was going to either have his heart stop or just faint. By the waters, he had to stay awake!

The baron banged his hand on the table, helping Eleksander stay in the room. "Aye, maybe we should. The lad doesn't look like much, but he counts as royal *but* has none of Lothiam's blood in him. A good thing considering how that bloodline of royals have behaved."

"Are ye sure that's the reason? Not your wish to keep ruling by birthright alive at any cost?" the warden said.

There were overlapping replies across the room that he couldn't make out. The pulse beat in his ears was increasing again.

The duchess pointed a ringed finger at Eleksander. "This young man is the son of a queen and a duke. He is a splendid candidate to start a new royal line. So, as I say, I suggest we prepare him to rule. While we do so, this council can lead Cavarra."

"You are only endorsing him because you want someone related to you, a raised Lakelander no less, on the throne," said the grand countess.

The warden snorted. "You reckon she really wants the family scandal on the throne? She must see potential in the lad. She's a shallow little gobshite, but not stupid."

"Hear, hear," said the baron with trouble-starting glee.

The duchess leaned forward so she could fix the warden with a glare. "I do not believe a dirty, backwater ruffian like you should be name calling. I have a much larger vocabulary and shall throw insults back at you twice over."

Eleksander tried to listen to the rest of their arguing, but the words mixed, like a soup of disjointed sentences. That weight on his chest was increasing, pushing on his heart and lungs until they felt strangled.

Were these people actually talking about him ruling Cavarra? This was pure lunacy.

He stood, knocking his chair over. "I... I cannot do this."

Heart-wrenched, panicked, and overwhelmed, he ran off without a destination.

Chapter Nineteen

UNSURE

Hale watched Eleksander run out and stood to go after him. Captain Naseer's warm hand on his shoulder stopped him. "Correct me if I'm wrong, dear boy, but perhaps Sander can use the advice of an outsider, someone with a little more experience?"

"Y-yes. Come get me if he needs me," Hale said, secretly happy that he didn't have to go.

He wanted to help. But how? He had no idea what Eleksander was feeling or how to fix the problem. Yet, it was as unnatural to not go after him as it had been to not fight for their right to be on the council. Fighting was his strength, after all. And shit, how he loved fighting to get what his fellow second wavers wanted and then feeling the pride of providing. What had kept him from demanding spots on the council was that he wasn't sure he wanted it. Why should they work so hard to sit on a council where they weren't respected or required, trying to convince their elders to even give them air to speak? It was demeaning and probably pointless, these ragworts would never listen to them.

He wished they were able to... what? Not go back to sea. He'd had enough of that. Maybe return to being students? Or start their own county, away from all these quarrelling boil-suckers making decisions and causing trouble. He wanted a life where his tasks were clear-cut and under his control. To keep himself and his loved ones alive. He could do that. He looked around the hall, at the spineless academics and power-hungry coinbags who were messing up his future. No, these people would never listen to them. Not unless they had real power.

He peered at the door where Eleksander had gone. If Eleksander became king, they'd have power, wouldn't they? Then they could set the rules, choosing on the day if they wanted to reform the tithe system, or go to sea, or stay in bed for an hour longer. They'd never be sent anywhere. Never be forced by others to kill or die.

The mere idea of it made his head swim.

There was a hard pit in his stomach too, one of worry for his Eleksander. He should have gone after him. Even if he didn't know what to say, he could have held him and kissed him. Shit!

Someone touched him. A small hand on his shoulder.

"He will be fine," Avelynne said.

Hale dipped his head in agreement, not sure of what else to do.

Chapter Twenty

SHOOT WITH YOUR STOMACH

Eleksander was halfway down the hallway when he heard steps behind him. A hand grabbed his arm, firmly but not painfully. "Easy there. It's all right, Sander. Take a breath."

It was Captain Naseer. Not at all who Eleksander had expected.

"I don't want to breathe," he snapped back, illogically. The hallway was blurry and he had to place a hand against the wall to steady himself.

"This may be hard to believe, but I understand why you're upset. I never wanted to be one of the foremost captains in the Hethekla fleet. When I was a little girl, I was told—"

"You mean a little boy." It felt good to disagree with this man who meant well but was the only target for Eleksander's scorching emotions.

"No, I was born a girl. Nothing that couldn't be rearranged as I grew up and went from Octavia to Octavius. Hethekla has many innovations for such things." Naseer waved the subject away. "Anyway, when I was little, I was told that very few are born fitting into the role fate will hand them. Most of us grow into it, with hard work, creativity, and support from others. Especially if that job is to lead."

Eleksander rubbed his forehead with the hand not pressed against the wall. He needed to sit down. "I don't care. That was you, this is me. I'm not like you. I'm not what they expect of me. I'm not capable of it!"

With that, he strode down the hall. He didn't want to run like a petulant child, but his mind kept telling him to rush somewhere safe. Somewhere where there weren't impossible expectations on him. Somewhere he could process having just met his birthparent and been all but shunned by him.

He wasn't sure how he got from that hallway through the many corridors to his and Hale's bedchamber, but he was happy the journey had passed in an unconscious daze. He closed the door behind him, drinking in how quiet this humbly lime-washed little room was. How safe. He had to be alone, had to clear his head, and focus on something else.

After a few deep breaths, Eleksander moved the water jug and objects for ablutions from the room's only table. He set it up as a desk, placing upon it a few pieces of parchment, a quill, and a freshly refilled inkwell. He started writing a list of things that made him unfit to lead but then the panic set back in, dizzying him, and he switched writing a letter to Ellenaria Aetholo. His older sister would know what to do. The words wouldn't come, though. He began to draw instead. He drew the set of marbles he had as a child, the ones given to him by the soldier he had to kill. That didn't help. All he saw now was death. He switched to drawing his compass, which had meant so much to him. But then that had been sullied by the king and the Twelve. Besides, he had lost the compass somewhere at sea. He envied it, hidden away from everything at the bottom of the cold, quiet ocean floor. Finally, he tried to sketch Hale's face, something he had never been able to do. He couldn't accurately show the mischief in Hale's eyes or the frequent little movements of his mouth, as eager to be on the move as the rest of him.

A forceful knock on the door made Eleksander jump. He hid his parchment under a blank one and called, "Come in."

Hale pushed open the door. His clothes were, for some reason, soaked. "Hey."

"Hi." Eleksander tried to smile, but it probably came out as more of a grimace.

Hale banged the door closed behind him with his usual inelegance. "Naseer said you didn't want to talk to him, so I came looking for you. I started out in the courtyard, I thought you might be out walking or shooting off some arrows."

"It's raining hard enough to drain the sky out there."

Hale shrugged. "I'd be outside anyway if I felt shitty."

"We're quite different."

"Yes." Hale deflated, his tanned brow creased and mouth drawing down.

"You found me, though," Eleksander said, trying to

cheer his lover up, despite that he himself felt about as cheery as the weather.

"True. I did! Another notch in my hunter's belt."

Eleksander tried to smile again but said nothing.

Hale approached and wiggled a hand in under Eleksander's braids to place it on his neck. The hand was unexpectedly cold. Was that because Hale had been outside or was it him who was hot from panic?

"Do you," Hale started, then coughed. "Do you want to talk about it?"

"I don't know." There was very little he knew right now.

Hale stood there awkwardly for a moment and then said, "Oh. Did you hear about Jero?"

"No?" Eleksander answered, happy to think about someone else than himself. "What became of him? Last I saw him he was limping off the battlefield."

By the waters, what if Jero's injuries had only seemed minor but actually killed him? Eleksander's heart sped up again, feeling tired and sore from overbeating today.

"He's fine. Other than a limp that apparently won't heal. Ave found ways to send a message to him and check." Hale let his hand caress up and down Eleksander's neck. "She said he's gone back to the Lakelands. Kae paid him a big reward for his service to Cavarra and he bought a farm with it."

Eleksander's respect for Kae increased.

"A farm? Sounds nice," he said, closing his eyes and enjoying the soothing of that hand and the change of topic.

"Mm. Ave got a letter from him where he described the farm and said that he bought it to be away from people and the 'big events of history' or something like that."

They both laughed a little, recognising the sentiment but aware that fate wouldn't allow them to do the same. Or maybe it was due to something inside them, and not fate at all.

"Jero thanked us for all we had done." Hale fervently shook his head, assumedly to dry it since the movement cascaded droplets of rain from his hair. "He said he'd stay in touch with Ave and that he'd hold a vigil each year for all those we lost at sea."

"A yearly vigil is a good idea. He was a smart man to get away from all of this."

"That's what I said. Sab didn't agree, though. She said she couldn't imagine just leaving this whole mess before it has been fully cleared up and handled properly."

Eleksander clicked his tongue. "I worry about Sabina. I thought she'd learned to let go of responsibility and control."

"Apparently not."

"I suppose that will take a long time to unlearn. If she ever manages it," Eleksander said with a sigh. "She does have a point, though. This mess does need clearing up. I just wish we didn't have to be the ones to do it."

"Mm-hm."

They were silent for a moment.

"Do you... want to talk about it now?" Hale tried.

Eleksander gave a hollow, despairing chuckle. "Fine. Yes. Let's talk about how they expect a young, meek, fledgling mapmaker to suddenly be king over a silver beast plagued continent of four ancient, ever-warring counties. Oh, and some sort of lake monster."

"Oxen-shit, sweetheart. No one expects that. Not yet.

You'd start off just being a princeling, learning the ropes and such." He stretched. "Besides, you're not that meek. Sweet as you are, you've got a backbone of steel and stand up for what's right when you need to."

"Governing a nation takes more than that."

"It takes someone like you. Did you read my tattoo when we were..." he gave a suggestive snicker before ending with, "... in the cave?"

"No."

Eleksander's cheeks burned, remembering putting his lips against the tattoo on Hale's lower belly, but never reading it.

"It says 'shoot with your stomach' in bold capitals."

He must've looked blank because Hale explained further. "Remember when we wrote letters to each other during the winter break? I asked you for archery tips and what to do when you can't decide how to line up a shot?"

Eleksander dug through his memories and remembered. He had sat on his four-poster bed back home in the Lakelands, with his sisters practising the lyre and the harp in the next room. He'd been preoccupied with pining for a lad he'd accepted would never be more than a friend and wracking his brain for a good answer to said lad's archery question. In the end, he had tried to explain why he always shot with his stomach. He'd written something like:

People speak of having a gut instinct. That is because your stomach feels what your mind is too addled with thoughts and your heart is too addled with emotions to handle. Your stomach will feel ill when something is wrong. Worry, guilt, indecisions, even anger. It will also lift and tingle when you feel something wonderful. It feels things the rest of you is too muddled to grasp, it cuts through the complexities and grasps the basics. So, when you're unsure about wind direction, the placement of the target, the sharpness of your arrow tip, the weight and shape of the bow, your focus, your stance... all you can do is pool what's in your mind with what's in your heart, and then let your stomach decide how to proceed. Does it feel right in your gut? In short, shoot with your stomach.

He rapidly lifted Hale's tunic. Yes. In a bold, slanted script—half buried in that line of fuzz leading to his pubic hair—were the words "shoot with your stomach."

"You tattooed that into your skin? To be there forever?" Eleksander squawked as he let the tunic drop. "But that phrase was only something I wrote off the cuff about archery. Not some motto to live by. I mean, I've said things to you that I've put a lot more thought and feeling into. Those would surely work better to live your life by."

Not that he thought anything he had ever said should be lived by.

"That's not for you to decide, sweet lad," Hale said, part admonishing. "For me, those words encapsulated what I've always tried to do in my life. You were right when you said that when everything else in you is muddled, your belly signals what's right."

"Stomachs aren't very clever or helpful though, Hale. They can feel uneasy and you're not sure why, or if it is just a passing sensation or something permanent. It can even be that you have simply eaten something that didn't agree with you."

"Having eaten something bad feels different and you

know it. And the unknown uneasiness is always a signal to stop and figure out why your stomach is that way, right?"

"Right," Eleksander said, distracted by the role reversal and what Hale was like when giving advice and support. There was a tutor vibe that was, well, *interesting*.

"Your gut is another line of defence, Sander. I've had to rely a lot on that in my life. Nomadic living in rainforests, grasslands, and deserts means you don't have time to sit down and draw up plans. And... um, I know we're talking about you and not me, but..."

"But what? Tell me, I love hearing about you."

Hale looked down at his hands. "My gut was what told me that the way I feel about you is more important than my worries about Woodlander society judging me for loving another lad."

Eleksander's breath hitched. He'd never get over hearing Hale say he loved him.

"Really?"

"Mm. Even before you nearly died, my gut was telling me that come what may, I should be with you." He oh so slowly dry-washed his hands, gaze still down on them. Eleksander watched those scarred, rough, warm hands too.

"You know, the first time I ever touched you was on our first day at the academy," Hale mumbled. "I patted you on the stomach, remember?"

"Yes." It had been more like a set of slaps than patting, but he didn't mention that.

"Our first touch. I know it's silly as shit but that feels like it has meaning." Was he blushing? Hale Hawthorn never blushed. He carried on, nigh inaudibly, "Now, my belly reacts every time we're together. It's never got that full-of-butterflies feeling around anyone but you."

"Not even Ave?"

"Not around any of the lasses I've liked. I've felt little tingles but nothing like when you admitted how you felt in that cave. Or when you shoot arrows so perfectly. Or when you take your clothes off. Or when you saved me when we went over that waterfall. Or... whenever you smile at me."

Hale oozed discomfiture. Eleksander didn't want him to stop, though, didn't want to diffuse the situation and make it all go back to normal. Perhaps it was selfish, but he needed to hear this.

"So," Hale said on an exhale, "I got those words tattooed on me when I thought they were just good advice on how to shoot and how to live your life." He chuckled. "Now, the tattoo has an extra meaning because it also shows... how I love, I suppose."

"With this?" Eleksander placed a hand on that stomach and, even through the tunic, felt every ridge of muscle.

"With my gut feeling, yes. I'm a creature of instinct. Somehow, you knew that about me right away. It makes it clear that you're the one for me. No one else can, with such ease, understand me. Or my gut."

"It's easy to understand this dear thing, half the time it's just hungry," Eleksander said, edging forward on the chair so he could kiss that hard stomach.

Hale laughed. "True. Actually, I'd like to eat something. Do you think the kitchens have started on our next meal?" He shook his head as if to clear it. "Hang on. That's not what we're talking about. I brought up shooting with your stomach because that's what you need to do now. You're overthinking as always."

"Maybe. That and I'm scrambled after, well, you know," Eleksander said, rubbing the aching spot between his eyebrows, where the tension had lodged.

"The reaction of that stick-up-arsed, swanky, shit of a duke who doesn't deserve you as a son."

"I suppose neither my heart nor head is serving me very well at the moment."

"Exactly, pretty lad. Your gut feeling, though? That has led our group so many times during these last six months. Your stomach will steer you right. It'll steer this whole snarled-up nation right."

"I don't know. I keep thinking about Lothiam and his forebears. They got so distant from the people that they began to use them, *us*, for their own gain without any qualms." He looked out their tiny window, watching the rain pepper the warped glass. "Maybe they had good intentions at first, though? And were corrupted by power, riches, or by the monster's spell? I don't want to end up like them, Hale. I don't want to make Cavarrians' lives worse."

"You won't. You're a good person. And shit, the fact that you're worried about this proves you won't." He cupped Eleksander's face with warm and surprisingly gentle hands and lifted it until their gazes locked.

"You can't be sure of that," Eleksander whispered.

"I can. You grew up a merchant's son. A coin-hoarder with more riches than your family could spend." He chuckled at Eleksander's grimace, then spoke on. "And the Aetholo's taught you how to make more. And here you sit, thinking only about the Cavarrian people and if you can be what they need. Not about power, coin, the people's admiration, or even making it into the history books." His hands took a tighter grip on Eleksander's face. "Sweetheart, I've never met anyone who is as furious when they hear about injustice as you. You'd be a just ruler."

There were still so many doubts and questions in Eleksander's mind. He took a moment to boil them down to their essence, gathered up the courage, and asked, "Can I... Can I be enough?"

"You'll be enough and more, lad. And if you ever find yourself struggling, you'll have reinforcements. Your family and your friends. You know, your people."

His people.

The weight of those words was immeasurable.

Hale's thumbs rubbed soft circles on his cheekbones. "Think of all we've gone through. All we've done. If you want to do this, and only if *you* want to, you can do it. Check with your big, warm heart and that scholar's mind of yours and then... shoot with your stomach."

Did he want to do this? He had been so busy with if he could and if he should, that he hadn't stopped to question if he wanted to. He closed his eyes. His stomach was saying yes, wasn't it? If not, why had he panicked so much about if he was able to do it, instead of about how to get out of it. This gave him a chance to finally make things fairer, right some wrongs, and look after the underdogs.

"I'm still not sure that, even with help, I'll be enough," he croaked.

"Start trying." Hale let go of his face to shrug. "Soon you'll see that I was right, *as always*, and you were more than enough. Wasn't it Ave who once said that leadership grows from confidence?"

Yes, she had said that. In the same conversation, she'd claimed that what separated good leaders from bad ones was often their intent. She had been talking about her parents, who cared for no one or nothing but power and the Ironhold name, but hopefully it held true for him as well.

Hale shuffled his feet. Fair enough, this was a lot of talking and thinking for a lad who got bored doing either. "Look, you can't know until you try. And, again, you won't be alone. You'll not only have us, although *I* reckon that'll be enough, you'll also have shit-heaps of experienced advisors."

He was right. There would be advisors. In fact, the advisors would be the people who'd lead Cavarra if he didn't step up. And honestly, he wouldn't trust them not to have their own gains in sight. Be those gains power, as in the case of the Grand Count and Countess of the Peaks, or fame like the Duke and Duchess of the Lakelands. Or focusing only on their own county–like the Woodland's Warden and the North's Baron and Baroness. Or, for the Twelve, a meticulously planned vision for the future to be made real no matter the cost to life.

Even if he agreed to be the official heir, these groups would surely want to control him. After all, if they didn't want the second wave on the council, they surely only wanted him on the throne as a figurehead while they ruled. Well, he wouldn't allow that.

"I'll think about it some more. Just to make sure," Eleksander said.

"Sure. Give your stomach some time to digest it all." Hale bent to cup his face again. "And remember, you have to do very little to be better than the arse-maggot who held the role before you. Just show up and give a toss about anyone other than you. Easy!"

With that Hale kissed him. Everything felt better when they were kissing and for a spell, Eleksander put everything else aside and relaxed into the affection.

When the kiss ended, Eleksander couldn't help it, he whispered, "Will you help me?"

"Goes without saying, love. Come what may."

So flippant. Had he thought this through? "It would be a different life than you ever expected."

"My expectations have always been to be the best I was able to be. To do more than anyone thought a dirty, clumsy, short-tempered orphan could do." He threw his hands out and gave a toothy grin. "Well, I've been a famous mapmaker and explorer. I have golden magic and I'm shagging the future king of Cavarra. I'd say I'm getting more than I expected."

Eleksander laughed along but soon felt it die away. He had to think about what was best for Hale. "You can still be that famous mapmaker and explorer, you know."

"That life wasn't for me. I grew shit-weary of the sea. And the idea of a life searching for new places and peoples, with all that diplomacy and cataloguing? Ugh, it makes me itch."

"Then why did you apply for the Hall of Explorers in the first place?"

"Easy. It was the highest level I thought I could reach. But, protecting you as you rule? While being in control of the nation I love *and* of my own fate and choices? There's no higher level." He scrunched up his currently clean-shaven face. "Besides, I was shit at mapmaking. I mean, all those precise details and calculating distances. Who has the patience?" He squinted out the window. "Still, I would've liked to make one map. Something to save for the future and to show the adventure we had."

"Oh?" The room seemed a little brighter. "In that case, I have something for you."

Eleksander rifled through his pile of parchments and found a crumpled, many times folded one. It was salt-stained and the ink had smudged in a couple of spots. He'd have to fix that. Maybe it wasn't ready to be shown?

"What's that?" Hale took the parchment.

"I, um, made a map of the little island we were stuck on." Eleksander loosened his braids out of the hair tie and retied it, needing something to do with his hands. "I planned it while I cared for you in the cave, memorising all the details for when I had parchment and time to draw it."

"And then you did this when you got home?"

"Mm-hm."

"Look at all the detail! You even drew a sea serpent coming out of the sea."

Eleksander peered down. "Yes, that was perhaps a little fanciful of me."

"More like accurate. Those things were forever popping out of the shitty waves. The proportions of the mountain are a little off, though." Hale's eyes widened. "If you don't mind me saying that. I wasn't criticising. I mean, you never went up there so you wouldn't know."

"It's all right, my treasure. I'm sensitive, but not that sensitive."

"I know. I just," he scratched his head violently, "don't want to make you feel worse right now. I never want to make you feel worse. My words are meant to help and strengthen you, never hurt you."

Eleksander's chest filled with warmth. "You know, you become sweeter by the day."

"Stop gibbering on. I'm rough, not sweet." The twinkle was back in Hale's eye though and he appeared truly thrilled about the map.

"You can correct the mountain if you like," Eleksander said. Hale looked unsure so he altered his words, "I meant to say that you absolutely should change the mountain. I want it to be right."

"Now that sounds more like an heir to the throne," Hale said with a smile. "Well done."

Eleksander stood and gestured for Hale to sit, pushing the quill and inkpot towards him. The lad he loved quickly drew a new top for the mountain and seamlessly made the old, incorrect top a part of the rockwork. They really did make a good team.

Hale sat back and regarded the map. "That's some truly grand work, handsome."

That term of endearment, that affection... It made Eleksander feel like he could take on the whole world as long as he had Hale by his side.

He pulled Hale up and into an embrace, one that soon became a kiss.

Hale stopped the kiss after a while and said, "By the way, I'll always be with you, protecting you, and advising you. But don't expect me to lead meetings, make deals with foreigners, or deal with whingy Cavarrians."

"You can sit by my side and nap while I do those things, my love," Eleksander promised. "Or sit and strategize about how my security and army should be trained and deployed."

"Now that's more like it," Hale said before resuming the kiss.

Eleksander's panic had drained down into the flagstones and been replaced by perspective. Hale always did have a steadying effect on him. In fact, he was starting to wonder if he didn't have that effect on Hale too.

Eleksander ended the kiss. "What happened after I left the meeting?"

"It was disbanded. Everyone needed to stretch their legs, eat, and drink. Sab, Ave, and Aurea went to get some food, actually. Can we... join them?"

"Of course. I know they'll be worried after I ran off like that."

"Sure. That. Also, I'm starving."

Eleksander laughed, giddy with affection. "Well then, let's listen to your stomach and get something to eat."

As they walked through the winding hallways, Hale said, "That map really was something else."

"Oh? Thank you."

Hale shoved his hands into his pockets. "You don't have to give it up, you know."

"Mapmaking or drawing? Because I think I shall be drawing for the rest of my life."

"The mapmaking. The way you excel at things, you can do everything you want. Rule. Make maps. Explore. You can even go teach centering classes, making me stand with my foot above my head while deep breathing like some Lakelander."

Ignoring the jest, Eleksander stopped walking. "I wish I shared your confidence in me. Do you really think I can rule this nation? With its warring factions, its bloodied history, and the silver beasts?"

Hale halted too. "Sure. If you can keep on top of me, you can keep on top of Cavarra."

Oh dear. The double entendre couldn't be resisted.

"*On top*?" he said, trying to make his voice take on that flirty tone he'd heard Hale and Avelynne use so often. It didn't sound right to him, but judging by Hale's expression, it didn't totally miss the mark.

"If you fancy being on top, pretty lad, I'll let you have a go," he said with a grin. "Just don't think you'll always be the one taking charge in this relationship, *your highness*."

"I won't. Whether or not I become king of Cavarra, you'll always be the king of my world," Eleksander said before claiming Hale's mouth.

It was during that kiss the pieces fell into place. Knowing that Hale believed in him and wanted him as king was lovely.

It wasn't enough, though.

He broke away from the kiss to ask, "When you vote for a new warden in the Woodlands, does every single person vote?"

"No." Hale made his pensive face. "That would be fairer, but we're nomadic and there's a lot of us so it would be hard. Every group has a representative and then, every five years, all the representatives gather and vote in a new warden. Why?"

"I'd like the people to get a vote on whether they want me as leader or not."

Hale sucked his teeth. "You heard the dust-brained, old folks. They think voting is a step too far."

"They think every change is a step too far."

"True." That pensive face was back. "I'm sure the people would love to vote in some fresh blood. Particularly the person who they've heard tales and songs of. The one who broke through Lothiam's spell and freed Cavarra from it. The clever lad who'll rid them of the silver beasts any mome—"

Eleksander interrupted with an involuntary scoff.

"You will," Hale said firmly. "You're the smartest person on Cavarra, your Hall of Explorers tests proved it."

"Intelligence doesn't mean as much as you think, my love."

"You're more than smart. You braved the seas and lived. You're the son of the queen they loved, right? The hero with the unique golden magic, the fighter who'll find a way to deal with the fiend in the lake, and the leader who was there to form the new council."

"That wasn't me alone."

"No. But if they vote for you, they get us other second wavers baked into the deal."

Eleksander gave him a quick kiss. "Lucky for me."

They hurried off towards Sabina and Avelynne. And, of course, the lasses' darling Aurea. He remembered her earlier plan to use the Hethklish printing press to get information out to all Cavarrians about Lothiam's spell. Could that be used in a voting process?

Thinking about the Hethklish brought back his time on their ships and his belief that there should've been a captain on each ship for better leadership. He remembered bringing a shocked sailor back into action during the storm. He had been just as shaken as said sailor but realised that displaying confidence you lacked was how you made people trust and heed you.

Maybe he could do this after all?

Chapter Twenty-One

GLAIVES AND FAMILY

Avelynne was out in the courtyard, enjoying the sort of bluish black sky that came right after sunset. It was windy but the rain had just stopped, leaving everything wet, chilly, and fresh. Everyone else was inside, reading by a fire or playing games, meaning she was left alone and unwatched out here to do one of her least favourite things–exercise.

To be exact, she was venting her unease and painful memories through weaponry training. Not with the pike she had picked up in battle since it felt ghoulish to use a dead soldier's weapon, not to mention disrespectful. She had sent that weapon to be buried with its owner. No, she had raided the Hall of Explorers armoury, just like before they sailed. This time had been different, though. She'd been so unaware back then, picking a weapon that was showy and impractical. Now, she knew to pick one that was light enough that she could carry and wield it without spending most of her energy. Nevertheless, she still chose a polearm. That wish to prove to Tutor Rogan, and herself, that she wasn't too reedy to use one still lingered. Besides, she liked the distance it put between her and her foe, affording her a chance to read their face and body language. And, yes, a polearm's size and intimidation factor made her feel powerful, why lie to herself about that?

She held up her chosen polearm so the metal glinted in the light of the courtyard's torches. A glaive. The slashing ability of a sword combined with the thrusting of a spear. This one was quite light and short, meaning she didn't need to ask Sabina to shorten the handle, as they had done with the war scythe before they sailed. This glaive would be a good weapon to bring when confronting the creature in the lake. Hopefully there would be no fighting though, there was still a chance that the creature held no malice against Cavarrians.

Avelynne took the correct stance, even more important on the rain-slick flagstones, and stabbed the target dummy's middle, once, twice, thrice. She withdrew the glaive and then slammed it into the side of the strawman's head like a club. She got ready to slash at the lower part of the straw figure when she heard someone whistle low.

"Ouch. What did that thing ever do to you?"

Avelynne turned and saw Aurea heading towards her with a friendly expression. She wore a cape and lowered its hood, the breeze rustling her copper hair.

Avelynne gave a polite smile, but it strained her cheeks, so she stopped. She knew she was allowed to do that now. "Good evening, Aurea. How are you?"

"Better than that target dummy." She squinted at it through the flickering of the torches. "I think you've killed it several times over. Impressive technique. I don't think I've ever seen someone of your lighter body type use that type of weapon?"

Lighter. A kind word for it. She couldn't stop being short, but she could at least re-build the muscle mass she'd lost while unconscious. Preferably with some haste.

"Some would say I shouldn't use polearms," Avelynne said, hearing her own terseness. "My parents most of all. They believe I should put down all weaponry and instead hold a sewing needle. Or a stack of written decrees to give to my servants and tenant farmers."

"Ah. Your parents. They're the leaders of the Peaks, right?"

Avelynne grasped her glaive until her knuckles clicked. "Yes."

"I see." Aurea said, surveying her.

Whatever she found made her refrain from asking anything else. She went around the strawman and checked its back. "Stabbed right through and has lost most of its straw. You might want to move on to the next one."

Dipping her head, Avelynne stepped over to the next dummy. While hefting the glaive in her hands, she considered what to do. She could keep training, maybe even ask Aurea if she wanted to spar, or...

Quiet as a mouse, Aurea shifted her weight from foot to foot. Her eyes, browner than their usual amber in this scant light, brimmed with curiosity.

Obviously Avelynne wouldn't keep training. She sighed out a small laugh. "You like to ask things, and I like to talk. So go on, say what you're thinking."

The held back words spouted out. "Sabina said your

parents treated you terribly as you grew up and when you finally stood up to them, they disowned you? Is that true?"

"Sabina doesn't lie unless she absolutely must," Avelynne said.

"Oh. I'm sorry to hear that, about your parents I mean. My mother threatens to cut me off from the family all the time, but it's a joke or a sign of exasperation, never real."

"I see."

Aurea hummed. "Having met you four, I realise that I'm lucky to have parents who are neither dead, extremely hard on me, or uncaring. Or as in Eleksander's case – have too many parents, all quite famous."

Avelynne wondered if it was her parents that qualified as "uncaring" or "hard on her." Her coin was on uncaring. Although both she and Sabina had parents who were very hard on them. The Aetholos had been quite hard on Eleksander too, but only to make him succeed and be the best he could be. And Sabina's because they needed her help and forced her to be a third parent. Her parents however... why had they pushed? Out of misery in their own lives? Out of loathing for her?

With a kind expression, Aurea waved a hand in front of her. "Hey? You still with me?"

"Yes. My apologies. I was thinking about my parents."

"Right. Well done for standing up to them, by the way. That was brave, no matter what the repercussions were."

Avelynne scuffed the toe of her boot on the flagstones. "It was necessary. They had to know that they couldn't control me any longer and how their behaviour throughout my life has ruined a lot for me. Had ruined a lot *of* me."

"Necessary or not, it was still brave. I hope I'd do the same in your position. My parents, loving as they are, tend to want to control me too. Luckily, they don't lock me up, starve me, and shout at me, as I heard yours did. They just guilt trip and come up with 'suggestions' on what I should do every two minutes."

There was a twitch at the side of her mouth, a wonderful little tic that Avelynne had noticed a few times before. It was exceedingly endearing, and Aurea's face was so open and kind.

Avelynne took a deep breath and tried to sum it up. Not the starvation or the imprisonment, but the everyday things that she hadn't told anyone about. The pinpricks that added up to be deep, unhealing wounds.

"I had to walk quietly, as to never disturb anyone. No loud noises, especially not laughter or singing, since both those gave my father headaches."

"Sounds like they didn't want to hear or see you."

"Or smell me," she said with a hollow laugh. "No herbal oils or scent bottles for me." She peered up at the stars, it was easier to speak when not making eye contact. "They didn't want me to take up room. Or perhaps, simply not exist."

"I'm so sorry," Aurea said softly. "That must've left its mark."

"Of course." One of the stars was brighter, it must be the Utter Northern Star. She remembered the night she spoke to Aurea about the stars on the Qetesh, right before the storm. "You know, lately I have thought a lot about how they punished me for my interest in the sexual, for being curious and enthralled by it." She caught herself. "I know that's not polite to speak about. Certainly not with someone you've only known for weeks."

"Oh, who cares about polite. And we know each other quite well after all we've been through. If you're all right to speak of it, tell me. I'm open about these things."

Avelynne knew that, of course, but it was nice to hear it. "Me too. I always had a fascination with physical pleasure in all its shapes. Touching yourself, kissing a lover, massages, or even something innocent, like a hot bath on a cold day." She wrapped her arms around herself, keeping her attention on that star as if it would wink out of existence if she blinked. "My parents punished me whenever they caught me reading a smuggled book about it, asking the kitchen maids a thousand questions, or sneaking out to kiss one of the stable hands. They value denying yourself anything pleasant. Be it food, amorous activities, or even rest."

"You talk about what they didn't want you to do. What did they want?"

Avelynne moved her gaze from the cold stars to the warm woman in front of her. Aurea was good at this, at drawing you out, at making you see things in a new way. If she wasn't careful, she'd end up playing counsellor to four nineteen-year-olds with sacks of trauma. Not that she hadn't already. How many discussions about blame and anguish over dead sailors had Aurea been forced to sit through? And yet, she stayed and listened, ever prompting them to talk. As much as Avelynne loved to listen to others, it was nice to be the one to be listened to for once.

"What did my parents want? They wanted me to be harder, colder, quieter, and more obedient. Despite that I obeyed every order they gave." She realised she was taking short, shallow breaths and tried to calm. "Then, to marry a rich Peakdweller noble. One whom they'd chosen, of course, and who would no doubt be male for breeding purposes. When married, I'd take on the leadership of the Peaks."

"They wanted you to take over while they were still alive?" Aurea said.

"Yes. That way I would do the tedious work in public and they could sit at home, in their austere parlour, calculating and pulling the strings of their puppet-daughter and son-in-law. And, as I said, breeding. The expectation would be a healthy heir and as many siblings as spares that my womb could survive."

The latter was a touchy point, of course, since her mother's womb had only managed one child.

Aurea's eyes shot wide and she scrunched up that sweetly upturned nose. "That's... quite the ask."

"I suppose it is."

Before she had come to the Hall of Explorers, that had all seemed so reasonable. Now, she'd rather die than be locked in that life.

After some silence, Aurea said, "Can you forgive them for how they've treated you, do you think?"

"I'm not sure if I want to. Or if they would want me to. I believe them glad to be rid of me. My cousin has already taken my place as the next heir and there are many other cousins to carry on the Ironhold name if need be. In their eyes, I kept failing. What good am I to them?"

Aurea didn't answer, only worried her lip.

"Say it," Avelynne prompted. "Go on. Whatever it is, I shan't be cross."

"Perhaps you should forgive them? Not for their sake or for your future relationship's sake. I mean, why would you want people like that around? But so you can start closing that chapter of your life and move on to the next one." She stepped closer, near enough that Avelynne could feel the warmth coming off her. Or perhaps that was in her imagination. Aurea took her hand, and that warmth was certainly real. "I know it's not comparable in anyway, Ave. But I had to forgive my parents for trying to make me stay on Hethekla and be solely a printer. For making me feel miserable about wanting to try different things, ones far away from them. I had to accept their behaviour and where it came from before I could move on."

Avelynne gripped her hand, worried Aurea would pull it back. "That's exactly it. I need to understand their behaviour. I don't think I can move on until I know why they behaved the way they did. What I had done to deserve —" She corrected herself. "I mean, what they felt I had done to deserve how they treated me." She looked skyward again. "Or perhaps there was no reason. Maybe they were miserable and lashed out at someone unable to defend themselves."

"Then I suppose you need to talk to them."

There they were. The words she had tried so hard to avoid. Avelynne sensed the wing containing the guest quarters behind her back. Her parents were in one of those rooms, despite that they had griped and requested the grand rooms of the empty castle. She could bang their door down and force them to talk to her. She saw the faces of the

Grand Count and Grand Countess of the Peaks in her mind. No, she couldn't. Besides, a little part of her, a child part of her, needed them to come to her.

"I know I do," she replied. "I will see if a good chance to speak to them comes up."

She worried Aurea would push her to do it no matter how good the situation was, but Aurea just inclined her head and said, "Another brave thing. Almost as impressive as your polearm work. Want to see if you can kill this strawman as effectively as the last one? Show someone who only knows the bow and the sword how it works."

Avelynne held the glaive out. "Perhaps you should try it yourself?"

"Really?"

"Why not? I'll teach you. Come here."

Aurea accepted the glaive and stood in front of the strawman. Avelynne got behind the ever so slightly taller woman and began adjusting Aurea's body with light touches, drawing a muscled leg back, moving an elbow into place, pulling a midriff back, pushing strong shoulders down.

"There," Avelynne said when Aurea was in the proper stance. "I suggest a firm grip but not so tight that your strength is focused on that. Take a deep breath." She felt Aurea's torso expanding against her own and said, "Good. Now, with the sort of force and effort level you'd use if you had to lift something very heavy from the ground, thrust the tip dead ahead."

Avelynne moved back and watched Aurea follow her instructions, with good results considering the middle of the target dummy was stabbed clean through.

"Dear me, you have just the right force and assertiveness," Avelynne said. "Your archer's aim clearly came in handy too. I kept jabbing too much to the side at first. Granted, that was probably due to that I couldn't hold a polearm up for longer than four heartbeats." She clicked her tongue. "Let's be honest. More like two heartbeats."

Aurea laughed. "I assume that would be an issue, yes." She shifted a little. "Is this the right stance, though? Should I not draw my arms further back before I thrust?"

"Not that much, no, you don't want to end up in an awkward angle. Especially when you're just starting out and your joints and muscles are yet to be used to the glaive."

Avelynne placed Aurea's limbs back where they had been before, enjoying the excuse for further physical contact and the fact that Aurea seemed to feel the same. The Hethklish woman leaned into Avelynne's hands and, when it was time to thrust again and Avelynne stood behind her, leaning back against Avelynne's body until they were as glued together.

It was nice to be moving and not talking right now. Avelynne was overwhelmed and somehow hollow after their conversation. Moving was much better. Furthermore, Aurea was warm in her arms, smelled so good, and was so pliable in her movements, going where her teacher led. It was funny, Avelynne was so used to being the one who followed in physical situations. However, with Aurea it was as with Sabina, who led and who followed altered. Like a wave moving back and forth, as natural and easy as the tides.

The familiar tingle and pulsating of arousal snuck up

on her and the moment she realised what she was feeling, she froze. She shouldn't be thinking of those two in the same way. Aurea was not her lover and she had promised Sabina to try exclusivity.

She stepped as far back as she could. "I think that's all the lessons you need, the rest you can pick up by observing and practising."

Aurea spun on her heels and watched her for a moment. "Yes. And the night is getting colder. Should we go in and find the others?"

She had said *the others* but Avelynne wondered if she hadn't meant Sabina.

"Wonderful suggestion. Let's do that. If they have time, which I doubt since Sander and Hale are stuck to each other like sap to bark. Nevertheless, if they and Sabina are free, we could play bottletop."

Aurea pulled her hood back up. "What is that?"

"It's a drinking game."

"Oh! I like those, we play them back on Hethekla all the time. Sometimes with alcohol and sometimes with a sort of spicy syrup that burns your mouth. How does bottletop work?"

"I'll show you. Either tonight or some other time."

They had plenty of time for games and getting to know each other better. The worst of their dangers were surely over.

Strangely, that thought didn't comfort Avelynne as much as it probably ought.

Chapter Twenty-Two

ABOUT THE MONSTER

Sabina shifted on the bench. Another day, another meeting of the council. So many things were becoming boringly familiar. The tension in the grand, draft-ridden hall. The sense of time being wasted. The annoyingly hard bench against her rump. And, of course, the judging glares at her, wondering if she was about to have another outburst.

The arrows slits were at least open today, allowing the morning sun to pitch shafts of light into the hall and show the impatient expressions on the attendees. Most of the leaders had to return home soon.

How long had it been since their last meeting? Only two days? Nevertheless, that had been enough time for the Twelve members to interrogate Lothiam's closest allies. Partly to see if any of them had been aware of their actions or if they were all just under the spell. But, mainly, to see what these people knew about the creature in the lake before the council approached it. Sabina took in the attendees. If these oldies had learned one thing from flinging the first wave and second wave out to sea without adequate preparation, it was that taking precautions before acting could save lives. Better late than never, she supposed.

Now, here they all were, about to discuss the results of these interrogations and how to approach the creature. Sabina noticed Eleksander's knee bobbing. These meetings got under his skin. Not in the same way as they did with Hale, who had sneaked in a tankard of goat's milk laced with brandy that he drank while prodding a new scar by his elbow. *He* was obviously bored. Poor Eleksander had worse reasons for dreading these meeting. Just like Avelynne. Sabina wanted to scream at the Ironholds to speak to their daughter, to apologise, to beg on their bony knees for her forgiveness. But they gave her barely a glance.

Kae stood at the head of the long table and waited until the chatter had dissipated, then she lifted her chin.

"As you know, we have interrogated Lothiam's nearest compatriots. Including Tutor Rogan, who in return for the severity of his sentence being decreased has told us what he knows. Even if he did get violent while interrogated." She indicated her swollen and bruised eye area. "Anyway, it seems the king's spell builds up over time, so short bursts of conversation might not be as perilous as we first thought. We have members of the Twelve carefully experimenting with that now."

"What did Rogan, and the other foul accomplices, say about the fiend in the lake?" the baron said, showing as much eagerness as his iceboar, which was snuffling the air in the direction of Hale's brandy milk.

"They all tell the same story, with personal embellishments of course. None of them have ever been allowed to see the creature. They have, however, heard Lothiam say that it has made deals with his forbears for many generations and that it is dangerous, with magic beyond our understanding."

"I could have told you that," the warden said impatiently. "What else?"

"It has lived for centuries but everyone asked believed it could be killed," Kae said. "The monster requires sacrifices but not for sustenance, as it apparently feeds on fish blood and magic. After some pressure, they also mentioned that Lothiam was terrified of the creature but tried to hide it. As royal advisors we also overheard some of Lothiam's conversations."

Here she looked to the much-tattooed Twelve elder, who rolled her eyes and said, "Yes, I recall the fool of a man saying that we would never see his 'special asset' as it only surfaces when he beckons."

Duke Phamaro's eyebrows moved up his smooth forehead. "So, we must bring Lothiam with us to call forth the beast?"

His voice was slow and silky but sounded contrived to Sabina. It hadn't been that measured when he was roaring about not having a son.

"I fear so," said the Twelve elder. "Which is why we have experimented with how much Lothiam can speak before putting one under the spell. We should be safe as long as he is gagged up until he must summon the creature and then gagged once more when he has finished."

The baroness banged both palms on the table, battle rush on her features. "All right, that's a start. What do we plan to do with the beast when subdued? Kill it?"

"Well asked, worshipped one," the baron said as he

wrapped an arm around his wife's shoulders. His hand slowly drooped, resting with its fingertips on the baroness' slight bosom.

Sabina tried not to roll her eyes. Every Northerner knew that those two were like newlyweds, even after all these years and even if they were in public.

"First of all, we interrogate it," said the duchess as she languidly toyed with a bejewelled, dangling earring. "We should learn all it knows about the spell, Lothiam, and the silver beasts. After that, we keep it on hand. To use its powers for the improvement of Cavarra."

"'Tis too dangerous," countered the grand count. "The fiend must be put down."

"Aye. I say we starve it of its food," said the baron. "Drain the lake of anything with blood and use the lake's animals to feed Cavarrians instead."

In her mind, Sabina saw the seas and fields of the North, frozen and barren for more than half of the year and understood the baron's suggestion.

"No, no, no. That takes too long," said the grand count-ess, as if speaking to a despised, witless child. "If it can die, it surely does so from being attacked with iron and magic."

The duke gave her an incredulous look. "Are you forget-ting how we just heard that the fiend lives off fish blood and *magic*? Think of how the silver beasts grow from magic. What if this creature does not die from such an attack but merely becomes stronger and enraged?"

The grand countess swatted that away with a gaunt hand. "Natural magic has that effect on silver beasts, yes. Is that not why we bother to take the children along? For them to use their odd golden magic in place of the normal kind?"

Natural. Children. Odd. Normal. Could the grand countess say one sentence without something in it making Sabina want to punch that tiny, bony nose of hers?

"Perhaps," Avelynne said with an unnerved but resolute air, "we should let it live and convince it to leave Cavarra?"

With venom, the grand countess hissed, "Be quiet you little—"

There her husband stopped her by putting his hand over hers and saying, "Steady, dearest." He addressed the rest of the attendees, "We can see what our options are when we have spoken to it. I doubt my wife is wrong, though. Slaying it is surely the soundest idea."

Avelynne's cheeks coloured and it looked like a smile tugged at her lips? Could she really be happy for something as small as her parents refraining from calling her a witless, soft-hearted chatterbox or whatever that bloodless grand countess had been about to say. Or was it that they actually entertained her suggestion?

"I agree with waiting to see what happens," said the warden. "To be sure, we must speak to it. If it then attacks, we counterattack with weapons and both kinds of magic. If it stays peaceful, we do too and see what solutions are best for everyone."

There were grumbles around the table, to which the warden replied, "Anyone got a better idea? I mean, we can always," here she grinned, "vote on it?"

The mood soured in an instant and the other leaders muttered loudly in their pairs.

"Enough of this. Every moment we sit here bickering,"

Taferia said, tapping her finger on the table, "silver beasts ravage Cavarra worse and our nation stands without a leader or answers to what sort of spell it has been under for generations."

"The Woodlander has a point," the baroness said. "I suppose we'll all go have a wee chat with the monster, then? None of us are going to trust just one group to go."

Everyone agreed, stood, and, with the aid of pages and servants, got ready for battle. Sabina knew the county leaders had warred against each other and remembered seeing most of them on the battle at the shore. She couldn't imagine the refined duke and duchess in battle, though. Not until they both grasped bows—ones perfectly hewn and beautifully inlaid with silver tracery—that had been leaned against their chairs. Those bows were the most elegant yet practical weapons Sabina had ever seen. And the duchess, who Sabina had thought vain and ridiculous before, suddenly looked formidable as she took her jewellery off and with practised movements strapped a quiver of arrows on her back.

Taferia nodded towards the second wave. "No doubt we'll need your golden magic. Are you ready and able?"

"Oh, we always are," Hale said, standing up. "Let's go to our bedchambers and fetch our new armour and weapons."

Sabina nodded, glad to see he'd barely touched his boozy milk. Partly because she worried about him drinking to cope with his problems, like on the ship, and partly because now was a time when they'd all need to stay sharp. Sharper than the most whetted axe.

Chapter Twenty-Three

PREPARED

Hale hefted and swung the sword Taferia had brought him, nearly slicing the tunic hung over the chair by the ablutions table. A simple but whetted to lethal perfection longsword with a solid grip made of hawthorn. Also, the pommel had HH, for Hale Hawthorn he assumed, engraved in it. It was love at first sight. Or, rather, first swing.

Eleksander, Avelynne, and Sabina had already armed themselves. They were now ensuring that their hair was out of the way for what was probably going to be a fight. He ran a hand over his own fuzzy scalp. Shaving it every few weeks was much more practical. He glanced at Eleksander's coiled, black braids which Sabina was tying up for him, and remembered how they felt in his hands. How, when shy, Eleksander would hide behind them, dipping his handsome face and then glancing up through long lashes at Hale with his features framed by those braids. Perhaps there was a point to long hair after all.

They were all in their new Hall of Explorers armour,

freshly smithed mail vests and crisp oil-imbued leathers that needed wearing in. Had that been laying in some cubby hole in wait for the third wave? No. They were all made in the exact measurements of the second wave. Ah. Who cared? The main thing was they were armed and finally doing something about the whatsit in the lake. Not just sitting around talking and doing silver beast shit about the problem.

A knock on the door snatched his attention. Sabina opened it to reveal Aurea and Octavius Naseer. Aurea gave a little bow. "Good morrow, second wavers." She peeked in over Sabina's shoulder. "Oh, nice outfits and weaponry. Is that a new bow, Sander?" When he nodded, she said, "I'm sure it will serve you well. Right, then. Are we all ready to make a new acquaintance of the watery persuasion?"

Hale grunted. This woman's enthusiasm and curiosity was no doubt a strength. But he found it annoying as shit at times.

"I suppose we'll have to be," Sabina muttered.

With her earlier chirpiness gone, Aurea stroked Sabina's upper arm. "I know this isn't easy for you. You won't be alone with the rest of the council, though, if that helps at all. Naseer and I are coming along."

Eleksander paused the adjusting of his jerkin under the new quiver. "You are? I thought you were working on the repairs of the Parataxia and the Qetesh down at the shipyard?"

Aurea tucked her thumbs into her belt, which held two of the long knives of the Hethklish. "Taferia and Kae came to us earlier, seeking our guidance since we have more experience with encountering new creatures. We had scarce advice to offer, I fear. Except for using caution, being adaptable, having an escape route, and of course – arriving with good intentions."

Sometimes the Hethklish were a little too warm-hearted. Hale wondered how long they'd make it here on Cavarra on their own.

Captain Naseer leaned against the doorframe. "After giving said advice, Aurea and I volunteered to come along for the confrontation. Perhaps our experience will come in handy. Also," he gave an embarrassed wince before adding, "Tutor Hathleen and Tutor Myle requested to not have to attend. And as Atha Santorine is still recovering from her time in Lothiam's dungeon—"

"And the Baroness and Baron of the North who should join us but have been... delayed," Aurea interrupted with a gleeful smirk.

Sabina scoffed. "Aye, they are notorious for wanting to bed each other at any given time. Especially before a possible battle."

Naseer waved that away with an air of dignity. "My point was that a few more people attending would seem useful."

A few more people? More like a few more fighters. Hale sheathed his sword. So, it would be the leaders of the counties, the four Twelve members, the Hethklish, and them. If it came down to a magic fight, they'd be fine. If it ended up being a battle of weapons, a lot of their fighters were older and out of practise.

"Certainly," Avelynne answered Naseer. "Diplomats, with experience of how to communicate with different beings will be most helpful. I worry the creature does not speak our language or that it will simply refuse to speak with anyone not part of Lothiam's bloodline."

"That's your worry?" Hale said, not hiding his astonishment. He imagined them all slaughtered by a monster ten times as deadly as the sea fiend that ate so many of their sailors.

"We don't have time for more worrying of any kind," Sabina said, tightening the straps holding Grimfrost on her back. "We must make haste."

That at least made sense. Thank goodness for his Northern sister in arms.

Hale made for the door. "She's right. Come on." He led the way to the courtyard, eager to get this done.

Chapter Twenty-Four

CONFRONTING THE CREATURE

Sabina tried to relax her shoulders down from her ears as their group walked to the lake that lay nestled between the royal castle and the Hall of Explorers. Grimfrost was reassuringly heavy on her back and Kall was by her feet. Both he and she were rested, fed, and their battered bodies had pretty much healed. They were ready for whatever would come. Or at least Kall was, he lived to fight. She wasn't so sure what she lived for, though.

Aurea kept leaning in as they walked and whispering things like, "You're barely breathing. Take a long, slow inhale."

No matter how she breathed, Sabina found no calm. Although Aurea's voice was soothing. So was Avelynne's hand, which had just grabbed hers. Sabina kept her gaze locked on the back of Lothiam, who was being dragged along in his chains by the baroness's snowbear. The bruised and bent former king tried to talk, or curse, but the gag made it sound like gibberish.

With a raised fist, Hale growled, "Quiet, corpse-maggot." After one last grunt, Lothiam obeyed.

Thus, in silence, they arrived. When they stopped by the water's edge, they were welcomed by crows cawing in the nearby trees and clouds filling the mid-morning sky, giving a grey, hushed light to the event. The lake was as tranquil, and free of any sign of an ancient monster lurking below the surface, as it had been when she and the other three snuck out to swim in it. On those carefree, moonlit nights, had the creature known they were in the water with it? Had it watched them? Seeing their naked legs kicking and studying their entire bodies under their see-through tunics? An icy shiver went down her spine.

Taferia took off Lothiam's gag. "Call forth the creature. And if you start saying anything else, we will kill you."

He smirked at her with blood seeping out from between his lips. Had the gag somehow hurt him or had something worse happened? Sabina didn't want to know. Cavarra truly was far too violent. She longed to be back out at sea, perhaps even sailing for Hethekla. She imagined it, seeing it in her mind's eye. Hoisting sails on a sunny day, untroubled and with someone else in charge. Avelynne and Aurea would be by her side, possibly the lads too? If she could convince them to leave land again.

She was yanked back into reality by Lothiam calling Taferia, "A dirt-poor, un-beddable sow", and spitting blood at her feet.

Calm as the glassy lake, Kae used the blunt end of her quarterstaff to jab Lothiam's lower back. "If you don't obey her and call the creature, I'll use the sharp bit."

He groaned with pain, then cleared his throat. He spoke, first quietly and then louder with each syllable. He was saying words half recognisable as old Cavarrian and half over-long words that slid into each other with a lot of sharp consonants.

Lothiam quieted and for a moment nothing happened, other than the sun piercing the clouds and shining right at the water's edge. Then the lake rippled. Through the circles surfaced what looked like a man but twice as large. Sabina staggered back, accompanied by the others. Her right hand flew back to grasp Grimfrost's handle while she stared unblinking at the water.

The creature surfaced up to the waist. He had sea-green, sleek hair so long it lay behind him in the water like a veil. His upper body was lean but muscled with skin that was grey and a tad iridescent, like fish scales. It must be some sort of skin, though, considering how it had wrinkles and veins, the latter appeared green rather than the blueish tint of human veins.

The monster's semi-human appearance made Sabina think of the selkies and mermaids that her people told stories of. Part human or human at certain times. However, this thing had a lower body like a fishtail and, along it, rows of tentacles. Not large ones to battle with, like the sea monster that had attacked the Wolfsclaw. No, this had thin tentacles that flitted in the water, like multitudes of eels had attached themselves on certain places on him. For some reason, they disgusted her. She fought not to look away.

The creature opened his mouth, revealing silvery, sharp teeth. He looked about to engage Lothiam in conversation, then noticed that the former king didn't stand alone. The monster's gaze found them one by one.

"Who art thou?" he hissed in perfect, albeit old-fashioned, Cavarrian. She wasn't sure why she was surprised. He had lived on Cavarra for snow knew how long. He might've invented the language himself.

Sabina expected Kae to answer since she had been happy to take charge up to this point. But no. It was Duke Phamaro who, with gliding steps, placed himself between the creature and Lothiam.

He held his bow, with an arrow at the ready but not fully nocked. "We are a council set to lead Cavarra since the former King Lothiam has been dethroned. Who, or rather what, are you, foul fiend?"

The creature jolted at the words "foul fiend" and now Kae did speak. "Hm. Excuse my associate's choice of words. Allow me to introduce us all fully."

She began to give a brief explanation of who they all were, giving only their surnames. The creature didn't seem to listen. He was staring right at the second wave and only them. His yellow-eyed gaze moved from Avelynne, to Sabina, to Hale, to Eleksander and then started over. The little hairs on Sabina's neck and arms rose more every time the gaze landed on her.

The creature interrupted Kae, who was explaining her own experience as a former advisor to the queen and one of the original Twelve, to say, "What brings thee to my lake? What made you summon me?" His speech was still a hiss, probably due to those needle teeth.

Hale sprung forward. "We're here for answers. We know

you caused the shitting silver beasts and that you helped this maggot control us all," he bellowed while indicating Lothiam, who was currently being re-gagged by the Woodlands' Warden.

Sabina clenched her jaw. She loved Hale but wasn't sure he should be the first point of contact for new races. Even if this lifeform did turn out to be evil and should be fought, they should at least try to start out civil to get the lay of the land. Or to keep the creature from becoming furious and butchering them right away.

The lake creature shook his head, as if arguing with himself. No. More as if an argument had been settled. "You humans. You are all alike, full of threats and demands. I am wearied to the brim of it!"

The creature lifted and held his hands in the same way one did to throw magic, making everyone dodge or take cover. But no magic, neither silver nor gold, came out of those grey hands. Instead, Sabina's head throbbed with a sort of pressure, as if it was being squeezed and squashed like an apple to make cider. She had only read of such spells in children's fairy tales. Snow below, what had they gotten themselves into?

Hale was the first to fight through the pain. He wailed like he was dying and threw a clumsy volley of magic, some of it hitting the spellcaster's right arm. The fiend shook it off and formed his hands for another spell.

Sabina had to act, she gathered herself enough to throw a magic cascade. When it hit the creature in the chest, he roared and momentarily dropped his hands.

The members of the Twelve, the Ironholds, and the

warden took her lead and threw magic until the air was filled with silver streams. The creature still managed another spell before he sank into the water to avoid being hit further. This spell was like a strong gust of wind, pushing them with enormous pressure. Sabina's eardrums vibrated and her vision shivered. The wind incantation tossed all of them backwards until they hit either the ground or the trees and bushes surrounding the lake. Sabina thumped into a tree and knew from the pain that her wounds from the battle hadn't healed as well as she thought. Kall ended up next to her, uninjured and growling at the lake.

The moment the fiend re-surfaced, everyone who could stand started attacking. However, volleys of magic, thrown knives, and fired arrows didn't subdue the creature. In fact, the arrows and knives bounced off like they had hit stone, not even drawing a drop of blood. The attacks with silvery magic did at least get a bit of reaction as the monster winced when they hit and sometimes was pushed back, creating waves in the lake. However, the sort of skilled and repeated magic attacks this creature had endured would have killed anything else Sabina had ever encountered. Even the sea monster had been more affected by magic blows than this fiend, losing tentacles and screeching in pain. Probably because it was blind and not half as clever as this lifeform. But maybe it was more than that. How old was this thing? How powerful?

The Duke of the Lakelands threw a volley of magic that hit the creature right in the mouth. The only reaction was a slight pushing back of its grey body and another head-squeezing spell being cast.

Holding the sides of her head until the excruciating pain passed, Sabina tried to accept that this creature was likely to defeat them. Or simply vanish into the water and not surface again in their lifetime. She checked on the others. The leaders of the counties and the Twelve members looked increasingly panicked. The Hethklish and the second wave were calmer. Although, Avelynne did pause her attack to groan and whisper, "This isn't working. We should have spoken kindly to it from the start."

"I know. It's too late to dwell on what we should've done, though," Eleksander replied, sounding surprisingly composed. "It won't help us now. We must focus."

Hale tried throwing a cage of magic, only to have the creature dive into the water and avoid the silvery enclosure altogether. This all seemed so easy for the fiend and its face showed superiority one moment and murderous rage the next. But not a flicker of fear.

Through tight jaws, Hale said, "Keep fighting and believe in your strength. It's time for us to show what solstice born can do."

"Do you think the golden magic will work on someone this powerful? And if it does, can we control it?" Avelynne asked. "What if it kills him? We need him to answer questions."

They turned to see the monster launch another shock-wave, this time at the members of the Twelve who were thrown back and thumped to the ground. Blood trickled out of their ears, and they all looked dazed and pallid.

The fiend stayed unmoving in the lake, once more turning its lighthouse gaze onto the second wave.

"I don't think we have much choice anymore," Eleksander said quietly. "We have to try something, before this thing kills us all."

In unspoken agreement, they lined up and lifted their hands.

No one around them spoke. Nor did any of the crows caw. The silence felt as treacle thick as the passing of time did.

Sabina focused inwards, drawing up any crumb of energy she could and imagining it going into her magic. This had to work. She held her breath.

The four of them threw their magic and, the instant their streams touched, it turned golden. As before, it grew brighter and more widespread when it touched water, even though the lake was only brackish and not pure saltwater. Soon the golden magic coated the whole lake's surface, like it had the sea, and then spread up onto the monster. It covered his body until he gleamed as if dipped in molten gold. And, just as if he had been solidified in metal, he froze to a statue. A statue sticking up from a lake surface of hardened gold. The sight was becoming familiar to Sabina, but that didn't make it less eerie.

"Now what?" she said on a shaky exhale.

Avelynne replied, "If the golden magic truly does obey our wishes, should we not be able to lower it? Freeing his face and throat so he can answer our questions, but keeping the rest of him frozen in place?"

Eleksander nodded. "That sounds like a good idea. You three keep your magic the way it is. I will try to dim my output and see if I can focus on moving it away from his face."

Out of the corner of her eye, she saw him scrunch his

face up, tense his big arms, and move his fingers. Gradually, the gold lowered, freeing sea-green hair and grey skin, until the creature's face and neck were visible. Eleksander had sounded so in charge and had managed the task beautifully. Sabina couldn't have been prouder.

Eleksander cleared his voice and called across the golden surface. "Kae told you who we are, so it's your turn now. What is your name?"

The trapped fiend squirmed against the magic and snarled, "My name? Of what importance is that to thou?"

"We humans finds that names help break down boundaries, I suppose? Besides, you have been a big part of Cavarrian history, I should like to know your name."

The creature's stilled. "Am I to believe thine curiosity is in good faith? Not a trick to curse me when you learn my true name?"

Lothiam had for some time been trying to shout through his gag and now raised the volume. It still came out as gobbledygook and everyone ignored him, including Eleksander who answered, "Do I look like I could trick a creature as powerful and ancient as you?"

"Nay." The creature looked down on his body and the lake. "Yet, this gilded magic, tis as astounding as it is intriguing. I have only seen it in visions, despite that I have dwelled in these waters for longer than I can say. How did thou come about it, child?"

Eleksander hesitated, clearly weighing each word he said to this being. "My three friends and I were all born within a solstice of heightened magic and turned out like this. We have no more answers than that. Now, may I know your name?"

The creature's expression was hesitant, but after a moment, the lakedweller said, "My name is Vattendal."

Eleksander dipped his head. "Thank you."

He sounded tired, so Sabina stepped closer to the water, keeping her magic output the same, and took over. "Aye, thank you. I'm Sabina Rosenmarck and the lad you just spoke with is Eleksander Aetholo." She made her voice unruffled, even though her heart was racing. Should she have given their full names? "If you swear not to attack *and* to answer our other questions, we will stop the magic that binds you."

Vattendal's yellow eyes narrowed. "Soon, thou will tire after expelling so much magic. Why should I not merely wait thee out?"

"Because, as you yourself said, this is not regular magic. Therefore, you don't know that we will tire," Avelynne said in a friendly manner before adding, "We won't by the way. Oh, and I am Avelynne Ironhold."

She didn't even stumble over not giving her title anymore. Sabina had to wonder if the Ironholds would ever let her be a countess again.

Avelynne added, "The hotblooded young man next to me, who was somewhat rude to you, is Hale Hawthorn. He meant no malice."

"Very well," Vattendal said, his gaze again travelling over the four of them. "Ask thine questions, solstice born. On one condition, remove that wretch." He nodded towards the chained Lothiam.

Sabina fully understood and respected that request. Actually, everyone but Lothiam probably did. Still, it was interesting to see the loathing on Vattendal's face. He was obviously no friend of the man he had colluded with.

As Lothiam was dragged away, Sabina realised that this was their fate – to just as they were about to get answers, get slapped in the face by more questions. Well, that wouldn't stop her from trying to get to the bottom of this and everything else.

Chapter Twenty-Five

FIENDS, FARSIGHT, AND FOUL MONSTERS

Eleksander was the only one not glancing at Lothiam being dragged away by the two biggest Twelve members. His focus was fully on Vattendal. "Why did you do it?"

"Do what, child?"

"Help Lothiam's royal line forge the curse that has kept us Cavarrians bound to him?"

Lit by a shaft of sunlight, Vattendal regarded the gold he was trapped in. "Once, in halcyon days, I was worshipped. An unalloyed holy god of water. Adored and feared in equal measure."

"Why does he talk like he swallowed a set of old scrolls and a bard and now they're battling to get out of his mouth first?" Hale whispered.

Eleksander shushed him.

"My worshippers were simple creatures with simple needs. They prayed and sacrificed to me in return for bountiful harvests and stout health. I luxuriated in their devotion and need. All was well." Vattendal's expression darkened. "Twas not to last. Through epochs, this landmass kept altering and this body of water dwindled, until, after one particularly bad drought, I found myself surrounded by land. I was confined in this lake."

"Why didn't you just walk, or um... slither, back to the sea?" Hale asked.

Humiliation flashed across Vattendal's face. "I can do many a thing—some wonderous, some foul—but I cannot touch land. That is the curse that has bound *me,* and it is infinitely worse than your piteous monarch and silly silver pests."

The duchess bolted forwards but was stopped by the baron and baroness, one of them apologetically saying, "We need information."

Eleksander's heart twinged. He would also be on the warpath if he had to listen to the creator of the silver beasts, which had killed and ate your newborn, call them "silly silver pests." He didn't dare look at his no doubt furious birthfather, but instead glowered at Vattendal, taking care to keep his many sharp replies under his tongue.

Vattendal, meanwhile, gazed skyward. "Grieving my freedom, I waited under the surface. I looked to the rains and assumed I would be reunited with the seas once more. During my fruitless wait, the land changed." He frowned. "This part metamorphosed into what you call the Centre, a dwelling for few people and none of them believers in anything but royalty or their next meal. I missed the sacrifices and prayers of thousands nigh as much as I missed the sea."

"So you decided to punish us all for it? Including children, like mine?" Duke Phamaro said, his normally silky-smooth voice breaking.

"Nay. This was never about thou and thine," Vattendal said, sounding affronted. "I had to make do with the only humans who attended me—your royals—and use more radical measures to ensure they made up for the lack of more worshippers. Foul, soulless humans they were, caring not one whit about helping me back to sea nor about gathering more devotees for me."

"Our royals were never known for being helpful," Avelynne said.

"That is the unblemished truth." Vattendal's grey lips took on an ugly twist. "They demanded something in return for their worship and sacrifices, a spell laid on the rest of the nation. One ensuring their bloodline was never questioned but ever heeded and loved. Resentfully, I accepted."

So, he was able to do all that but couldn't get himself to the sea? Nor find himself more followers? Nature played strange tricks on its creatures. Still, Eleksander supposed it was a relief to know Vattendal wasn't all-powerful.

"The sacrifices you mentioned," Sabina called over the growling of Kall by her feet. "It was their loved ones? Killed in your honour?"

"Precisely so. The true sacrifice of the heart."

"And they prayed to you? Even our former king?" Sabina said with a dubious grimace.

It was hard to imagine Lothiam venerating anything but himself. Add the fact that Cavarrians had sworn themselves off the idea of gods so many generations ago and Eleksander understood Sabina's scepticism.

"The worship diminished each generation, as they stopped being afeared and grateful. As they forgot just how mighty I am!" Vattendal said with a snarl. Then, his yellow eyes glinted in competition with the gold that covered him. "Yet, I have some farsight and it showed me the end of their wretched line."

Eleksander almost lost the flow of his magic stream. "What did you see?"

The former god smirked. "That their end would be brought forth by the fruit of the zenith solstice."

"The zenith solstice? The one we were born during?" Avelynne asked, as much of the other second wavers as of Vattendal.

"It must be so," Vattendal said. "You possess the magic of gold. It draws its energy not only from the user but from the sun and the water."

"That's why we don't tire from this as much as from normal magic," Avelynne mumbled, seemingly more to herself than anyone else.

"How does it work?" Kae asked.

Eleksander wasn't sure if she was asking on their behalf or because the Twelve wanted to know so they could replicate and use the golden magic.

"That, I know not. Had I that knowledge, I should have trained myself to fight it so thou were unable to capture me. My farsight gives only glimpses." He strained his neck, as if uncomfortable in his golden prison. Was releasing him too much of a risk? Before Eleksander could decide, Vattendal spoke on, "My glimpses showed that the gilded magic, which stems from the most magical phase in this land's history—the zenith solstice—entered every child born at that time but was the strongest in the most magical four children. One from each county."

"That... sounds like it was done by design," Eleksander said.

Vattendal locked their gazes, making Eleksander shiver. "Perhaps. Or perchance 'twas a coincidence of nature. I have no answers to grant thou."

Eleksander wanted to ask follow-up questions, but Hale cut him off by barking, "Enough of this confusing shit. Explain what the silver beasts are. How were they created?"

Vattendal moved his focus to Hale. "All formidable spells come at a cost. My price for casting this one was worship, taking the form of a sacrifice; a beloved person beheaded in my name around every fifty years. However, my price wasn't the only one exacted."

He quieted, wearing an expression that seemed to say they should understand the rest.

Hale groaned. "Go on. What else?"

"Thou should know that nothing comes from nothing. If thou were to place more magic into the world, well, the world would hunger for more. I birthed a mighty spell and it caused a magic surge in the land, infusing everything."

"Everything? Not just the insects?" Sabina asked.

"When I sighted this side effect of the spell, I assumed the magic would permeate everything. Yet, magic holds a sort of vague consciousness."

"That explains why our golden magic follows our lead and wishes," Eleksander said, mostly to himself.

"It does," Vattendal said. "And as humans kept overusing thine own magic and consuming the world's resources—bleeding nature dry of all it could give and leaving nought but wastelands—the magic countereffect of my spell entered insects."

"Why?" Hale roared.

"Is it not obvious?" Vattendal said with brutal glee. "They are the creatures thou see as mindless, over-breeding pests. I had presumed it would be rats and mice, but then... starving humans doth sometimes eat those. Wasps, centipedes, and cloth-eating moths, however, they are just nuisances to thou, only taking and breeding. Like thou." He gave a metallic laugh, showing those needle teeth. "The magic overspill had a sense of humour, making those pests into thine worst enemies. If thou had not ventured down this path of halting the spell, I believe they would have kept growing, until they were bigger than thou and more powerful."

"Exterminating us like we were the bugs," Hale said in stricken tones.

"Thou made them as greedy and magic-hungry as thou art."

"Don't you dare lay this squarely at our feet, you water-logged gobshite," the warden said from somewhere behind Eleksander. "Your spell created them as a charming little side effect to the binding of us all to a self-absorbed tyrant."

Vattendal frowned. "Speak not of him to me. That uncouth brute threatened to have my lake drained unless I strengthened the spell to make the entire nation not only have affection for him, but to rapidly forget any grievances they had against him." The frown deepened. "It took nigh my entire might to achieve and will have created more silver beasts."

"You didn't want to do it?" Avelynne asked.

"Nay. I acquiesced merely to save my life and in the knowledge that this endeavour was not to last long, since

236

my farsight told me his power would be ripped from him soon."

"I'm not surprised that a shit—" Hale stopped himself. "I mean that *someone* like you would do what Lothiam wanted. The surprise is that self-loving Lothiam found a loved one to sacrifice."

"Mayhap the brute loved the idea of his queen? I gathered from his salivating words that he loved her visage, at least," Vattendal said offhandedly.

Eleksander's breath hitched at the mention of his birth-mother. Would that ever stop happening? Vattendal still spoke and Eleksander focused back to hear him say, "Love can be different things. Some of the royals sacrificed a pet or a faithful servant." Vattendal wriggled within the gold. How long could they hold him?

"I'd like to ask..." Eleksander began. What did he want to ask, though? How to get to the truth? Where to start? He finally picked, "Entering the deal with the royals, you only did that because you became stuck in this lake?"

"Indeed. I am a solitary being, made to travel the vast, endless sea and only converse with others when I require worship. My overlong confinement here and the work I was forced to do for thine heartless, feeble royals has nigh slayed me. I was once much more formidable."

"I see," Eleksander said. "Well, what can we do to make you never enter such deals with other Cavarrians again?"

Vattendal grimaced. "I would rather lie with a haddock than venture into covenants with Cavarrians again."

"Does that mean he *doesn't* shag fish?" Hale mumbled from the corner of his mouth.

"Be that as it may," Taferia said, speaking over him. "We

can't simply trust you and leave you here to cause other mischief. Or use your power against us."

Vattendal's head jerked back. "Doth thou believe I wish to remain here? Have thou not listened?" He gave a hissing, snarling sound. "My farsight has showed that the younglings wielding the gilded magic can aid me in returning to the sea."

"What?" the baroness spluttered as she stroked her snowbear. Probably in an attempt to keep it from giving those noisy, rumbling growls. "Do you truly believe we will let ye simply swim off, circling Cavarra and returning when it pleases you?"

Vattendal sneered. "I swear upon the water I dwell in that I never wish to see Cavarra ever again."

"What about your punishment for what you have done to us, hm?" the duchess drawled, however, there was rage in the undertones of her slow, elegant speech.

"I have been captive for generations, bound to do the bidding of creatures I loathed, bestowing upon them the power I could not wield to free myself." Another sneer. "I have been punished. Furthermore, tis up to the *solstice born* if they wish to aid me or not, only they can do it."

While searching the faces of the other second wavers, Eleksander pondered their options.

One: release Vattendal and trust that he neither returned nor went elsewhere to treat other races as badly as he had them, unwillingly or not.

Two: murder him.

Eleksander looked down at his hands, which still fired magic and juddered a tad with the effort. He ached at the thought of more blood on them and more dead souls to his name.

"If we did release you, how would that work?" Sabina asked.

The warden waved that away. "Never mind the 'how.' I'm stuck on the 'why.' Why should we let this gobshite go? I say we make him work for us!"

Eleksander groaned inwardly. Up to this point, the warden had been his favourite county leader.

"Ah. There it is. The exploitive nature of humans that I was awaiting," Vattendal said with an acerbic, wry half-smile. "Perhaps I may appeal to your transactional nature and offer a deal?"

In that moment, Eleksander believed fully that Vattendal wanted nothing more to do with humans.

"Less of your disdain, curse-caster," said the grand count, his moustache quivering. "State what you will give us to release you instead of slitting your foul, grey throat here and now."

"What say thou to me eradicating the silver beasts as well as the spell making everyone adore thine former king? As well as swearing to never return to Cavarra, of course."

The baroness folded her arms over her chest. "I thought you swimming off would stop the spell? Or killing Lothiam?"

"I fear not. The spell was cast and lives on whether I or thine former king perishes."

"We only have your word for that," Duke Phamaro said.

Vattendal raised his chin. "I suppose thou must trust me."

The members of the Twelve were whispering to one

another, then Kae said, "Judging by the information stemming from our interrogations and from what we royal advisors have overheard Lothiam say, the spell is indeed its own creation and can only be undone by its maker."

"Tis so, distrustful humans. I can lift the spell and revert the silver pests back to the harmless little insects they once were. Would thou like that?"

His tone was that of someone offering greedy children sweets and it made Eleksander's chest burn with rage.

The grand count stepped closer to the lake, his bearing as ramrod straight as Eleksander knew he had forced Avelynne's to be. "Are we to believe that all you ask in return is to be moved to the sea?"

"A being's freedom and return to its home is no small thing, human. I have been confined to this fetid lake with thou fetid humans. My one desire is to swim as far away as my body and my power can take me."

Hale, still shooting magic at Vattendal with great ferocity, tilted his neck until it popped on both sides. "I repeat what Sab said. How the shit do we move you? Is it even something we can do?"

"Not so hasty, young Woodlander," the grand countess snarled. "We must discuss this. This water-ogre has not been punished enough and may commit more crimes in the future. We either force it to stay in our employ or we execute it."

The mutterings of disapproval and murmurings of approval sounded like an ill wind rustling through leaves to Eleksander. He was about to speak but to his surprise, Avelynne beat him to it. "We do not enslave, remember? All four counties swore to never do that again."

Everyone fell silent.

Avelynne, her gaze down on her magic-shooting hands, continued, "When it comes to death, I think we have had enough of that lately. And hundreds of years imprisoned is surely punishment enough?"

The grand countess scoffed. "You are not—"

Avelynne cut her off—actually cut her mother off—and said, "Also, murdering someone for something they *might* do in the future cannot be right. Furthermore, I'm not sure we even can kill him, Mother." Avelynne's voice only trembled a little as she said that last word. "We are using all our power just to bind him, but the magic doesn't seem to have done any permanent damage."

"Do not tell me what is possible, girl. You do not even know what you are doing," the grand countess said. "Everything can be killed. With enough experimentation, I am sure someone could end this ogre, even if you cannot."

Sabina stomped her foot, making her magic stream dance. "Your daughter, not that you deserve to call her yours, is one of the only four people who can even touch Vattendal. He said so himself. Only the golden magic, remember?" Sabina glowered at the grand countess and added, "She's right too. Even if it was ethical to kill him, the magic is only freezing him in place and we're not even sure how it does that. We may not know how to move Vattendal to the sea, but at least we have him to tell us. When it comes to killing him, there is no one to instruct us."

"Enough squabbling," said the warden. "As much as I want this fiend punished and unable to do more harm, there's sense to what the wee ones say. The most important thing is for him, the shitty silver beasts, and the even shittier spell to be long gone. Our only choice is to take his deal."

"It is not," the grand count whispered through tight jaws. "Leave this to me and my wife. The rest of you stand quietly and do not tell it that we cannot kill or enslave it, you remove all our bargaining chips and weaken our position."

"Nay," said Vattendal with solemn weariness. "Unlike humans, I stand by my agreements. I shall break the spell because I wish to. I want nothing more to do with thou or the spell but only to return to the sea. Tis that simple."

Taferia gestured to him with an open hand. "There you go. We must let the second wave release him and leave the rest to the hands of fate."

Eleksander wasn't sure if it was because Taferia was over thirty years of age or because she had more gravitas but now everyone, even the leaders of the Peaks and Lakelands, began to agree. He wondered if it would be her or someone else who would step up and make the final declaration. Most of the others looked to Kae, but she was looking at... him.

He wasn't witless, he knew her motives. She was grooming him to be the future king. Still, if he made the deal, he could at least be sure it was honestly meant. And he, with the other three, would be the ones to follow through.

"Go on, Sander, make the deal," Aurea whispered from somewhere behind him.

He wetted his dry mouth and addressed Vattendal. "Free us from the royal spell and the silver beasts. When we have confirmed that this has been done, I swear on my birthmother's head—Queen Lea who was sacrificed to you —that I and the other solstice born will return and bring you to the sea."

"I believe this promise is from the heart, child. Nevertheless, I cannot trust thine fellow humans. How do I know thou will be allowed to keep to the agreement?"

"Well, if the promise is broken, you can simply recreate the silver beasts and cast a worse spell," Kae said with finality.

"Tis true, I suppose," Vattendal said, gazing skyward. "I must take into account the glimpses my farsight has given me too. In gloried visions I saw these four younglings taking me away from all monsters and back to my home."

Eleksander jolted. Monsters? They were monsters to him just as he was one to them. As much as there was to learn from exploring the seas and new lands, there was much to discover by speaking to others.

"Again," Sabina said, her impatience showing, "how do we do that?"

"When thou knoweth I have held true to my part of the accord, return here and call my name – no need for that maladroit former king to do it. I shall then instruct thou on how to move me across the accursed land."

So, they were to take it one step at a time. That made sense.

"I'm so shittingly glad we don't have to bring Lothiam with us to call him next time," Hale said to the rest of the second wave.

"Agreed," Eleksander replied. "We will release him from the magic now? And then leave?"

He waited to see if anyone argued but no one did. The

four of them let their hands drop and their focus on the magic wane.

The gold slipped off Vattendal and the water and then vanished. Their surroundings got darker without the glinting gold and Eleksander's eyes took a while to adjust.

"Back away with your attention set on him," Sabina said quietly. "Be ready to combine our magic again if he tries any spells or other attacks."

They all voiced their agreements and kept Vattendal in their sights until they were far away enough to barely make him out. The four Twelve members were at their backs, leading the way and warning them of any obstacles. Eleksander believed their group could trust the former god but respected Sabina's wish to take precautions. Carefulness truly did lead to safety, an idea his parents had long tried to pull out of his careful personality. Perhaps a balance was desirable.

Away from the lake but not yet at the Hall of Explorers, Avelynne fell behind. A hint of worry brushed Eleksander as she made step with her parents. Although, she would of course need to speak to them, even if it was just to clear the air or to say farewell. Sabina and Hale didn't look as sure, concerned as ever for their sweet Avelynne. They never understood how strong she was.

"She'll be fine," he reassured. "She knows what she's doing. More so than us three most of the time."

They both agreed but still cast glances back at Avelynne, who walked with proud bearing and, for once, had her parents' attention and whatever politeness they could muster. His two fellow recruits needed distraction.

"We still know so little about the golden magic," Eleksander said. "What we did back there really brought that home to me."

Sabina murmured "stay" to Kall, to keep him from hunting a passing mouse, and petted him. "Aye, and we know even less about the zenith solstice. Was it merely a coincidence of nature that it had more magic than other time periods? Or was some sort of higher power involved?"

"Shit, I doubt the latter," Hale said with a chuckle. "This world, and our situation, is too much of a messy heap for me to think anything, or anyone, with a plan exists."

Eleksander pulled his jerkin tighter. "I wonder if we need to know."

Sabina stopped stroking, her hand between two of Kall's grey stripes. "What do you mean?"

"Well, we don't know where our silver magic came from. Or our eyesight. Or our ability to walk or talk. And we're not tying ourselves in knots wondering about that."

"This is different. Those are all common things among Cavarrians and are being studied and hypothesised about by scholars. This... this is new," she said. "I want clear answers. Now."

"Of course you do," Hale said with another chuckle.

She knitted her brows. "What does that mean?"

"I mean that tracks with what you're like."

"Again, Hale, what does that mean?"

"I can't explain it," he said with a groan. "Never mind."

Eleksander moved so he walked between them. "I think he means, with the deepest respect, that you often feel that you must know everything so you can control situations. Usually in order to help others."

"Exactly," Hale said with relief. "You just can't leave things be."

Sabina's shoulders hunched and her brow creased deeper.

"And that's fine," Eleksander added, seeing her reaction. "Accountability and caring for others are not only core parts of your personality but they're admirable, wonderful traits. But for your own sake, there must be limits and some sort of... balance?"

"You're kind." Sabina sighed. "And probably right."

"No matter what my sisters claim, that does happen on occasion," Eleksander said.

Sabina snickered but then grew grave again. "No matter the reason, I do need answers. There must be some out there," she looked towards where the sea would be if they could see it from here.

Hale clapped her on the back, hard enough that a lighter woman would've flown forward. "Then I'll get you your answers. No matter the cost. Maybe we can question Vattendal when we get him back to the sea?"

"Perhaps," Sabina agreed.

Warmth blossomed in Eleksander's chest. This was how Hale showed love. He couldn't talk much about feelings, even though he was learning. And, socially, he was clumsier than an ox with leaden feet. But he would climb mountains of glass shards to get Sabina her answers. And... he would stay with Eleksander, in the viper's nest that was the Centre with its power plays, stuffy rooms, and hours of debating and decision making. Hale would protect him and go everywhere with him, never expecting anything in return.

The question was if Eleksander wanted to ask that of him. He regarded the royal castle in the distance. Did he want to ask that of either of them?

"Hey." Hale leaned over to say, quiet enough that only he and Sabina could hear, "Do you know that you're really tempting when you're deep in thought? The furrowed brow and great arse combo works for you."

"Ugh, you two are incorrigible," Sabina said with a laugh. Giving them a morsel of privacy, she and Kall walked a couple of steps ahead.

Hale winked at him, slow and with sumptuous amounts of meaning, before wrapping an arm around him and mumbling "I love these wide shoulders," into his ear.

That warmth trickled into Eleksander's chest again, but this time it spread. Oh, it spread all the way to his loins. He worried his arousal might become obvious. The powerhouse that was Hale Hawthorn was heavily flirting with him. In public. Eleksander's cheeks burned and he had to look away so Hale didn't see his awkwardness. That was when Avelynne caught up with them.

Chapter Twenty-Six

CLOSURE

Avelynne covered her middle with her hands. Nausea, relief, and a hundred other feelings and sensations were crowding inside her.

"What did your parents say?" Sabina asked the instant they were next to each other.

"Well, um, they expressed some admiration for my use of the golden magic, how I survived the deadly sea journey, how I had brought the Hethklish and all their riches here. And, of course, for defeating Lothiam."

"Some admiration?" Sabina said, barbs in that husky, sweet voice of hers.

Avelynne tried not to sigh. "That is all I can expect, snowdrop. You know what they are like."

"Cold and horrid as frozen..." Sabina trailed off.

"Frozen piss?" Hale suggested in a furious mutter.

"I was trying not to say that," she replied.

Avelynne fidgeted with her hair. It was one thing for her to complain about her parents, but she had an odd need to defend them when her friends criticised them. Even if they were right.

"They did ride into battle to fight with us that day on the shore," she finally said. "Both of them risking their lives and the main Ironhold bloodline. And you know how much the latter means to them."

None of them disputed that. Granted, her parents' actions could've been a matter of honour and not looking bad in front of the other leaders. However, the Ironholds usually sent their army to do their fighting. In fact, her mother had only last year said that she was beginning to think that women were better suited for politics and leadership than something as menial and filthy as combat. Yet, her mother had sat on that battle horse, ready to get her heirloom armour and her great-grandmother's sword dirty. That had to be about more than principle and keeping up appearances.

Eleksander gave her an encouraging squeeze of the shoulder. "So, what was the outcome of your conversation?"

"Well, they declared that parenthood had been extremely hard for them. When I asked if that was because I was a substandard child, they said no. With much squirming."

Everyone gave snorts or mirthless chuckles at that, and she knew they understood.

"They admitted they had never wanted children but required an heir," she said. "So, they parented the way their own parents had, but maybe with even more antagonism since they didn't want that life. And since I never lived up to their expectations." There was a surprising lightness in her chest. "They said that this wasn't my fault, though. That they had understood that there was 'some merit' in me being who I am and that they had been wrong to expect anything else of me."

Eleksander whistled low. "Where does that leave you?"

"They, well, they said they were considering allowing me back at Ironhold castle and returning my title."

"That's big of them," Hale grumbled.

"Yes," Avelynne said, trying not to laugh. "I'm afraid they are quite hopeless. Still, they are the only parents I have and in their own way, I do believe they have missed me. Maybe even, in my absence, have noticed that they sort of love me."

Sabina kicked a pebble, dejection in her posture.

Hale meanwhile looked up at the clouds. "Shit. Well, I hope you'll still come visit us. Wherever we all end up."

Avelynne balked. What? "Hang on, you do grasp that I *obviously* said no."

They all spun towards her.

She held her hands out. "If I went back there, I would try to live with whatever morsels of affection they could throw my way and be constantly fighting for my wishes and rights. Or live my life the way they wish, always trying to impress and please them. Which I have learned is impossible." She shook her head a little. "Even now, when they were expressing some pride in my accomplishments, they criticised my appearance and pointed out that I was still far too weak-hearted."

Hale held up his clenched fists. "I'd love to knock some sense into those arseholes."

Avelynne noticed there were tiny hairs on his knuckles. He grew furrier every day, like a sweet, little bear cub. Not that an outsider facing him when this enraged would see this muscled, scowling, rough-haired man as sweet. She knew better, though. The second wave knew better.

"Anyway," she said, brushing her hand soothingly over Hale's back. "I am gladdened to have spoken to them and found out why they behaved as they did." She thought for a beat. "And that I need not measure my life to their standards or make them try to understand me. I've moved beyond them and their opinions."

It was mainly true. She'd seen through their power moves and how it all came back to their own unhappiness and inherent coldness. Yet, she knew that in darker moments, she would always hear their raised voices berating her. However, it would be only in her mind. Her body would be far away from them, exploring the seas and embracing lovers.

Free.

Eleksander reached a hand towards her throat and before she had time to wonder what he was doing; he had flipped her necklace. The tiny silver quill had clearly hung incorrectly, something it wouldn't have done if she'd been doing her normal fretting with it.

He smiled at her. "I'm proud of you. Are you certain, though? That you don't want to mend your relationship and get your home and title back?"

"Ironhold castle was never much of a home and I was a terrible countess and would make an even worse grand countess. When it comes to mending my relationship," she glanced back at her parents, "they have recognised that they had a pretty good daughter and made a mistake in disowning me. Meanwhile, I've forgiven them as much as I can and realised that I don't need them. Or owe them anything. I consider that as mended as it is going to get."

"Hm," Eleksander said. "Family is an odd thing. Especially the blood-based ones."

"That's why we should stick to the family we made," Hale said, almost as an aside.

Avelynne thought of the four of them. Then of the lovely Aurea, of Taferia, of Naseer, of the Hethklish sailors that she was getting to know. Before she came to the Hall of Explorers, she had been lonely to the point of despair. Her parents had seen to it that she had no friends, only a maid who disliked her. Now, she had a group of truly wonderful people around her. They wanted her company, they let her help them, and they cared about her. Stars above, some of them even loved her. How had she gotten so lucky?

Hale rubbed his stomach. "I'm starving. Someone go get Aurea and we'll sneak to the kitchen and convince the wonderous, pretty kitchen maids to feed us."

Eleksander raised an eyebrow. "Wonderous? Pretty?"

"Not as pretty as you, sweetheart," Hale said. "But they do possess the wonder of the keys to the larder. Which, my cherished lad, you do not."

"Fair enough," Eleksander said, laughing.

Avelynne looked to where Aurea walked with Naseer behind them. Aurea was watching the second wave and Avelynne's heart pounded in double time as their gazes locked. Those clever eyes, that lithe body, that soft fawn-coloured skin, and those striking aging scars, it all made Avelynne quite dizzy. She remembered their talk about her parents and suddenly couldn't wait to tell Aurea all. She moved to go get her but Sabina, followed by Kall, reached Aurea before her.

"Too late, Ave," Eleksander said, knowingly.

"Oh, shush you," she said, linking her arm in his and leaning her head on his shoulder.

That lightness in her chest stayed. Right now, she could take on the world.

Chapter Twenty-Seven

TO KEEP THEIR WORD

The next day they were back at the Hall of Explorers' great hall for another meeting. Sabina crossed her legs under the table, then uncrossed them again. It was a warm afternoon, making the hall stuffy as the members of what was now called the Council of Cavarra gathered.

The Ironholds and the Duke and Duchess of the Lakelands sat exchanging comments about if Vattendal shouldn't be killed after all, as well as some empty platitudes about future cooperation. The baron, baroness, and the warden walked in together, arguing over which made a person tougher, extreme heat or extreme cold. The Twelve members were speaking in hushed voices to the tutors, more scheming no doubt.

For the first time, Sabina wished she wasn't present for the decision making. She had to be part of it to ensure everything turned out all right, but she wanted to be out in the fresh air, using her body and her wits to take on new challenges. She was starting to feel like Hale. Although, he wasn't as restless as everyone had expected. He sat with an air of contentedness, drinking a tankard of water and flirting with Eleksander, even gazing admiringly at his Lakelander while he thought no one saw. They really were maddingly in love. Although, she supposed it was only maddening because she wanted that sort of relationship for herself.

She looked back to Aurea who stood behind them, propped against the wall. She had been invited as advisor in Naseer's place since he had developed some mild ague and taken to his bed with a fever.

Now, Aurea was able to give her that sort of relationship, they could be an actual couple and one day share wedding vows. No. That wasn't possible. She couldn't stop loving Avelynne. Also, she was quite sure that Aurea was falling for the former Countess of the Peaks as well.

Aurea caught Sabina watching her and leaned forward to say, "If you look any more like a handsome, brooding hero, I'll have to commission Avelynne to paint a portrait of you."

Sabina snorted. "Brooding hero?"

"Yes. You were all furrowed brow, set jaw, and solemn eyes. Distractingly dashing."

"She always is," Avelynne said, letting her thigh touch Sabina's under the table. "Even when she sleeps. Although, I'd say she is more beautiful than dashing at that point."

Sabina didn't know what to say or where to look. "Stop it, you two. You're only trying to cheer me up."

"I can only speak for myself but," Aurea moved nearer so the breath of her words ghosted against Sabina's ear, "I meant every word. Nevertheless, if cheering you up was a side effect, I'm glad for it."

"I couldn't agree more," Avelynne said, brushing her thigh against Sabina's again. She lowered her voice. "You deserve to be cheered up, since you're forced to sit here with these quibbling so-called adults who appear addicted to platitudes, repetitions, and arguing."

"Not to mention," Aurea interjected, "that you deserve to not to be in a room with a couple who wear enough rose oil to coat the inside of your nose."

Sabina had to admit, it pleased her that Aurea knew her well enough to pick up on her aversion to rose scents. It wasn't so nice that the duke and duchess must've actually bathed in rose oil this morning and the room's warm air was ladened with the sickly-sweet smell.

Standing erect, Kae gave a single clap of her hands for attention. "We all seem to be gathered and settled. Perhaps we can begin?"

When no one disagreed, she sat down while saying, "Good. Over to you, Taferia."

Next to them, Taferia rose. "Thank you for agreeing to attend this meeting."

Hale slammed his tankard down said with theatrical shock. "Agreeing? We were allowed to say no?" This drew quiet laughter from around the table, breaking the ice a little.

Taferia cuffed him gently on the shoulder before speaking on, "I know everyone's time is valuable and that you leaders of the four counties need to return home soon. So, I will quickly go through the updates." She held up a vellum scroll. "Good news first. We have had reports coming in from all over Cavarra. Seems there have been no silver beasts spotted anywhere and the spell is breaking, meaning more and more people are questioning the king and waking from their devotion. Vattendal held his word."

There were expressions of delight around the table and clapping from the two tutors.

Taferia read on. "More and more people now believe the accounts of the labour camps and have collected their loved ones from them, dead or alive. They are realising that the claims that their family and friends deserved what happened to them were lies."

The smiles and gleeful utterances grew muted. No wonder. Sabina's stomach was roiling. Systematic cruelty and injustice had been stopped, but for many who had died from executions or torture, it came too late. Their loved ones were left not only with grief but also guilt for believing the king's propaganda and thereby aiding in the terrors.

Eleksander had gripped the table, his lips pressed together into a hard line.

The only thing he hated more than the silver beasts was injustice and terrible things being allowed to happen to innocent people, she thought. That nothing could be done about it, and that those who could actually do something... didn't care enough to do it.

She watched the disbelief on his face turn to relief as he mumbled, "They're really gone. No more children maimed or killed? No more worrying your throat might be sliced open by a razor-sharp wing or your eye pierced by a dagger-point stinger?"

"No more," Sabina agreed. "And no more starvation because they eat all the food."

One unchallenged injustice gone, at least.

Eleksander put a hand on his chest and breathed shakily. They were all breathing somewhat shakily in their dazed relief. Their elders began discussing how to re-grow crops and how society would change now that the silver beasts were gone.

"They're talking about the next steps for Cavarra?" Eleksander said, sounding concerned. "Vattendal kept his word. Our next step is obviously to keep ours."

"Yes, before he thinks we mean to break our vow and he brings all the silver beasts back," Avelynne said with dawning realisation. She put her hand on Eleksander's arm. "You should say something. Now."

Eleksander looked around the room, his gaze lingering on his birthfather. "I can't."

"You can, love," Hale said. "Shoot with your stomach."

Sabina wasn't sure what that meant, but it had an effect. Eleksander very carefully, very slowly stood.

The clamour in the room quieted and the eyes of everyone turned to him.

Sabina saw his throat bob before he said, "So, um, Vattendal kept his side of the bargain. Next, we keep ours and release him from the lake, right?"

Sabina hurt for him. Why had he made that a question and why had he sounded so unsure? He was right and he knew it. She wished she could give him the confidence in himself that he deserved to have.

Hale sat forward. "Right. We of the second wave will release him. Today."

The grand count brushed a finger over his neat moustache. "We still don't know how that will work. Will it be safe? Will returning the sorcerous fiend to the sea with this new golden magic even work?" His blue-veined hand waved in Avelynne's direction. Was he even aware of that? "We must be cautious. There are magic forces here that we know little of."

The duchess gave a bell-chiming giggle. "Do you mean Vattendal's spells or the golden magic that your own daughter has bandied about without your knowledge?"

The grand count glowered at her, but she merely adjusted the flared sleeve of her silk gown, clearly pleased with her comment.

Startling everyone, the warden slammed down the knife she'd been toying with. "Shitting silver beasts, this again? Did we not decide to release Vattendal? And that we must trust our young mapmakers? Who, by the way, have shown themselves more capable and trustworthy than most Cavarrians."

"Capable and trustworthy is one thing, flinging around magic that no one knows anything about is something quite different," the grand countess said.

The warden rolled her eyes. "Well, I have confidence in *my* mapmaking magician. So much so that I have decided to hold a yearly celebration to his bravery and skill." She pointed to Hale with the hilt of her knife. "I never knew your parents, lad, but I'm sure they'd be proud of you. And since they're not alive, I and everyone in the Woodlands will be proud for them."

She began cleaning her nails with the knife, as if she hadn't just changed Hale's life with one single comment, and added, "Now, can we move on with this? I have work to do."

Sabina watched the colour rise in Hale's tanned cheeks. Then he slowly and gingerly smiled, as if afraid to feel this joy and pride lest it be snatched away again. He had never felt wanted or appreciated when growing up. Now all of the Woodlands wanted and appreciated him. Sabina clapped him on the back, Woodlander style, and got a nod of appreciation back.

"Aye, we should trust them to get the job done and to control their magic," the baron said, his iceboar grunting to punctuate the sentence. "I say we all head to the lake after this meeting, accompanying and helping our mapmakers any way we can." He looked to them. "These bairns have been forced to do too much alone and without their elders to stand by them."

The baroness took her husband's hand but fixed her gaze on the second wave too. "We'll not keep you away from the action. But we will carry some of the burden and take some of the responsibility. To make up for no one having done so before."

Sabina thought about all their lost sailors. About months and months of grief, worries, anguishing decisions to be made, and hurts to endure. She regarded the parchment-dry, pale faces of her county's leaders and was glad to see the support and care coming from them. It was late, but it was finally here.

"Thank you," she said.

She would take the chance to ask them to help her family before they went back to the North. If her parents got more coin for food and firewood, maybe they could work less and spend more time with her siblings.

Taferia rapped her knuckles on the table. "We *did*

decide. And obviously we should all go. Why are we wasting time re-debating this?"

Hale toasted her with his tankard of water. "Glad someone finally said it."

"We gathered to get an update on Vattendal's spell-breaking and then to decide when to release him," Kae said. "However, it seems that we must hurry to do it before our decisions are unpicked and become matters for discussion again."

"There was another vital point," the massive Twelve member said. "What to do about Lothiam. Do we hold a hearing? One where we vote on his punishment?"

The grand countess sneered. "We have no time for drawn-out processes where there can be only one end result—execution. Thus, let us simply get on with it. Behead him, like he did with my kinswoman."

Her kinswoman? Oh, right, Queen Lea. Sabina pondered how the late queen not only had to die a public and fearsome death but then had her name slandered for years.

Arguments broke out in the hall, echoing off the walls and the high ceiling until it was impossible to tell who was saying what.

"Yes, have him killed!"

"Lock the worm-licker up in his own dungeons."

"Do not be absurd, he should at least be tortured."

"I say we send him out to sea in a rowboat without oars."

Then, Eleksander stood again, and silence fell.

Chapter Twenty-Eight

SPEAK UP

Weighed down by the intense attention, Eleksander held on to the table edge. "I think the fairest thing would be to have him spend the rest of his life in one of his own labour camps. Perhaps one of the copper mines?"

When the words were out, he shut his mouth with an audible click. He'd gotten this idea after hearing that Tutor Rogan's sentence, for aiding Lothiam and for viciously attacking several Twelve members during interrogations, was twenty years in one of those camps. Now, however, everyone was staring at him. Was it a silly suggestion?

"Go on," Aurea said. "If you pardon an outsider for saying so, it sounds like a good idea."

"I believe it is," Eleksander said, a tiny bit more confident. "Everyone knows Lothiam is lazy and detests manual labour. So, make him break his own back instead of those of his former peoples' for a change. Whilst being of service to Cavarra by mining our metal."

"Good idea? It sounds like an excellent idea," Sabina said, sitting forward. "Baron, did I overhear you say that everyone who hasn't committed an actual crime has been released from the copper mines in the North? There must be plenty of room, then?"

The baron grinned. "Aye, loads of room. Lothiam's wee hands have been soft and clean, if you don't count the metaphorical blood on them, I reckon it's about time we change that. Let the idle shite work!"

"Not that I think he'll be very productive," said the baroness while adjusting her snowbear's weapon-carrying harness. "But the Lakelander lad is right, let's send Lothiam down one of the mines and see how the soft-skinned layabout fares."

A rush flushed through Eleksander. They liked his suggestion.

The debate returned to full swing again. It took a while but soon everyone, even the more blood-thirsty of the council, agreed that Lothiam should spend the rest of his life working in one of his own labour camps. Also deciding, on Aurea's suggestion, that the labour camps should be overhauled to be more humane and only be for the worst offenders.

When that was settled and everyone sat about congratulating themselves and each other, Kae got up. "If we are all ready, let us armour and arm ourselves once more and head for the lake."

Without a word, everyone else stood too and headed for the door.

Chapter Twenty-Nine

SMALL PROGRESS

Avelynne's chest tightened. As the others filtered out, her parents stood and so did she, that big oak table between them. They kept looking at her and she recognised the twitching of her father's moustache and that set of her mother's mouth - they were disappointed with her. What was it this time? That she hadn't taken their side when they were disparaging the golden magic? Or because she was about to embark on something they didn't believe she could succeed in, thereby shaming the Ironhold name? She tried to guess and...

No. It didn't matter.

She looked them both square in the face, starting with her father. His features slackened into neutrality and then he turned his attention elsewhere. Ignoring Avelynne's presence had often been his default. It was different with her mother, their gazes stayed locked for a long time. The room was quiet and stuffy with dust motes in the air between them. Avelynne lifted her chin and saw a shift on her mother's face. Was that a pull at the lips? Yes, and the wrinkles by her eyes deepened. She blinked and the expression had vanished, her mother now engaging in discussion about what weaponry to bring with her husband. Slight and fast as it had been, that *had* been a smile. One of appreciation. This shouldn't matter to Avelynne, but of course it did. The tightness in her chest gradually loosened.

The council members either walked off together or dallied in groups in the corridor, debating weaponry and tactics. They were missing two people, though.

"Where's Tutor Myle and Tutor Hathleen?" Avelynne asked when she joined the other second wavers and Aurea.

"They, um, once again excused themselves from coming along," Aurea said.

Sabina was crouched down, picking a leaf from Kall's fur. "They scurried off after saying that when Tutor Santorine was fit enough to return from bedrest, she would be a better candidate for this sort of task."

Avelynne couldn't be angry or disappointed. Both Ithikiel Myle and Elya Hathleen were scholars, experts within their fields. They were not fighters or diplomats.

Everyone else really should get ready for the task, though. Someone must hurry the others along, so Avelynne loudly said, "Come, let us get ready," to the rest of the second wave and Aurea.

As they left, Hale paused by where the duke and duchess stood arguing with the warden about some border dispute and said, "You might want to make some haste. We don't want to go on our own, but we will if we have to."

He said it without aggression or curse words. He was indeed learning to control himself. She still worried he had upset them though, but then she un-tensed and settled into a more relaxed walk. He hadn't been that rude and, besides, their elders should heed, or at least respect, them. They were to be in the second wave's debt if they rid Cavarra of Vattendal. *If.* Could they do this? If they failed, Vattendal would bring back the silver beasts and maybe even the spell. Perhaps he would inflict worse things on them in his wrath? She pinched the back of her hand to make herself stop. She mustn't question their ability to do this, mustn't doubt herself.

"Are you all right?" Aurea asked, touching Avelynne's hands and making her stop the pinching.

"Yes. Or rather, I will be when we get this over with. You will be there, right?"

Aurea smiled shyly. "If you all want me to be?"

"Of course," Sabina and Hale said at the same time and in the same matter-of-fact way.

Eleksander patted Aurea's back. "You are as close to an honorary member of the second wave as anyone can be and we can certainly use your experienced and level-headed advice."

"Then I will go wherever you lead," Aurea said.

It was meant for them all, of course, but her hand... it had grasped Avelynne's.

Chapter Thirty

EXODUS OF A FORMER GOD

When everyone was uniformed and armed, they went straight to the lake. Eleksander walked with his sights on the water and his senses working overtime. The cawing of ravens in the trees made him jump and he tried to masquerade it as an itch on his neck. The expectations on the second wave hung like a wet, woollen coat with rocks in the pockets on him, weighing his whole body down.

He heard the steps of the rest of the council behind him. Supposedly they were there for support and aid, but Eleksander couldn't help but feel they were there to watch and judge. To see what this contender for the throne was able to do. To watch him fail.

They stopped a few paces from the lake and in a grave and firm voice, Sabina called for Vattendal. Nothing happened. Was he making them wait? Would he not appear? Eleksander could hear weapons being drawn behind him and tried not to sigh. What did they think that was going to achieve?

He took another step toward the water's edge. "You have

kept your end of the bargain, Vattendal," he said. "We have come to keep ours."

The former god surfaced slowly and with an air of ceremony. When risen to his chest, he connected their gazes, his yellow eyes blinking with at least two sets of eyelids. "Well met, son of a murdered queen."

"Oi. How do we release you?" Hale said.

They really did have to work on his pleasantries if they were going to stay at court.

"My visions have shown me that tis a simple thing. I am a creature of water and thine formidable gilded magic works best via water, with water, in water." Vattendal's hands skimmed the lake's surface. "Thus, thou must make a bridge of water across the land between this lake and the sea. Binding me in the gold that overcomes all curses, and then using it to carry me along this bridge of thine."

A simple thing? Magic shot like an arrow or formed into a shape for mere heartbeats, it didn't move water and it certainly couldn't be sustained for more than a handful of minutes. Eleksander calculated how long it was from here to the shore. Not long on horseback, but on foot it would take hours. *Many* hours.

"Shit." Hale threw his hands out. "Haven't I kept saying that it was witless to place a seafaring academy like the Hall of Explorers somewhere landlocked? If the sea was here, this would be over in the snap of my fingers."

"You're right. It would," Avelynne said in that careful, maternal way that she had with Hale. "However, if the sea was nearby, I am sure that Vattendal could have dragged himself into it. After a few attempts."

"The reedy child is correct," Vattendal said.

Avelynne ran her hands over her narrow waist with her face scrunched up in annoyed offence.

"Don't make comments about her appearance," Sabina said. Then she tapped her fingers against her lips and almost to herself said, "Thinking logically, the golden magic doesn't tire us like silver magic, and it has obeyed our wishes and thoughts before."

Avelynne replied, quietly enough so only they could hear, "Do you really think we can draw water out of the lake to then spread it across the ground under him the entire way to the sea?"

To Eleksander's shock, they all turned to him. He knew that the elders did so because they wanted to see what the would-be-heir would do, but why would these three do it? The natural leaders in their group were: Sabina if practical sense was needed. Hale if swift action was needed. And Avelynne if knowledge or empathy was needed. Yet, they were all waiting for his verdict with worried anticipation.

And he found he had one. "There's only one way we can tell, we try. Besides, Vattendal saw us do it in his farsight. That must account for something." Somewhat soothed by his own words, he stood taller, trying to look confident. "This special magic of ours has slain sea monsters, toppled an unbeatable crownbearer, and bound a former god in place. It has more might than we know. And so do we."

"You're right," Hale said.

The other two added their agreements while stretching their fingers and planting their feet.

He watched the figure in the lake. Vattendal lifted his chin with a questioning expression. The stares of the rest of the council were boring holes in Eleksander's back, making him slouch. Avelynne's hand, placed on his lower back, helped him straighten up and the sight of silver magic glinting around the fingers of Sabina and Hale told him they were ready.

It was now or never.

Eleksander lifted his hands and let his silver magic stream towards the water. Soon the others added their streams to his and that feeling of power filled him as the magic changed. As the gold lit up the water, gasps came from those behind them. Had they gasped when it happened before too? Eleksander had been in such a panic at those times. This time, he was equally filled with fear but his heart drummed steadier. They were using their magic for a good cause, for peace and aid, not violence. There was a solid confidence in doing what you knew was right.

When the gold had spread across the lake's surface and reached Vattendal, beginning to climb up his torso, the former god said, "Next, thou must focus on drawing the water out of the lake and laying it on the ground. Before thine magic ends up trapping me again."

Eleksander obeyed, carefully setting his intent, and assumed the others must have done so as well. The water came out of the lake in a line of gold-covered water, forming a thin creek between their feet.

"Is that heading in the right direction?" Sabina asked, a warning in her voice.

Eleksander closed his eyes, envisioning the many practise maps they had drawn of the Centre. "East. Right, Ave?"

Wetting her pale lips, she croaked, "Correct."

"I'm sure you know this," Aurea said, compass in hand while indicating with the other one. "But east is that way."

"Make it go where she's pointing," Eleksander said before staring down at the line of golden water and willing it towards the sea.

Their creek made a sharp turn towards the correct direction. So far so good. Now, they must get Vattendal out of the lake that had imprisoned him for hundreds of years.

"Try to make the magic remaining in the water encase and lift him," Sabina said, flitting her attention between their creek and Vattendal. "See it in your mind."

Hale went first, one hand still pointed to the water on the ground and the other extending towards the water. Eleksander followed suit and imagined the gold covering and then gently picking up Vattendal, like the magic was an extension of his hands. He needed a clearer image. He tried to relive when his sister Ellaria had tripped and broken her ankle at a market, and he had lifted her up and carried her home. It worked! Vattendal was out of the water, the gold-covered water dripping off his fin and his willowy tentacles. His landing wasn't great, causing more of a thump than Eleksander would have liked, but he seemed unharmed.

The instant Vattendal had recovered, he began sliding along the trail of water they had created so far. "Marvellous work, even if it took longer than desirable. Now, focus on creating my path," he said, slightly out of breath from slithering and dragging himself along.

The gold water pearled off his grey, iridescent skin and the reedy tentacles flailed as if angered by the lack of water. That in combination with Vattendal's unnatural dragging movements and his superior smile which showed those needle teeth of his, was... eerie. Eleksander steeled himself, he mustn't be unnerved. The second wave spun to face east and walked on, creating the creek ahead by hauling more water from behind them and forging a safe path away from brambles, trees, and stones.

Behind him, Eleksander heard the sloshing sound of Vattendal's movements and beyond that, the tentative foot-falls of the rest of the council. He realised that Vattendal hadn't even looked at the others, hadn't cared about them enough to even ask them to put their weapons away.

Eleksander focused back on trying to get as much water as possible for Vattendal to slide along. His stomach churned at how this was starting to feel much harder than the things they had so far done with the golden magic. Anything before had been fast and vehement, often fuelled by anger. This was for a better cause, yes, but it seemed they would need more concentration and stamina. What if the golden magic started to tire them the way silver magic did? No. He must keep his confidence.

"When we get further on, we should re-use some of the water we've used along the way instead of drawing it from the lake," Sabina said.

They all agreed but Avelynne murmured, "Assuming we can keep this going for that long."

So, Eleksander wasn't the only one who had been thinking about that. Would Vattendal die if they failed? Very likely.

"It'll be fine," Hale said. "Trust and keep the faith in yourselves."

They walked on, hands moving the gilded lake water along with them. Time passed but Eleksander only knew of it because of the sun's movements across the sky and the changing landscape around them. He was focusing on his task too hard to be able to tell time and the intense effort was making him sweat despite the gusty spring day. This had to work. He kept his gaze on the ground to steer the magic and water but needed to look up occasionally to see if they were still heading in the right direction. He wished he could stop and check his compass, but found it wasn't necessary. He had a sense of where the sea was as they drew nearer to it. Was that because he had travelled this way before? Or was the golden magic drawn to water?

No one spoke as they drudged on, only the sounds of human steps and Vattendal's splattering was heard as a beat to their march. He understood why the second wave weren't speaking, this took far too much of their energy and Vattendal probably felt the same. It was astounding that the Twelve and the county leaders weren't quibbling, gossiping, or lecturing each other, though. Was that out of respect for the second wave? Or fear of what would happen if they broke their concentration?

Eleksander's feet were so heavy and his focus ever harder to maintain. He told himself to take it one step at a time. Move the water from behind them to in front of them, avoid any obstacles on the ground, and ensure they were heading for the sea. Then do the same all over again, step by step. The breeze had stopped. Now, the sun above made his braids hot against his scalp and sweat coated his neck. How far had they walked? After a while, his eyesight began to blur with fatigue and over-concentration. He had to keep going.

It was a relief large enough to make him whimper when

he could finally smell a hint of salt and seaweed on the air. Worrying about the others, he said, "I can smell the sea. We're almost there."

Avelynne and Hale hummed wearily.

"Take heart," Sabina said in a tone that was positive despite its clear exhaustion. "You've all done amazingly up to this point, just keep going a little longer. We can do this!"

The other two now gave whooping replies.

Eleksander made a mental note to give more praise with his encouragements in the future. Particularly good for armies and court councils, he guessed. Oh, by the waters, he was preparing himself to lead? He focused back on the task.

It took them longer to move the water now due to increasing fatigue and the problem of some of the water getting separated from the golden magic and thereby leaking into the ground, giving them less to work with during each relocation. Still, the smell of the sea got stronger with every step. They must not falter or stop.

He hadn't glanced back to check on Vattendal. Partly to not disrupt his own focus and partly because those tentacles and that strange slithering still made his skin crawl. Shame struck him. Vattendal couldn't help how his body looked or moved and Eleksander shouldn't judge, or avoid, someone who was different.

To lead was to step up but also to care. So, he made himself turn his head and say, "Vattendal, are you all right? I'm sure you already know this, but we are almost there."

"Yes, child, I know. I am managing but thou cannot tarry. Concentrate."

There was gratitude in his voice and appearance but

also extreme exhaustion. There was so little water left. Would Vattendal survive this? Eleksander re-doubled his efforts.

They strode on, the golden water finally carving a line across sand instead of earth. Crashing waves and squawks of seagulls could be heard. Then, with a sigh of relief from several of them, their Hall of Explorers boots trod in wet sand and soon the gold touched the shallows. The magic grew brighter and stronger, carrying Vattendal along on it. When out in the waves, the golden magic didn't coat as much of the sea as it had the other times. Eleksander wasn't certain if that was due to their lack of energy or simply because the magic somehow knew that it didn't need to.

Vattendal submerged himself the moment the golden magic bore him into deep enough waves. He moved fast in the water, with grace and power. Eleksander was happy he hadn't watched this humbled, and probably humiliated, former god hobble along in the dribble of water they'd been able to provide. He could only hope the others of the council hadn't stared at Vattendal during that long, frightening, and probably mortifying ordeal.

From the corner of his eye, he saw Avelynne slump down into the sand with as much refinement as she could muster. He called her name right before Sabina did, but she waved their worry away, "I'm fine. Simply tired."

"I know the feeling," he said, dropping down next to her. The other two joined them, Hale even laying down, his boot so near the water that waves lapped at it.

Aurea came rushing over. "Are you all right?"

The moment they had confirmed that they were, she continued, speaking fast and gesticulating wildly as ever.

"That was incredible! I have seen a lot of magic and a lot of rescues but nothing like that. The way you used magic to siphon water out of the lake and then kept reusing it to make a path. It was quite extraordinary!"

She continued talking, saying something about breaking boundaries for what magic can do and that people on a faraway island she'd come across years ago could move fire by magic, but he barely heard her. He was too busy trying to get his breathing back to normal and watching Vattendal, who was swimming about the waves like an exile who had finally been allowed to return home. Which of course he was, but it was more than that. When the former god occasionally resurfaced, he seemed to be growing and his grey skin shimmered more intensely. His long hair appeared thicker and was moving on its own accord like it was dancing in the wind, and his eyes were lighting up like candle flames. Had he been like this back when the lake was still connected to the sea? Eleksander could understand all too well how his ancestors would have worshipped Vattendal when he saw him like this. The former god dove again, cleaving through the foam of a wave.

"Shit, that was hard work," Hale said. "I'm proud we managed it, though."

The Woodlander lay splayed out on the sand with his chest heaving and the waves now travelling over his big boots to lap up along his britches. His lips were parted as he panted and his sweat-slick tunic clung to his muscled torso and arms. There was a drop of sweat on his nose, too. How Eleksander loved that curved hawk nose. He closed his eyes and chuckled under his breath. He had never felt like this for anyone else. When he opened his eyes, Hale was looking at him, smiling from ear to ear. Eleksander wished Vattendal was his god, if he had been, Eleksander would've prayed to see that smile every day of the rest of his life.

Their elders, as quiet as they had been during the entire journey, gathered around them. About half of them watched Vattendal powering through the waves while the rest were staring at the four mapmakers. He was happy to see that Avelynne's parents regarded her with a hint of worry on those callous faces.

The baron and baroness were unpacking sacks they had carried slung over their shoulders. The baron took out two waterskins, handing one to Sabina while saying, "Well done, lass. Have some oakenberry juice to get your strength back."

He gave the other one to Eleksander, who drank greedily. The juice was still quite cold and he could've scoffed a whole lake's worth of it.

"Oh, I'm sorry I didn't bring you anything to drink," Aurea said.

He told her that was fine and handed the skin over to Hale. Aurea watched the exchange and asked, "This is probably a bad time for my incessant curiosity, but why are these oakenberries everywhere in your diet?"

"They make you feel more awake, lass," the baroness said. "And it's one of the few foods neither our livestock nor the silver beasts would eat. I don't know why."

Avelynne, who had been leaning against Sabina, sat up. "I read it's because the nutty, bitter taste of the berries' juice tastes like poisonous fruit to animals. We humans, however, found oakenberries to have an interesting flavour as well as giving an energy lift and, well, got rather addicted."

"Aye, sounds about right," the baroness said, crouching on her haunches next to her snowbear. "Cavarrians are oft drawn to things that are bad for us."

Her husband agreed from where he stood behind her, attempting to keep his iceboar from snuffling too much in the sand.

The others on the council were still higher up on the beach, whispering among themselves. What were they saying?

"Don't worry yourself about them. Just get your strength back. They can wait," the baron said, clearly having followed Eleksander's gaze.

The four mapmakers emptied the two bottles quickly and the baroness dredged out another pair from her sack.

Meanwhile, Kae broke away from the group and came over to where they sat in the sand. "Well done, second wave. We are all grateful and impressed."

"We? As in you of the Twelve?" Hale said while subtly watching the warden, who was keeping an eye on Vattendal out in the waves.

"Every last on one of us, even the leaders of the Peaks and Lakelands. You will be an asset to the council."

From a neat little satchel, Kae produced a brown loaf and tore off a piece for each of the four mapmakers. It was incredible to think that bread might not be a scarcity now that the silver beasts were gone. And they could grow all kinds of grains and plants, including fruit that wasn't these eternal oakenberries. Cavarra's future would be interesting, he was glad he'd be here to see it.

Hale ripped into his bread like a starving animal. Then, around a mouthful said, "Vattendal is staring at us."

Eleksander paused with the bread at his lips. He looked into the former god's yellow eyes and called, "Is, um, everything all right?"

"All is well, child of a murdered queen." Vattendal bowed his head and then gave something that was probably a smile of gratitude. It seemed menacing though, since the needle quality of his teeth had increased. How did he avoid ripping his mouth apart with those things?

"I would thank thee for thine aid with a gift," Vattendal said. "Perchance by telling thou what my farsight has shown me?"

Hale swallowed the bread with an uncomfortable-sounding gulp. "Of the future?"

"Of *thine* future, protector of the overlord."

Hale didn't react to the curious nickname but instead said, "Can it be about the golden magic? I promised... someone I'd find out more about that."

Not mentioning Sabina by name would have been more subtle if he hadn't glanced at her right as he said "someone." Still, Eleksander was sure she appreciated the attempt.

"Thou cannot request what thou wish to know," Vattendal snarled. He paused before indicating the second wave with a webbed hand. "I have seen thou four forced to separate. Thou," here he fixed Eleksander with those glowing eyes, "must ascend the copper throne. Other futures await the rest. Yet, thou four will weave in and out of one another's lives until thine death. Thou will perish within a fortnight of one another, much as how thou were born."

"At a ripe old age, no doubt," Hale said, more to the other second wavers than to Vattendal.

Vattendal spun in the water and was about to dive when Avelynne called, "Farewell. Oh, and good luck."

Over his shoulder, Vattendal dipped his head. "The same to you, smallest of the triad." Then he swam off with the speed of someone leaving a sinking ship.

A "goodbye" lingered unspoken on Eleksander's lips.

From higher on the shore, Avelynne's father was loudly complaining about that she had wished Vattendal good luck. "Imagine wishing a monster who bound us in misery and enslavement for generations *luck*. Such rot."

Aurea scoffed and sat herself behind Avelynne to then put her arms around her in comfort. Or protection? Avelynne seemed quite unaffected by her father's words but happy, as always, to be embraced. She leaned her head back on Aurea's shoulder and caressed Aurea's arms with a happy sigh. This intimacy made Aurea jolt, but she soon looked quite delighted.

Eleksander glared at the Grand Count of the Peaks. Not for the first time did he disagree with that man. He was happy that Avelynne had said what she did. There could be no doubt, though, both they and Vattendal were better off with an ocean between them.

He mulled over Vattendal's words as he ate some of his bread. So many questions. Copper throne? The only throne he knew of was Lothiam's. That monstrosity was old as time itself, made of tarnished gold, and covered in velvet cushions for a man who believed movement, or any type of effort, was for peons.

"Look at that, a soul we helped and saved." Sabina nodded towards Vattendal's fin vanishing into faraway waves. "Does that make up for the ones we let die?" she asked quietly.

Surprisingly, it was Hale who answered. "Shitting silver beasts, Sabina. I adore you but you *have* to stop being so hard on yourself. It's not a tally. You've been in the middle of a homicidal conspiracy, a sea wreck, monster attacks, and a rebellion that became a sort of war." He paused for breath, to no one's shock since he rarely spoke this long. "You did your best and tried to keep everyone alive and safe throughout. No one could've gotten away without a shit-heap of death to their name after that lot. Trust me."

Eleksander's affection overcame him again. His heart, and his gut instinct, had made the right choice.

"Hale's right," Avelynne said. "This is what I've been trying to tell you, snowdrop. The fact that there were deaths, and other types of losses, is not your fault. I know you were raised to be responsible and that you take on every ounce of guilt you can find, but you have to let some of it go. Before it drowns you."

Sabina snapped her head back. Eleksander had noted that ever since the Wolfsclaw went over the waterfall, she had struggled with the word drowned. For Hale and himself, that disaster had been a panicked blur. Avelynne had been unconscious. But Sabina... what had happened to her deep in the belly of the sea?

"Also," Hale said with an expression of someone wondering if he was stepping into a bear trap, "no offence, but you have to realise that not everything is about you or because of you. Deaths happen. Shipwrecks happen. You can't fight it, you're good but not that good."

Sabina gave him half a smile but then her features hardened. "I don't want to talk about this. Forget that I brought it up and hand me some of that juice."

She took it and drank fast, hiding her face with the waterskin.

Eleksander decided to put her out of her misery, but what could they talk about? He was too tired to think. The sight of a seagull soaring over the waves made him ask, "What do you think Vattendal's words about his farsight glimpses meant?"

Hale merely shrugged and ate the last of his bread.

"Let's see," Aurea said, furrowing her brow. "He mentioned you four parting but weaving in and out of one another's futures. And, um, dying around the same time?"

"Yes. Also, something about you alighting on something copper?" Avelynne said as she tapped Eleksander's knee with her index finger.

"Ascending, not alighting. And it was a copper throne," he amended. "Which I've never seen. Have any of you?"

Sabina hummed. "The only copper I know is our compasses. Oh, and this." She tenderly ran a hand through Aurea's hair. She caught herself and pulled her hand back as if it had been burned, looking first to Aurea and then to Avelynne. The latter was still sitting wrapped up in Aurea's arms and legs and only gave a good-natured laugh. Aurea, meanwhile, merely smiled and smoothed down her hair.

Yes, Eleksander had to agree that it was copper-coloured. But it had nothing to do with thrones.

As if she had heard his thought, Avelynne said, "Well, as someone almost sitting in Aurea's lap, I suppose one might say I have ascended a sort of copper-coloured throne?"

"Wait. Was that a joke about pubic hair?" Hale said with clear appreciation.

Avelynne beamed mischievously while Aurea gave her a playful slap on the arm.

Time for a change of topic, Eleksander decided. "What are the rest of the council talking about? They've been deep in conversation over there ever since Vattendal left."

Sabina scowled, but he wondered if that was about the council or her love life. "They better not be making decisions without us," she said, standing and brushing the sand off herself. "I'm going over there to make sure."

"Um. We should join her," Aurea said, letting go of Avelynne and rushing after Sabina.

Avelynne bit her lip and then with a watery smile at Hale and him, joined the other two lasses.

"Oof," Hale said, watching the three women approach the rest of the council.

"Agreed," Eleksander said.

He worried for them, not only for the two who had become his extra sisters, but for Aurea. She was outside the bond of the second wave and a foreigner on these rough shores. The strange romantic situation the three of them found themselves in couldn't be improving her situation. What would happen when she soon left for Hethekla?

Hale had pulled that new longsword of his out and was needlessly polishing it with his sleeve. "Well done, by the way."

"Pardon?"

"You know, for taking charge in the whole release process." He replaced the sword and grasped Eleksander's hand instead.

Intertwining their fingers, Eleksander said, "Thank you. Honestly, I thought Sabina or you would step up."

Hale grinned as he stood and pulled Eleksander to his feet. "Sab has enough on her plate and me, well, I don't have anything to prove."

"What? Have I got gilded lake water in my ears or was that Hale Hawthorn saying he had nothing to prove?"

"I don't want to be... the child that I had to be." He looked away, clearly done with the topic.

Eleksander thought he knew what he had meant. He didn't want to be the forgotten orphan who had to be the loudest, the strongest, and the best to get any attention or affection.

He squeezed Hale's hand. "And here I was thinking that you meant you had nothing else to prove because there's going to be a Woodlander festival for you each year?"

Hale's black eyes glinted in unison with his toothy smile. "Well, there's that too. Do you think there'll be a statue carved out of hawthorn at the festival?"

Eleksander was about to reply with something kind but changed his mind. Hale would prefer banter. "You mean of the tentacle monster that made you drop your precious crossbow?"

"Huh? Oh, shit! You little troublemaker. I'm going to..."

Eleksander tried to raise only one eyebrow. "You're going to what?"

That was when Hale leaned in to whisper what he was

going to do him when they were alone. To Eleksander, it didn't sound like a punishment.

"Fine," he heard himself say in a husky voice. He cleared his throat. "You can do that. Later. For now, let's see what the council thinks of what just happened."

"And then go to bed?"

"Well, we are all tired after this arduous day."

"That oakenberry juice and bread didn't give you a little energy to expel before we nap, Lakelander?" Hale said, winking.

Pleasant chills went down Eleksander's spine. "I have enough energy to take my... punishment, if that's what you mean." He looked towards the warden and the duchess, who had both spotted their approach, and added, "Now shush."

Hale quieted. To Eleksander's joy and relief, he didn't let go of his hand despite the many eyes now watching them.

Chapter Thirty-One

THE HEART SHE HAS GIVEN YOU

Sabina's tense muscles were at last relaxing. She was back in the Hall of Explorers, sitting with Avelynne in their quiet bedchamber and drinking leaf tea before dinner. They were on Sabina's bed, discussing the day's events and Vattendal, concluding that they were happy he'd been spared execution and was free. Nevertheless, the resentment over the spell and the silver beasts was still there. Sabina feared it would stay with them forever.

She regarded the leaf-muddied tea that was left in her tin tankard. "All in all, I hope to never see him again."

Avelynne toasted her. "Agreed."

They drank the last of the tea and Sabina regretted it the instant the bitter leaf taste filled her mouth. She swallowed again to clear it. "I'm glad that all the council discussed without us were the possible repercussions of letting Vattendal go. Back there on the shore, I mean."

"Yes. Although, while they didn't admit to it, I think they also spoke of us." Avelynne drummed her fingers against her tankard. "I think we passed a sort of test for them. Oh, speaking of that, I have something to tell you about my parents."

Sabina swallowed again. "Tell me while I rinse these leaves out of my mouth."

While Sabina got some water from the jug by the ablution table, Avelynne explained that she had convinced the council, starting with her parents, to set up a fund for the families of the sailors they'd lost on the Wolfsclaw. Including, of course, Ivar Nore's family.

Sabina saw the sweet old sailor in her mind's eye, petting his ice wolf or teaching her good rowing form. She couldn't save him. Nor forgive herself for his and the other sailors' deaths. But she could find ways to honour him.

"Good," she said. "We can never return the lives lost, but maybe we can give their families some solace and safety."

They sat quietly on the bed for a long time. While seeing the faces of all the lost sailors in her mind, Sabina took her hair out of her loosening braid. Her impossible mane needed combing, smoothing with scented oils, and then re-braiding. She left it hanging loose, though, too forlorn to bother with it.

"You know," Avelynne began, leaning nearer to tuck some of Sabina's hair behind her ear. "It is high time for you to decide what to do about Aurea. Before she sails."

"Back to Hethekla?" The grief and guilt retreated a few steps, making way for a whole other set of emotions. Ones that made her heart thump like a trapped bird against her ribcage. "Has she said when she's going?"

"Soon. She's been tending to the poorly Naseer and

getting on with the ship repairs, but both are nigh mended."

"Oh." Sabina ran a hand through her hair. "I, um, I suppose I should talk to her before she leaves."

"Of course you should. Snowdrop, she's one in a million. Sweet, funny, intelligent, understanding, loving and, well, very easy on the eyes."

"You sound almost in love with her yourself."

"While I don't fall in love like that," Avelynne's tone was quiet but sounded less guilty and confused than before, "I do think the world of her and wish I could somehow be with her. But, like you, she deserves a committed long-term romantic partner, since that is clearly what she wants."

"What about what you want?"

"I don't exactly know what that is yet," Avelynne said sadly. "I do know that I don't want to hurt anyone, but I don't want to be locked in a relationship either."

Sabina tried to think of every lesson she had learned lately. Every wisdom that others had hammered into her stubborn head. "I will let you go. And I suppose I should let Aurea go."

"Dearest, no. You shouldn't let her go," Avelynne said as if it was obvious.

"What?"

"You need to let go of some of your guilt, accountability, solemnity...and probably me. Not Aurea! You need someone who relaxes you, cheers you up, and soothes you." Avelynne leaned in closer. "Meanwhile, she needs someone quieter who will make her stop to think and to calm down, but who also appreciates her bubbly, curious nature. You two are made for one another. Two intelligent warriors ready for adventure and a long life together."

When Sabina didn't reply, Avelynne lovingly tapped her on the nose. "If you are determined to take on every possible responsibility, then take charge for the heart she has given you."

"She hasn't given me anything, Ave. We've only known each other for a couple of months."

"Cavarrians have married after shorter courtships than that. And she fell for you right away back on that island." Avelynne ignored Sabina's derisive huff and spoke on. "Sometimes, two people are so well matched that it doesn't take long for them to know they don't want to be apart. Perhaps I'm wrong and you will hate each other after a year, but I do believe you have to find out."

"But she's leaving."

"To sail and explore," Avelynne said slowly and clearly. "The very things you yearn to do. It's perfect."

"You're saying I should go with her? I have to stay here and be on the council."

"No. You do not. I will be on the council and so will Hale and Eleksander. Taferia too, and I believe you can trust her to want to cut through the corruption, selfishness, and dawdling bureaucracy, snowdrop."

"All right, but... That isn't all. There's also the golden magic. It won't work unless all four of us are together."

"We do not need the golden magic, not unless there is a threat that cannot be vanquished with normal magic. Besides, you wouldn't leave for the rest of time. You'll miss us and come back. I am certain of it."

Bewilderment dazed Sabina. "I... should stay."

"If you do, your tendency to sacrifice yourself for others won't stop with the council and the second wave. You'll soon return to the North, to help raise your siblings and cater to your parents, while also trying to help them as village warriors." Avelynne's pretty mouth turned downwards. "You'll wear yourself down to the bone until all that is you is gone. It's a waste of all that *Sabina Rosenmarck*. You need to find out what responsibilities you have to yourself." She paused, probably to let Sabina digest. "And let others learn to look after themselves without you always stepping up. That includes me."

"You've learned to look after yourself just fine," Sabina said. It was true but she heard how distant and wavering her voice sounded.

There was so much to think about.

Her heart would break if she left Avelynne. But then, didn't it break a little each day when Avelynne couldn't give her the relationship she needed? Perhaps she must give her up? Then, Avelynne would be free, while she could be with Aurea and have an exciting future at sea.

She watched Kall on the floor. He laid there, looking up at her as if he was waiting for a command. She pondered the ones he knew best.

Stay.

Hunt.

Which one was the right one now?

He gave a slow blink. The equivalence of smiling in the cat world. Kall loved being around Aurea. Avelynne too. But Avelynne would never marry his mistress. Aurea, however, would. There was a possibility here for everything Sabina had ever wanted. Sailing with the Hethklish, exciting challenges and new horizons, getting far away from the responsibilities of her family and of the council, seeing the incredible modern Hethekla with Aurea as a guide? As a... possible fiancée?

"I should at least try to see if she wants me, shouldn't I?" Sabina said, unsure if she was asking Kall or Avelynne. Or herself.

With a sombre expression, Avelynne took her hand. "Yes. You said after the battle that you would stay with me until I told you to go. I'm... telling you now, my dearest, and you should hurry before she decides to make sail."

The idea of Aurea leaving without this all being aired hit Sabina like being dunked in ice water. She got up and Kall did the same. With a passing farewell for now, Sabina headed for where Aurea no doubt was, by Naseer's sickbed. She ran through the myriad of long, identical corridors of the Hall of Explorers until she came to the rooms given to the Hethklish. She knocked on Captain Naseer's door, her heart pounding hard enough to hurt.

Naseer bade her come in and she saw that he was sitting up.

"Hi," she panted. "You look better than when I saw you last."

He smiled. "I feel better. Only the last vestiges of the fever left, I think."

Sabina looked around the room. "Um, is Aurea here?"

"I'm afraid not. She went down to the dockyard to sign off on the final repairs."

Sign off. Final. How had she not realised the Hethklish were so close to leaving?

Naseer rubbed his sallow, unshaven face. "I'm glad I am not sailing with them. Some bedrest will do me good."

"Aye, it no doubt will." She grabbed the door. "Um. I..."

"Have to go talk to Aurea. Agreed. Hurry along," he said.

Sabina gave as short a farewell to him as she did to Avelynne. The sense of time running out, thereby bringing the risk of losing Aurea, was growing. This is what indecisiveness got you. She convinced the stable grooms to let her borrow a horse and rode for the shore. Kall ran beside her, seeming happy to finally get to sprint with full power and not hamper his speed for slow humans.

When she came to the dockyard, workers rushed about, reminding her of when she had first seen the Wolfsclaw being built here. She had been afraid and excited then too.

The Hethklian ships were elegant and quiet in the dimming light of dusk, The Qetesh closest and the Parataxia slightly behind its sistership to the left.

Sabina tied up the horse and headed for Aurea who stood by the Parataxia's moorings with the quartermaster, pointing to something up in the sails.

"Aurea," she called.

The magnificent new captain of these, almost as magnificent, ships turned when hearing her name.

Sabina tripped at the sight of her. What now? What should she say? Should she be all passionate, like in romantic tales? Should she try to be calm and reasonable? No, that wouldn't be possible. She banged her fist against her thigh. It didn't matter how she said what was on her mind, she just had to say it for snow's sake. Quickly.

Aurea squinted at her. "Hello you. Are you all right? You looked flushed."

No words came from Sabina's useless mouth. Instead, she dashed towards Aurea, not sure what was going to happen when she got there.

Aurea tentatively held her arms out, not all the way, clearly worried she was misreading what was happening here. Sabina tumbled into her embrace to prove that she wasn't misreading a single thing. She absently saw the quartermaster board the ship but cared only about the feel of Aurea's body and the pine soap mixed with Aurea's natural scent.

"What a wonderful surprise," Aurea said. "May I ask, though, why you were in such a rush to give me a hug?"

"You're leaving," she gasped.

"In a few days, yes."

"But the final repairs are done now?"

"Sure. That doesn't mean we're sailing at any moment, though." She sounded as if Sabina had lost her mind, and maybe she had. "Naseer is just now recovering, most of my sailors are off exploring Cavarra, and we haven't gotten the stocks of food the council promised us. Also, well, I don't want to leave before I've spent some more time with you."

You. That could mean just her. Or all of the second wave.

The weight of foolishness filled Sabina, and she nestled deeper into the hug. "Of course. You wouldn't just leave without warning. Sorry."

Aurea's mouth was close to Sabina's ear as she softly said, "Don't apologise, dear heart. You've had a long day and some awfully eventful months."

"Aye, that I have."

Snow below, this woman felt so wonderful in her arms. She moved her head to burrow into Aurea's neck on the other side, but accidentally bumped their faces together. Sabina couldn't help herself; she turned the mishap into a kiss, fumbling and brief. She pulled away to check Aurea's expression and give her a chance to say *no*. Or *yes*. Or *not right now*.

Instead, Aurea kissed her back. Her lips and mouth were cooler than Sabina's after that long ride but just as silky soft as Sabina had imagined.

When they parted, Aurea whispered, "Sorry if I'm bad at kissing. I haven't had that much practice."

"I thought you mentioned having a long-time partner when you were my age?"

"Sure. My two relationships were both long and very committed but lacked the amount of kissing that other lovers seem to rack up. I like physical affection, but it's not my favourite thing."

Sabina hummed a wry, little laugh. "I spent the last hour chatting to Avelynne, who loves the physical affection but not committed, long relationships. Am I the weird one? I mean, am I strange for needing both?"

"No. I think that's quite common. You're not weird or strange in any way, sweet treasure."

Those words loosened old knots in her chest. She looked into Aurea's reassuring, open face. Time to roll the dice. "Do you think there's a chance that I... Could I, um, try having the long, committed relationship I need with you, do you think?"

Aurea's eyes shot wide. "Oh. I'd love that!" She bit her

lip around a shy but gleeful smile. "Wait. Would you then sail with me, or would I stay here? Because I have a responsibility to my sailors to get them home now that Naseer is staying here in Cavarra."

Light-headed, Sabina staggered a little. It had been that easy? "I meant to sail with you. If you'll have me?"

"Gladly. But what about your responsibilities? Being on the council and steering Cavarra right? Your parents needing you to look after your siblings? Or the rest of the second wave not being able to use their golden magic without you?"

She had to smile at how Aurea's mind went to exactly the same things hers had. "I spoke to Avelynne about all of that. I need to let go. And besides, I'll be back. We would come back to Cavarra, right?"

"Of course! I obviously haven't planned any of this, but I guess we'd divide our time between Cavarra, Hethekla, and being out at sea exploring. Does that sound reasonable?"

"Aye, sounds perfect."

Aurea held up her index finger. "I do want to say that this plan is for us as a couple *or* as friends. Let's not commit to too much too soon. You have never been completely free and on your own. You might want that at some point of your life."

"You don't want to wed me?"

"Wed? You Cavarrians move so fast. At some point, I may want to. We don't need to be thinking about that now, though." She took Sabina's hands. "Doldrums, when I say you can stop being so serious and accountable, that includes relationships. Stay with me, have fun with me, but you don't need to plan your entire future with me today.

You're nineteen, I'm twenty-two, we have time before long-term commitments are needed."

"I suppose so. Unless a sea creature eats us."

"Granted. Tell you what, if I see a sea creature looming ahead as we sail, I'll get my quartermaster to marry us on the spot. Sound good?"

They both laughed. Aurea's aging scars, despite raising up instead of dipping in, reminded her of Avelynne's dimples then.

Avelynne.

Sabina cleared away the lump that had just formed in her throat. "I do worry about leaving something, or someone, behind. Even if I'm only gone for a short time."

"Avelynne."

"Aye. Not for her sake. I mean, she might be lonely for a while, but she'd soon find plenty of new lovers and friends. And she doesn't need me to protect her, she does that herself." Sabina looked in the direction of the Hall of Explorers. "But I'm not sure if I wouldn't always be leaving a part of me behind, the part of me that I can be around her. The part of me I gave to her."

"I understand. You've shared a lot and she truly is quite special."

Sabina chuckled.

"What?" Aurea asked.

"You both keep saying that about each other. 'She's special' or 'she's so unique.' You're fascinated by one another, probably smitten too."

"Or perhaps we're extraordinary people and have picked up on that about each other. Did you think about that, huh?" She poked her tongue out at Sabina, clearly a gesture that meant the same in their cultures. "Anyway, I'd also miss Avelynne. Have you spoken to her about her choice?"

"Her choice?"

Aurea bent over to pet Kall as she said, "Yes. I assume you would like her to join us and so would I. So, have you asked her?"

"Join us? As in sail with us?"

"Sure, that too, but I meant *join us*."

They looked at each other while Sabina's brain scrambled to catch up. Was Aurea saying what she thought she was?

Aurea righted herself again. "I mean, I know she doesn't like committed relationships, but she could be a sort of occasional guest?"

No. Her brain wasn't catching up. It had been through too much lately and had now retired to some warm, dark corner for a nap. "Guest? In a relationship?"

"Sab, we've spoken about how your Cavarrian ways differs from ours."

"Mm-hm."

"How do relationships work on Cavarra?"

Sabina contemplated how to answer. This was sort of like trying to explain how walking or jumping worked. "Men and women engage in courtship. After some months, they usually wed each other and set up a family, often—but far from always—with children who are either biological or adopted."

"The marriage consists of one man and one woman?"

"That's the norm," Sabina said with a shrug. "Same-gendered relationships exist in all four counties but are slightly frowned up in the Lakelands and the Woodlands. People of the same gender can marry in the North and in the Peaks, though, where those relationships have been common for generations."

She realised how lucky she was and how much worse things had been for Eleksander and Hale.

"Huh, that's a lot of focus on gender. Who gets to marry here?" Aurea let go of Sabina's hands to indicate their surroundings. She didn't sound condescending when she spoke but then she never did. Despite that, Sabina had the feeling that she pitied Cavarrians.

"Here? The Centre consists only of the court, the Hall of Explorers, and a harbour. Other than the royals, people only come here to work. Except for the royals, who have usually stuck to opposite-gendered marriages for easier, well, breeding."

"And these marriages are only for two people at a time? You don't have threefolds? Or fourfolds?"

"What are those?"

"I guess not, then," Aurea said, clearly fascinated. "In Hethekla there are different kinds of marriages. They're all equally valid, common, and have no restriction of genders. Two people in a wedlock is called a twofold. Three make up a threefold. And four people married to each other is a fourfold."

Sabina gaped. "Oh. Um. Well, why stop at four?"

"Why did you stop at two?"

"I don't know," Sabina said sharply. Why was she defensive? "Because it was the number needed to make a baby?"

"Ah, that would make a sort of sense, I suppose."

"Your marriages weren't based on that?"

"I think they were once." Aurea scratched the back of her head. "That thinking has been obsolete for a very long time, though. We've come across other civilisations who stuck to just pairs with the main focus on childbearing, though. Naseer is sure to share all our findings with your council."

Again, no condescension or pity in her tone but just the zeal of giving information and the curiosity to learn. She wasn't the only one curious right now. Threefold. Could that work?

Sabina wet her suddenly dry lips. "How, um, how do you keep relationships with more people working? How do you make sure no one feels left out or cheated on?"

"How can I be both a printer and a sailor? I take turns giving them my full focus or sometimes try to combine them," she said with a smile. "Look, in all seriousness? You take it day by day. Everyone shares their thoughts and puts the work in, like with any relationship." Aurea caressed Sabina's cheek with a knowing expression. "It isn't the *responsibility of one person* to make it work, so you'd be fine."

Unsure of what to say to that, Sabina just kissed her.

The sound of hooves and creaking wheels drew their attention to the approach of one of the smaller Hall of Explorers carriages. It stopped abruptly and out of it stepped Avelynne.

Sabina was about to say that Avelynne had a knack for showing up when someone was talking about her but stopped. There was acute distress on Avelynne's face.

Chapter Thirty-Two

CLOSE QUARTERS

Avelynne bade the carriage driver to return to the Hall of Explorers. Then, with her heart in her throat, she strode over to Sabina and Aurea. They both looked so strong and secure, so perfect for one another. She was glad that she had pushed them together. However, stars above, it had made her feel lonely and abandoned. She was being ripped apart from within by it, like when she as a child had been locked into her room for weeks without human contact. Curse her selfish weakness, but she hadn't been able to stay away and leave these two to their happiness. Not quite yet.

"Good late afternoon, sweetest of ladies," she called, trying to force merriment into her voice.

"Hello you," Aurea said, beaming. "We were just talking about you."

"You were? Only nice things, I hope?" The banter was as forced as her tone, and she wanted to kick herself.

"Of course, Little Countess," Sabina said, stepping forward to take Avelynne's hands and kiss them in turn. "I'm glad you're here. Why are you here, by the way?"

She was relieved to have come up with an excuse on the way over. "Oh, to call you to dinner. It's already being served in the great hall. I assumed you would be joining us? It would be a good time to say... farewell."

Sabina and Aurea shared a look that she couldn't interpret.

The quartermaster shouted about something he had made fast from the Qetesh and that he was going over to the Parataxia. Aurea called a "thanks" back to him. Then all was silent again and those two kept looking at each other.

"Is something amiss?" Avelynne said. "Are you trying to tell me you won't be coming along to dine?"

"No," Aurea said quickly. "We'll definitely be eating with all of you. We're only quiet because there's something we need to ask you."

"She's being kind," Sabina said. "*I'm* the one who should ask you. I've known you longest and I'm the one who's in love with you."

Ah. Were they about to ask for her blessing to sail off into the sunset and be a couple? How sweet. How excruciatingly painful. She might not be able to love them the way they needed, but she would miss them with her every fibre. She prepared herself to be brimming with reassurance and to show none of her hurt.

Sabina scuffed her boot on the harbour's sea-stained planks. "Do you think you might want to, um, join us?"

She did a full reroute of her emotions. "Join you? In what way?"

"On our journey but also with us as lovers," Aurea said. "I was telling Sabina that on Hethekla, it's common to have relationships with three or even four people. Now," she held her hands up, "I know you don't do relationships. But what if you came with us, traveling like friends and possible lovers?"

Lightness rose through Avelynne. "As friends and lovers?"

"Yes. You could dip into our relationship when you wished," Aurea said. "No pressure, no commitment."

"I'm new to this idea too but I think it could work," Sabina said, rubbing the back of her neck and avoiding eye contact. "She and I will be a couple in love, and you can just, you know, cuddle or do more sexual things with us when you feel like it?"

It sounded too good to be true. Avelynne wasn't sure if her involvement in their relationship might upset the balance, might disturb their happiness.

"And there's... room for that? For me?"

Aurea, misunderstanding, said, "Being the new captain, I get the captain's quarters. Plenty of room and privacy for us. Come have a look."

Avelynne decided not to correct her. Sabina and Aurea knew their own minds and needs better than she did. Besides, if she found she was being a thorn in their happy relationship, she could always bow out and be just a friend. There were plenty of charming sailors she could bed instead.

With her swift and energetic movements, Aurea walked the gangplank up to the Qetesh. She, Sabina, and Kall followed. Kall somewhat reluctantly as he had been busy sniffing at a bush with mice scurrying about.

It was nice to be back on a Hethklish ship. Avelynne tried to imagine staying on it, not like before when she had to in order to return to Cavarra, but because she wanted to be here. To explore, to draw maps, to feel the sea breeze in her hair, to use both her polearm skills and her practise of diplomacy from many a year of living with her parents.

After all, what was the alternative? She wasn't going to return to her parents and to Ironhold castle. So what then, live at court with Hale and Eleksander? A third wheel who frequently had to be around her parents during council meetings and, woe betide, had to demand tithes from them and the other county leaders? Taking new lovers each week, only to break their hearts if they, as per Cavarrian custom, expected love and marriage.

No, this chance, this adventure, this freedom, this opportunity to be with these two incredible women without heartbreak. It was the biggest of gifts. She filled her lungs with the smell of wood, tar, and fresh sea air. Home.

"If I came with you," she said to Sabina as they walked towards the captain's quarters, "we would be leaving Hale and Eleksander alone."

"I thought about that too. As you very well know," Sabina said with a pointed look. "We wouldn't be gone for long stretches at a time, though. Besides, we could ask them to come along for some of the sails."

Avelynne considered that. "True. Although, I am not certain how the council would feel about their heir risking his life out at sea."

There. She had dared broach two thorny subjects. Firstly, that Eleksander might be the next king and during such an undertaking might need their support. Secondly, that it was all very well to say that they wouldn't be at sea for long, but there was a risk of dying out there. It could happen during a storm, from a sea creature attack, or they might go ashore on some strange land and find its inhabitants as violent as Cavarrians.

"Life is full of risks," Aurea said, holding open the door to the quarters. "We all have to decide which ones we are comfortable with. Eleksander's life is his own. Just like yours belongs to you." She gazed from Sabina to Avelynne. "You both need to stop living for other people. Now, step on in."

They did and Aurea lit candles for them to see by. The captain's quarters turned out to be an unadorned room containing a bed and a small desk which held stacks of maps, a half-full wine bottle, and three emptied bottles containing beeswax candles that now burned brightly. As expected, the space wasn't large but certainly private compared to where the rest of the sailors slept below deck.

Avelynne stifled a smile, remembering the sailors bedding one another in the hammock next to hers that morning of the sea serpent attack. This was a much better place for that sort of thing. While Sabina and Aurea spoke about the room and how many chests for clothes and books could be fit in it, her gaze fell upon the bed. It was a plain, wood frame with a straw mattress and pillows clad in linen bedding that looked freshly cleaned. It was also wide enough to take up half of the room, easily fitting two people, three even if the people in question were on the slighter side. Like them, even with Sabina's muscles and curves.

That smile was impossible to stifle now as Avelynne's heart raced and there was a warming between her thighs. It had been so long since she had...

Sabina stepped into her line of sight. "Are you listening, Avelynne?"

"Oh. Afraid not. What was that?"

"I was asking if we shouldn't get back to the Hall of Explorers? We don't want to miss dinner."

Avelynne regarded the other two women, who looked calm but a tad perplexed. Had they really not noticed her expression, the fact that she was staring at the bed, the colour no doubt rising in her cheeks? Oh, but they could be so oblivious and sweet. And she was being too lascivious. Or perhaps just enough? Yes. She was done apologising for what she was and what she wanted.

"We could go back and eat," she said. "Or we could stay here and check if an important part of our arrangement works."

"Which part?" Aurea asked. Then it seemed to dawn on her. "Ha. I think I'm understanding why you went quiet while staring at the bed."

"I'm guessing you're not talking about if we all fit in the bed to get a good night's sleep?" Sabina said.

"No, that wasn't quite what I was referring to," Avelynne replied, excitement boiling over within her. "However, if neither of you are in the mood, we can simply return to the Hall of Explorers for dinner and forget all about it for now?"

They all shared glances. It felt strange to be discussing this as if it was a matter brought up in a council meeting and not an act of pleasure and intimacy.

"I think going to bed would be a great way to seal and celebrate this arrangement of ours," Aurea said, her anticipation and eagerness obvious.

Sabina, however, wrapped her arms around herself, making Avelynne bite her tongue. Oh, how witless! She had forgotten that this would be Sabina's first time doing more than mere kissing and touching.

"Oh, snowdrop," she breathed. "I understand if this is not how you want your first time to happen. Perhaps it would be better with only the two of you, in love and alone?"

Those strong warrior arms released fast and were instead stretched out towards Avelynne. "No! No, I want you to be with me, my countess. Everything is safer and better when you're there." Sabina smiled over at Aurea. "I'd like it to be all three of us. What is better than your first time being with someone who makes you comfortable and confident?" She paused for effect. "Being with two people who have that effect on you. And, aye, I'm ready for it to be now."

"I am too," Aurea whispered, reaching out to touch Sabina but then shying away.

Avelynne studied her. Aurea was normally so bold, chatty, carefree, and happy to make the initial move. The brave captain and famous printer. Now, she blushed like a timid young maiden. Avelynne sought Aurea's gaze to assess if she was all right, while Sabina ushered Kall out of the small quarters and told him to stay on deck. Aurea's breathing had picked up, her bosom rising and falling with it like storm-ridden waves. Her rosy lips parted and Avelynne waited to hear what she would say.

Chapter Thirty-Three

FIRST TIME

Sabina, having deposited Kall outside where he curled up and fell asleep, came back into the captain's quarters. She was hit by the scent of burning honey coming from the beeswax candles and by the way the other women watched one other. Absorbed, marvelling, eager.

Aurea's lips were parted and, after a moment of pregnant silence, she breathlessly asked, "Why do you always look at me like that?"

Avelynne's slim eyebrows lowered. "Like what?"

"Like you can see right through me."

"She often does that," Sabina said with a snicker. "And I think she actually can see through people. She certainly reads me like a book, one with simple words and big pictures."

"I merely take note of body language, personality type, and past behaviour, and then make guesses," Avelynne said. "To start our involvement off on the correct foot, I'll be completely honest. I was actually admiring that lovely tic of yours."

311

Sabina knew what Avelynne meant. When Aurea was stressed or nervous, there was a tiny twitch on the left side of her mouth. It was twitching double time now.

"Ah, that," Aurea said on a sigh. She curled in on herself. "I've had it ever since I was little. I hate it."

How could anyone hate something so charming?

"Oh, you shouldn't," Avelynne burst out. "It's adorable. I worry it means that you are nervous about what might happen here, though. Are you certain you want this?"

With her shoulders back again, Aurea got a playful expression. "I can be nervous, aroused, and eager for this all at the same time. I am an excellent multi-tasker."

"Now there's the Aurea I know," Avelynne said with a laugh. "Anyway, I didn't mean to stare at your tic, it's just that I... cannot help but want to kiss it." Her attention was now very clearly on Aurea's mouth. "If I did, would it still? Or would it move faster? Fluttering against my lips like butterfly wings?"

"I don't know." Aurea touched her fingers to the movement by her lips. "I feel like I should know that. Could you help me find out?"

Avelynne moved closer to Aurea, who slowly opened her arms in invitation. Avelynne's hands grasped Aurea's waist and both their eyes closed as their faces neared.

Sabina watched, her heart pounding in time with what was between her legs. Avelynne was going to kiss Aurea, right here, right now. And, by all snow, Sabina wanted her to. She was thunderstruck by the fact that didn't feel jealousy at that thought, only desire and affection.

Avelynne placed a chaste kiss on the twitch on the side of Aurea's lips. It was hard for Sabina to see, but she thought the tic stilled. Then their lips connected and a kiss, first hesitant and tiptoeing, grew confident and hungry. One of them let out a soft moan into the kiss, Sabina didn't know which one and it didn't matter, all three of them felt the same way, she was sure of that.

She walked up behind Avelynne as if in a daze and put her arms around the two shorter lasses. She kissed Avelynne's neck and felt Avelynne's knees buckle. No matter, she was pressed between Sabina and Aurea, and they were both more than strong enough to hold up the slighter woman. Sabina couldn't get enough of Avelynne's soft skin and kissed all over her neck and around the shell of her dainty ear, burrowing under the red-black hair to get more access. Meanwhile, she let her hands roam Aurea's hips and down over as much of the thighs as she could reach.

Throughout, Avelynne was arching her back, nestling her rear into Sabina's pelvis. They continued like that until the kissing and touching became frantic. That was when Avelynne pulled away from the kiss, gasping, "I need both of you naked. Now."

Neither Sabina nor Aurea argued but started pulling their own and each other's clothes off in time with Avelynne. The Hall of Explorers uniform and the outfits of Hethklian sailors weren't pretty or sophisticated, but it must be said that they were relatively quick to take off.

When naked, Sabina felt exposed in more ways than one. The other two were so beautiful. Her body was heavier with muscles and curves, and her skin marred with more scars, as well as dips and growth lines in her thicker parts. The hair between her legs and under her arms was blonde while the other two had darker shades. Was it normal to have body hair so pale?

Her discomfort faded when Avelynne raked her eyes over her body and moaned, "Oh stars above, look at you," with a gaze so lustful that Sabina felt like food for someone ravenous. There was a rush of power in how desperate for *her* that Avelynne looked.

"Doldrums." Aurea had whispered the Hethklish swearword. "You're both stunning."

Sabina stepped closer to the bed and the other two followed suit. This was actually happening. A thrill rushed along her bloodstream and her mind dizzied as if she'd been drinking. She made herself savour the moment, to take a heartbeat to admire these women's naked forms. Aurea's eyes, usually astute and curious, were lidded and tranquil, appearing golden in the candlelight. She had Hethklian aging scars not only on her face but between her breasts, there shaped as a sun with rays reaching towards her nipples. Her light brown skin was taut over a chiselled stomach and wide hips. Such a contrast to Avelynne, with her thin body coloured the white-silver of the moon with blue veins just showing through, like faded lines on a map. She had left her silver quill necklace on. These two were so unbelievably precious to Sabina, so perfect. She trembled. There was so much to see, so much to take in. Did everyone who was new to bedding feel this overwhelmed?

Aurea grasped a hand from each of her lovers and pulled them down on top of her on the bed, murmuring sweet words.

Then there was no more time for Sabina to worry or to think. So many hands and fingers, on and *in* her, two whole bodies for her to worship, two soft mouths seeking hers, and all those reassuring gazes from sex-drunk eyes. It was impossible to keep track, or control, or even her wits about her.

Sabina relaxed her mind and her every muscle and simply... let go.

When all three of them were spent, they laid tangled up in the linen sheets, legs intertwined and hands holding onto each other.

This is right, Sabina mused. *The three of us are meant to do this.*

At least for now. The future was full of possibilities. She marvelled at the thought. She'd worried her life would always be her stuck in that cold, dark cottage in the North, looking after her siblings until her parents died and she took over their jobs as village warriors. That wasn't her path, though. She, Avelynne, and Aurea were meant for something different.

"You know what we are?" she asked.

"Tired and blissful?" Aurea suggested.

Pondering a little longer, Avelynne said, "A triad? Like Vattendal said when he nicknamed me 'the smallest of a triad'?"

"Aye, all of that. But I was referring to that we're sailors, explorers, mapmakers, and adventurers. I, Sabina Rosenmarck, was made to hop on a ship bound for exotic shores with a beautiful woman at my side and simply sail into the sunset!"

The others looked a little confused at her gusto. Had she overdone it? That was probably cringey. Soon, however, the other two agreed, Avelynne only adding, "Two beautiful women, thank you very much."

Aurea laughed. "Yes, we are indeed all those things. I am also very thirsty," she said, untangling herself and getting up to snatch the bottle from the desk.

They sat in the bed and gulped down the rich red wine. That wasn't a sensible idea on an empty stomach and when so exhausted, but who cared? Everything would work itself out.

She smiled to herself as she handed the bottle to Avelynne, wondering when this carefree new Sabina Rosenmarck would fade away and bring back the usual practical, responsible one.

Aurea sat herself closer and ran her hands along the length of Sabina's loose hair. Her braid had come undone? How had she not noticed?

"How I love this wild mane of yours," Aurea said, letting her fingers burrow into the hair and comb down, her fingertips skimming the skin of shoulders and chest underneath.

Sabina's breath-catching pleasure was interrupted by the sound of distant, affronted mewling, followed by scratching on the door from heavy paws.

The three of them giggled before Avelynne said, "Let the overgrown kitten in before he claws the door to firewood."

Aurea nodded. "Just don't let him up in bed while I'm naked and—"

"Wet all over?" Avelynne suggested with a mischievous raise of one eyebrow.

Aurea's only response was to bite the former countess's shoulder and then suck until a red mark adorned the white skin.

Half watching them, Sabina let Kall in, petted his big head and commanded him to stay on the floor.

Avelynne was waving at him, uselessly as he didn't understand the concept of waving. Avelynne had to stop treating the snowtiger like a toddler. Although, granted, it was quite cute when she did it and Kall must agree since he was slow-blinking back at her.

Sabina swallowed a swig of wine. "Right. We need to go back to the Hall of Explorers." She searched for her clothes. "When there, we'll eat something to soak up the alcohol and then talk to the lads about our plans. They'll need to decide whether they want to sail with us."

There. The old her was back. That was all right, she decided. It was fine for her to be responsible, as long as she relaxed sometimes.

"Yes, we should get back there," Aurea said, scratching one of her pointed ears. Was it the one that the silver beast injured? "There are spare horses in the shipyard."

Avelynne stretched, giving a far too enticing view of her body. "I'm glad I sent the carriage back. If we were sat in one of those, I wouldn't be able to keep my hands off you two."

"Woman, you are insatiable," Aurea said.

Sabina fretted that Avelynne would take that as a criticism, but no. Avelynne smiled, dimples in full view and said, "Yes. Aren't you lucky?"

"Very," Sabina and Aurea said in unison.

And they were. Even removing bedplay from the equation, Sabina felt luckier than she could ever have imagined. Before they left, she would steal a few more kisses from these two, as a celebration of her good fortune. Responsibilities could wait a while longer.

Chapter Thirty-Four

DECISIONS

That evening, Eleksander sat on his bed in the bedchamber he shared with Hale. Sadly, still with separate beds. Hale was asleep on his ruffled bedsheets, sprawled out on his back and making tiny, snuffling snores. After dinner, Hale and he had gone back to their room to rest, mainly because Hale had overeaten. In celebration of food soon not being scarce anymore, the staff had put on a feast for the ages and many attending had eaten their fill and then some.

Avelynne, Sabina, and Aurea had entered the great hall right as everyone else was finishing up the meal. They were as dishevelled as they were flushed. When asked about that, Avelynne said, "We've been out riding."

Hale and Taferia had both scoffed, but no one had disputed the claim. The three lasses looked happy and that was all Eleksander needed to know. Well, there was something else they wanted him to know apparently, but they said they could talk to him about that after a meal and a bath.

Their late arrival meant they had missed something big.

About halfway through the pheasant dish, Kae had stood up and clanked her tankard with a knife. "Sorry to interrupt everyone's meal. I just think it may be time to give our young mapmaker the good news." She turned to Eleksander. "I shall keep this brief. I have been in discussions with the full council, barring the second wave, and everyone is in agreement. We will appoint you the next heir to Cavarra's throne."

At that point, he dropped his fork. Hale picked it up for him and then took his hand under the table.

With a worried frown, Kae said, "This is obviously an honour you can decline. However, if we don't crown you, we will pick another heir. Cavarra is not ready to choose its leaders by popular vote."

Who would they pick? There weren't many choices with royal blood. Cavarra had only three bloodlines that, following ancient lore, had been chosen by the soil of Cavarra to inter-marry and lead the country. Lothiam's line, Lea's line, and a third which had died out ages ago. Of Lea's bloodline, only Eleksander and a decrepit old uncle were alive. In Lothiam's bloodline, there was only one survivor: a cousin of the king's, who was said to be halfdead with some sort of wasting sickness. It would seem intermarrying the same three families for decades and decades didn't lead to plentiful and healthy heirs. Or good rulers?

"He'll think about it," Hale said.

"Sure. Think on it, lad," the Warden of the Woodlands said around a mouthful of pheasant. "Talk it over with your friends and give us an answer within the next three days."

"The next three days?" Eleksander spluttered.

"Yes," said the grand countess, who had barely touched

her food. "After that, we all return to our counties, thus making conversations slow and cumbersome. It is ever the case that things become misunderstood, forgotten, or left unsaid when communicating by messenger ravens."

After that, Kae had sat down, and everyone had carried on eating or drinking. Everyone but Eleksander, who had lost his appetite.

So now Eleksander sat here, watching Hale sleep, unable to read his books or write letters to the Aetholos or even to rest. How could anyone do so, knowing that their next decision would have to be whether or not they could make a good ruler. Or, he supposed, if they even wanted to be king. This decision was for life and he, well, he couldn't even decide on whether to have cider or wine with his meal tonight.

He left the bedchamber, closing the door behind him with a silent click, and paced aimlessly. In his second corridor, someone short collided with him. Or perhaps it was more accurate to say someone young, he realised as he peered through the torchlight at the lass before him. He swallowed hard. This sneering child was his half-sister by blood, the youngest of Duke Phamaro's daughters.

"Good evening, my lady. My apologies for walking into you."

He shouldn't apologise of course; she was the one who had barrelled into him.

She somehow gave the air of looking down her nose at him despite that she had to crane her neck all the way back to even see his face. "Why are you wearing *that*?"

He pulled at his jerkin. "It's my uniform. We wear—"

"Are there toys here?" she interrupted.

Eleksander thought about the academy's various objects and could only think of maps, weapons, and navigational instruments. "No, I think not. There are some books, though. Some of them have pretty pictures of the stars. Or of the creatures who live in the seas."

The girl scrunched her face up. "Ugh. Dull."

He hoped she meant the books and not him. He remembered being an overindulged child compared to many others, since he grew up in a wealthy household. Nevertheless, he had been raised to be polite and respectful. And been taught how to entertain himself with whatever was around, even if that was only pinecones for dolls, rocks for building blocks, or a book he couldn't read. A gust of night air came in from the nearest arrow slit and he noted that he'd never been left alone to wander maze-like corridors of a menacing training academy after nightfall either.

Certainty struck; he was lucky to have grown up with the Aetholos instead of the duke. As grim as his fate had been those first years when hidden and nigh killed—not to mention living his life wondering who his birthparents were and assuming they didn't want him—he wouldn't change his fate even if he could.

He met the fixed stare of the lass. Was she aware that they had the same jaw-shape and that when they frowned, they both pursed their lips in the same way? The latter he had found unattractive when he'd caught his own reflection while frowning. However, seeing it mirrored back on her face, he had to admit that there was an adorable quality to the gesture. He must remember that next time he hated it.

Did she recognise the similarities between them? No. Small children wouldn't think of that and she didn't know about him. She wouldn't be searching this stranger's face for her own features.

He crouched down and smiled at her. "I'm sorry you are bored, my lady. May I ask if you're here alone? It can be very confusing in these winding corridors, and I wouldn't like you to get lost."

"She is not," a voice called from further down the corridor.

The Duke of the Lakelands strode towards them, making quick work of the corridor with his long, powerful legs. He wore a long, opalescent silk cloak over his usual immaculate garb, and as he rushed along it splayed out behind him like an ethereal veil. His strong-boned face wore an expression far from ethereal, though. It was set in hard discontent.

The breath caught in Eleksander's chest, sitting there mingling with his emotions and feeling like an infection about to overcome him.

Breathe, he told himself. *And stand up tall, try to look your best.*

"There you are. Return to your mother," the duke said to his daughter. "It's late and also filthy out here. You shall ruin your pretty dress. Again."

She groaned and stomped her little foot but obeyed.

The duke watched her go. "She's a princess at heart. As spoiled as royalty, as devious as a monster, and with the sweetest face. She and her sisters have been raised to crush hearts and conquer with iron fists clad in silk gloves." He sighed. "I hoped to marry at least one of them off to whomever Lothiam adopted or sired, that plan is foiled now that their half-brother will take the throne."

Replies crowded on Eleksander's tongue.

You do admit that I'm your son, then?

You will be open about that we're of the same blood?

You always planned to have one of your children on the throne?

You're convinced that I'll agree to be king?

He said none of them. His mouth wouldn't work, his mind was muddled, and his heart was beating far too fast again.

Instead, it was the duke who spoke again, seeming incredibly reluctant to do so. "I knew nothing of you, you understand. I ended my brief romantic entanglement with your mother when I heard she was promised to marry the king one day." He clasped his hands behind his back. "I now understand that my parents found out that she was with child but kept that from me, deciding to take care of the issue without my involvement."

Eleksander tried to school his face. Take care of the issue. That was an interesting way of saying that they decided to have their five-year-old grandchild killed.

"A-and now that you know?" he stuttered.

"I do not believe it changes much. You are full-grown and have not wanted for neither coin, comforts, education, nor affection. The latter, I admit not being something I..." he trailed off.

The ensuing, stifling silence was only broken by a whitengale singing heart-piercingly outside.

"What will happen between us?" Eleksander blurted. "I mean, will I ever see you? I mean, would you want that?"

He staggered back at his own words. "My apologies, I don't know what I'm..." He ran a hand over his hot, damp forehead. "I suppose I'm asking if you will publicly acknowledge me as your son?"

That wasn't what he had been saying and they both knew it.

Nevertheless, the duke played along. "Yes. I see no point in denying it and neither does my wife. It strengthens your claim to the throne, and it aids my family in keeping the Duchy of the Lakelands under our control." He fastened and unfastened the silver clasp of his cloak, a gesture that would be fidgeting on someone less elegant and measured. "Obviously, we shall be happy to advise you if you ever need that. We could also offer some financial aid, or access to our connections. If the cause is beneficial to us, perhaps even some political backing."

Eleksander sagged with disappointment but wasn't surprised. Duke Phamaro would provide clout, opinions, and coin, especially if it served the Duchy of the Lakelands, but never offer to be a father to Eleksander.

Fine. The rules were set. And that disappointment melted away fast.

"Thank you," he replied, standing up tall again. "If I do decide to take the throne, I am sure to need advice and supporters."

The duke held up a ring-clad finger. "Ah, yes, the question of accepting the crown. I spoke to Taferia Palm. She mentioned that you for some unfathomable reason struggle with the idea of being the next heir." He curled his upper lip in disgust. "And your unseemly departure from the council meeting where it was first brought up proves as much."

He was dismayed with how Eleksander had fled the room, then? But what else could he have done? Should he have ignored the need to leave and simply sat there dying inside but not speaking, like a useless statue, like he himself had?

"I am still deciding what I want to do," Eleksander said, somewhat tersely. "I take the responsibility of being king very seriously and wouldn't want to accept the burden unless I believed I was right for the task."

The duke gave a little sniff and turned to run his fingers over the woven lines of the tapestry next to them, like his mind was already on anything else less pathetic than Eleksander. "We have seen you take charge and achieve great things. The battle on the shore. Your handling of that vile man-creature in the lake. Your achievements on your sea voyage. You have done more than the last five generations of Cavarra monarchs put together."

Eleksander shifted his footing. He'd done none of that alone. And he had gotten nigh all his sailors killed on that sea journey. "I am not sure that's enough to make me a good ruler."

"No one knows who is fit to rule. It is subjective." The duke pulled his fingers back from the tapestry, grimacing at the dust on them. He wiped them on the stone wall. "You are clearly dedicated and quick to learn. The fact that you want our ruler to be 'good' means you will not gladly step over dead bodies to get to power and fame. That's an improvement from what we have had."

That nonchalant tone, it boiled Eleksander's blood.

"You make it sound trivial. So many lives hang in the balance, so many people could be miserable or dead if their monarch makes the wrong choices."

The duke's thick but immaculately trimmed eyebrows rose. "My, my, such urgency and passion. How... quaint. I am clearly not the right person to speak to you about this. How fortuitous then that I passed on a message to someone who, metaphorically, speaks your language." He inspected his fingers, probably for lingering dust. "In fact, I am rather surprised that you have not been called to see them already. They must've arrived by now, even accounting for the slowness of cheap horses."

"Who?"

"The Aetholo family." He made an airy hand gesture. "I had them sent for."

Had them sent for. Like he had summoned a pet or ordered exotic bottles of wine.

Eleksander had only sent them short letters by raven in the days since he got back. The Aetholos were busy. His father as a high-ranking merchant and guild leader. His mother as head of several charitable organisations. His sisters in their studies to be scholars and physicians. They never let sentimentality stop them from their work. Now he wondered, however, if love was a different matter.

Eleksander studied the arrogant nonchalance of the duke. It made it hard to believe that his invitation of the Aetholos was a kind gesture. Was it just so they would talk him into wearing the crown and so ensure someone with Phamaro's blood took the throne? Or a way for the duke to show Eleksander who his family was and who he was expected to turn to in the future? It didn't matter. Seeing his mother, father, and sisters was all he cared about at this moment.

"I see. If they've arrived, where would they be?"

"How should I know?" the duke drawled, sounding a lot like his wife. "I asked one of the servants to tend to them when they arrived and to inform you. It has nothing to do with me. Now, I must go wash my hands and see to my family."

Without a farewell, he sauntered back to whence he had come with a gracefulness that belied his strapping build. And, of course, that gossamer cloak billowing behind him.

See to my family. That was overkill. Eleksander had already understood the separation between them. The grief of being dismissed by his only living birthparent was heavy —and would have to be dealt with gradually and for a long time—but it wasn't as debilitating as he had thought it would be.

His real family were here. They had come all this way to see him. Despite that their schedules couldn't allow for such a thing.

He ran towards the servants' quarters, searching for someone to ask. He found a cook he'd spoken to often, since she also had a crush on an oblivious man and so had helped sneak Eleksander food to woo Hale with. She asked around and found out that a wealthy looking group had arrived out of the blue and had been brought to wait in a lesson room. She took him to it and was there rewarded with many thanks from him and a sizable amount of gold coins by his mother.

Then, the Aetholo family was alone and reunited. It

was odd to see them in this sparse, murky, and dusty lesson room. He saw his father, mother, and sisters in the quiet, tiled rooms of their large villa in the central Lakelands. Reading in the well-lit library, going off to trade in the city centre, giving the poor reading lessons in the Aetholo grounds, or practising centering in the sun-drenched, walled garden. They were strange in this dark, foreboding fortress of an academy. Strange, but still a tonic for his burdened heart.

He rushed over to them, trying to keep the dignified bearing and reserved composure he'd been raised to have, despite that all he wanted to do was scoop them into an embrace and cry and laugh.

Ellenaria met him halfway across the room. She was the one least out of place as she had come with him and worked here. She was now studying to be one of the Hall of Explorers tutors. He was confident that she would be the best one there had ever been, and any future waves of mapmaking magicians would be in good hands.

She looked him over and he waited patiently for his ribbing.

"Ah. Look at you, your braids are a mess," she finally said. "You can wield some sort of superior magic and rescue lake gods but cannot keep yourself presentable? Pish. I'll have to help you with them as soon as we're done speaking."

He couldn't stop himself any longer. He put his arms around her and gently pulled her into a hug. She smelled of home. She stiffened, as any Aetholo did at unexpected physical contact. Within their family, affection was shown by words and actions, not physical touch. Still, her stiffness faded and she returned the embrace, whispering, "I've been so worried about you, little brat."

"I'm sorry to have worried you," he replied. "I missed you."

"We missed you too," said his father, right before joining in the hug in the awkward way that Ekon Aetholo always hugged. Eleksander felt other arms around him as his mother and younger sister added themselves to the group cuddle.

"I'm so glad you're here," he half-sobbed.

"My poor, sweet little son," Elebna Aetholo answered, patting the back of his head from within the cramped embrace. "What a time you've had and how brave you've been."

He would normally have told her to stop talking to him as if he was six, but found it soothed him and so kept quiet.

The hug ended and everyone stood beaming at one another.

Eleksander opened his mouth to ask how their journey had been. Or why they hadn't sent message that they were coming. Or how they could leave their duties and come here on such short notice. Instead, he found his own tale spilling out. Most of it they knew from city gossip and his letters, and they filled in as much as they could when his voice broke or when he was lost for words.

It was a relief to tell them about all the death, the fear, the guilt, and the constant questions. But also to share all the good, the people he had met, and the wonderous things he had seen. He left out the part about Hale finally returning his feelings. He'd tell his sisters about that when they were alone. His parents could find out later. Hopefully by someone else telling them.

"I am so sorry that we have not come to you before," his mother said. "And that we didn't believe you when you sent Ellenaria those letters about the former king's spell."

His youngest sister Elissee blurted, "I believed. Ellenaria and I kept reminding each other of the truth to render the spell useless. We wanted to come fight the king when you returned from sea. But, *apparently*, I'm too young and not a warrior. Despite being the best archer of anyone my age."

Elissee's tendency to rapid-fire words like a volley of arrows had annoyed him in the past but now he adored it. He took in her sweet thirteen-year-old face and wanted to spare her from everything he had suffered but show her all the incredible things he had seen.

"We may not have sent your sisters, or come to fight ourselves, since battle is not an Aetholo strength," his father said. "But when the Twelve warned us of the king's scheme and how he was gathering forces to apprehend you on the shore, we used up every favour and put all our funds into rousing the Lakelands army to fight for you."

"Someone had to," his mother said with a grimace. "The duke and duchess were the last county leaders to agree to fight and dethrone Lothiam. Only when our merchant guild pressured them did they join the fray."

"Speaking of the duke," Ekon Aetholo gripped Eleksander's upper arm, "I'm sorry you discovered who your mother was, only to find she had died. And that you father was our arrogan... hm. Our duke."

Eleksander stared at him. "I found my birthparents, yes,

but they could never be my mother and father. That's you two."

His mother sagged with what must be relief. "Oh, thank the waters," Elebna Aetholo breathed. "I fretted you'd either not care about us anymore or somehow harbour resentment because we never found your birthparents. We did try our best. You know that, right?"

Eleksander scrambled to take both his father's and mother's hands. "Of course! And I wouldn't turn my back on you two. You cleaned up my every wound, wiped every tear, and scared off any monster under my bed. You loved me and taught me everything with skill and patience. You were the best parents I could ever hope for."

He didn't mention the nigh impossibly high expectations the Aetholos had for their children, nor how it made him, Ellenaria, and Elissee work themselves half to death trying to excel in everything. No one was perfect. Besides, that one flaw in the Aetholos' childrearing had at least made their three children hardworking and, often, successful.

"We worried," his father said quietly, "that we had somehow inadvertently turned you against your birthparents since you never helped when we looked for them. In fact, you seemed to want us to stop searching."

"No. I mean yes, I did. I mean..." He stepped out of the embrace and rubbed his eyes to hide that they were tearing up. "I never wanted to find my birthparents because I was sure they had abandoned me. That notion didn't come from you, it came from deep inside of me."

"Do you know what it was based on?" Ellenaria asked, ever examining.

He considered for a moment. "How I was found, I think. Naked, lost, and so alone. I remember that most vividly, how *alone* I was. How wrong that felt, how unfair. Like I'd been punished even though I had been good and done what I was told to."

What he was told to do. He couldn't remember that, but Taferia's tale had filled in the gap. The wet nurse hiding him had been ordered to drown him but had instead pulled Eleksander out of the lake and told him to run as fast and far as he could. That it was a game and that she'd come find him soon.

Thank the waters that Ekon Aetholo, travelling the early morning roads to trade in the neighbouring city, had stumbled upon him. Eleksander could still remember the words his father had said after having checked that this crying child had no parents in the vicinity. "Come with me, little one. I have a daughter, only a couple of years older than you, called Ellenaria. Come keep her company until we can find your parents."

Ellenaria. Another child orphaned by tragedy, Eleksander mused. She'd been the sole survivor after her family home burned down. Young Elissee, however, was an Aetholo by birth. Still, she had never been treated any different from her older siblings for it. Both he and Ellenaria had been chosen, he realised with the glowing warmth of pride. His parents could have dropped them off at an orphanage, but they got to know them and then chose to keep them. How many non-adopted children could say that?

Now, a grown man, Eleksander felt like he had been found again, once more taken in, and given the sort of unconditional love that he was sure the duke couldn't give.

"I'm sorry you felt that way when you were found. And yes, it was unfair," his mother said. Due to his height, she had to stand on her tiptoes to smooth his braids. The ones she had taught him to braid in the same fashion as her own, giving the two of them a sort of family resemblance. "You have always been enraged by injustice, my sweet Sander. It is what makes you such a good fighter for what's right. That fight has given you purpose and joy." She wavered; the next words seeming hard for her to say. "Perhaps it is a heritage from your birthmother, who started the Twelve and ended up sacrificing her life for what was right?"

Eleksander took the hand caressing his braids and reverently kissed the back of it. "Or perhaps it came from the woman who raised me? The one who runs charities and taught her children to fight injustices?" They smiled at each other. "Either way, it doesn't matter from where it came. What matters is that I grew up with parents, and sisters, who helped me harness it into something I could use to try making the world a better place."

"Something you can do best if you're in a position to lead," Ellenaria said.

The words hit him right in the chest. *A position to lead.*

What had his mother said before? *That fight has given you purpose and joy.*

They watched him. None of them would tell him what he should or shouldn't do. It was clear to him what they thought, though, and that their reasons for thinking it were the same as his own. His thoughts halted. It was more than that they felt he should do it, both for others and because it would allow him to follow his passion, it was that they... must be convinced that he could do it.

He had been thirteen when he wanted to enter an archery competition and his parents and Ellenaria said it was his choice, but kindly suggested that he shouldn't because he wasn't ready. They had been right. Despite that it had hurt to hear it. If they thought he couldn't be a good crownbearer, they would tell him so.

"If I agree to be king," Eleksander blew out a shaky breath, "it'll be so hard. What if I let everyone down?"

To his surprise, his father laughed. "You? Let people down? You have never done anything but exceed everyone's expectations."

"Father, I got most of my crew killed and my ship crushed."

"You're a featherbrain," Ellenaria stated. "That's the wrong way of seeing it. The truth is that you managed to help some people survive an overwhelming disaster."

There was a tightening around Eleksander's heart. "I suppose so?"

"No supposing about it," his mother briskly said. "You did more than many in your situation would or could. We heard about you staying level-headed enough to tie ropes around the waists of your sailors and thereby securing them. With enough time, you would have saved more."

"And," his father added, "if you take the throne, you can honour your lost sailors by ensuring that others aren't sent out to sea without preparation or proper equipment. You can honour their names and make sure all of Cavarra remembers them."

"If I'm crowned, I will do that," Eleksander vowed. He thought on. "Me taking the throne would also stop the four counties from fighting over who else to make heir. In general, I can quell their fighting, instead of encouraging it like Lothiam did."

"Uh-huh. You should do it for that reason," Elissee said, jittery and clearly bored. "You should also do it so you can follow your path of fighting injustice. And to ensure there's a modern thinker in power, one who wants to let the people have a say." His youngest sister formed her hand as a duck beak and slapped her fingers together as if it was talking. "Blah blah blah. There are a million reasons why you should be crownbearer. Do you want to be, though?"

Eleksander put a hand to his stomach. He would never admit this to his logical family, but he was gaging his gut feeling. He took his time, knowing they would wait. Even Elissee.

He dropped his hand. "I want to do it. I want to be king. If I fail, I will at least know that I tried the best I could."

"And that you did it for the right reasons," his father said.

"So, your mind is made up," Ellenaria said. She rolled her eyes. "About time. By the waters, you'll need plenty of advisors to speed up your decision making."

He laughed. "Good thing I have all of you, then."

They all agreed, without showing any hints of ambition or pride. There was a job to be done and who better to make sure it was done properly and fairly than the Aetholo family?

Eleksander risked everyone's slight discomfort and pulled them all into another scrabbling group hug. In the safety of this embrace, Eleksander made another decision. He would only take the throne if the council would agree to certain demands. Convincing them would be quite the challenge but he did, to his own surprise, believe he could manage it.

There was a timid knock at the door.

"Yes?" Eleksander said.

Tutor Myle opened the door. "Sorry to bother you, Master Aetholo. I mean, um, your highness?"

Eleksander winced. His former tutor calling him that was unbearable. How was he going to get used to that?

"Master Hawthorn has been storming around the corridors searching for you," Ithikiel Myle said. "Do you wish to speak with him? If so, I can direct him to this room."

Eleksander imagined a drowsy Hale with sleep-creased clothing barrelling through hallways, shouting for his beloved while yawning and rubbing his eyes. He was so often like a bear after hibernation when he awoke.

"Please do," Eleksander said, his cheeks straining with the wideness of his smile.

Both his sisters must've noticed as they made mocking cooing noises and comments about lovebirds. Their parents merely looked confused.

"So, that ill-tempered but handsome Woodlander is on his way?" Ellenaria said. "Let him come. I'll shake some sense into him like I did the first time he and I spoke. He needs to be open about... certain choices."

Eleksander let gleeful laughter bubble up. "He's open with it now. We're taking it all slow and easy, but we have committed to each other." He froze, then slow-turned towards his parents, who he had just remembered could hear him. "Um. Mother, father. When he finally arrives, I'd like you to meet my... Hale."

His mother opened her mouth and Eleksander truly didn't know what was going to come out. It turned out to be the same teasing bird cooing as his sisters had made, to everyone's amusement.

In the distance, bumbling footsteps were heard and the echoes of Hale shouting, "Sander?"

"Master Hawthorn has arrived," Myle said.

Eleksander admired this man's gift for stating the obvious. "I know. Let him in, please?"

Myle stood aside and Hale bounded in. He had a crease from his pillow on his cheek and his black eyes were bleary. Neither of which took away any of his handsomeness. He shut the door behind him, right in Myle's face.

"Be nice," Eleksander admonished.

Hale gave a half-shrug. He had scant appreciation for Ithikiel Myle ever since they saw his simpering kowtowing to Lothiam.

Hale spotted the Aetholos. "Shitting silver beasts!"

"Mind your language, Woodlander," Ellenaria said, a wry smile playing at her lips.

"Right. Yes. Sorry," Hale said. He wasn't looking at Ellenaria, though. He had met her plenty of times. He was looking to the other three, especially Eleksander's parents.

"This is Hale Hawthorn," Eleksander said, following up with introducing his family members one at a time.

"A pleasure to meet you," Elebna Aetholo said, a mere beat before her husband did.

For some inexplicable reason, Hale gave them a stiff little bow each and didn't say a single word. His stubbled cheeks showed a hint of reddening. Eleksander wracked his brain. No, he couldn't remember ever seeing Hale shy around strangers before.

"We should leave you two to speak alone," his mother said. "We need to get going anyway. We have been promised a guided tour of the Hall of Explorers and its surroundings by Ellenaria."

Eleksander had to ask. "You'll still be here later?"

"Of course. You won't be rid of us that easily," his father said with a chortle. "Your mother and I have arranged for others to take on our duties for the next ten days. And your sisters can study while here."

Ellenaria nodded. "The Hall of Explorers library has books that I could not find in the Lakelands."

"Not to mention that there's no socially expected dress code here." Elissee put her small hand on his arm. "Also, you know, it's not *terrible* to see you and get to be around you."

"By the waters, it is a gift to be with you and to see you well," his father said. "I have never been as frightened as when your ship didn't return when expected."

Eleksander's mother wrapped her arms around herself. "It's true. None of us could sleep until we heard you were returning, safe and sound."

"I hope to never scare you so again," Eleksander said.

Whatever his family was going to answer to that was never to be heard as everyone was distracted by a loud thump, followed by a muffled scream. Hale had knocked over a full inkwell that fell right on Ekon Aetholo's sandal-clad foot.

Chapter Thirty-Five

INKWELLS, COPPER SHIELDS, FAREWELLS

Hale held his breath. How could he be so clumsy? He shouldn't do things when he was barely awake from a nap. It never ended well. Shit, last time he had gotten his hand stuck in a jam jar.

No one spoke as Eleksander's father bent and picked up the inkwell. Thank the trees it hadn't opened and splashed ink over this coin-bag's sandals or that fine cloak fastened with a copper shield pin engraved with E.A. The Aetholos were all so nicely dressed. Not showy like the Duke and Duchess of the Lakelands, but with austere clothes that looked expensive and somehow cleaner than any clothes that Hale had ever seen. In comparison, he was an utter mess.

"I think you dropped this, young mapmaker," Ekon Aetholo said, handing the inkwell over.

"Didn't drop it. I knocked it over. From that table. Some bonehead had put the inkwell right on the edge, like a bonehead." He patted the table to indicate it. Why was he doing or saying any of this? Shit. He had to get himself together, fast.

Ekon gave a warm, bellowing laugh. "I stand corrected." He put the inkwell back and then pointed to Hale as he said to Eleksander, "Your Woodlander has a sense of humour. That's always a good start."

Hale tried to not look confused. Sense of humour?

"He does," Eleksander said, preening. "He's also an outstanding navigator and the best fighter I've ever seen. He has great skills in determining flora and fauna and—"

"You can carry on boasting about him another time," Ellenaria said and headed for the door. "We should take that tour and, as mother said, let you two talk."

They said their farewells and left, conversing quietly about if they should visit the library first.

"Ugh. Well, I made a shitty first impression," he muttered when the door had closed.

"No," Eleksander said, rubbing Hale's shoulder. "You were sweet. That's a good start and they'll like you even more when they get to know you."

"I hope so," Hale said. He'd make sure to be ready next time. Or at least awake. "By the way, why do all your family members have names that start with E?"

Eleksander gave that delicious lopsided smile of his. "It's a sort of inside joke. When my parents fell in love, they realised they'd have the same initials and thought it would be fun if everyone in their family did. That way, we could all have the same family emblem."

"Emblem? Is that like Avelynne's family thingy?"

"No, not quite like the elaborate crests that the noble class has, with colours, mottos, and symbols on them,"

Eleksander said, leaning against a desk. "Most middleclass Lakelanders have taken a sort of family mark, though, especially merchants. It gives you something to stamp the wax seal on letters with and is useful in guild business to distinguish between high-ranking members."

Hale recalled the pin on Ekon's cloak and vaguely thought he had seen the same in rings on both his and his wife's fingers. "And your parents have their initials?"

"My parents chose a copper shield with an E and an A in swirling letters as their emblem. As I say, my parents think it's funny that we all have the same initials. That's just their sense of humour."

"Why copper?"

"Father's main trade is in copper. And it's a shield because mother believes that the strong and lucky should be a shield for those who are less fortunate."

"Huh," Hale said, distracted by how much easier the classless and nomadic Woodlander society was. "Wait, were you not called Eleksander when the Aetholo's found you?"

"I could only remember being called 'sweetling.' Obviously, that was what the wet nurse called me as she raised me during the search for a discreet family." He frowned. "After it was decided I should be killed instead, well, I suppose it's easier to order the death of a child with no name."

Hale grabbed him and pulled him into the tightest hug he could give. "Are any of the maggot-eaters who were involved in that still alive? I'd like to... *talk* to them."

"Save your fight for a more urgent cause," Eleksander said against Hale's ear. "I do wonder, though. Before they took me from Queen Lea, did she give me a name? Even if it was just in her mind?"

Hale thought hard. What would he want to hear if he was Eleksander? "I wager she did. She probably gave you the finest name she knew."

Eleksander hugged back even harder. Hale could never get over how nice it was to be held by someone wider and taller, like being cocooned. And his sweet Lakelander always smelled so good. After a while, Eleksander pulled back for a quick but heartfelt kiss. Hale just had time to notice that Eleksander's face was wet, before he turned away to wipe his cheeks, seeming embarrassed.

Hale put two fingers under his chin and moved that handsome face back towards his own. "Could you... not do that? Hide your feelings from me, I mean. Please? I need to see or hear what you're feeling. Because I sure as shit can't figure it out myself."

"Actually, you do quite well at it these days," Eleksander said between muted sniffles.

The pride at those words was stronger than Hale had expected. It was time to change topic, though. They shouldn't be talking about him right now.

"So, um, what did your family say?"

"We talked about the duke, the past, family relation-ships, and so on." Eleksander looked to the door they had left from. "The key thing right now, however, was that after hearing their advice regarding my ability to rule, I consulted my gut instinct on if I *want* to be King of Cavarra."

"And?"

"I've decided that I do."

"Excellent!"

"You sure? You still ready to waste your time at a stuffy court?"

"Not all my time," Hale said with a snort. "You'll be the sort of king who travels out to meet his people. To keep an eye on the county leaders and to see what Cavarrians need."

Eleksander picked up an abandoned quill from the desk and tapped it against his lips. "I hadn't thought of that, but you're right. And when I'm needed here, I can send you out. Possibly with Avelynne or Sabina, in case you need assistance."

"You mean in case I say something stupid or coarse and offend people," Hale said, snickering at the truth of it.

"I meant so that you don't have to handle the unruly children we call elders without someone by your side to help carry the load."

"Sure. Well, that shouldn't be a problem. There'll always be someone around to tag along with me," Hale said, rubbing the last of the sleep grit out of his eyes. "Besides, not all the over-twenty people are awful. Taferia's great. I could see myself travelling with her if Avelynne and Sabina are busy."

"We'll work all that out later," Eleksander said, smoothing Hale's creased tunic. "One step at a time. First, I have to actually be crowned."

"True." Hale inspected the room. "Wait, is this where we used to have navigation lessons? Was this where I got tree sap on my astrolabe?"

"Yes, I think it is. I'm still not sure how you managed that."

There was knock on the door, so quiet they barely heard it. What bonehead knocked like that? When Eleksander said, "Come in," the spineless Tutor Myle stuck his head and shoulders in. Of course, *that* kind of bonehead knocked like that.

Myle bowed, nearly falling flat on his face. "Pardon the intrusion. Miss Ironhold, Miss Rosenmarck, and... the young Hethklish lady are here."

"Aurea," they heard the woman herself say from somewhere in the hallway. If she was offended at her name not being remembered, it didn't show in her cheerful tone.

Hale stared at their former tutor. Was Myle just hovering outside the lesson room to let people in? Or was he vying for a role at Eleksander's court? Wasn't he busy with his drawing and tutoring? Oh, shit, right. There were no more recruits to tutor. Hale stretched and yawned while considering if they should keep the Hall of Explorers open. If so, should they teach more subjects than mapmaking and exploring? After all, without silver beasts, the need to evacuate Cavarra was gone. But then, exploration was important. Ugh, this was too much for his poor head.

He noticed that Myle was still talking, saying something ending with, "If you would like some?"

"Yes," Eleksander replied. "Water or oakenberry juice, perhaps? Thank you."

The tutor bowed deep. "Of course, your grace. Or is it your highness?"

"For now, please stick with Eleksander. Or, as per Hall of Explorers custom, Master Aetholo."

"You intend to keep that surname?" Myle said with

astonishment. "Many of us pondered if you would take the duke's name. Or the late queen's one?"

"I have the right name."

At Eleksander's tone, Myle said no more but bowed even deeper and slunk away.

Hale went to add more firewood into the lesson room's tiny hearth just as the three young women came in.

"Well met you two," Sabina said with unusual exuberance.

Avelynne and Aurea strutted in with equally cheery greetings. Had they gotten into the stash of brandy? They smelled of the outdoors, fresh and cold to his nose. Avelynne caught him watching her rubbing warmth into her hands. "We went for a walk after dinner. It's turned out to be a crisp and clear spring evening, marvellous for stargazing."

Aurea took Avelynne's hands in her own and blew hot air on them. She then seated herself cross-legged on the nearest chair and nodded to first Sabina, who shook her head. Aurea next nodded to Avelynne, who only blanched and worried her lip.

Eleksander chuckled. "One of you has to say whatever it is you've come to tell us."

"We do have news," Avelynne finally said.

"Is it that the three of you have finally decided to be together?" Eleksander asked. "Because that much is obvious even to a sleeping man."

Hale stopped stoking the fire mid-movement. Because, wow, it wasn't shitting obvious to him.

Pink covered Avelynne's cheeks and was currently spreading down her neck. "Sabina and Aurea will be together. I will be a friend who, well, visits into the relationship on occasion."

Hale scratched the back of his neck. Three in a relationship? No, not three because Avelynne would only visit? What the shit? How would that work? Was it just shagging? He let go of his neck and shrugged. It wasn't his problem what they did as long as they were happy. He finished up with the fire and joined the others.

"There's something else too," Sabina said. "We've laid out a plan for the future. Or, well, at least for next few years."

"No point in you doing that before you know Sander's plan," Hale said. "He's decided that he'll agree to be king. So, we'll all be staying here and helping him rule Cavarra."

"Ah, we thought you might make that decision," Avelynne said. She went to Eleksander and took his hand in both of hers. "I am so glad and proud that you will lead this nation. We will of course aid you in that. However... perhaps not from the Centre. Not all the time anyway."

"What are you saying?" Hale asked, suspecting that he wasn't going to like the answer.

"I think," Eleksander said slowly, "that they're saying the three of them will sail away together. My question is if they are going to Hethekla or out exploring. And for how long they'll be gone."

Hale looked to Sabina for confirmation. With a grave expression, she said, "Hethekla, at first. I'm not sure how long we'll be gone."

Something ruptured in Hale. "Y-You're leaving us?" He banged a fist against the wall. "Now? When we need you the most?"

"Dearest, that's not quite fair," Eleksander said, downcast. "They have their own lives to lead. And we do not need them more than we have at any other time."

A twisting knot was forming in his stomach. "Oxen-shit! We are the second wave. We're the solstice born." He hit the wall again, not even caring if it fractured his hand or made the others flinch. "We were chosen to be together. We swore to be a team and face every fear together."

"And we still will," Avelynne said. "Two of us shall simply be on the move sometimes. Either to explore, which can be in the service of Cavarra, or to visit Hethekla, where we can be part of the diplomatic effort as well as the cultural and resource exchange."

"Besides, we'll come back soon," Sabina said. "We love you and we *are* a team. We couldn't stay away from you for long even if we wanted to."

Eleksander slumped down on a chair. "You make good points. And while I'll miss you frightfully when you're away, I understand it's what's right for you. You two took to the sea much more than Hale or I did." He smiled a little. "Even more so when it came to the adventure of exploring."

Hale looked at his feet. He was still relieved to have them on firm land, where there were trees and fields. If humans were meant to be at sea, they would've been given fins. It astounded him that not everyone else understood that. He switched his gaze to the women of the second wave. A vague thought hovered just out of touch. Something about that they both had cages here in Cavarra, ones that they were free from when they travelled. But did that mean they had to leave him?

Eleksander turned to Aurea, "And you must be eager to

go home, to get your sailors safely back to Hethekla and their families."

She uncrossed her legs, wearing an apologetic expression. "Yes. I don't wish to leave you two as we're just getting to know each other. And I certainly don't want to take Sab and Ave away from you," she said, wringing her hands. "But I'd love to show the two women I've fallen for my home and how my life as a printer looks. I want to take them to the places that matter to me, to share things with them."

Hale groaned. This was starting to make sense to him. Shit. No! He gave the wall another thwack. "Why now? Huh? Just wait until Sander and I are in place at court, and everything has calmed down. We need you. What if there's some sort of trouble?"

"Like what?" Sabina said.

"I... Shit, I don't know. An uprising against his rule? Or some other heir wanting to fight Sander for the throne." He could hear how loud he was getting but didn't care. "Then we may need the golden magic and you've just sailed off and left us all alone!"

This time, he hit the wall so hard that his knuckles crunched. The pain shot through him like shards of shattering ice. It didn't matter. It was nothing compared to how his stomach hurt.

Chapter Thirty-Six

RESPONSIBILITY

Wearied and worried, Eleksander ran a hand over his face. The reasons for Hale's anger were obvious. It wasn't just that most of his negative emotions were funnelled into rage but also that he had a lifetime of being left behind, of never having anyone pick him and then stay with him. Obviously, he would react like this. Nevertheless, Hale had no right to shout and be violent simply because his friends were going to travel. There would no doubt be many of these moments in their relationship and time ruling the kingdom together. Eleksander steeled himself to say something, but Avelynne beat him to it.

"Hale," she said softly. "I fear it must be now. Aurea has to captain the ships back to Hethekla. Her sailors do, as Sander said, need get home before their families think them lost at sea. However, we will come back soon."

"Not if you die," Hale yelled. "You two almost drowned after the waterfall. How can you want to go back to the sea? How can you risk your lives when you matter so much?"

Sabina snorted, like a half-crazed horse. "I nearly died

in battle back on that beach. I brushed death in this very academy fighting one of its tutors. You can die anywhere, it's a question of where you want to live. And how."

Eleksander couldn't argue with that, and he was sure Hale couldn't either.

"We will be careful and try our best to survive," Avelynne said in her most soothing tone of voice. "And as soon as we have had a few days in Hethekla to see the most important sights, we can return to Cavarra."

Hale's hands had fisted at his sides and his knuckles were whitening. "And what if we need you during that time? What if we come under threat and you're not here? You have a responsibility to—"

"Don't you dare use that word," Sabina said. "The second wave have been used as pawns, sent into danger, and ordered about, aye. But you forget that Ave and I grew up with it too. We've had nineteen years of never getting to decide for ourselves!" She stomped her foot hard enough to make the desks shake. "It's time we do what we want to do. Golden magic or no. Love for you two or no. We have to be allowed to pick what *we want* to do."

Eleksander put his hand on Hale's arm, feeling the tensed muscles. "She's right, love. You know, I've really only noticed one difference between how Cavarra treats men and women." Hale looked at him as if he was changing the subject, so he hurried to clarify. "I grew up with sisters and a mother. They were expected to consider mine and father's needs first and care for us, like Avelynne does. And to be the responsible ones who often sacrificed what they wanted, like Sabina does. We have to stop that."

Hale's expression grew even more thunderous. "That's

the way it is in your counties. In the Woodlands it's nothing like that shit." He thumped his left fist against his thigh. "I'm not saying they should stay with us because they're lasses. But because we, the second wave, save each other, need each other, and love each other. We're a... team."

Eleksander suspected he'd been about to say another word than team and it made his heart ache.

"You'll stay a team even if they're at sea or in Hethekla, Hale." Aurea shifted on her chair, seeming unsure if she should be voicing her opinion. "They won't be taken from you. They'll only be physically further away for a while."

She understood what Hale's outburst was, then? Good. Eleksander knew the other two did as well. It would be a shame if Aurea thought it was the whim of a spoiled child or violent outbursts from someone who could not control themselves.

Avelynne cupped Hale's cheeks. "You won't need the golden magic while we are away. There are no other magical creatures here and any human who attacks Sander, well, the royal army and a certain Hale Hawthorn can handle them."

Hale tried to pull his face out of her hands, but not with any great effort.

Her logic wasn't having any effect, something she clearly noticed since she sighed. "Listen to me. If we leave, we will always come back to you. And, if you want, you have a standing invitation to come with us. No one is leaving you behind or forgetting about you. We will always be more than a team, we're your *family*."

There it was, the word Eleksander was sure Hale had actually meant before.

Now, Hale hummed noncommittally and peered from Avelynne to Sabina.

Avelynne backed away so the white-haired Northerner and the black-haired Woodlander could stare at one another. Sabina's body language was much like Hale's, closed fists and feet planted squarely apart. Perhaps they noticed their similarity, or something else passed between them that Eleksander could not understand, because slowly their hands loosened and their shoulders relaxed.

"I don't want to force you to do anything," Hale murmured after a while. "And I don't want you to feel trapped here."

"I know. And I understand why you want us to stay," she said. "Avelynne is right, we're family and we love you, you bonehead." He snorted and she gave him a melancholy smile before continuing, "You will always be our brother. And we want to help you and Sander rule. We need our freedom, though. So, we'll leave, but we will write letters and we'll return to Cavarra between travels."

Hale wasn't meeting her eye. "D'you swear?"

"I swear upon the snow."

"The snow can go to the shit-heap," Hale said, his voice cracking. "Swear on Kall. Swear you won't forget about us, about me, and sail off into the horizon and never come back."

She came over and grasped his shoulders. "Of course. I swear on Kall."

He threw his arms around her and pulled her against him. She, as usual, showed no reaction to the clumsy roughness but only gripped him equally hard.

"Can I ask," Aurea whispered to Avelynne and Eleksander, "if they're hugging or wrestling?"

Their answering laughter broke the room's tension like a rock against a thin layer of ice. There was still the solemnity of farewells lingering in the air, though.

Hale pulled up a chair and sat down next to Eleksander, leaning his head against his standing lover's hip. Eleksander ran his fingers through the short hair, caressing the troubled head over and over.

Sabina joined Avelynne over by the room's small fireplace. Perhaps it was his imagination, but they looked stronger, more willing to fight for their wants and needs than when he'd first met them. These two had worked hard to grow back the wings their parents had clipped. Now, they needed to fly. The fire burned high in the hearth and the glow made golden shadows flicker across the two women's faces. He thought of that first time when they turned the sea into magical gold and how it had made him feel. They were special together. Without them, he was only the unsure and timid Eleksander.

Kall came up to him and licked his hand with that strangely coarse tongue.

"Hello, sweet chum," Eleksander said in the cooing way he had heard Avelynne speak to this lethal predator. The snowtiger let him pet his head, even bowing so Eleksander got better access. Eleksander nuzzled his face into the fur, something he had never dared do before, and kissed that wide head. There was a comfort in the reserved animal's complete trust in him. An encouragement of sorts.

Eleksander faced Avelynne and Sabina. "As much as I

shall miss you, I believe it's right that we separate for a while."

"I'm gladdened to hear it but I'm curious to why you think so," Avelynne replied.

"With our golden magic, I believe we're meant to be together. I also think we must go through some tests to determine how our solstice power works, check its limits and possibilities. Probably working with Atha Santorine to get to the bottom of it. But right now, well, it's not the time."

Hale leaned back in his chair. "Why the shit not?"

"I'm not ready for that on top of figuring out how to rule a kingdom and... certain changes I will demand from the council before agreeing to be king." He nodded to Sabina and Avelynne. "And you two should go to Hethekla. Both for yourselves but also for me and Cavarra."

Sabina gave him a gauging look. "Why do I think you mean for other reasons than trade and diplomacy?"

"I don't fully trust the Twelve or the county leaders," Eleksander said, keeping his voice down despite that they were alone. "I want to know that we have the backing of the Hethklish if needed. Especially if the council pushes back on the deal that I will suggest in return for serving as king."

"You trust *the Hethklish,* more?" Hale asked. "You've only met a single group of them and never even been there."

"It's our trustworthy faces," Aurea said.

Eleksander laughed along with her, glad she hadn't taken offence, then went back to where Hale sat and continued stroking his beloved's head, feeling that big scar from the fateful night with Tutor Rete. "You're right, my love, I haven't been there. I hope you and I can change that by travelling to Hethekla with Ave, Sab, and Aurea one day."

If he ascended the throne, he would see many of the places in this world and make personal connections with their leaders. Eleksander Aetholo would not be the sort of king who hid in his castle and ate oakenberry tarts all day.

His hand stilled on Hale's head. "Until then, while I don't fully trust them, I find it easier to trust strangers who have so far been more honest and helpful than my own people who have lied and manipulated me."

Hale shrugged. "Fair enough."

Aurea jumped up from her skewwhiff sitting position. "I am sure you'll get Hethekla's support. One of my country's flaws is that it likes to meddle. You should use that. Although, you won't need it. From what I've seen, you're more than competent to control the quarrelling county leaders and the scheming Twelve. Furthermore," she went to her lovers and wrapped an arm around each of them, "I promise you, Hale and Sander, that I'll bring these two back within a year. Then, we'll stay for a while and help you with anything you need."

"Good," Hale said. He then, under his breath, repeated the words, "Within a year."

Eleksander regarded the three women. They made sense together, rounding out the other's flaws and bringing out their virtues. And so what if they formed an alliance different from the usual ones? The second wave never did things the way everyone thought they should but forged their own paths. Clearly, so did Aurea.

He smiled at Aurea. "We appreciate that. And as much as I want you to focus on bringing them back, also make sure they're happy and safe while they're out there and do the same for yourself. Please?"

"I'll do my best."

"As that seems to have brought us back to the topic of responsibility," Sabina said, a deep crease between her eyebrows. "I agree with you, Sander, that we should wait to test the golden magic. But we cannot wait too long. If one of us dies or is incapacitated, we can no longer use the golden magic. Therefore, we must do any tests in the near future. Just in case."

"Oh, would you relax?" Hale said with a cheeky grin.

Sabina seemed about to shout at him, but then just went over and pinched his ear, to his great amusement.

Avelynne smiled at them both. "We can start the tests when we return after this first journey. Unless Eleksander needs our full focus to aid him with his duties as king at that point, of course."

"We'll have to see how things look then," Eleksander agreed.

He kept caressing Hale's cropped hair and scarred scalp. Slack-faced, Hale had closed his eyes, appearing wholly contented. There was not a single trace of rage, fear, or grief anymore. How easy it was for him to let go of his distress. Eleksander hoped that would rub off on himself one day and that his more fretful nature wouldn't drag Hale down. He didn't doubt that Hale would be good for him, but would that go both ways? Such a big part of Hale's nature was freedom.

"You know," he let his fingers brush Hale's temple, "it's not too late for you to change your mind. To decide to sail with them and either come back to me later or... stay out there and explore and adventure with them."

His heart thudded and his mouth got dry. Hale had sounded sure when they spoke of this in their bedchamber, but much had happened since.

Hale started. "What? This again? Shit, no. I told you, I want to stay with you and help you sort this place out. Besides, I've had enough of that maggot-shagging sea."

"It did not seem to suit you," Avelynne said with that expression she got when studying people. "Too vast, uncontainable, and exposed?"

"Exactly," Hale said, standing up to stretch. "Sander, remember what you said when we were on the Hethklian ship? When I felt weird and surrounded by that endless amount of shitty water?"

"Hm. I'm afraid not?"

"You said, 'we'll be home soon, and you can train with all the weapons in the armoury or eat all the newly made oakenberry pie in the great hall,' remember that?" He grasped one of Eleksander's loose braids and rolled it between his fingers. "Well, *that* is what I want, love. And I want to do it with you."

"I'd like that," Eleksander said, somewhat choked.

Hale let go of the braid and rolled his shoulders, making his bunched muscles dance in a very rehearsed way. "Not to mention that what I do best is protect and defend. So, I'll stay here and protect and defend you."

"My heroic knight," Eleksander said, admiring every visible part of the man he loved.

"Not a knight. I asked Taferia about titles," Hale said, pushing his chest forward. "When someone without a drop of royal blood weds a royal, the non-royal one becomes either the Queen's Consort or the King's Consort. The last one being the case with us, of course."

"I see," Eleksander said. "It's a handsome title but perhaps a little long?"

Only when he had said that did he realise that Hale had assumed they would marry. And the idea hadn't made either of them flinch or question it. It simply felt... right. Should that scare him? By the waters, how did it not scare Hale? But then, when Hale had decided on something, he didn't waver.

Eleksander jolted as something else hit him. If they didn't wed, he would always be the solitary ruler and Hale merely his lover. That wasn't right. They would both rule, even if Hale only wanted a small portion of the burden and the glory.

"I don't think 'the King's Consort' is too long. I like it," Hale said, blissfully unaware of Eleksander's serious realisations. "Consorting sounds like another word for shagging."

Avelynne tilted her head. "I believe you're thinking of 'cavorting,' actually."

Eleksander's worries melted away. "Cavorting or consorting, either way I shall ensure you do plenty of it," he said, a rush coursing through him.

"Ugh. We can hear you, you know," Sabina said. "We're *right here.*"

Avelynne and Aurea, meanwhile, both looked like proud and delighted mothers.

"I talked to Taferia about something else too," Hale said, suddenly serious.

He was so relieved that Hale had found an older Wood-lander to run things by and to confide in. "Oh, yes? What was that, then?"

"We should build a statue of your mother. Put one in each county and one here outside the court."

Any remainder of that aroused rush vanished. "My mother?"

"Mm. I mean Queen Lea. Although I'm sure Mrs Aetholo deserves a statue too for raising you finnicky three brats."

"That's a good idea," Sabina said. "Lea was the first person to stand up to Lothiam and his line. She figured out what he was doing, she founded the Twelve to stop him, and she birthed the worthiest leader this nation has ever seen."

Eleksander couldn't look at her when she said the part about him. "I like the idea of erecting statues of her too. I have a condition, however." This was good practise for his upcoming deal-striking with the council. "We make it a statue of her but on its plaque note that it honours *everyone* who perished due to Lothiam's, and his forebears', behaviour. Like our lost sailors and," he stroked Hale's cheek, "your parents. Who could no doubt have been saved if there were educated physicians, and the aid supplies they'd need, out in the counties. Something which we will invest in as we rule."

Hale's lips parted and his jaw worked. No words came, though. Instead, he only smiled and for Eleksander, it gilded every part of this rough and ravaged continent.

"Well," Aurea said, ending the comfortable silence that had reigned. "That's a lot of big decisions in one night.

Perhaps we should go to bed early and digest everything with a long sleep?"

Hale laughed. "Sure. We lads will go to our bedchamber and you lasses to yours, inviting Aurea of course, and then we'll sleep. That's what we'll be doing in those beds."

With that Hale slapped Eleksander's rear. Eleksander considered that they would have to be more considerate around others, who may be sex-repulsed or easily offended. Because if there was one thing that he and his friends seemed to be absorbed with ever since they stopped being in mortal danger, or steeped in unrequited love, it was bedplay. Not that he was complaining.

Avelynne smirked and said, "To bed we all go, then."

They all said goodnight and filtered out towards their bedchambers. Hale had been right, Aurea followed Sabina and Avelynne into their room and suggestive murmurs as well as giggling could be heard as the door shut.

As he walked hand in hand with Hale to their bedchamber, Eleksander quietly told him what his requirements for taking the throne would be. Despite Hale's enthusiasm for each of the four demands, Eleksander wondered if the council would acquiesce? If not, he and Hale must stake out a different future for themselves, for they both agreed that he couldn't be crowned without these terms being accepted.

Then Hale pulled him into bed with a hoarse whisper of, "I love you, my clever, brave Lakelander," and all thoughts left Eleksander's mind.

Chapter Thirty-Seven

DIVING IN WITHOUT REGRETS

Closing the door behind her and so shielding them away in their little bedchamber, Sabina pulsed with nerves, affection, and arousal.

Whispering wicked promises about what she was going to do to them, Avelynne lit a candle and, shielding it with one beautiful hand as she moved, put it on the ablutions table.

With a delighted giggle, Aurea went over to the beds. Without having to discuss it, Sabina helped her move the two beds together to make one big one. She loved how they so often were of one mind and ready to take action.

Avelynne stayed by the table. She fingered the necklace at her throat, and said, "We are doing the correct thing, are we not?"

"Do you mean..." Aurea indicated the bed.

"No," Avelynne said. "I meant about the sailing. It is all right that we aren't staying to help Eleksander and Hale rule, right?"

"Aye," Sabina said. "We must live *our* lives. We are doing the right thing."

"Of course, snowdrop." Avelynne's tense body language melted, and she crossed the room until she was near enough to pull Sabina onto the joined beds and kiss her.

"And remember, nothing is set in stone," Aurea said, undoing the laces of her britches. "You're free. The world is full of options for you to pick from now." She moved onto the bed with such calm, unassuming confidence. The same trait that Sabina had first fallen for with this woman.

More laces were undone, straps unstrapped, garments tugged down. Mere moments later, that feeling of four hands on her body overtook Sabina.

Even though they were too far away from the harbour for it to be more than a hallucination, she thought she could hear waves and smell the sea air. Kisses were peppered across her breasts and over her heart. That heart which was so light that it might simply soar out of her chest and head for the Qetesh and Parataxia and yank their anchors and mooring ropes up.

There was no doubt. This was the right decision.

Like a wave, she rolled one of her lovers over, then parted a pair of warm, trembling thighs and dove in.

Chapter Thirty-Eight

SHALL HE BE KING?

The morning sunlight was uninvited, but Eleksander was finally up and facing it. It had been hard to get out of bed and equally difficult to wash and dress. Why would he want to start a day like this one when the option was to stay here, safe, warm, and in the arms of the man he loved? And Hale was being as distracting as only he could, pulling out all the stops to get every bit of attention and affection Eleksander had. Not to mention every bit of arousal.

Now, though, Eleksander was ready to go break his fast. Then, it was time to give the council his ultimatum. Unhelpfully, his stomach roiled.

"I'm not sure I'll be able to eat anything," he said, pulling his boots on.

"What?" Hale said, stopping in shock with the tunic halfway over his head. "Unable to eat. Um. What about drinking something? Just to have something to power you?"

"Mm. I'll try."

He didn't fancy the odds of keeping anything down, though.

When in the great hall, the mingling odours of porridge, boiled eggs, oakenberry marmalade, and other foods dished up along the table assaulted his nose. Why couldn't he just get this meeting over with?

Aurea, Sabina, and Avelynne were already there. The latter put her tea down and patted the bench for him and Hale to sit next to her. He kissed the top of her sleekly brushed hair before sitting down and pouring himself some milk and dolloping in some birch sap for sweetness. Around him, the members of the council ate and spoke. The scene looked like just another morning, not the day when he asked for the throne, and could be denied it if they didn't like his demands.

Time trickled by like thick honey over level ground.

Half an hour later, breakfast was cleared away and Eleksander downed his sap-ladened milk. A few people filtered out to answer calls of nature, including Eleksander, and then they were all back for the meeting. The smell of Hale's recently devoured goat's cheese sandwich still lingered at their end of the table, making bile rise in Eleksander's throat.

Everyone was still speaking in groups, for example the baroness and the duchess, who sat arguing over some band of nomads who had settled on their counties' shared border and whose responsibility they were.

Eleksander couldn't stand it any longer. He went to the head of the table and borrowed Kae's trick of clapping his hands together once. It worked. All eyes were on him.

"Good morrow." He schooled his voice, which was threatening to creep up in pitch. "This meeting is called for me to either accept or refuse the throne of Cavarra and I'd like to answer without preamble. Get to the meat of it, as they say here in the Centre."

The baron, who was feeding his iceboar some egg he had squirreled away in a pocket, bellowed, "Sounds like you're pre-ambling to me, dear lad. What say you? Fancy a crown?"

No one had a right to be that merry and laidback right now. Eleksander glared at the egg. Or so unhygienic.

Putting away unkind thoughts, he squared his shoulders. "I do accept. *If* a few conditions are met."

The warden narrowed her eyes. "I see. What might these conditions be, then?"

"There are four of them," he said, a little too quietly.

The grand countess leaned forward. "Oh, do speak up."

He would have to work on getting her respect. Or at least her politeness.

"I have four conditions," he repeated. "I'll start with one I think you'll find acceptable. I want official court roles for everyone in the second wave and for Aurea to have some sort of diplomatic title. Just so that if something happens to me, they cannot all be side-lined but will still have a say in Cavarra's governing."

Kae looked to the others of the Twelve, who nodded. "We find that reasonable."

After some mumbling in smaller groups, everyone else approved too.

"Wonderful," Eleksander said, his stomach still lurching. "Condition number two is your support in my plan to put most of the tithes from the counties back into to the counties. To take care of the poor, the orphans, and the sick. To educate and to house. No more spending all the tithe coin on wars or on pomp and festivities."

To his surprise, everyone agreed with that, although the duchess and duke did so through gritted teeth and with scowls. They'd have to fund their own social events in the future.

Eleksander steeled himself. This next one was going to be as popular as a bread-and-butter pudding filled with nails.

"The third condition is that after five years of me ruling, we will have set up a system for the citizens of Cavarra to vote for their leader. Like the Woodlanders do, but on a national scale. So, more like the Hethklish."

"Pardon? Vote on who will be the crownbearer?" the grand countess spluttered. "No. We honour Cavarra's choice. The land has chosen its leaders by favouring the three bloodlines. For example, Lea's, meaning *yours*."

There was the argument he had been waiting for. "That's just it. We have no proof that Cavarra chose those bloodlines. It's an old myth, furthered by the royals. For example, Lothiam used Vattendal's spell combined with the Centre's robustness and lack of silver beasts to prove that Cavarra favoured him - when in fact this place thrived because he leeched coin out of the counties and spent them on the Centre."

Furious remarks could be heard from more than one direction.

Eleksander could still taste milk and birch sap, but the sweetness was now souring on his dry tongue. "Look, monarchy and the three bloodlines have had their advantages. At this point, though, the people of this nation must be heard." He looked to Sabina and Avelynne, who had given him this idea. "For too long, Cavarra's population has done as it was told and followed tradition. It should be offered the power and freedom to choose."

The duke threw his arms out in a despairing gesture. "By the waters, how would that even work?"

"I'm not sure. Which is why we would need five years and all our minds set on the task. If you want, I could be one of the candidates when the voting starts." He picked up the speed as at least six members seemed about to interrupt him. "Thus, if the people felt I'd done a good job in the past five years, they could vote for me. That way, I would know I ruled because my subjects thought I was the best one for the task, not because of the blood in my veins."

Arguments broke out like forest fires.

The Northerners both spun their heads towards the warden before the baroness shouted, "You have influenced him somehow, Woodlander. I see your work at the heart of this."

The warden only laughed, so loud in fact, that the disputes between the Peakdwellers and the Twelve members were drowned out.

The duchess could still be heard though, as she continuously called Eleksander a merchant changeling who had betrayed his noble blood. The two tutors, whom everyone usually ignored, were speaking too by the looks of their moving mouths, but they had no chance to be heard. Finally, there was something that Hathleen and Myle cared about enough to get involved. Eleksander wished it hadn't been this, though.

Hale banged a fist on the table. "You trusted Eleksander to find you new lands and to either negotiate with foreign races or to slaughter them, *in your name*. But you won't trust him, your heir, with this?"

"Those things are not comparable, dear child," Kae called back to him with a disciplining tone.

"Child? I'm nineteen," Hale barked back.

More shouts joined the fray and soon it was merely one big clamour.

Eleksander steadied himself, imagining his mother's voice as she reminded him to breathe slow during centering practice. He placed a hand on his middle, feeling the breath move it. Then, he deepened his voice and let it come from the depth of his stomach. "Enough!"

Everyone quieted. The only sound in the high-ceilinged hall now was the echo of that loud, deep, and clear *enough*.

Until the cursed iceboar began casually snuffling around the floor for any dropped egg, of course.

The humans were rapt, though, and that was all he needed.

"I will not take the throne without all my demands being met," Eleksander said, less loud but equally clear. "If you do not allow voting in five years, you need to find another heir. There are two others with royal blood, I believe."

The grimaces around the room told him that he had judged the situation correctly. He was their most palatable choice. Mainly because he was the only one not at death's door.

"I suppose we must stomach that," the grand count said through tight jaws. "After five years, perchance we can find a good solution to how this 'vote' shall take shape."

Eleksander tried not to smile. The grand count meant to change his mind during those years. Little did he know of Eleksander's strategy. On their return, he'd ask Avelynne and Sabina to write a report on Hethklish voting to provide something that the second wave could emulate. Then he'd show the plans to representatives of the people, middle-class as well as working-class, and set the voting system up, with or without the county leaders and the Twelve. He would drag this council into the future if he had to. But his elders didn't need to know that. These people knew only manipulation and lust for power. Well, he had seen plenty of merchant negotiations growing up, he could play that game.

To amuse himself, Eleksander tried to emulate how his birthfather usually responded to the grand count. He didn't go as far as airily gesturing with a bejewelled hand, but he did raise his eyebrows and with slow, irreverent, regal elegance said, "Indeed. In exactly five years to the day, *I* will provide the council with a solution."

He almost sounded like the duke, he realised, but his own voice was stronger and warmer. More red-blooded human. He found he liked that about himself.

The warden was scratching the baroness's snowbear behind the ear, much to the baroness's chagrin, and said, "I counted three demands there, lad. What's the fourth?"

He had saved the safest bet for last. After all, Vattendal had seen this one come true with his farsight.

"The throne. I mean the actual physical seat in the

castle. Lothiam's line has had that golden monstrosity up high on its dais for generations. I won't go near it." Eleksander kept his chin lifted, not a youth asking, but a grown monarch ordering. "I want a simpler one and I'd like it closer to the ground so people can come nearer. Oh, and it must be made of copper."

Next to him, Hale gave a hum of recognition. "Copper for the Aetholos. Nice."

The grand countess leaned forward. "What was that?"

"My future King's Consort," Eleksander said, unable to resist trying it out. "He pointed out that the emblem for my family is a copper shield. I will rule as the heir of Queen Lea and Duke Phamaro, but I'll do it on a throne of Aetholo copper."

"Highly irregular," the grand count griped.

"I see what you're thinking, lad," the baron said. "But we want Cavarrians to see that you are a king of royal bloodline, carrying on that heritage. It will make them feel secure and trust in your leadership, despite your young age and all the turmoil lately. That golden throne is a symbol for continuity."

"No," said a smooth voice. "We start a new future and a new way of ruling Cavarra. It should be on a new throne. Why not create one that honours our growing merchant class and the people who raised our king?"

Eleksander did a doubletake. Of all the people to say something like that, Duke Phamaro was the last one he would have expected.

"Oh. Well, yes, exactly," Eleksander said. "I'll leave you to discuss whether to accept my terms. I'll return in an hour."

"And don't try to figure out ways to negotiate," Hale said as he stood. "This is the deal. Take it or leave it."

Hale held the hall's heavy doors open for Eleksander, his gaze boring into each leader of the counties and member of the Twelve in turn.

As Eleksander left, he signalled to Avelynne, Aurea, and Sabina to stay. They could be his infiltrators. Then, he took Hale's hand and held it tight as they drifted aimlessly down the hallway. What were they saying in that room? Would they accede to his requests? Had he pushed too much too soon?

"Let's get some air," Hale said, leading them to the nearest door to the courtyard.

When out in the crisp morning, they both took deep lungfuls and blinked at the pale sunshine.

"You did really well," Hale said. "You asserted yourself and showed them who you are and who you can be."

Eleksander held his middle, his stomach still painful. "Thank you."

"Now, you can relax and wait for them to fall in line and toss that crown to you." Hale leaned against the stone wall and, shading his eyes with his hand, watched some crows in the apple trees. "In fact, you can probably have them make you a nice copper one if you fancy. Lothiam's gold one won't fit you anyway."

Hale was so unworried and made everything seem so easy. It was lovely just to be in the presence of that.

"I suppose you're right." Was his stomach settling a bit?

"I am," Hale said. After a moment, he snorted out a laugh. "That snooty grand count thinks he can put a stopper in your voting scheme. That's good. He and the others who're against it can stay busy doing that while we get on with making the plans."

Eleksander regarded Hale. He had seen through the grand count too? "Once again, you're absolutely right." With that, he took Hale's hand and fervently kissed its scarred knuckles. This would work. They would rule well together. They would *love* well together too.

"Of course I'm right," Hale said. "Even a sightless silver beast finds its target once in a while."

"Ha, I haven't heard that saying in ages." The bright blue sky above them was as free of clouds as it was of silver beasts. "Let's go for a walk, my love, and discuss how the voting will work."

"That's my lad," Hale said before leading them towards the gate out into the grounds.

Chapter Thirty-Nine

FREE TIME

When the Hall of Explorers' oversized sundial claimed an hour had passed, Hale led Eleksander back to the great hall. There, he stood by Eleksander's side, so close their arms pushed together. The council, barring Avelynne, Aurea, and Sabina, were all grim-faced.

Slowly, Kae stood up and Hale felt Eleksander stiffen.

There was a hint of a smile on that stark, lined face of Kae's, though, and it calmed him at least. It didn't seem to do much for his poor Eleksander.

"After heated discussion and deliberation, you have been granted your demands," Kae said. "And thus, we have been granted a new king. Also, a king's consort as a bonus, I gather."

Aurea started applauding and, one by one, everyone along that extensive table joined in. Even the Duke and Duchess of the Lakelands patted their hands against the table in some sort of aloof version of clapping. No, wait, not everyone. Not the Ironholds. They probably weren't even able to applaud. It'd probably fracture their frail hand bones. Still, they didn't look quite as dour and sour as normal.

The applause rose, filling the hall and his ears.

The stiff Eleksander seemed to sway, so Hale wrapped an arm around him.

Eleksander turned to him and with a stunned expression said, "Fancy building a new future for our nation with me?"

"Sure," Hale said, his chest swelling with pride. "I've got some free time."

Chapter Forty

CROWNKNIGHTS AND CORONATIONS

With the meeting over, Avelynne was walking with Sabina and Aurea to Naseer's quarters. The other two were discussing how happy they were that Eleksander's demands were met. She, however, was more relieved that Eleksander now clearly wanted to be king. She'd feared he would agree to it simply because he felt he should. But no, yesterday as well as today, there was clear enthusiasm in his demeanour. Especially a moment ago when he and Hale had rushed off to... celebrate.

When the three of them were outside Naseer's room, there was no need to knock. The man himself swung open the door. "Hello ladies. I thought I heard steps coming my way."

Aurea looked about to jump up and throw her arms around his neck, but their strict hierarchy wouldn't let her do that to a former captain. "I am so glad to see you up. And with some colour in your cheeks too," she chirped instead.

Avelynne agreed that Octavius Naseer was less ashen

faced. However, the tall man drooped so that he was nigh their height and his cheeks were gaunter than before, making his aging scars stand out like a tiny spine laying along each cheekbone.

"Not as glad as I am," Naseer said. "Clearly my body wasn't prepared for Cavarrian agues and couldn't resist them as well as my young sailors could. Now, I am much improved but also famished and exceedingly bored of my bed."

"Come with us to the great hall, then," Sabina said. "We'll ask for some bread and cheese for you."

"And, if they have some, those buttered parsnips you like," Avelynne added, trying to be the best hostess possible.

"Marvellous." He closed his door behind him. "Let's go right now."

They sat around the hall's oblong table, Naseer catching up on the meals he had missed during his convalescence while Sabina, Aurea, and herself took turns filling him in on everything. He listened and advised them to do pretty much what they had already done. A useful reassurance, to Avelynne's mind.

After a while, Naseer pushed his empty plate away. "Ah. That was superb. After eating only broth for days, chewing was a welcome change."

"I can imagine. I'm glad to see you regain your appetite, Captain," Sabina said after swallowing a mouthful of oakenberry juice. Avelynne had ordered a tankard for them each, to keep Naseer company as he ate.

"No need to call me 'captain' anymore. In fact, after everything we have gone through, you should call me Octavius." He leaned his forearms on the table. "So, when will you sail?"

Avelynne and Sabina busied themselves with their oakenberry juice.

"We haven't decided," Aurea said. "We want to go soon, as the sailors need to get back home. However, Sab and Ave should probably be by Sander's side for a while. At least until he's crowned."

Avelynne drank to hide her relief. She had worried Aurea was chomping at the bit to set sail today or tomorrow morning. Clearly, she had seen that Avelynne and Sabina wanted to delay.

"The sailors will surely understand a short delay," Naseer said. "I must speak to them today anyway and can bring it up then."

Aurea nervously tapped her tankard. "You think they will be amenable? They've been out at sea for a long time."

"I'm sure you and I can make them understand."

The doors creaked open and Taferia poked her head in. "Ah, there you are. Sorry for the intrusion but as soon as you four have time, I need to speak to you. It's about your future titles."

They got up from the table and moved closer to the doors.

Titles. Avelynne understood why Eleksander had insisted on them having court positions, and they may be necessary one day. However, she had just gotten used to not being a countess. The idea of another title made her uneasy.

"This is so very exciting," Aurea said in her usual gleeful, rapid way. "I've been a printer, a second in command of ships, a daughter, and even a betrothed lover once. But I've never had an honorary title given to me by another nation before. What will it be?"

Avelynne had snagged on a word there. Betrothed? There was so much she still had to learn about Aurea and that should no doubt be worrying. Yet, she found it nothing less than thrilling.

"Since the meeting, I've been visiting the other council members and polled them on title suggestions," Taferia said. "For you Hethklish we found something that was agreed upon by all council members. We kept it simple and stayed with 'diplomat.' Will that work for you?"

"Of course. Clear and simple is always good," Aurea said.

Taferia was mainly focused on Naseer, though. "As long as it is acceptable to you to have the same title as someone younger. Someone who also used to be your subordinate?"

"Certainly," he said. "I'm glad there will be two of us. 'Cavarrian Diplomats for Hethekla.' It has a nice ring to it, doesn't it?" He bumped Aurea's arm and she agreed.

"Good. We'll make it official during the next council meeting. Now..." Taferia trailed off, meditatively rubbing underneath her chin. While Naseer had lost weight, Taferia had gained quite a bit. It suited her. "The problem that we ran into," she finally said, "was your titles, Sabina and Avelynne."

"Ah. Aurea and I shall give you privacy to discuss that

while we go speak to the other Hethklish," Naseer said. "I'm sure we can convince them that they should stay and witness something as unique as a coronation."

As they left, Aurea's hand brushed first Sabina's arm and then Avelynne's lower back. That one touch was enough to make Avelynne want to clutch Aurea and kiss her dizzy.

She composed herself and followed Sabina and Taferia past the doorway as to be out of the way of the servants who had come in to clean the hall. As the servants worked, they sang something in perfect four-part harmony. It took a moment before Avelynne recognised it as a lullaby from the Peaks. One of the servants, a blonde about her own age, was with child, explaining the choice of song. It was beautiful and she wished someone had sung lullabies to her when she was a child. If Hale and Eleksander decided to have children, she would sing to their little heir.

"As I mentioned," Taferia raised her voice enough to be heard but not to disturb the servants, "we have come on to rocky ground regarding your titles. We cannot pick usual Cavarrian ones, as they are either royal or used in the four counties."

"And I bet the county leaders were adamant that we couldn't use their titles," Sabina said.

"Very. So, we, or rather I," she said, sounding embarrassed, "came up with a new word signifying how you will be our future crownbearer's eyes and ears out in the world as well as his extra pair of hands here at court. Crownknight."

"Crownknight," Avelynne said, rolling the word in her mouth. "Crownknight Avelynne Ironhold." It sounded less vague than countess and more useful too. It was a title that sounded *earned.* "Yes. I like that a great deal. Thank you."

"Aye, it's good," Sabina said. Then she shook her head. "Imagine me with a noble title. Next you'll tell me goats are to be given gem-studded horns."

"I know how you feel," Taferia said with amusement in her voice. "Our soon to be King Eleksander has asked me to be the top advisor to our soon to be King's Consort Hale. *First Royal Advisor Taferia Palm.* Can you believe it?"

"First royal advisor?" Avelynne said. "That is such wonderful news. Both for you and for Hale and Eleksander."

Taferia bowed her head. "Thank you."

Avelynne had meant it from the bottom of her heart. This considerate and sensible Woodlander was going to be a wonderful aide for Hale. It was a relief to know Taferia would be there for Hale and Eleksander when she couldn't be.

"Taferia," she began cautiously. "You know that the deaths of our sailors and everything we have experienced has weighed on us, right?"

"Of course." Taferia Palm looked offended down to the bone. "I was there. By your side."

"I know. I also know you were the one to stop Hale from drinking so much, making him talk instead. Can I prevail upon you to do that again? They both need to process the grief and guilt. And to find ways to honour the sailors we lost."

"Agreed. I will do what it takes to make our royals open up and deal with what happened."

Would she ever get used to hearing Eleksander and

Hale be called royals? That reminded her of what she needed to ask.

"Oh, Taferia, there's another thing. We've just been discussing something with Aurea and Naseer, I mean Octavius. They are trying to convince the Hethklish sailors to stay a little longer in Cavarra so we can be part of the coronation. Is there any way the ceremony can be pushed forward?"

Taferia frowned. "Hm. So you can attend it?"

"Yes. I know coronations take a great deal of planning and have historically happened months after an heir was named. However..." Avelynne *was* going to ask for this, she was allowed to do so, and by the stars, she would do it. "I think Cavarra needs leadership sooner. I also know that our future king needs us by his side on that big day. So, it makes sense to have the coronation as soon as possible."

Taferia went from frowning to pensively pursing her lips.

Avelynne pushed on. "It also means that the county leaders shan't need to travel the long way back to their seats, only to return soon. I mean, I'm not saying that the coronation has to be tomorrow. But perhaps within the next week or so?"

"How does seven to eight days sound?" a voice behind them asked.

They turned to see Eleksander approaching.

Avelynne put a hand to her chest. "You startled me, Sander. When did you get here?"

"Never mind when," Sabina said. "How did you do it without us hearing your steps?"

"The Duchess of the Lakelands gave me these," he said,

pointing down to his feet which were clad in a pair of beautiful silk shoes.

Sabina bent to peer at them. "Pretty but about as practical as a rowboat in a desert. They still don't fully explain your stealth, though. I'm trained to hear any approaching footfalls."

Eleksander shrugged those broad shoulders of his. "The singing servants masked some of the sound, I guess? Anyway, I heard those last words of your conversation and I repeat my answer. Seven to eight days."

"You mean your coronation is booked? To take place in a week?" Taferia said without hiding her incredulity.

"It seems so," Eleksander said. "Before coming here, I was summoned to the guest quarters in order to speak to the county leaders. They want the coronation to happen as soon as possible to save on travel time, as Avelynne intimated." He paused to smile at her. "The baron and baroness then brought up the topic of my copper throne. They have just sent a messenger raven to their coppersmiths to start working on it, hence the seven to eight—"

"The North is making your throne?" a clearly chocked Sabina interrupted. "What did the other leaders say about that?"

"They were busy fighting over who would get to give me and Hale other gifts," Eleksander said with obvious embarrassment. "The Woodlanders will craft Hale's throne and crown. The Peakdwellers want to make my crown and a new set of royal regalia. The Lakelanders want to shower me with art and decorations for the castle as well as clothes. Like these shoes." Eleksander lifted a foot and waved it about.

So, while they were watching Naseer eat, Eleksander and Hale hadn't been allowed to celebrate but been swooped up by the county leaders. Avelynne wasn't even a little surprised.

"I'm sure they all think they can buy me, or at least some favours. But we know they can't." Eleksander stopped admiring his shoes. "Anyway, the baron said that their seasoned, quick coppersmiths use magic in their work and have heaps of supplies on hand. More importantly, they have their smithy on the border between the North and the Centre, only a couple of hours ride from here. Therefore, with working full days and nights, the throne should be here in a week."

"Full days and nights?" Avelynne asked.

Eleksander sobered. "I have ordered the baron and baroness to pay the coppersmiths exceedingly generously. Which they claimed they would've done anyway."

"They probably would have," Sabina said. "Despite their other flaws, the baron and baroness are known to be fair and rewarding of hard work."

"Back to us and you attending my coronation," he said. "I've been hoping you could be there, but I didn't want to put pressure on you by asking."

"You can ask us anything," Avelynne said, stroking his arm. "We are your Crownknights and so at your command."

"You will always be my equals. My second family, closest friends, future travelling companions, and, most of all... my role models. Never at my command," Eleksander said.

And of course, that was true, she could feel it in her very marrow.

"Traveling companions?" Sabina said with, for her, unusual exuberance. "Good! I can't wait to travel with our marvellous king and bring him to meet new trade partners."

Taferia, no doubt focused on the here and now, seemed less thrilled. "A week? The people won't appreciate the amount of pomp that'll need to be cut. We cannot train ravens to do tricks, build rows of seats in the royal court-yard, or have a thousand cakes from every part of Cavarra."

"Well, as the future king, surely I get to decide when my coronation is? We'll simply have to create whatever pomp we have time for. Depending on if the Hethklish sailors agree to stay that long, of course," he added with a worried look. "Then we can set a date later in the year and make that a day of celebration each year, or even a fortnight long celebration. We can have our trained ravens and thousands of cakes then."

Taferia hummed. "Not a bad idea."

"Actually, I quite look forward to that now," Eleksander said. "Cavarra can use a long celebration to mark the end both of Lothiam's reign and the plague of the silver beasts. A celebration where the question of governing is already settled, so there's no worry or debate." He straightened his back, looking quite... well, regal. "I'll be crowned and then we can start planning a celebration where the focus isn't on me but on Cavarra's bright new future."

"We'll leave you two to discuss this," Sabina said. "We should go see how the Hethklish are getting on."

Yes, they should. Avelynne was now very invested in

attending the coronation. It must be possible to convince both the Hethklish sailors to stay and the council to help move the coronation. Or had they already pushed everyone around them too far too fast? Could a coronation even be planned within a week?

As she waved to Taferia and kissed Eleksander's cheek, she forced her worries down. She cracked her neck, held her head high, and strode after Sabina. Trying was the only way to find out, and she was ready for the challenge.

Chapter Forty-One

THE ROYAL CASTLE

Hale ran a hand over his scalp, lingering at each scar or overlong strand of hair. He was meant to be outside sparring with his old mentor Ghar, who had come over from the Woodlands, but instead he stood here in the royal castle's throne room.

Six days had passed since the decision was made to push the coronation forward. So, tomorrow, Eleksander would be king. There would be a day and evening of coronation celebrations. Then, the following morning, Sabina and Avelynne would sail away with the Hethklish. Everything was happening so shittingly fast.

His hand dropped to his side. Only one day until everything started anew. And here he was, uselessly fixed to the spot in this echoing, lonely chamber. Everyone else had a task. The servants were busy working. Avelynne, Aurea, and Sabina split their time between preparing for their journey and welcoming the guests who had been able to make it in time for the coronation. The rest of the council were busy arguing over flowers and food, despite that it had all been decided days ago and anything they said now would be ignored. Hale should've gone along with Eleksander who, together with a squadron of royal knights, had ridden to the shipyard to meet the workers there and invite them to the coronation, an idea that was as brilliant as it was late. Still, they'd find room for another fourscore of people.

Hale slow-spun on the spot, taking in the extremely long throne room which was quite bare. The tapestries and decorations of the past royal line had quickly been removed and Lothiam's pus-ugly throne taken away to be melted back into useful gold. In mere moments, the new copper throne would be brought in. Next to it would be placed a throne for him, one Eleksander wouldn't describe. Apparently, it was a surprise. Hopefully it would at least be comfortable. What else would they fill this room with? For the ceremony, the walls would be lined with tables ladened with food and brim-full bottles. Had anyone thought about what would hang on the walls, though? Maybe they could hang some weapons and shields? Or a tapestry of the second wave using their golden magic to slay monstrosities? No, that took ages to weave. And might be boastful? He'd ask Eleksander. A discussion during their coronation garb fitting yesterday had shown beyond any doubt that Eleksander had better taste than him.

Through the open door he heard servants outside talking about the ceremony and how much they had to do before tomorrow afternoon. Hale had asked if he could help them with anything earlier and they had bowed to him, *bowed to him*, and told him to rest and enjoy himself. It was odd as maggot-shit and twice as uncomfortable.

He took a step towards the open door. Maybe they'd let him sweep the floors if he said it was a royal decree?

A voice that wasn't a servant rang out. "You there. Where might my mapmaker be?"

Hearing the Woodlands accent, Hale had at first thought it was Ghar coming to find him. But no, the voice was female and more authoritative. The Warden of the Woodlands. His knees weakened a tad. The servants told her where he was, and she stomped into the throne room with her usual air of someone with more pressing tasks to be finished elsewhere.

"Young Hawthorn, there you are. I wanted to swing by and wish you luck tomorrow." She hooked her thumbs on her weapons harness. "About time we got another Woodlander ruling this nation. It's been three generations since the last time."

The last time had been a Woodlander *woman* marrying a Northern *man*, though. Cold sweat broke out all over him and his ribcage tightened.

He firmed up his stance. It didn't matter if she and other Woodlanders disapproved of his love, it was his and it was right. "It'll be the first time a Woodlander rules with someone of their own gender, though."

During a long beat of silence, she squinted at him. "Been worrying you, has it? I can see why, to be sure. Our kind haven't been very open to that sort of thing. Luckily, you can change that."

"Luckily?"

"Sure. You know as well as I do that nature works best when it has all kinds in it. Show the Woodlands that your kind is as good and natural as theirs."

Theirs. Not ours. Huh. Why had the warden never married?

"Anyway," she said, "best be going. I need to claim the coins I won from the baron playing cards last night and then send some letters back home. I'll see you at the ceremony, boyo. Make the Woodlands proud." She marched off, adding, "As you seem to keep doing."

He stood staring after her for a long time, the icy clenching of his ribcage slowly dissipating, making him light and warm as summer winds. He yanked himself out of the sappy softness. There was work to be done. His man would be crowned. Then they could set about improving Cavarra and open all those narrow minds. It would be good to get stuck in and stop this shitty waiting about.

There was one hitch, though. A deep-rooted niggle. Things would not be official, would not be right. Although, there was a way he could fix that. And why not do it at the same time as the coronation? Why not make sure it was all tied up neatly on one glorious day? They could make everything perfect. If Eleksander would say yes. Shitting silver beasts, what if he didn't?

Awed gasps and whispers from the servants outside told him that someone even more impressive than the warden had arrived. Hale rushed to nonchalantly lean against a wall and arranged his face into the cocky smile he knew Eleksander liked.

"Good morning, my love," the heir to the throne said as he strode in.

Eleksander kissed him hello and Hale took a firm grasp of the other man's waist, to keep him from leaving him taskless and alone in this empty place again.

"I met Ghar outside and he said you hadn't arrived for your sparring session?"

"Right. Shit," Hale said. "I need to find him and apologise."

"No need. Ghar seemed happy for the postponement and said he was going to get some food and would find you later."

"All right." Hale thought hard. He needed to talk about something else before he launched into the big question. "So, um, how did you fare with the dockworkers?"

"Quite well, I'd say." Those perfect oak-brown eyes of his lit up. "They seemed receptive and not too intimidated to ask questions. I got the chance to be honest with them about our past and how I plan to be a different ruler. One who listens." Eleksander suddenly squirmed. "Do you mind easing your hold on my middle a bit, my sweet?"

"Shitting silver beasts, I'm so sorry." Hale loosened his hands and rubbed where they had gripped.

"It's all right, I'm fine. You seem tense, though. Fretting about tomorrow?"

"No. Not really. I'm nervous about right now."

Eleksander jerked his head back. "Whatever for?"

"I have something to ask you."

"Oh? What is it?"

Shit. How was he going to phrase this? He should've started this better, should've planned it. "I, um, well, tomorrow you'll be king, and I'm meant to become the king's consort."

"Meant to?"

"Yes. I mean, I won't really be unless we're..." He couldn't finish the sentence but had a feeling that Eleksander knew where he was going with this. Why else would his throat bob like that and those eyes, still distractingly perfect, widen so much?

Hale tried again. "Unless we're... wed to one another."

Eleksander's eyes stayed wide, unblinking. "Uh. I thought we, *I*, could make a royal decree that made an exemption?"

"You could. If you want that. I'd like, well, to go the customary way. I know we're young and we haven't known each other for ages but," he tried to slow down, to not stumble over the words, "Cavarrian royal marriages are usually set between people younger than us, right?"

"Right," Eleksander croaked.

"And often ones that barely know each other. You and I have faced shit-heaps together and been friends before we were lovers."

Eleksander still wasn't blinking. "True."

"And no Cavarrian royals have ever taken the throne without being married. Tomorrow, there will be guests—including your family—and food, booze, a royal advisor with authority to swear things into law, and festive decorations everywhere. Isn't that what you need for a wedding?"

"It is," Eleksander said, dragging the two words out.

Hale would've given anything to be able to read people right now.

"I wouldn't want to get married without Ave and Sab," Eleksander said. "I'd like them to be the ones to lay the wedding flowers under our feet. So, we either wait to wed until they come back from Hethekla, or we do it before the coronation tomorrow. But sweetheart, isn't it a little short notice? Won't people mind?"

"P-people mind?" Hale stuttered. "Does that mean that you don't mind? I mean... that you want to?"

Eleksander gave his sweet, crooked smile. "Not if you're asking like that."

Hale's heart leapt. He focused on what to do. Shit, what were the traditional steps and words? Recollecting as he went, he dropped to his knees, bowed his head, and spread his arms open. "Eleksander Aetholo, would you grant me the privilege of being your spouse? Your companion in all hardships as well as all celebrations? Your staff to lean on and your blanket to be sheltered in?"

"I will." Eleksander also kneeled and took the same position, repeating the same words. Although, he only got two thirds in before Hale interrupted with, "Yes! Stop talking so I can kiss you."

Eleksander complied. The kiss was intense, deep, and lasting until they were both breathless. Hale threw himself into it with one thought repeating in his mind: *he chose me, and he wants to keep me.*

When the kiss ended, Hale found his vision blurry. Thank the trees that Ghar wasn't here to tease Hale for going soft. Not that he cared. He would gladly be soft if it meant being this happy.

They stayed kneeling in front of each other, holding hands, and everything was... perfect.

Until the joy on Eleksander's face dimmed. "Can we just decide to do this, though? Add a wedding to a coronation without asking anyone? With one day's notice?"

Hale surveyed his treasured one. The way Eleksander's shapely brows furrowed, the way his strong jaw moved when he was uneasy, those soft lips that would soon quirk into that lopsided, shy smile – at least if Hale managed his task of making him smile again. Hale's studies led to one conclusion. This was the most beautiful and wonderful creature in the world and Hale would make it his mission to keep him safe and happy.

"You'll be the king soon. Sure you can," he replied. "All we need is some rings, which the royal coffers are brimming with. Everything else will already be in place. Cavarrians will expect the royal couple to be wed, so if anyone complains, say it's the will not only of their crownbearer but of the people."

"You're right," Eleksander said, placing a warm hand on Hale's cheek.

Hale kissed the nearest digit, then gave a little chuckle. "I'll enjoy going through the heaps of rings in the treasury. It'll be like when we picked out our weapons for our first sail."

"Yes. But we'll be picking out something for love and not survival this time."

"You're right. As always." Hale took that gentle hand from his cheek and helped Eleksander to stand with him, sparing their knees from the throne room's stone floor.

He had never thought the day would come when he'd rather pick out a piece of jewellery than a weapon. It felt good, though. This was his. His relationship, his lover, his *beloved*, his future. Shitting silver beasts, it would even be his kingdom in a way. Not bad for an over-active orphan who had always messed things up by being too clumsy, too rough, or by saying the wrong thing. He hadn't messed this up, though.

"What if we *are* too young?" Eleksander said quietly. "What if the marriage doesn't last?"

Hale shrugged, certain that it would last for as long as his heart still beat in his chest. "Then we find that out together and take action. It won't be the end of the world."

"I suppose not."

To break the serious mood, Hale let his hands slip down to Eleksander's rear. "So, tell me, is it the night before or after the wedding where we experiment with all the exotic sorts of bedplay that I've never tried before?"

Eleksander played with the laces at Hale's tunic collar. "Behave yourself and help me get through the next few days, and it might just be both nights. And many to follow after that, until I've thoroughly exhausted you."

Hale pumped a fist into the air, seeing Eleksander laugh, and noting that he was happier than he'd ever dared think he would be.

Chapter Forty-Two

SILVER, GOLD, COPPER

Coronation day. How Eleksander had dreaded and desired this day in equal measure.

The throne room was packed to the brim. The midday light pierced the thick and warped glass of the throne room's windows as Eleksander Aetholo took the echoing steps towards his seat of power. The pale shafts of sunlight looked silver against the grey stone beneath his feet. A mere two years ago, he had come to the Centre as a naïve, frightened lad. Today, he was a battle-scarred warrior, an explorer, a grieving sea captain, a rebel, a married man, and an heir about to be king. In short, he was still frightened. But now, able to handle it.

Every step felt momentous as he strode along the oblong room with guests standing to attention on either side of the walkway. During the wedding, they had been cheering and singing. At this ceremony, no one even so much as coughed. His palms dampened. He tried to dry them by moving his fingers and felt the wedding ring hugging his finger in support. He'd found one that fitted nicely, a golden one with engraved swirls that reminded him of streams of magic.

Hale Hawthorn stood ahead of him, right in front of their thrones. A large, copper one for himself and a smaller one carved out of hawthorn wood—made in the Woodlands of course—for Hale. His handsome husband was clad in the garb quickly sewn up for the new king's consort, green linen trousers and tunic, the latter tight over his muscular chest, both with leaves and crowns embroidered in copper thread all over, something which had cost more than either of them had wanted to spend on clothing. He wore the same finest leather boots in a greenish brown as Eleksander. There was copper dust sprinkled over Hale's short, dark hair, glinting in the sunlight. The new copper-trimmed sheath for the longsword Taferia had given him also caught the light. No coat, of course. Hale would only have taken that off and left it somewhere. His clothing colours matched Eleksander's silk trousers, gossamer-thin tunic, and long cloak. No more Lakelander blues and whites for him. Now, he and Hale wore their colours: the green of hawthorn leaves and the copper of the Aetholos. Those colours would replace every bit of Lothiam's red and gold in this castle.

The room stayed silent as a tomb as he approached Hale and their thrones, the only sounds his pristine boots clacking against the stone. His husband smiled at him and at least half of the nervousness faded. Eleksander could do this. As long as he wasn't alone, and he knew he never would be.

Close to the thrones and even closer to one another, stood Avelynne, Sabina, and Aurea. They would sail for

Hethekla tomorrow, but he knew they wouldn't stay away for long. On the other side of the aisle were the Aetholos, all looking so proud.

As he sat down, he noted that neither his nor Hale's thrones were very ornate due to the rush to create them. Good. It set the tone of this era. He meant to be of service, not revel in riches and beauty.

Some pomp had been necessary, though. A choir, with singers from each county, stood at the other end of the room and sang the coronation song in raising voices. The walls hadn't been decorated with weapons as Hale had suggested, but with fabrics dyed with the rarest dyes and hanging flower arrangements that filled the space with sweet scents. The royal knights, his protection squad, were in extra polished armour while the royal advisors were dressed in their white formal garb with trim as silver as magic. Taferia stood nearest Hale, as his first royal advisor, while his own first advisor, Kae, stood next to him.

Kae looked formidable as she, with great ceremony, handed him the freshly smithed monarch's orb and sceptre. The polished copper regalia, studded with green gems and pearls, were slick in his over-heated hands. He was busy with how to best hold them and barely realised what was about to happen before his newly made crown was placed on his head. The copper crown, with emeralds in every shade of green, was heavy but fit well and wasn't nearly as uncomfortable as he had assumed it would be.

He was now the Crownbearer of Cavarra.

He took a shaky breath but sat straight-backed, watching the assembled while Hale got his, more modest, copper crown. The hushed crowd was made up of nobles, merchants, and the dockworkers he'd met. Inviting commonfolk hadn't been popular with the council, but he was going to be a king for all of Cavarra. Behind Sabina, Avelynne, and Aurea stood the leaders of the four counties and their families. The Twelve, those who weren't royal advisors and so up by the thrones, stood with Naseer behind the Aetholos. Hale now had his crown, and so everyone's eyes were fixed back on Eleksander. Expectant. Judging. Icy panic crept into his edges. Then he saw something in the expressions of the Aetholos, and the same on Avelynne's face. And Sabina's. And Aurea's. And Taferia's. And Octavius Naseer's. And, most of all, on Hale's face. Belief, trust, and encouragement. Their confidence in him was almost palpable and he drew every morsel of strength from it that he could. This was a new day, and he should allow himself to enjoy the excitement and hope of it.

Eleksander readied his voice to be clear and strong to speak his first words as ruler of Cavarra. He knew a scribe was jotting down his every syllable and the speech would be spread across the land by use of the printing machine that Aurea had spent the past few days describing to the scholars and crafters. As soon as the device had been built and tested, of course. Invention was going to be one of his priorities. Research and experimentation too. He caught the eye of his former tutor, Atha Santorine. She was still haggard after her captivity but had sworn her life and loyalty to him and he knew she would one day help them unearth the answers about their golden magic. Today, though, he had to say his first words as king and the crowd was waiting.

He lifted his chin. "To everyone who has gathered on

this day of my wedding and my coronation, I thank you. Cavarra has changed, swiftly and completely. No more silver beasts causing peril and starvation, no more spell to keep us all in the thrall of unjust monarchs, no more unreasonable tithes exacted." He paused to let them cheer and whoop, only speaking again when they had quieted. "A new Cavarra is born. One that no longer is weighed down by calamities on the home front or infighting. We are now a nation that will look outwards. We will meet other races, learn of modern inventions, and import new goods, for we no longer fear leaving our shores. I intend to be the king that makes Cavarra stand tall, with curiosity and kindness in our hearts, and reach for a better future for all."

As the applause and cheers rang out, he couldn't help it. He thought of the massive coronation revelry—filled with music, food, and entertainment—that was to be held after this. People from all around Cavarra gathering everywhere in the Centre to dance and drink the day and night through. Before he and Hale retired for their wedding night, he longed to sneak away to drink oakenberry brandy and play bottletop with his friends. One last game before the women took on the challenge of sailing and the men took on the burden of staying home and ruling. No, not a burden. Not only a burden, anyway. An honour. One worth celebrating.

Chapter Forty-Three

NEW

The next morning found Sabina, somewhat unsteadily due to too much brandy last night, stepping out of a carriage onto the salt-stained planks of the shipyard. A sack hung heavy on her back and a long, linen-wrapped package was grasped in her hand. By the reddish light of the sunrise, she watched the carriage trundle back to the Centre. There, Eleksander and Hale would still be sleeping after the late night. The many games of bottletop they'd played had been the evening's highlight for her. Just the five of them—Aurea being taught the game as they all got drunker and drunker —having fun and laughing over silly things. The farewell hugs afterwards hadn't been as fun. Still, they wouldn't be parted for long and both Hale and Eleksander understood why they had to leave. Later today, those two would be arguing with the council, setting rules and intentions for Cavarra's future. That wasn't her problem. Not her responsibility. Her gaze slipped off the carriage and towards the Hethklish ships.

She took a firmer grip of her package, called Kall to her

side, and followed Avelynne and Aurea, who had already gone up the gangplank to the Qetesh and were standing by the ship's wheel, comparing their compasses. Avelynne dropped hers and Aurea caught it, handing it over with more caressing of hands than needed.

They both turned at the sound of her and Kall's footsteps.

"Ah, there you are, sweetling," Aurea called to her. "I worried you'd gotten lost somewhere on the gangplank."

Avelynne put her compass away and came to meet her. She took Sabina's free hand. "I understand why you've tarried. It's a lot to leave behind. But we'll be back soon, snowdrop."

"Aye, we will," Sabina replied and kissed her.

Aurea hummed happily. "You two are so beautiful when you kiss. I think I shall never tire of seeing—"

She was interrupted by her quartermaster clearing his throat from behind them. "Captain Heraclius. Shall I go over and take charge of the Parataxia for the unmooring?"

"Yes, go ahead," Aurea said.

Sabina had so rarely heard Aurea's surname. It was nice, but not as *nice* as seeing her lover in charge. There was easy but impressive power in Aurea's stance and her voice as she said, "I'll swing over when we have cleared the shallows."

Sabina looked to the ropes in the rigging. It wasn't the safest way to travel. "I can go over there now and captain the Parataxia if you'd like?"

Aurea wagged a finger at her. "You are not to take responsibility for anything for a while. Make yourself comfortable somewhere and let that gorgeous salt white hair down."

"Salt white?" Sabina said.

"Yes," Aurea said. "Like the sea salt that covers anything that tarries long enough by the sea. You were made to be a sailor."

"I've always thought of it as white like snow," Avelynne said, caressing Sabina's braid.

Aurea paused with her hand on the ship's wheel. "I've only seen snow from a distance, on islands we have travelled by."

"What?" Sabina said. "Well, we'll change that. When we come back to Cavarra, I'm taking both of you to the North. To see my village."

And meet my family, she added in her mind.

"Really? That's wonderful," Aurea said. "I hope there'll be icewolf pups. Oh, and snowtiger cubs of course," she added while petting Kall.

Sabina jolted, recalling what was on her back and in her hand.

"Before we sail, I have something for you two," she said, handing the long package to Avelynne. "Here's yours."

Avelynne thanked her and began unwrapping.

Sabina took the sack off her back and gently placed it in front of Aurea. "And yours is here, on top of my things. Open it with care."

Aurea sat down and did just that. She squealed like a child at the icewolf cub nestled on top of Sabina's clothes and books. They were lucky it had slept long enough not to ruin the surprise. Sabina hoped with all her heart that the little thing hadn't done its business in the sack. Maybe she shouldn't have given it such a big breakfast?

"Thank you so much. It's beyond adorable," Aurea chirped, waking the cub. "Look at all that white and grey fluff and those sweet little ear tufts!" Aurea touched the pup's ears and the wolf sniffed her fingers to her great elation. It, or rather *he*, jumped out of the sack, his tail wagging to show he was as excited as his new owner.

"You're welcome. When I spoke to the baron and baroness about providing for my family, I also asked them to send for an icewolf pup. This wee lad arrived with Eleksander's throne two days ago and the baroness has been hiding him for me since then."

Sabina ordered the pup to sit and was relieved to note that it had been given some training by the breeder.

"I've never had a pet," Aurea said, gazing lovingly at the mini wolf climbing up into her lap.

Sabina's heart swelled. "I'll help you raise it like we do our companions in the North, that way it'll be even more than a pet. And Kall can be a role model, teaching it not to eat the ship's goats. I have only one request."

"Anything," Aurea said, petting the cub's little head.

"That you name it Ivar or Nore. After Ivar Nore, the man who, with the help of his brave icewolf, stopped a sea monster from killing me and Kall."

"I'll pick Nore. I'm glad to honour a man who saved someone whom I love." She made kissing noises at Kall, then said to Sabina, "Oh and you too, of course."

"Very funny," Sabina retorted.

Aurea was lost in the pup again, though. "Just look at his beautiful apple-green eyes."

Sabina left her to it, her cheeks still burning at the words, "someone whom I love." She turned to Avelynne instead; she had waited quite a while to hand over that particular gift.

The former countess held it out in her open palms, like it might vanish if she gripped it. "A war scythe? Thank you, snowdrop. It's truly magnificent."

"Not just any war scythe, not like your old Hall of Explorers one that rusts at the bottom of the sea. This one was made for you, forged by a weaponsmith right on the border between your county and mine."

Avelynne's slender fingers slowly curled around the handle. "Really?"

"Aye. I put in the order for it right after the battle against Lothiam. It has a Northern blade with a carved snowflake just like Grimfrost," she thumbed towards the axe strapped to her back, "and a Peakdweller hilt made from the iron pines that I'm told grow only around the Ironhold Estate?"

"Yes. Iron pines take a lot of special care and so have died out everywhere else." Avelynne eyed the scythe again. "Wait, if it is half Northern, is it named like your weapons are?"

Sabina's cheeks heated again. "Read the hilt."

"Countess," Avelynne whispered.

"Same as you. I told you, no matter what your parents or anyone else says, you'll always be a countess to me."

Aurea, who was still petting her pup, smiled up at them. "Crownknight *and* countess? Two great titles for an even greater woman. Although don't you have to be a countess of something? What about this journey? Or this ship?" She hummed pensively. "Or wait, you can be the Countess of War Scythes."

"I quite like that." Avelynne leaned the polearm against her shoulder in a cavalier way, pushed her chest out, and quirked a seductive eyebrow. "Kneel before the Countess of War Scythes."

An interrupting ruckus came from the Parataxia. The sailors on the other ship were shouting at each other about something but Sabina couldn't tell if they were happy or angry. She put a hand on Aurea's shoulder. "Your sailors sound restless. Shouldn't we set sail?"

"In a while. Let them blow off some steam before they need to focus on sailing," Aurea said, watching her pup curl up next to a befuddled Kall. "I think that's best. If they disagree, they'll let me know."

Sabina wanted to argue but then... just allowed herself to enjoy the moment and watch Nore, an untroubled new little life, fall asleep with his head on Kall's back leg. Aurea's lack of need to be constantly perfect and useful was a gift, one that none of the second wave had been given. Not even Hale. Avelynne moved close to Aurea too and Sabina realised that those quick fingers of hers were no longer fidgeting with her necklace. In general, Avelynne seemed more comfortable in herself than ever before.

Sabina let the hand on Aurea's shoulder squeeze a little. "Thank you. For allowing us to come with you and for letting me, um, court you."

Aurea smiled. "Actually, I thought I was courting you." She kissed Sabina, who let herself be pulled into an embrace. After a while Sabina, distractedly, noted that Avelynne went to help a passing sailor carry some crates.

The old Sabina Rosenmarck would've stopped the kiss and assisted. Or worried that Avelynne felt left out. This Sabina Rosenmarck deepened the kiss. Everything else could either work itself out or wait until she had time to deal with it.

When the kiss ended, she searched Aurea's face. "Will you be happy with this?"

Aurea tilted her head. "What? With you and I being together and Avelynne taking part when she likes? I'm overjoyed with it."

"No, I meant with sailing back and forth. Don't you want to return to being a printer?"

"Printing can wait. Barring any deadly misfortunes, we have our whole lives ahead of us. For now, I want to show you and Avelynne more of the sea. I want you to see that it's not just monsters, tempests, and shipwrecks."

"I look forward to that."

They shared another kiss, until Aurea pulled away and said, "Everyone has quieted down. Time to set sail."

"I'll leave you to your work. Let me know if I can help."

Aurea caressed Sabina's cheek. "I told you, no helping for at least the first few hours. Go relax." She turned and called to her sailors to take their places and prepare the rigging.

Sabina walked away, calling Kall and Nore to her. She rolled the last tension out of her shoulders. Grimfrost sheathed to her back didn't feel heavy anymore, the weapon was a part of her now, simply another tool in her arsenal of things this ordeal had given her. Some of those things were benign, some weren't, but she'd try to find a way to use them all for good. To help people, perhaps

411

including herself? The snow knew she could do with more life and joy instead of death and remorse.

Sabina headed for Avelynne, who stood with a sailor and asked questions about the safety boats that hung off the side of the Qetesh. Avelynne's expression was melancholic and no wonder. Could they have saved more of their sailors if they had those on the Wolfsclaw? Sabina sighed at the amount of damage she and Avelynne carried. Still, they would now have the time, and Aurea's help, to talk things through. Maybe even forgive themselves. If they could help each other to heal, they might be able to aid Hale and Eleksander do the same when they got back. She missed those two already.

Chapter Forty-Four

THE UNSAID

Hale's head throbbed and his whole body was heavy as stone. Shit, that had been too much brandy. And only a couple of hours sleep. Although, he couldn't regret the latter considering what he and Eleksander had been doing instead. Now, they walked hand in hand towards the royal war room for a quick meeting with the council before the county leaders travelled home.

There was someone up ahead, leaning one hand against the corridor wall with their head bent. *Her* head bent. Hale nearly tripped over his own feet at the sight of Atha Santorine. Or at least the bony shadow of her, cheeks hollowed out and dark circles under her unblinking eyes.

"Your royal majesties," she said as she unsteadily curtsied. "I have feared this first meeting with you. I have much to explain."

Eleksander held up a hand. "There will be plenty of time for that later. Besides, you have been punished enough."

"I still wish to make amends. I want to be more honest and responsible than the rest of the Twelve."

"Then repay us by continuing to study our magic and stay in our employ," Eleksander said. "Our future will be filled with new things requiring research and experimentation."

She bowed. "I shall give you, and this work, all I am and all I can offer." Her head twitched as if she had thought of something. "On that note, may I share with you what I have found regarding the magic of the solstice born?"

She'd kept researching? She was meant to be recuperating.

"Mm. Make it quick. We have a meeting, remember?" Hale said, wondering if he was meant to always let Eleksander take the lead. No. Eleksander wouldn't want anything to change between them.

Atha Santorine leaned a hand against the wall again. "Everything so far points to that it was a mere coincidence. The magic energy of our world simply flared that one summer, like a heatwave or an unusually cold winter. I can keep studying it if you like, but I think the main question now is what the limits and possibilities are for your magic?"

Coincidence? Yes, actually, that felt right. His whole life had been entrenched in nature, he knew its randomness. It didn't matter why the thunder struck twice in a day, it mattered what you did with the consequences of the strikes.

"We will discuss this in detail later," Eleksander said. "And when Ave and Sab return, we can conduct experiments and trials. For now, we really must get to that meeting. Are you ready, Tutor Santori—I mean Atha?"

"I am a little weary. Let me catch my breath before I join you." She glanced toward the war room. "I am not used to being out in public nor of having the pressure of how to behave in front of a group of dignitaries. I..." She was struggling, in more ways than one.

Eleksander put a hand on her arm, steadying her. "Take some time to collect yourself. As soon as the meeting is done, I order you to rest and eat up. Cavarra needs you at full strength, as it does all of us."

She gave a weak but earnest smile. "I knew you would be a good leader, a better one than this nation deserves. I didn't expect you to show such forgiveness and care for me, though."

"Then earn it," Hale said, putting iron in his tone.

Her back straightened. "I shall."

They nodded to her and continued on towards the castle's war room. Despite that, of course, it was where they belonged, it was shittingly odd to Hale that they were meeting there instead of in the great hall of the Hall of Explorers. The war room had its perks, though. Like chairs instead of long benches and, since the castle's arrow slits were only in the outer walls, it was less plagued by draughts.

"What are you so lost in thought about? Santorine's research?" Eleksander asked.

"No. Draughts."

Eleksander chuckled. "Ah. I knew it would be something profound."

"I talked to Avelynne about draughts once, saying that I liked that the breeze could come into the rooms through cracks and such. She didn't."

"I fear most of us wouldn't," Eleksander said. "Especially not in winter."

"She said it wasn't normal that the Hall of Explorers was so draughty. That Ironhold castle was better insulated."

"I'm sure it is. Less dank too, no doubt. Both Ironhold castle and the royal castle were paid for by aristocrats to have a place to live in and to show off to guests." Eleksander rapped his knuckles on the thick marble wall next to them. "They would spend more on them than on an academy built for coinless scholars and young recruits."

"I suppose."

Hale's already unruly stomach clenched, but this time it was due to emotion and not the hangover. Avelynne should be here. So should Sabina. He shook himself off, he needed to get over it. There was work to do. Still... he had to ask.

"Do you think Ave, Sab, and Aurea were right in that they'll be back within the year?"

"Yes. It wouldn't be like them to say it otherwise, would it?"

"No." Hale ran hand over the stubble on his cheek, remembering his friends kissing him goodbye there last night. "There's so much I didn't ask them about before they left. So much I didn't... say. And now, they won't know about Santorine's findings for another year."

Eleksander halted. "Tell you what. I'll meet with the council on my own, meanwhile you can do something else time-sensitive and important."

Hale stopped too, ready to be of service. "What?"

"Send a message to them with the castle's messenger ravens. Let's see if these birds are up to par with the ones at the Hall of Explorers."

"Sure. I'm on it! Who should I send a message to?"

Eleksander gave him a long, meaningful look.

"What?" Hale asked, more irritably than he probably should've.

"Who were you just talking about?"

"Oh, you mean send a message to Sab and Ave? But they'll be far out to sea?"

"Not that far. It can only be a couple of hours or so since they set sail."

"Will that be close enough for the messenger ravens to fly?" Hale scratched at the stubble again, this time on his chin. "Do ravens have the energy to make the trip out there and back with a reply?"

"Listen to you, you're becoming nigh as much of a worrywart as me or Ave. Messenger ravens can fly for days, remember? Try it. If the raven gets fatigued, it'll return with the message untouched. But at least then you'll have given it an attempt."

"You're right." Hale considered the war room ahead of them. "I feel bad about skipping our first meeting as royals, though. How much do I have to pay you as penalty?"

"Nothing. I promised that you didn't have to attend any —" Eleksander stopped himself. "I mean, there will obviously be a cost. Two kisses. One payable now and another when the meeting has concluded."

Now that was the deal-making of a king. Eleksander would be a great leader and he, well, he would be the best consort Cavarra had ever seen. And, most of all, they would be happy. Excitement, contentment, and pride spread through Hale, warming and dizzying, like he'd just downed a glass of brandy on an empty stomach.

Wasting no more time on words, Hale grabbed that tall husband of his by the waist and drew him into a passionate kiss.

Chapter Forty-Five

MAPMAKING MAGICIANS

She leaned against the mainmast and inspected the fraying rope she'd been brought by a sailor. It should have been replaced when they were in drydock. No more of the lenient second in command, from today on she'd have to be the harsh but fair *Captain* Aurea Heraclius.

She hung up the rope and crouched to pet her little Nore, mainly to distract him from bothering Kall. She heard Avelynne laugh and followed the sound. Sabina and Avelynne were helping the boatswain with the rigging over by the foremast. Or Sabina was helping, Avelynne was apparently laughing with the boatswain about her own lack of upper body strength.

A shade over two hours. That was how long Sabina and Avelynne had managed to not work. Doldrums, these second wavers were a hardworking bunch. And, it must be said, stubborn as mountain mules.

"Something's flying straight for us," came a call from the ship's lookout. "Looks like one of those Cavarrian messenger birds."

She shielded her eyes from the late morning sun and found that her lookout was right. What were those birds called? Ravens? This one was headed for the Parataxia but both Sabina and Avelynne gave some sort of whistle through their teeth, and it headed for them instead. The raven landed on Avelynne's outstretched arm. With deft fingers, she took off a message tied at a tiny collar around its neck.

Avelynne and Sabina read the message and when Aurea saw tears falling into their smiles, she hurried over to them. "What does it say? Who's it from?"

"It's from Hale," Sabina said. "Written in his usual short sentences." She gave a happy little hum. "He says that he wishes he would've been there to wave us off. That the castle has less draughts? And that Atha Santorine says our solstice magic was a fluke of nature, but that there will be more examinations into what it can do. Just like he promised me." Sabina's voice broke on that last word.

Avelynne carried on reading instead. "He wants us to draw him a map of Hethekla. He also says he wants to sail with us so we can use our golden magic in the saltwater where it works best. Finally, he asks if we really are coming back to Cavarra within the year."

Avelynne looked to Aurea. "That *is* feasible, right? Being back before a year has passed?"

Aurea did the calculations in her head. Sail to Hethekla. Show these two a few things, tell the government about Cavarra, and restock at least one ship. Or, more likely, be fitted with a new ship and other sailors. Then that ship, with some Hethklish diplomats and themselves, could sail back to Cavarra. "Yes. Weather and sea willing, we could be back in less than a year."

"Then let's hope for no monsters and no doldrums," Sabina said. "Why don't you go write a quick reply and tell him that we should be back within the year, Little Countess?"

"Of course." Avelynne let the bird fly over to Sabina, then went to the captain's quarters where the quill and ink were. And, Aurea's mind couldn't help but add, where their shared bed was.

Avelynne was by the door when Sabina called, "Oh and tell Hale... that I love him and Eleksander."

"I was always going to," Avelynne answered and hurried in.

Aurea picked up the whimpering Nore and was about to bring him over to Sabina when she saw her sweetheart squint towards Cavarra, which got ever smaller as they travelled.

Worry spread through Aurea like a poison. "It's not too late for us to turn around, you know."

"Huh? No. I desperately want to sail to Hethekla. It's just that I'm..."

"Missing Hale and Eleksander?"

"Aye."

"They'll sail with us soon enough. Our government will be eager to host the King and King's Consort of Cavarra."

Sabina's face lit up. "Aye. That'll be good. Until then, I get to spend more of my time with you." She leant over to give Aurea a gentle kiss, the bird cawing plaintively on her arm.

The bird's noise made Nore go berserk so Aurea put the wriggling puppy down.

"Behave yourself, you naughty little wolf," Sabina said in that stern voice which made Aurea tingle.

"Done," Avelynne said as she walked back out on deck.

She fastened the missive to the raven as she told them what she had written. Declarations of love, guarantees of a map of at least the first harbour they saw, a brief line on the horrors of draughts, and the promise of that they would be back before a year had passed.

With the missive attached, the raven took off.

Aurea put her arms around the shoulders of her two mapmaking magicians, her gaze still on the raven heading for the royal castle. That was where these two would return to after each trip. Not to their families, not to the council, not simply to Cavarra. They'd return to Hale and Eleksander. And it was a comfort to Aurea that she would be invited to go with them. These Cavarrians might just be the steady home that had always eluded her.

Avelynne gave her a kiss on the cheek and said, "Could you teach me how to steer the ship? That way I can be of more use onboard."

"Ah, good idea! Teach me too?" Sabina asked.

"Gladly. We'll go relieve the quartermaster and I'll give you your first lesson."

There was so much she wanted to teach them but also, so much they could teach her. About strength, resilience, loyalty, and standing tall despite the odds being against you. She was excited to observe Hale and Eleksander setting up their new government and to see how their nation would interact with her own. This day marked not only a new future for Cavarra but a new future for her and for the second wave of mapmaking magicians. And Aurea was certain of this: those four were ready for whatever would come their way and she, well, she would be proud and glad of heart to witness their journey.

REVIEWS

I sincerely hope you enjoyed reading Copper Throne.

If you did, I would greatly appreciate a short review on your favourite book website.

Reviews are crucial for any author, and even just a line or two can make a huge difference

ALSO BY EMMA STERNER-RADLEY

Korinne Woodsorrow is trapped. Not only at her parents lumbermill but also in a village where she's shunned. Worse than that, she's stuck sacrificing the life she wants for the person she loves.

Next to the lumbermill looms the deadly Whispering Wildwood, with its magical creatures and mystical plants. The wildwood is not to be spoken of and not to be entered.

Yet, when disaster strikes, Korinne has to take her brother--who is all muscles and heart but not much brain--with her into the wildwood on a death-defying quest. Guided by a dashing rogue of a pirate and hunted by mysterious monsters, this quest soon goes deeper into a world of fairytales, danger, and wonder.

Korinne quickly has to figure out who and what to trust. As well as her new future, her sexuality, and of course - what happens if a quest changes into something completely different while you're on it?

SUPPORT ME ON PATREON

Being an independent author writing LGBTQIA stories you don't always get the exposure and financial support that other authors achieve.

Because of this, many of us rely on support from the reading community through sites such as Patreon.

As a patron of mine you will receive exclusive behind the scenes news, updates, my latest book releases for free before anyone else, and even free audiobooks!

If you are interested in supporting me then I'd be extremely grateful.

https://www.patreon.com/emmasternerradley

ABOUT THE AUTHOR

Emma Sterner-Radley is an ex-librarian turned fantasy writer. Originally Swedish, she now lives with her wife and two cats in Great Britain.

There's no point in saying which city, as they move about once a year.

She spends her time writing, reading, daydreaming, exercising, and watching whichever television show has the most lesbian/sapphic subtext at the time.

Her addictions are reality escapes, coffee, protein bars, sugary snacks, and small chubby creatures with ridiculously tiny legs.

www.emmasternerradley.com